THE

MERMAID'S DAUGHTER

THE
MERMAID'S
DAUGHTER

ANN CLAYCOMB

WILLIAM MORROW

An Imprint of HarperCollinsPublishers

P.S.™ is a trademark of HarperCollins Publishers.

HarperCollins books may be purchased for educational, business, or sales promotional use. For information, please email the Special Markets Department at SPsales@harpercollins.com.

FIRST EDITION

Designed by Diahann Sturge

Library of Congress Cataloging-in-Publication Data has been applied for.

ISBN 978-0-06-256068-1

17 18 19 20 21   LSC   10 9 8 7 6 5 4 3 2 1

*For Ryan, who doesn't read fairy tales but believed in this one,
for Erin, who does read fairy tales and believed in this one,
and for Ellie, little mermaid swimming free.*

"I know what you want," said the sea witch . . . "You want to get rid of your fish's tail, and to have two sup-ports instead of it, like human beings on earth, so that the young prince may fall in love with you . . . I will prepare a draught for you . . . Your tail will then dis-appear, and shrink up into what mankind calls legs, and you will feel great pain, as if a sword were passing through you. But all who see you will say that you are the prettiest little human being they ever saw. You will still have the same floating gracefulness of movement, and no dancer will ever tread so lightly; but at every step you take it will feel as if you were treading upon sharp knives, and that the blood must flow. If you will bear all this, I will help you . . . Put out your little tongue that I may cut it off as my payment; then you shall have the powerful draught."

"It shall be," said the little mermaid.

—HANS CHRISTIAN ANDERSEN, "THE LITTLE MERMAID"

The water is wide, I can't swim o'er.
And neither have I wings to fly.
Give me a boat that can carry two,
And both shall row, my love and I.
There is a ship and she sails the sea.
She's loaded deep as deep can be,
But not so deep as the love I'm in.
I know not how to sink or swim.

—"THE WATER IS WIDE" (SCOTTISH FOLK SONG)

THE
MERMAID'S
DAUGHTER

Act 1

KATHLEEN

Aria for Soprano

"Kathleen," she says, "you are going to go mad."

I have only just finished singing and I feel like I have surfaced from deep water, gasping like a fish desperate to be submerged again, to still be breathing the song. For a moment, hearing her words, I am terrified to have it confirmed. I am going to go mad: she knows it just looking at me, just hearing me. *How does she know?*

There are only a hundred people in the audience, but they are all clapping, many of them on their feet. I can feel my voice recede from my throat like a tide dropping. I take shallow sips of air, keep my eyes on the woman who is holding my hands. She is smiling at me, shaking her head. Her voice, trained to fill much larger spaces than this one, cuts easily through the applause, silences it. Her hands are warm around mine.

RUZENA IS A great soprano, an international diva, brought in to do a master class with three young singers handpicked by the faculty to show off the caliber of the school. Ruzena's job was to listen to each of us sing, correct us on breathing, stance, tonal quality, pronunciation, gestures. Then she would pronounce judgment.

Carianne has a light, sparkling voice, a true soubrette. The diva promised her Mozart roles and worked with her on balancing out the weightlessness of her voice with better breath control, especially when she sings longer phrases. Hyung is a mezzo with a break in her voice that she has learned to sing around. She masks her weakness with a huskiness that untrained audiences hear as sexiness. Ruzena saw right through it, took Hyung to task for not stretching her range, for not doing more vocal exercises to increase her flexibility.

She had no corrections for me. When I finished singing she moved gracefully from where she had been standing behind the piano, put her hands on my shoulders, and turned me toward the audience. Then she took a step back and made a grand gesture of her own, of presentation. It's the gesture the conductor usually makes when he presents the star: the falsely modest step back, the satisfied smile, the sweep of the arm inviting applause. She did nothing in this class but make this familiar gesture, award me her unqualified approbation, but it was enough—my God, more than enough—and she knew it. People stood for an ovation, some of my friends even whistled. In the front row, Harriet Evans, the mezzo who should have been picked for this class instead of Hyung, was one of the first to stand. There was nothing forced about her smile, like there would have been about mine if I'd been consigned to the audience. No, Harry just beamed, her cheeks flushed with love and pride. When she caught my eye, she stopped clapping long enough to blow me a kiss. Then Ruzena turned me back around to face her, took my hands in hers.

"YOU ARE GOING to kill yourself," she says. She puts her fingertips on my throat, her touch light and reverent. She is performing. She does not know anything real, is not predicting anything about me. She is talking about the roles I will play: Lucia, Mimi, Butterfly, Violetta, Norma, Manon. She is offering the highest possible praise.

"You will stab yourself," she says, "throw yourself into the sea."

Too close to home. I was only a baby when my mother filled her pockets with rocks and walked into the sea to die. I have no actual memories of my mother at all, but I tried to follow her when I was six, swam out until I couldn't stand and let myself go under. The water was warm against my face and colder down below, where the sun had not touched it. The dark ribbon of cold seeped into my feet until they barely hurt at all, and my feet always hurt.

They hurt now, as I stand with my fingers still loosely clasped in another woman's hands. I can feel the rings she wears against my skin. If she squeezed my hands tight, the press of her rings would hurt, but of course it would: that kind of pain makes sense. My feet don't make sense. They don't ache or throb with the ordinary discomfort of walking too far or wearing bad shoes. When it's really bad it feels like I've stepped on a broken bottle and not only have I cut my feet, I'm still walking on the shards. I wear ballet slippers all the time and pick through dirty Boston snowdrifts in them rather than resort to heavy boots. There's no shoe in the world that can cushion my feet from jagged glass that isn't there. In my little ballet shoes, though, I can step lightly enough to almost tiptoe, almost prance, without anyone noticing I'm doing it.

I am supposed to smile at the litany of terrible fates in store for me, to show that I am in on the joke. I avoid even glancing over at Harry, who will have registered both the prediction and my reaction. I hate moments like this, when we are both recalled to my general—what?—*precariousness*? I like that word better than other possibilities.

"I was thinking of throwing myself into the sea tomorrow." I smile back, performing too. "It's spring break and we're going to drive to the beach."

"Well!" She squeezes my hands, releases them. "Enjoy it. Enjoy your vacation. But when you come back, you must promise to keep singing. Some day we will be cheering you on a much larger stage than this one."

"Once I'm resurrected from my tragic death?"

"My dear," Ruzena says, and now she turns a little to include the audience, "you will die a thousand tragic deaths onstage. It's the curse of the soprano. The tenor makes a fool of himself for love, the baritone must perfect an expression of evil glee, but we are the ones who die, my dear, every time."

I do glance at Harry now. For a moment I think I catch a glimpse of the fear that she generally hides so well, or masks with impatience and insistent caretaking. But then she rolls her eyes and grins at me, mouths a single word: *sopranos!*

OH YES, WE are drama queens, every one of us. Harry is not. She's a mezzo, for one thing—the loyal friend, the cousin, the lady-in-waiting. And she's far too sensible to rush headlong toward a tragic, early end. In the crush of the reception after the class, she skirts the crowd around Ruzena to find me sitting in a chair by the windows with my shoes off and my feet tucked up under my dress.

"Good," she says, "you're sitting down."

Harry and I will have been together a year in April, long enough to have started squabbling about the little things: my inability to put anything in our apartment away, her insistence on spending grocery money on healthy foods that neither one of us ever wants to eat. But we joke about those things; we don't fight about them. We fight about this: my unexplained illness that's never going to go away and her hovering over me about it like—and I did call her this once when I was really angry—a puffed-up mama hen. "Peck," I said. "Peck, peck, peck." Harry drew in a breath through her nose and for a minute I thought she'd snap back. But instead she pressed her lips together and left the room. I sprang after her and she shut the door in my face. I was so stunned that I stopped short. My feet hurt and my mouth hurt that day, badly. My skin burned as if with a rash, though in the mirror I saw only what I expected to see: my white skin stained red with temper along my cheeks and at my temples, my hair fairly crackling around my shoulders, my eyes black and dilated from the pain and the pills I'd taken. OxyContin, I think, that day, more than I'd been prescribed, and from a prescription I wasn't supposed to have anymore.

That was a bad fight.

Now I try not to bristle, but I'm raw from the strangeness of the diva's words, the sensation I had onstage that her predictions were settling over me like a net so finely woven as to be inescapable.

"I only sang a master class, not a whole performance," I say. "I'm not tired."

"But your feet were bothering you," she says. She sits down beside me and touches my hair. Even in the midst of her anxiety, she can't stop her face going soft when she touches me. We've been together nearly a year, but *that* hasn't faded, thank God. I still want to touch her as soon as she touches me, wind a finger in one of her blond curls, push her back or down against something, and let my long hair fall like red curtains around our faces.

I turn my face to kiss her palm, but then she ruins it.

"Are you all right? I mean, I know what she was doing with the things she said, but still. I could have killed her. She could have found another way to tell you how wonderful you were."

"She couldn't have known. Come on, Harry. It's not a big deal."

"It is if you take what she said serious—"

"Is there champagne?" I ask. "I thought I saw champagne going around, in real glasses, no less, not the usual plastic cups they use at these things. Can you get me some?"

She lets her hand fall from my hair. "Are you sure that's a good idea?"

Champagne, like the pills and the pot and the other things that I've tried, doesn't work on the pain. Harry thinks that if I'm going to self-medicate, at least it should help. I grant her that. But still, would it kill her just *once* to let it go? I unfold myself to get up, shrug my shoulder so my hair falls between us. "It's just a glass of champagne," I say. "I'll get it myself."

"Kath"—her hand is on my arm then—"don't. Stay here and rest your feet. I'll get us both a glass."

When she's gone, I slip out into the art gallery adjoining the room where the reception is being held. I don't want to get caught alone by a board member; they tend to fawn over me, which is flattering but tiring. The gallery is small and pretty, lots of blond wood and stark white walls. I walk from one painting to the next not really seeing them, because Harry was right, of course: my feet are throbbing so badly it's hard to focus on anything else.

There's only one thing, besides singing, besides the taste of Harry's mouth, that really distracts me from the pain and suddenly here it is, in front of me.

The sea.

It's not a big painting, not big enough to get really lost in or to evoke the smell of the water, the chilly, damp feel of the air above the waves. But it's enough to stop me, enough to make me feel again the pang of longing I felt when the diva said I would throw myself into the sea. I thought then of Moira, my mother, and also felt the shock of desire I always feel at the thought of immersion.

Paintings of the sea make me long for it and realize all over again that I can't ever have it. Why, when people paint the sea, do they always include sunlight on the water and a cliff or rock for the waves to hurl white foam against? That creates a remove, an emphasis on the way that the sea is different from the land, from the air, and conveys such a flatness to the surface that it's hard to imagine the depths

I know are there. Paintings of the sea, even photographs or movies that venture underwater, are nothing like my dreams of it.

I dreamed of the sea before I ever saw it, lovely dreams of a blue-lit world where everything undulated softly all around. Swimming through murky castles and fields of black sea grass, I was happy. As soon as I started reading picture books, my favorite ones were all about the sea and fish and underwater creatures. And when I could put words to the pictures, I interrupted my father during bedtime reading with endless questions about the sea: *How many fish are there? In the whole ocean, how many fish? Can any of them talk? Can people live in the ocean? Why not? Why can't we ride seahorses? Are you sure there aren't any bigger seahorses? Why are they called that if they're fish and not horses? Where is the sea, Daddy? How big is it? Could we go there? When? When?*

Robin, my father, didn't figure out until it was too late that what I wanted was not the seashore or the beach, but the sea itself, underwater. I was five when he took me to see the ocean off the coast of Nantucket. We drove straight to the beach, took off our shoes in the car. I remember running toward the water, abandoning him in my eagerness. And then I stopped. I wish I didn't remember this too, the shock of disappointment that knocked me off my feet, the tears that wouldn't stop. I cried as though my heart would break, cried until I could barely breathe, and my poor father, having caught up, knelt beside me and stroked my hair, utterly perplexed.

It was nothing at all like the beautiful underwater world I had dreamed. From above, from even a little distance, the ocean smelled sad to me, like dead things and things left behind. I had imagined its depths and its tides of shifting color, but it was nothing but a ragged gray blanket. Robin tried to calm me down, and when that failed, he said gently that we could leave now, it was all right, he was sorry, we could just go home.

But I couldn't leave without touching the water. I got up, still hysterical—*No, Daddy! No, no! I don't want to leave! I don't want to!*—and stumbled into the surf. My wet pants dragged around my ankles and my feet felt funny, tingly and buoyed up. I sat down in the sand and a wave rushed up and soaked me to my shoulders. My father's shadow fell over me and I heard him asking anxiously if I was all right. The salt water, my first taste of the sea, filled my mouth. I waited for each new wave to drape itself over me, and whenever and wherever my skin was actually in the water—even under the layers of clothes—I felt wrapped in comfort.

"THERE YOU ARE." Harry comes up beside me, stops when she sees the painting. Knowing Harry, she's seeing a great deal more: my hands clenched at my sides, feet shifting up and down as I try to take my weight off them, my throat working against the nausea that rises when I recall the taste of the sea in my mouth and then feel its absence.

For a moment, though I know she sees everything, she says nothing. Maybe she has decided she doesn't want to fight either.

"Is your mouth bothering you too?" she asks finally. That's the other phantom pain, the sudden blinding agony that started when I was a teenager and only flares up occasionally, thank God, or I *would* be crazy. As it is, the pain in my mouth makes me scream, makes me throw up, sends me to the hospital for Demerol and yet another psych workup.

I'm a singer, after all, and I've let more than a dozen doctors examine my mouth. There's nothing wrong. No reason why I should sweat and gag against my own tongue, the pain the same with every attack, as if it were happening anew each time.

I shiver, thinking about it. Swallow.

"No, my mouth's okay."

"You want me to leave you alone a little while longer?"

She doesn't say that she already took as long as she could, probably stopped and talked to people, soaked up the praise of my singing for me. She's got two glasses in her hands but she's not even offering me one yet. She's trying to help me come back to her, to the room, the party next door.

I shake my head, feel tears brimming because my feet hurt and the sea in the painting in front of me is small and far away and Harry, beside me, is gazing at me with love and worry in her gray eyes. She doesn't approve of how I handle the pain or the need for the sea, but she believes me. She doesn't think I'm crazy. I take a deep breath, then another, and try to come back.

"I'm okay."

"Champagne? As requested?"

I take the glass she offers, and she tips her face up to kiss me. I curl my free hand around the back of her neck, kiss her more insistently than I know she planned in public, touch her tongue with mine.

"Stop that, you," she whispers as she pulls away.

I take a drink of champagne and bat my eyes at her over the glass. "I'll never do it again."

As soon as we walk back into the reception, Carianne

comes over to congratulate me, fizzing with her own excitement and post-singing high. Behind her, Tom, the tenor who considers it his personal mission to make sure none of us take ourselves too seriously, sighs loudly and declares that now I'm probably going to be even more insufferable than I already was.

"Listen," he says, "the only thing that's saving you from a terminal case of 'soprano-itis' is the way you walk, that bouncy thing you do on the balls of your feet."

Another moment not to look at Harry. "How is that saving me?"

"Because it's not compatible with wilting, darling. I mean, you haven't got the bosom to sail around like a Wagner soprano, thank God, but if you didn't have that funny little-girl-in-high-heels walk you've got, you'd be in sad danger of permanently drooping, all flower-needs-water, you know?"

I sigh, shake my head sadly. "I do. I often feel just the urge to wilt and I have to stop myself. But you know what the worst of it is?"

"What?" Carianne asks.

I lean in and they all crane forward to hear my stage whisper.

"Sometimes, when I'm not paying attention, I catch myself wringing my hands."

Even Tom laughs at that, then lifts his glass to me before taking another sip.

"Have you noticed how good this champagne is? Far above the usual swill they serve at these things."

"It's Veuve Clicquot, Tom," Harry says, amused. "I saw them pouring a tray behind that screen." She gestures with her glass and we all turn to the staging area from which the waiters have been emerging with trays of champagne flutes and passed hors d'oeuvres.

"It's not surprising, really, is it?" Carianne says. "I mean, they couldn't exactly serve *her*"—she nods to Ruzena, who's talking to our program director and two board members— "boxed wine and expect her to pick up cheese and crackers off a big tray, could they?"

"No," Tom says thoughtfully. He's assessing the screens, his eyes narrowed.

"Tom," Harry says, "absolutely not. Don't even think about it."

But he just grins at her, tosses back the rest of his champagne, and starts making his way through the crowd.

"What's he doing?" Carianne asks.

Harry shakes her head and I laugh, both of us watching him duck back behind the screen.

"He's going to steal some champagne," I say. "I hope he gets a couple bottles. This stuff is amazing."

Tom has a liquid tenor voice and the body of a barely pubescent boy. When we get going, the two of us are insatiable instigators—of parties, excursions into downtown Boston, spontaneous performances of operatic death scenes on the sidewalk. Anything to distract us when we're not actively singing. Tom is the only friend I have who *needs* to sing the way I do. When he's singing he's not short or slight, his penis isn't too small to get the boys he wants, his father hasn't disowned him for being a faggot.

Tom and I come off the stage like we're coming down from a drug trip. We need champagne to drink and sprays of roses to clutch, the stems dripping on our clothes, the thorns poking our forearms, the fragrance of the wet petals at once fresh and sharp and deliciously artificial, the smell of a lover who wears too much perfume.

I watch Tom appear from behind the screen again, this time carrying a case of empty champagne bottles, with several collapsed boxes tucked under his arm and a trash bag in his hand. He's "helping" the catering staff, who are always panicky and stretched too thin, but I'm guessing that the bottles in the box aren't all empty. He winks at me as he heads for the back hallway to dispose of the "trash."

"Kathleen," Harry says, "remember you have to call your father."

"I will. I'll call him when we get home."

"Well, if we're going to try to drive out to the Vineyard, we still have to pack, there are at least three loads of laundry to do, and the place is a disaster." She sets her glass down on the windowsill and I take my cue.

"Let's go then. Anyone you need to say goodbye to, or can we just slip out?"

"Why don't you go out the back like Tom did?" Carianne suggests. "Maybe if they see all the students leaving that way, it'll throw them off his trail."

MY FATHER WAS a pianist when he first came to Boston from Ireland, twenty years old with a baby and a scholarship to study an instrument he'd never owned. He'd only ever played the piano at school or at church and he'd never even seen a grand piano. For the first few years we were here, he left me with a sitter while he was in class or playing in various nightclubs or Irish pubs to pick up cash. Then when I was four or five, he started taking me with him to work, making a nest for me behind the piano using our coats and scarves, feeding me bar food for dinner. I tease him that it's his fault I can't catch even a whiff of chicken wings without gagging.

When I tell people at the conservatory that my father is Robin Conarn, their eyes widen. He switched from straight performance study to composing when he applied to graduate school, and now he's one of the most admired composers of contemporary classical music in the country. My first year of college, he was interviewed in the Arts section of the *Boston Globe*. A composition major down the hall thought he was so cute that she cut out his picture and pinned it to her door, so I got to pass by my father every day as I rushed to class. His smile in that picture is shy, almost apologetic, his blond hair cut long over his forehead and falling close to his eyes. It was the same smile he used to give me when he would notice me watching him play at a bar, as if he was embarrassed to be caught doing what he was good at. Then he'd wink at me, or make a silly face, and be my daddy again.

I call him while Harry picks up the laundry scattered around the room and sorts it by color. He says hello so distractedly that I can see him perfectly. He can't be actually composing; he doesn't answer the phone at all when he's at the piano. But he's clearly working through something. I picture him standing at the kitchen counter with a knife in his hand that's dripping mustard onto the piece of bread he's supposed to be slathering. When I was living at home, I'd find him like that all the time: frozen midaction, frowning slightly, listening to music unfurling in his head.

"Oh, Daddy," I wail, "it was just awful! She was mean to

me, said I was the worst singer she'd ever heard, made me stop singing after only a few bars and put her hands over her ears."

Busy piling clothes in a laundry basket, Harry snorts with laughter. At the other end of the phone there is a moment of silence; then Robin says dryly, "That's terrible, Kathleen. Surely she could have let you down a bit more gently."

"No," I say regretfully. "She just told me I had to stop singing right away. She told me I was going to go crazy if I didn't, or kill myself."

Dammit. I wasn't going to tell him that.

Harry's head snaps up and there's another silence from Robin, this one not amused.

"Daddy. It was a joke. She was talking about all the roles I was going to play."

My father has a musician's internal ear for rhythm, for pitch and tone, that he usually reserves for music he's listening to or creating himself. But when he gets frightened for me, he tunes that ear to my voice, my movements, even my breath. Even when I was a little girl, I couldn't fool him. I'd lie awake in bed with my feet out from under the covers because even the drape of the sheet made them hurt, convinced that if I turned on the light and checked I'd see blood. I couldn't even hope to sleep. I would concentrate on just lying still and breathing deep the way Robin had taught me—a singer's breathing—and willing myself not to cry. And all he had to do was pass by my doorway and he would know. He'd come in, pick me up, take me to the bathroom, and run water in the sink, then hold me there, in the dark, with water running over my feet until the pain eased enough that I fell asleep and he carried me back to bed, my feet still wet.

I told Harry about this before she met Robin. After she met him, she said, "I wonder how long he stood there at the sink those nights, after you fell asleep."

I don't know. I don't remember. But I know what she was telling me, and she was right: he would have stood there all night.

"I did hope we were still in the joke," he says now, and I talk too fast, talking over him to fix it.

"It was her joke, actually. She was very grand, very conscious of herself onstage, you know. And she was praising me, that was her way, by talking about all the roles I'll play where I die or go crazy . . ."

I trail off, hoping the explanation has done its work. He sounds thoughtful when he answers, but still tense with that humming silence of his that means he's listening to me with all his senses.

"All your roles, hmm? So she wasn't *totally* negative about your future as a singer?"

"Well . . ." I smile, knowing he can hear that in my voice too. "Not *totally*."

"I'm not a fan of Lucia," he says, "though of course it's a natural part for you because of the red hair, the Scottish setting. It's about as close to Ireland as you're likely to get in an opera. There's that one short piece about Deirdre, but that's not a full production piece. It's a good piece, though."

"You'll have to write me a part, then, Daddy," I say. "Deirdre's good. How about Emer and Cuchulain? I could do a good Emer, don't you think?"

"I'll get right on that," he says. "You know, in my spare

time. Maybe I could just do an Irish story for this latest commission. Do you think they'd notice?"

Robin's writing an opera based on *The Scarlet Letter*, which means he had to read the book this winter. Harry was delighted; she's a fiend for books and kept calling out to me while I was on the phone with Robin to find out what chapter he was on so she could know what he thought.

"How's that going, by the way?" I ask.

He doesn't answer right away. I can hear the muffled sound of another voice in the room, his girlfriend, Tae, then Robin answering, holding the phone away from his mouth. "It's Kathleen. She did the master class today." I hear him laugh, say, "I'll tell her," then he is talking to me again.

"Tae got an e-mail from her friend in the Boston Symphony today who was there. What's this about a standing ovation?"

"Oh, well." I flush with pride and mortification now, though I didn't during the master class. When the audience rose to their feet this afternoon, I convinced myself that it was an ovation for the diva, acclaim for her mere presence. Plus, she was telling me that I was going to go mad.

"'Oh, well'?" Robin says. "That's all you have to say for yourself? The last master class I gave, half the audience fell asleep. One fellow in the front row was reading the paper. And you got a *standing ovation*? How many people were there?"

I don't want to talk about it, don't want to remember those moments onstage, Ruzena's hands imprisoning mine.

"You know," I say, "I don't bug you about the whole 're-nowned composer' thing."

Robin laughs. "I tried to get a vanity plate with that on it, but I couldn't condense the words enough."

I hear Tae in the background again, Robin answering her.

"What?" I ask. "Does Tae have a solution?"

"No," he says. "She thinks we both suffer from a short-age of artistic ego. But she knows plenty of conductors who have extra."

"Ouch."

"Yes," Robin says. "So are you and Harry still planning to try to catch a few days at the Vineyard this week?"

"Well, if you count throwing things in a duffel bag and driving out there without even a ferry reservation, much less a hotel room, as 'planning'—then yes." The impulsive trip was my idea, of course, and Harry is racked with nerves over the possibility—okay, probability—that we'll end up stranded in a crummy hotel on the mainland or have to just turn around and come home. She's not big on uncer-tainties. I know we should just stay in town, but I need to see the ocean. Call it a fix, which is how I put it to Harry when I suggested the trip. Just joking, of course.

"Can I offer an alternative?" Robin asks.

"Sure."

"One of my board members has a timeshare—"

"One of *your* board members?" I find this hilarious. Harry has disappeared with the laundry and I am lying on the bed with my feet up in the air, flexing my toes like a dancer, as if that will help, which it doesn't. It just doesn't make it worse.

"Stop it, Kathleen," Robin says. "You sound—"

"Happy? Silly? Manic?" I let my legs fall back to the bed. He's onto me, as usual.

"You sound like you need a break," he says. "It's a long winter up there—"

This is also hilarious. "Up here? In the frozen north that is Boston? Is it warmer down there in tropical Philadelphia?"

"—and one of my board members has a timeshare at a resort on Sanibel Island. He's been trying to get Tae and me down there. He called last night and tried to persuade us to go this coming week. He and his family were going to but something came up with his kids and they can't. So the place is going to be empty."

"Sanibel Island?"

"Gulf coast of Florida. A lot warmer than Martha's Vineyard this time of year. You'd actually be able to go in the water."

I sit up. "Seriously? Really? We could go? When?"

Now he knows he has me. "How about tomorrow? I'll call and confirm, then make plane reservations. I've got enough frequent flyer miles to take several people to Tokyo and back, or so Tae tells me."

"I have to ask Harry. Hang on."

I leave the phone on the bed with the line engaged, go out to the kitchen to find her. I *am* manic now, thinking about the Florida sea: warm enough to swim in, clear and blue enough to see through to the bottom where it's not too deep. My feet burn and the pain inside my mouth flares up. I swallow it back, hold on to the counter and resist the urge to put up a hand to feel for my tongue.

Harry comes in the front door carrying the empty laundry basket, sees me, and stops. She puts the basket down, goes to the sink, and fills a glass with water.

"Drink."

"I—"

"Don't try to talk. You know you can't; it just makes it worse. Drink."

I drink a few sips, then the rest of the glass in gulps. It helps, not like seawater would—*will*—but some.

"Robin's still on the phone," I say. I can talk if I think carefully about how to shape each word. "He wants to know if we want a free trip to Florida."

Harry raises her eyebrows. "And did you tell him yes?"

I shake my head, still carefully. "I wanted to check with you first. We'd have to leave tomorrow." My hand hurts, clenched around the glass, a silly, ordinary pain from holding on too tight. Harry leans over the counter and tucks my hair behind my ear.

"I am frequently surprised that you're not more of a brat," she says, "considering how incredibly spoiled you are."

She lets her fingertips linger on my cheek. I can't even register her touch, I'm too focused on hearing her say it's okay, we can go. Of course she's going to say it, of course she will, this isn't a self-destructive impulse, this is a *vacation* . . .

"I guess I have to rethink my packing strategy then," she says, and I grab her hand and kiss her palm, fly back to the phone on feet so light they barely hurt at all, and tell Robin yes, *yes*, we want to go. I say thank you and tell him to tell "his" board member thank you, feel my tongue working again, though I trip over it every other word.

I have to pack. Bathing suit, three kinds of suntan lotion for my Irish skin, sandals, sundresses, and ponytail holders for my hair. One more day before I am in the sea again, for the first time in nearly a year. I sink down onto the bed, shaking, holding a folded pair of shorts in my hands. Just a night in this bed and a ride in a cab, then a plane, another cab . . . one more day.

Here Below they speak of us—when they dare to speak of us—with scorn like a shell encasing their fear. They call us scavengers, bottom dwellers, scuttling crabs. They deny the value of the things we collect, in jars and nets and sharp-edged bowls of coral, until they need something. A salve for a wound that won't heal, a glimpse of things that have not happened yet, a swift-acting poison. Then they sidle through our gates, crab-like themselves in their clenched longings, their furtive needs.

We have always preferred it so. We desire many things, but have never wished to be at the heart of a story. Magic collects at the edges of stories, eddies before them and surges in their wakes. We are content—more than content—to lurk, to hover, to come behind and pick up the pieces.

Nor did we mean to wrap ourselves into this story, though we still recall the beginning clearly enough to know that we could not have avoided our part. We sold a potion to a love-struck mermaid, took payment from her, sent her on her way. Yet since then, seven daughters of seven women—beginning with that foolish, beautiful girl—have been bound to us and we to them. We have felt their pain when they have eased it in seawater, for pain travels swiftly on the coldest currents. Kathleen's, which must travel a long, long way to us, tastes of the sweet petals and bitter hearts of black anemones, which should be impossible. The flowers grow only in caves on the ocean floor and were once steeped in blood and water by warriors Below for courage in battle.

We would gladly be free of this story. Instead we must keep telling it—we, who have always kept to the edges, must tell the tale to those who are living it. For years now we have been trying to tell it to Kathleen, but an ocean separates us and there are limits to our power. We have sent dreams and we have snatched at her whenever she has swum in the sea, but it has not been enough. She must know the whole story she is living, so she can see how to end it. And we must give her the knife we made so long ago, the knife we have given them all, the knife that has returned to us seven times now, once for each useless death.

She must come home.

She is, for better or for worse, very strong. As strong as Fand was, though the time has not yet come to speak of Fand. Strong enough to will herself into frigid water when she knows that it is water she needs. Strong enough to resist the pull of immersion because immersion means death. Trapped, then, by her own strength, between the water and the land.

All the others gave in long before. Kathleen is older already than her mother, Moira, was when she left her husband and her baby daughter sleeping and walked into the sea. She drowned standing up, only a few yards from the shore.

We heard her coming, and we watched, for we could

do no more: the small, slender woman clambering bare-foot over a rocky stretch of shoreline to reach the sea. She staggered, off balance because of the stones in her pockets, catching herself on one rock as she moved to grip the next with her toes. She had red hair like a cloud or a puff of seaweed. It floated around her all the way to her waist. Tears ran down her cheeks but she made no sound until she reached the water, and then she let her breath out in a whimper. Her feet hurt so much. The cold, lapping touch of the water eased the pain. She walked out into the sea and the stones in her pockets helped her to keep walking until the water was over her head. Everything around her was cloudy, her hair floating into her face and the light from above yellow-green. She walked forward into darker water and waited, immersed.

We cast a gleaming green net for her and brought her down to the bottom. Her eyes were still open, her lips parted to let the water in. We took her fine, soft hair that curled and rippled in the deep currents. We wove her youth into it, and her clear, high voice that was like the sound of a flute, and also her despair. Then we let her go. Black silt rose up and settled, and the sea lettuce enclosed her.

Moira would have said that the sea called to her, but the sea calls no one. At its depths where it is blackest and coldest and truest in its nature, the water is neither hungry nor needy for life or warmth or quick-moving creatures like ourselves. The water just is, like the implacable old mountains Above, against which people fling themselves and up which they crawl, as though the mountain itself must tremble under their fumbling feet. The mountain does not care. Nor does the sea. What Moira felt was her own need, the same need that has driven them all, first Fand, who knew what she had done, and then those who followed her, who were not so fortunate: Victoria, Muirin, Ceara, Caolinn, Deirdre, Moira.

And now Kathleen.

We have a chance to reach her now such as we have not had in a long time. She will be swimming in clear water, amidst shells leached so utterly of life and color that a finely honed spell of summoning might run through them like a current. We shall not overreach our power. We shall not try to do too much. All she need do is listen, and hear us.

Come home, Kathleen. You do not know your own story, nor that you have a choice in it. Come home so we can give you the knife, still as sharp as when we forged it, sharp as the choices it offers. Come home.

KATHLEEN

Aria for Soprano with Choral Intrusion

We cross the Sanibel Causeway in late afternoon and I lean out the window, yearning toward the water. The bridge skims so close that I imagine that I could reach out and touch the rippling surface as we speed past. The smell in the car is sweet and wet, cut flowers and rain, and sunlight flashes back up from the water, broken into splinters of color. My eyes tear up but I can't stop staring. It's been so long since I've been this close to the ocean, nearly a year. How did I stay away so long?

I am crying. I don't realize it until Harry touches my face to blot a tear.

"I should shut the window," I say, but Harry stops me.

"Leave it open," she says. "The air feels good."

I can feel it on my skin, in my hair, which is tangling in the sticky air and starting to cling to my cheeks and neck.

And I can almost taste the water if I breathe in deeply and then close my mouth. The flavor on my tongue is salty, the taste of the sea.

"Good Lord," Harry says, and I wrench my eyes from the water to follow her gaze to the road ahead. The entrance to the resort is banked with hibiscus on either side, with the name carved into a stucco sign in elegant script. Once through the gates we wind past palm trees, golf courses, swimming pools, ornamental gardens, and tennis courts on our way to the main building to pick up our key. Harry leans into me, her breath stirring my hair.

"Wow," she murmurs. "This place goes on forever. And the flowers . . . Toto, I don't think we're in Boston anymore."

"You need a flower in your hair," I tell her, "and then you'll forget all this nonsense you're spouting about this place—what do you call it?—'Boston.' It sounds very grim and depressing and I'm sure you're making it up."

Harry laughs. "Do I get to put flowers in your hair too?"

"Only white ones. Everything else will clash."

At the front desk, waiting for our key, I am like a child. I can smell the ocean, hear the ocean. I even caught a glimpse of it around the corner of the building when the car dropped us off. I bounce on my toes, spin around in little circles; I cannot keep still.

Harry shakes her head at me. "You're adorable," she says. "I've never seen you like this."

"Like what?"

"You're so excited. I mean, I knew about you and water—I *thought* I knew about you and water—but now I see that I had no idea."

"You make it sound like we're having an affair."

"What, you and the ocean?"

"Yes."

"Well . . ." She turns her back to the counter and leans on it, grinning at me. "Are you?"

A family—mom, dad, three kids, inflatable swimming toys, towels—invades the front lobby on their way out to the pool. I shudder at the thought. Why, especially with the sea so close, would anyone deliberately subject themselves to water leached of its softness and smell? At some point when I was in elementary school, Robin signed me up for swim lessons at an indoor pool. My therapist at the time had suggested that any water would satisfy me. After the first lesson, I hid in a locker in the ladies' room and wouldn't come out until the teacher sent Robin in to talk to me. I made him promise not to bring me back. I've avoided swimming pools ever since, but even now the merest whiff of chlorine makes me gag.

Still, this family has the right idea: they are all barefoot. I kick off my ballet flats. Better. I stuff the shoes in the out-side pocket of my carry-on.

"I can fit yours in the other pocket," I offer to Harry.

"I'll leave mine on for now," she says. "Somebody has to be the adult here."

I stick my tongue out at her and she laughs at me again. Then the woman returns with our key and paperwork and points to a motorized cart, already loaded with our bags, waiting for us in the driveway. We loop around the cul-de-sac in front of the main building and head down a smaller road toward the beach. The driver points out our block of condos on the right, but straight ahead is the water. It's a vivid Florida ocean here, the blue as bright against the white beach as the flowers—in pink and purple and orange—are bright against their backdrop of green. I am out of the cart while it is still moving, and I don't know if my movement precedes or follows Harry's murmur to me to "Go, just go. I'll catch up."

I run down to the water and into the water and I only stop then because the relief of feeling it on my feet makes me reel.

"Colder than you were expecting, huh?" a man asks, sounding amused, but I don't even register his face. He's standing in the surf next to me and talking about how even though it is Florida it's also only March, and the way the tides and currents move, this water is actually cooler than water farther up the coast . . . It is cold, but not the gasping cold of the Atlantic Ocean in New England. And I've gone swimming in the pewter-colored water off Nantucket in every month of the year, gone out when the few other people on the beach shuddered as they watched me plunge in.

I wade out farther and the man's voice fades away. The sun on the endless, glinting blue surface of the water is too bright, the light where the two meet hard and sharp and sparkling. I look down, and the water is clear enough that I can see my jeans, heavy and black, and my bare white feet beneath them. When I am far out enough to pick my feet up off the bottom, I unfasten the jeans and kick them off, shrug off my sweater and shirt, shimmy out of my underwear, and duck my head under. At last. Immersion.

Naked, I dive under and swim out into deep water, behind even the biggest swells of surf, where I have to come up for air. I stroke the water with my feet and hands and it strokes back, the cold current pulling at my feet and ankles. I give in and go down again. I never close my eyes underwater if I can help it. I'd rather blink against the salt sting and be able to see where I am down here. The sand is still white beneath me, as white as an endless new carpet, no seaweed or small plants to break it up. On the plane Harry read to me about the island being famous for its seashells and about how people come here just to collect them. She joked about taking up seashell crafts, making picture frames or vases. There are shells and pieces of shell everywhere, shifting slightly in the sand as the tide moves over them, as if settling themselves more comfortably. I surface for a breath, then swim straight down to the bottom to pick up a conch shell.

I have a whole collection of these at home. Harry will tease me for picking up another one. I push my hair off my face and tread water. The sunlight seems already to have bleached the shell from the color and sheen of a pearl to the colorless white of a clean bone, but for the pleated curve of the interior, which is pink and satiny. I tuck my fingers inside so I can hold it in one hand and swim with the current for a while, paralleling the beach but not moving any closer to shore. The sun will be setting soon, but it still burns on my cheeks and my shoulders wherever my hair has not mantled them. I am not swimming toward anything, but, with some effort, I am not swimming away from anything either. Not the white beach I can still see out of the corner of my eye, nor the people on it, who I always try to pretend will have forgotten all about me, so that when it is time to come in, I will be able to slip past the "only an idiot would swim out that far" line that they've drawn in the water with their eyes and join the rest of them in the shallower water, all of us floundering together up onto the stinging sand.

Of course my little attempts at camouflage rarely work. I've learned, over the years, to pay attention to whistling sounds or amplified yelling, so that a lifeguard doesn't actually get into a boat or onto a surfboard to "rescue me." Even so, I have their attention. Maybe it's the red hair, hard to miss out here in the middle of the water. Whatever it is, whenever I give up and swim back to the beach, people come over to me: "I thought you were heading out to sea!" "Are you crazy? Swimming that far out all alone?" "Are you a triathlete?" And I smile vaguely and say that I just love the ocean. I know that they are afraid of the sea and they know that I'm not afraid of it and that makes them more scared for me or of me, because . . . well, because you ought to be afraid of the sea. The sea can kill you.

I do feel, for a moment, small and hollow when I realize how far out I am in the water. It's a weird sensation, like I've just made a wrong turn on my way to a place I know, a wonderful, safe, familiar place, and now instead of being there, I'm nowhere. I've felt it before and it's always bad, like vertigo or reaching out across the bed for your lover to find her gone.

I turn my back on the sea and swim toward the beach—a little closer, anyway, close enough to make out Harry standing in the surf, watching me. She is holding something in her arms—my discarded clothes—and even from here I can tell that she is holding herself stiffly, the way she does when she senses trouble. Like I'm about to crumple in a heap on the floor and refuse to go to class because my feet hurt too much. Or like I've emerged from a practice session talking a mile a minute and singing full voice in the hallway because I've taken a pain pill without telling anyone and washed it down with too much caffeine on an empty stomach. Times when she has to manage me.

Well, she can't come manage me now. She can't make me come out. I wave to her. She's still dressed in the khakis and navy blue cotton sweater she wore on the plane and she could be a page out of a J.Crew catalog. The wind is playing with her hair, blowing the short blond curls in her face as she tries to wring out my jeans. She must have gone into the condo already, because she has a towel over her shoulder. Of course she would have thought of that.

I swim farther in and wave to her again, showing off my shell, but when my feet brush the bottom I stop. I will go to her soon. Just not yet. I go under again and focus on how good the water feels under my hair, lifting it off my neck and shoulders so that its weight no longer tugs my head back. It's a discomfort I don't even notice until it's gone. I close my eyes and feel the water on my eyelids, just a faint pressure, and the drag when I open my eyes again. I turn toward the open sea again, one cupped hand still holding the conch, and pull the water apart like a curtain, kicking my legs behind me. I used to swim like this for hours, coming up for air only when I absolutely had to, deliberately keeping my back to the shore, and to Robin waving me in.

He is so protective that I wonder sometimes why I don't chafe at his concern the way I chafe at Harry's. Of course, he's my father, not my girlfriend. And he reveals himself in ways that wouldn't be obvious to someone who didn't know him, or me. Like the house in Philadelphia, which he bought when I was in college, and which he kept calling his "dream house" and teasing me about over the phone— how there was a room in it for me, but if I didn't come home often enough he was going to turn it into a music library. It wasn't until I spent my first summer break there that I saw through him. The room is painted blue and green in gradually intensifying shades down the walls, like you're going deeper into the water as you get closer to the floor: custom-painted room, with blue lights and blackout curtains and my own bathroom with a sunken tub big enough to submerge in.

The house is also only fifteen minutes from one of the best psychiatric hospitals in the country, although of course I didn't know that when I first came home that summer. I'm sure Robin knew, though, before he bought the place. There are things we don't talk about, my father and I, because it's always been just the two of us and we don't need to say anything. And then there are the *other* things we don't talk about. Water. The sea. The pain in my feet and my mouth. My mother and the pain she felt in her feet and in her mouth until she drowned herself to be free of it.

In place of memories of my mother, I have only the few pictures Robin has, and those not very good. His favorite is a Polaroid that's been leached of color over the years so that it's practically sepia-toned. In it Moira stands beside the crib Robin has just put together, cradling her incongruously rounded belly. She is clearly delicately built, her arms thin, collarbones hollow, fragile even in late pregnancy. The expression on her face could be the half-smile of a shy teenage girl—she was only twenty when I was born, after all, and self-conscious about being a freckled redhead. Robin says she didn't know she was pretty or believe anyone who told her so. She could also be smiling as much as she is able, which is only halfway, a smile attenuated by the strain of concealing despair.

She was dead just a year later.

When I was sixteen, I finally asked Robin the obvious question. "Did Moira have pain like I do?"

He shook his head miserably. "I don't know for sure. She had days when . . . when she wouldn't talk to me. When you were little, when you first started complaining about your feet hurting—I made some connections. She was so quiet anyway, Kath."

But she knew what would happen to me. She had to know. She knew, she felt it, and she left anyway, didn't even warn us.

Damn. I've bumped blindly into this train of thought, like a fish nosing through dark water. I surface abruptly, treading water, and shake my hair back. The conch shell is an awkward burden in my hand. I hold it up and explore its strangeness, the abrupt unfolding of one texture from the other at the edge of the inside pleat, from rough to silky. I put it to my ear to hear its whispery echo of the sea—

Come home.

The voice is right in my ear, as though the woman is leaning over my shoulder. I jerk the shell away from my ear and spin around, abruptly aware of how far I am from shore. The sunset splinters on the water, blinding me, but still I can tell there's no one there. Yet I heard the voice. The only other explanation is so stupid that I put the shell to my ear again.

Come home.

A different voice, also a woman's, and then another and another while my treading legs lose their rhythm and I sink down into the water, where the voices grow louder—

Come home come home come home.

I drop the shell and kick out for the shore in the same motion, swimming away from the voices—

Come home come home come home.

The problem is that the voices are not in my head, or in the shell anymore. The shell is behind me, turning as it falls and settling into the sand, and I feel a pang of loss almost as sharp as physical pain. Why did I let it go? Stupid, stupid, stupid.

Come home come home come home.

Except that when I dropped it, I didn't know the voices would follow me. It's as if the shell was just a homing device, some way of locking onto me, and now the voices trail me through the water, murmuring, as if the women speaking are so close behind me that if I just turned and glanced over my shoulder there they'd be—

Come home come home come home.

Nope, nobody there, the voices are still behind me and around me, each one imperative, but all of them together—I can't count how many there are, there's a young one and an old one with a quaver to it and an impatient one and a gentle one and one that maybe wants to laugh, that thinks this is funny—loop and lap one another into a single urgent cadence—

Come home come home come home.

My feet and then my knees snag on the sand and I come up abruptly into the air, exposed suddenly nearly to my waist, my breasts tightening painfully and my hair heavy again across my back. The voices fade, as if the speakers are moving away.

I forgot I was naked. Harry wades out, shaking her head, and wraps me in an enormous towel, half-dragging me the rest of the way out of the water so the towel doesn't get wet. It comes below my knees and I clutch at it as I scramble up onto the wet sand of the tide line, then stop and turn around, facing the sea again.

"Did you get your fix for the day?" Harry asks.

I shake my head. "Shh . . ." Now that I am completely out of the water the voices have stopped. I wait for the tide. As it surges over my feet, the voices clutch at me—*Come home come home*—and then wash away with the receding wave.

They are in the sea then. Not in the shell, not in my head. Maybe. But though I want to make sense of them—they were loudest when I was fully immersed, then fainter and fainter as I emerged—they are still impossible, because why can I hear them when only my feet are in the water? Can you have aural hallucinations that only show up—what's the word?—*circumstantially*?

"Kathleen?" Harry is saying, a hint of impatience in her voice now. I can't imagine why, except that she's gotten her clothes wet, first holding my wet clothes and then coming in after me. She needs to get inside, get changed into dry things, get some dinner. She must be starving. I scoop up the ends of the towel and reach for her hand.

"It was so warm," I say. "I'd forgotten how warm the Florida ocean is."

A wave rushes in and I dance out of the way too late.

Come home come—

Harry is amused. "Seriously? You don't want to get your feet wet?"

The important thing is to make sure she doesn't know. We're on our first real vacation together. I can't be hearing voices in the sea. And even if one were to concede that I *am* hearing voices in the sea—I dodge the next wave successfully and tug Harry up onto the dry sand, which feels like broken glass under my feet—I can't let Harry know.

"I've had enough of the water for one day," I tell her. "Unless you count a shower. Or maybe"—I walk closer, deliberately bump her with my hip—"a dip in the hot tub. Isn't there supposed to be a hot tub on our deck?"

Her hand tightens on mine; her smile deepens. "There is," she says. "It's big enough for a party of twelve. And there's a privacy screen all around it."

Maybe tomorrow they'll be gone. Maybe they have the wrong person. I could come back tomorrow and try telling them that. This makes me shiver with only slightly hysterical laughter.

"Cold?" Harry asks. "Is the hot tub calling us?"

If you only knew, I think, and this, combined with the difficulty I am having walking on the sand without crying, makes me laugh harder. "If I wouldn't shock everyone in sight, I'd race you to it," I say. "But I think I'd better keep the towel on."

"It's a good look for you," she says. "Sort of half-drowned regal rat."

This time the laughter loosens something clenched inside of me, so that I remember to walk lightly on the sand, which hurts less. I'm cold and hungry and so is Harry, and if there are voices in the sea they can just damn well wait. For what, I don't know, but I will stop thinking about them now. I follow Harry up the deck stairs, hitching up the wet towel as it threatens to trip me.

"If we get in the hot tub now, I'm not sure you'll be able to drag me out," I say. "Does this place have room service?"

SHIELDED FROM THE beach and the neighboring condos by a curved wall of sun-bleached planking, the tub has the allure of a secluded grotto. The churning of the jets drowns out the sound of the surf, but I can still *see* the waves over Harry's shoulder. Closer up, below us and around us, the water is blue-green and gilt in the glow of the lights set into the sides of the tub.

We began on the bench against the wall, but the water wanted us floating, not sitting, and so we've given in and slipped into the middle of the tub, where we touch bottom and then push off, touch bottom and push off, turning slowly, legs tangled together. Mine are longer but hers are stronger, our hands clenching and kneading, from thigh to butt to back to breast. I arch backward and grip her close with only my legs while her fingers circle and circle and draw points that she takes in her mouth. I am wet all over, from her mouth and the water and the cloak of my hair. I tug her head up and kiss her, taste salt from my skin on her lips, sink into the melting dance of my tongue against hers, slide down and against her in the tub, down and up again, her hands gripping me tight, fingers tucked into the hollows of my thighs from behind, holding me still. I scoop up water in my cupped hands and pour it over us, between us, against us. The feel of her against me underwater is a friction like pain and the relief from pain together. I touch her hair where it is wet and tightly curled against my own, both slick as seaweed. I feel boneless and liquid, like I have spilled out—we have spilled out together into the water, we are the water, glinting and foaming in the dark.

Afterward, she insists we shower, moisturize, dry our hair so it doesn't soak the pillows. I can only convince her not to do more kitchen cleanup by promising to do it myself, though of course I cheat. I stuff all the containers of leftover food in the refrigerator and fill the sink with soapy water so she can't see the dirty dishes. Harry will end up doing it properly herself tomorrow morning, but tonight she is so tired that she is asleep even before I shut off the light in the kitchen and grope my way down the hall.

The bedroom is bright with moonlight streaming in through the French doors and Harry is curled up right in the middle of the bed. She is lovely in her sleep, more softly so than when she's awake and worried or busy. She is wearing an old T-shirt and no bra; the contrast with her boy's haircut is delicious. Her eyelashes are surprisingly dark for someone so blond, something I noticed the first time I watched her sleep. I pull the curtains closed, take off my robe, and slip into bed beside her, bracing myself for her to roll toward me as she always does, my body a magnet for hers even in sleep. I love the feel of her, but sometimes I can't bear any contact, not even her breath on my neck or her hand on my waist. I can tell this is going to be one of those nights, but I wait for her to sink deeper into sleep before I wriggle away.

How did I ever fall in love with a woman like this?

So levelheaded, so stable. When she decides to lose five pounds, she loses five pounds. When her voice teacher suggests a certain role or song cycle to her, she doesn't just read the libretto and find a recording to listen to, she spends a week in the library, researching text, music, interpretation, everything. Even her voice reflects who and what she is in a way mine doesn't. She has a voice like the inside of a New England church. I can hear *her* in her voice. And though everyone—especially Harry—loves my voice, my voice lies. I am nothing without my voice, but it lies all the same. I stand onstage, my skin chafing against the fabric of my costume and my feet hurting so much that I can only will myself to stand still by picturing the blood soaking my shoes and seeping through the soles. But when I open my mouth to sing, the sound that comes out is unmarred, a stream without even a pebble to disturb its ecstatic flow.

Even that one morning—the morning when pain was a fire in my mouth and a river of pain poured out of my mouth—

Shit. What was I thinking about? I was thinking about singing. I was thinking about Harry and singing and voices and my voice.

Everyone says, "Such a beautiful voice." Even that morning it was beautiful.

I try not to think about that morning, or about the dream the night before, of the sensation of someone actually catching hold of my tongue with wet, bony fingers. The nails pinched and I tried to twist away but then there was a quick decisive motion, another arm and hand descending, and my tongue was gone, my mouth full of blood, and

I woke up screaming. The scream was like a song. I could hear it, and the song was incandescent in the air as Robin came running.

I am not supposed to think about that morning, my sixteenth birthday, of all days. One therapist suggested that I found the dream so traumatic that I developed a kind of stress disorder. Even recalling the dream or the pain that followed can trigger another "episode." I taste wet iron in my mouth, feel it filling with saliva the way I was sure it was filling with blood as I screamed.

Unearthly. That's what Robin called it. He picked me up out of bed that morning, held my arms in a grip that left bruises, and still the scream went on and on. It only stopped when I began to gag. When I did, I could feel that my tongue was still there, flattening out as I retched. At the emergency room, one doctor said it was swollen and bruised as if someone had indeed pinched it with something sharp, but of course, I must have done that myself, in my sleep.

I swallow the metallic taste in my mouth and shove my feet out from under the blankets. I am clammy the way you are after you've just thrown up, too hot and too cold all at once. Stupid voices in the water. If it wasn't for them I'd be asleep by now, not thinking about things I'm usually good at holding at bay. I breathe deeply and carefully, in through my nose, out through my mouth, using my stomach muscles as if I'm warming up to sing.

Harry tries to snuggle closer again. When I flinch away she sighs and rolls over. Then of course I immediately want her to come back to me, though I can feel that finally, lying very still without anyone touching me and my feet kicked out from under the covers, I am beginning to sink toward sleep. I hate the conscious knowledge that I am Harry's weakness, that she's abandoned her rational approach to the world to love me as she does, without questioning the stuff that doesn't make sense, pain and nightmares and phobias about having my tongue cut out. And I hate that she is my weakness too, that she has gotten not just past the lies I'm so used to telling about my physical symptoms, but inside the struggle to hide them from everyone else, that she loves me *more* because she thinks I'm brave and strong. Hardly. A few months ago I began to feel her swimming beside me in my dreams. They are the same dreams I have always had, dreams of deep water and shifting blue light, but now Harry is there too. I point things out to her as we pass them: shimmery schools of silver fish, the flat shadow of a ray or an eel that swims away before you can be sure of it. But then I turn to face her fully and she's gone, of course she's gone, and when I wake up, weeping as always, it's because I've lost both Harry and the sea.

I WAKE THE next morning from one of these dreams and lie quietly for a moment, feeling the slight warmth and weight of Harry's hand, which has again found its way onto the curve of my hip. I dry my eyes with the edge of the sheet.

Then I hear the surf and I have to know. I shrug back into my robe, let myself out the French doors onto the deck, and run down to the beach and into the surf. It laps around my feet and ankles, deliciously cold against my skin, and for a moment it is just the sea. I grin and walk in up to my knees. Then a wave knocks me over and as I struggle to untangle the belt of my robe from around my thighs a woman's voice snaps at me—*Kathleen! Come home!*

I am still so shaky from the dream and so angry at the damn voices for ruining what was supposed to be a perfect vacation that I scream back.

"What do you want?"

A wave rushes me and I swallow a mouthful of seawater, which feels wonderful in my dry mouth but seems to make the voices slide right down my throat, murmuring *come-homecomehome*. I stagger to my feet and smack the surface of the next wave. "Stop it, do you hear me? Stop it. Leave me alone!"

But it's just more of the same, murmured urgings to *come home* trailing me as I stalk back up to the beach and sit down just out of reach of the surf. I pull my knees up and press my face so hard into them that I see spots. I need Harry. I need Harry to help me with this one, and I can't let her help me. The trouble is that I'm not levelheaded or reflective or logical—not about much of anything, really, and certainly not about my, ugh, my *problems*. When I first told Harry about all the weird pain, she immediately started asking what the various doctors had said, what medications I'd tried, the questions I guess it makes sense to ask. And somewhere in between answering her and stifling the urge to scream at her to stop asking me these stupid questions, I realized that she wasn't doubting me, which was what I'd assumed she'd do. She was asking because she *believed* me. It didn't make the answers any easier, since no one has a good explanation and nothing has ever helped, but it made it easier to give them to her.

But what if I tell her about this latest development? *Honey, I'm hearing voices in the sea. Whenever I touch seawater,*

I hear women telling me to "come home." What do you think that symptom means?

Nope. Uh-uh. Can't tell Robin either. Because what if this was what finally made Moira crack, hearing women in the water whenever she soaked her feet? Can psychosis, or whatever, be so specific from one generation to the next?

On the face of it, just as a simple fact, hearing women talking to me while I'm swimming isn't so bad. It's better than feeling like your tongue's being cut out. But—*try to think logically here, Kathleen*—voices in the water are not real, they can't be real. Yet I'm definitely hearing them. And that pretty much squashes flat the whole shaky thing I've built, with Harry and Robin's help, out of all the other symptoms, the idea that somewhere there's a medical condition we just haven't found, a syndrome or an allergy or an autoimmune disease that causes flaring pain. Add in *hearing voices but only while touching seawater and only saying one thing, repeatedly, except for occasional use of subject's own name*, and there's nothing left but, well, Crazy. With a capital *C*.

A particularly enterprising wave reaches up and circles my ankles: *come home*. I put my hand down as if I could pin it there, get the sea's attention that way.

"You know," I say out loud, "for the record, part of what makes me mad here is that I hate to be a cliché. I mean, voices in my head . . . for God's sake, it's not even original."

Another wave makes a foray, soaking my butt this time. The tide must be coming in.

Come home.

"And if you're trying to get me to drown myself, you're not going about it well at all," I tell this one while it is still foaming around me. "I may be crazy about the ocean, but it's not *home*."

The wave recedes, still murmuring, and I wonder if it, or they—the voices, I mean—know that I can't come up with someplace that *does* feel like home, not our apartment in Boston or my beautiful bedroom outside of Philadelphia that's meant to trick you into thinking you're sleeping at the bottom of the sea.

WHEN I COME back up to the condo, Harry is sitting out on the deck with a book and a cup of coffee.

"I made a whole pot," she says. "Did you have a good swim?"

"One of these days I'm really going to have to consider a bathing suit," I say. "Let me go change."

When I come back out in dry clothes, she has lowered her book and is watching a scene play out down at the beach. There's a little girl down there now, hardly more than a baby, sitting in the wet sand at the water's edge and shrieking with excitement whenever a wave washes over her. Her father dances from foot to foot behind her, ready to snatch her up.

Harry turns to smile at me. "That poor father! He's so nervous for her and she's having a ball. And I love her pig-tails. My mother used to put my hair in pigtails like that, sticking right out of the top of my head. They were completely ridiculous."

"But cute," I say. I nudge her foot with my toes. "Admit it, you were very cute."

I've seen pictures of Harry as a little girl, her face puffed out with baby fat, dimples in her elbows and her knees.

To hear Harry talk, she went from being an "ordinary" person, a little girl with dimples, to being an artist. She still finds it strange and wonderful to call herself a singer. It's a transformation that most singers talk about, even the ones who claim to have been born with perfect pitch or whose parents swear they sang before they walked or talked. But it's something I can't understand.

I've had rapturous moments of progression in my singing, like when Robin and my voice teacher explained to me that I could make singing my job. And there was that terrible day when my voice was forged—all in an hour, apparently, all in a scream. My voice teacher was absolutely baffled the next time he heard me sing. Since my voice changed, there is always a moment when I'm singing when I feel the music itself settling like a web around my voice, holding it in. If I'm singing with another person, the sensation is different; the other voice is a weight pulling mine down. I don't think that without the weight or the web of constraining sound that I would necessarily sing *higher*. I would just sing something *more*. There is song rising in the back of my throat at that moment—I can feel it there and I can hear how it might sound. But I can also hear how it would overwhelm the music around me. So I swallow it back.

But the sense of being a person separate from your voice and then gradually becoming the person who can lay claim to that voice, by virtue of hard work and strenuous vocal exercise and study: I can only imagine how that feels. When Harry and I moved in together, her mother sent several boxes of Harry's books from her parents' house, including a photo album. I sat beside Harry on the floor in

our new living room and stared hard at those pictures—at
HARRIET, 3 YRS., AT THE FAMILY CLAMBAKE, a chubby
blond baby in a green and white gingham dress with a wide
pink collar embroidered with black to look like two slices
of watermelon framing her face. Her face is scrunched up
in what she must mean to be a smile for the camera, and she
is smudged and sticky with sand at the ankles and wrists.

I searched for the shadows of her voice around her, for
a glimpse of it in her dirty little sunburned face. There's
a capacity for wonder there already, the wonder that's in
her face and in her voice when she talks about the great
mezzo Lorraine Hunt Lieberson. But the voice itself, what
I would have thought had always been *Harry's* voice—it's
not there yet. It's floating somewhere outside of her, waiting
to be a part of her sometime later.

"Are you hungry?" Harry asks. "I had a bowl of granola
already."

"I'll get something."

"Who were you talking to?"

I carefully pick up my coffee cup. "What?"

"Down at the beach. I thought I heard you calling me
and I woke up."

"I didn't mean to wake you! I'm so sorry."

"It's fine." She shrugs. "I got plenty of sleep. But then
when I came out here you were sitting down there talking."

"You talk to yourself all the time."

Harry laughs. "True. It's just that you usually don't."
And the inevitable zinger: "Are you okay?"

"I'm fine," I say. This is what will make me crazy, having
to lie to her about not being crazy. I take too big a sip of
coffee and it burns all the way down.

We felt the spell catch, a tug on the line we had flung across the ocean like the jerk a fisherman feels—she heard us, at least. Now we wait and wonder how to do what must be done.

We are not accustomed to doubt like this, to disagreements among ourselves that send fine fissures skittering across the surfaces we have rubbed to a silken sheen—tables and mirrors and bowls. We know what we must tell Kathleen, but we are uncertain—have we not acknowledged already that we are not storytellers?—how to spin the tale. Some of us want to begin at the beginning, when the little mermaid put a shaking hand to the string of teeth and bones at our front gates, setting them to chattering out her need. Some of us wish to unravel the story further as we have already begun to do by speaking of Moira first.

We rub the fissures out and agree (some of us murmur that we concede) that as we have begun, so shall we go on. From Moira back to her mother, Deirdre, to Deirdre's mother, Caolinn . . . all the way back to Fand. That story, of course, is its own telling and counter-telling, against the way it has been told until now, and is best saved for last.

Deirdre, who was mother to Moira and grandmother to Kathleen, tried to drown herself every day. She huddled *in her bath until the false warmth had gone and the cold had set in, bowing her head and setting her teeth against the chill because the shivering of her body did not feel real. Beneath the shivering was something more, something that she could not explain, about the feel of the water—even such stripped and colorless water as that— against her skin and in her mouth and her eyes and even her ears if only she could stay there. When she gave in, Deirdre chose this false drowning and made it real. She filled the bath and used the knife, which sent swirls of bright color into the water. It faded to pink, and her skin to white. We knew of Deirdre's death when the knife returned to us, but she gave nothing else back to the sea.*

Caolinn—slender, bright, and fair, just as her name promised—loved a woman. She thought that this love might save her, or at least that the curse might end with her, but she sang too long in the pub one night and was pushed against a wall on her way home, fingers scrabbling uselessly on stone and pain tearing through her while the man at her back tried to make her feel how her voice had torn a hole in him.

Her lover promised that they'd grow old together, two spinsters in a cottage. The baby could call her Auntie. Instead, while Caolinn was heavy with child, her lover left her forever, forced by her own father to don a black dress like a shroud, to cover her hair, and to live surrounded by other women, but without her beloved, without Caolinn.

Caolinn named her daughter Deirdre, which means "child of sorrow." One night she nursed the baby, wrapped her warmly, and left her on the doorstep of the village church. Dry-mouthed, she gulped all the pills the doctors had given her for pain after the birth. She stole a rotted-out rowboat and let it carry her, shivering in her bare feet and her thin dress with icy water slopping in, as far as it could before the bottom gave way. She gasped when the cold enfolded her, but she slept like a child all the rest of the way down. Her hair was thick and straight and a dark red that, underwater, was the color of blood. She died with her hands clenched, the one around her nightmares of a man's reeking breath on her cheek and the other around a lock of her lover's hair. These things we pried out carefully and saved.

HARRY

Aria for Mezzo-Soprano

The first morning in Sanibel, I woke abruptly thinking Kathleen had shouted for me. She wasn't in bed and she didn't answer when I called her name, so I got up, pulled on a pair of shorts with my T-shirt and went out on the deck. When I saw her down on the beach I was relieved at first. Then I heard her talking angrily, gesturing as if she was arguing with someone. When a wave came up to soak the spot she was sitting on she seemed to flinch.

That was when I knew something was wrong. Kathleen flinching away from the touch of the water? I watched her a little longer, then I went inside to make some coffee and tried to feel annoyed with her at the crappy job she'd done cleaning up the kitchen. It didn't work though, because the worry trumped everything else.

I'd been worrying about this trip as much as I'd been looking forward to it. Kathleen was on a high when we left, which meant there was a low coming. When I got into bed the night before we left, she was already asleep, her feet twitching beneath the blankets. That might have meant that her feet were hurting, but Kathleen was always a restless sleeper, practically swimming across the bed at night. Some nights the weight of the blankets was intolerable, sometimes the touch of the sheet itself made her cry. Watching her sleep for a moment before I turned out the light, I thought about Florida, hoped the sheets were soft. I thought about how if a low was coming, it was going to come anyway, in Boston or Martha's Vineyard or Florida. I thought about how it was impossible to say no to Kathleen.

This morning, as I made coffee and rinsed the dishes from the night before, then put them in the dishwasher, I wished I'd thought more—thought of how far we were now from her father, from a hospital that had her records, from our friends. I'd gotten swept away by her excitement. No, to be fair, it had been more than that. I wanted to be here with her, to watch her in the ocean, make her happy by sharing it with her. Last night in the hot tub I'd felt her pulsing, abandoned around me like she never was in a bed. I flushed all over again, thinking about it.

I balanced a book on a bowl of cereal, my coffee cup in my other hand, and went out to sit on the deck. In the end, though, I didn't open the book. I ate my breakfast and watched Kathleen apparently arguing with the tide coming in around her.

MY PARENTS, WHO have only met Kathleen once when they came to my recital last fall and took us out to dinner, aren't sure they approve. My mother worded it cautiously.

"I just don't want you to sacrifice your own happiness

for someone else's," she said. "That's all. Make sure you're *happy* with her."

Even our friend Tom, who loves Kathleen—he practically *is* Kathleen, only male—told me that he's not sure she's good for me.

"Don't get me wrong, Harry," he said, "and don't frown at me like my high school English teacher. I adore her, you know that. But I love you too and you put up with way too much of her shit. Tell her no, for God's sake, tell her to lay off the drama once in a while."

There's a line at the end of *Jane Eyre* that I could have used to answer them both, if I was the sort of person who went around quoting my favorite books, which I'm not: "To be privileged to put my arms round what I value—to press my lips to what I love—to repose on what I trust: is that to make a sacrifice? If so, then certainly I delight in sacrifice."

I LOVE KATHLEEN the way I once imagined people only loved in books. Maybe that's why I "put up with her," but I think it's because it feels like a gift, to feel this way. That's so hard to explain that I've never tried, not even to Kathleen. She likes to tease me that I love books more than I love her, or that eventually I'm just going to have to succumb to my longing to be an English teacher, singer on the side.

If I *had* just majored in English as I'd planned, Kathleen and I would never have met. But I was also a cellist, good enough that by the end of my first semester in college my cello teacher had convinced me to pursue a double major. This meant taking "foundations of vocal music," a required class for all music majors except voice majors, nearly all of whom were exempt. The students who did take it were a bit of a motley bunch, vocally: violinists who could sing just fine, trumpeters who could carry a tune and not much else, and a few drummers and electronic musicians who made the professor wince when they opened their mouths.

We had to sing for her on the very first day of class. Her name was Alyce Koros, and I thought she was sexy. She dressed like a gypsy: kohl around her eyes, short, messy black hair, rings on every finger, and long flowy skirts all year round. When it was my turn to sing, she put me through twice as many vocal exercises as anyone else, then told me bluntly that I needed to change my major to voice.

The strange thing about a moment like that is how little choice you really have. I was a good cellist, a fine cellist. And I was a good writer, a fine writer. Teachers had the same compliment for my playing and my writing, said how "thoughtful" they were. I always knew that meant that I had to work at my playing, work at my writing, to be any good. The only thing I didn't have to work at was reading, which wasn't exactly a foundation for a career.

And then along came Alyce Koros, with her excited dark eyes and her revelation that I had a gift. A talent. An instrument, which is how people in the singing world refer to the human voice, that would let me do more than play music. It would turn me into a "mezzo-soprano," a term I'd never even heard of before. It would allow me to use words, beautiful words, terrible words, and make them more my own than I'd ever felt able to do on the page.

I double-majored in English and voice, then went on to the New England Conservatory. I'll have my master's degree this summer, and I'm already contracted with Central City Opera in Colorado for their summer season. The strangeness of actually *being* an artist has never really gone away for me, though. I still hesitate when I introduce myself to people. I say that I'm studying voice, but then sometimes I add, "But I was also an English major, so . . ." as if to assure them that I have something to fall back on.

There's another weird thing that happens when you start doing this thing that you love, something I wish Alyce had warned me about. It becomes hard to be a fan, to be un-critical. It's not because I think I'm that good, because I'm not. It's just that I know too much about singing, and about what singing ought to sound like in some ideal world. Even listening to great professional singers I find myself get-ting distracted, listening to their breathing, thinking about their phrasing and expression. I can pick up a poem or a novel or a libretto, read it, and just think, *Wow, amazing!* I wish I could do that with music too. By the time I got to grad school, though, I'd pretty much decided that it wasn't going to happen, that I was too trained to ever be swept away by a voice. Then I heard Kathleen sing.

IT WAS APRIL, but it felt like summer outside. I was on my way to one of the practice rooms in the basement. My end-of-semester recital was in less than two weeks, and I was still having trouble with the Bach that I'd chosen. Maybe, I remember thinking as I collected a room key from the student at the front desk, I shouldn't have picked all my music in January. Boston in January and Boston in April are almost different places. And Bach is best in the cold.

Kathleen was practicing in a room about halfway down the hallway. The doors of the practice rooms are designed to be fairly soundproof, but the joke among students is that the air-conditioning system is older than the building itself, so I wasn't surprised to see the door ajar. Standing just outside the room, I could hear her clearly.

The voice itself was a clear, pure soprano with a lush fullness to the vowel sounds where many high voices go thin or shrill. It clearly revealed training and control, but it was the natural sound of it that was so exquisite. That was why her choice of aria was so jarring. She was working on "Suicidio!" from *La Gioconda*, in which the heroine lists all the reasons she wants to die: the man she loves doesn't love her; another man has blackmailed her into sleeping with him; her beloved mother is missing and may be dead. *"Piombo esausta fra le tenèbre! Tocca alla mèta,"* she sings—*I fall exhausted into darkness! I am reaching the end.*

It's an aria with a lot of emotional weight, obviously, just the kind of risky, unexpected choice that might get a young singer noticed. But it was so wrong for the voice on the other side of that door. The expressions of utter despair rise both on the scale and in volume, over and over again, with more muted expressions of how hopeless she feels in between crescendos. Kathleen hit all her notes and held them when she needed to, her voice bursting out through the doorway with enough force to make me feel the power of it. But the aria demanded that she sing with such bitterness. Every time she came down on the phrase *fra le tenèbre* she put the emphasis on the deadened *r* in *fra* rather than on the vowel. I knew it was the right interpretive choice, but I hated it. The sound clashed with the serene, liquid beauty of her voice so badly that I wanted to push the door open and beg her to stop singing, to sing something else, please, anything else.

I wouldn't have, of course, but then, I didn't get the chance. I was glancing up and down the corridor to make sure no one else was around to notice me shamelessly listening to someone practice when the singing stopped mid-word. A moment later the door was jerked open the rest of the way and Kathleen flung herself out into the hallway. She practically ran me into the wall at my back, and I was so startled that I didn't think to do anything to minimize the obvious impression I gave of having been standing there listening to her. But she was headed for the water fountain, so our first-ever exchange of words was a mutually flustered series of "Oh! Excuse me! Sorry! Excuse me!"

She unscrewed the cap to her water bottle and filled it at the fountain, leaning down occasionally to drink from the top of the arc of water. I stood there like an idiot. I think by that point I had some vague intention of confessing that I'd been eavesdropping and telling her what a gorgeous voice she had. In the meantime, I noticed that she was as beautiful as her voice. There was also an intensity to her physicality that helped explain to me why she wanted to sing "Suicidio!" She was two or three inches taller than I was and slender. Her coloring was startling: dark red hair, white skin, and no freckles—at least none that I could see, though I blushed already at the thought of finding them.

When she straightened up and turned toward me I saw that her eyes were dark blue and thickly lashed. The hair at her temples was damp with sweat.

"Is it as hot in your room?" she asked, and I blanked, until I realized that I held the key to the practice room I'd reserved dangling from my fingers.

"It's hot in this whole building," I said. "I'm sorry if I was eavesdropping. It's just that your door was open—"

"Oh God, you were *listening*?" she exclaimed, and instead of horror, delighted relief lit her face. "I can't get it right," she said. "I've been working on it for weeks on my own, because Bella won't help me, and I'm starting to think I'm going to have to admit defeat. But damn"—she grinned at me, a reckless, mocking smile—"I hate that."

"Bella"—Isabella Menotti—is one of the top vocal coaches in the country and a professor at the NEC. She works almost exclusively with sopranos and is known for the things a lot of top vocal coaches are known for: exacting standards, a talent for the excoriation of her pupils, and a flair for the dramatic in her self-presentation. In Bella's case, this means that she wears vivid draped shawls or wraps over all-black clothes almost every day. She loves to toss the shawls over her arms or fling them around her neck to punctuate a point.

I wasn't surprised that this girl was studying with her, but I was intrigued to hear that she was fighting with her.

"Why doesn't she want you to sing it?" I asked.

"I don't know." She shrugged, then made a rueful face. "Yes I do. She thinks it's too far into the dramatic range for me. Every lesson lately she storms around ranting about how you have to earn certain roles through pain and how I can't possibly have had enough in my life to sing *La Gioconda*."

"Enough pain?"

"Yes." She shrugged again and tipped her head back to take another drink. When she was done she smiled slightly, just a twist of her mouth. "Whatever."

I didn't know what to say. I thought Bella's critique was

probably true, especially now that I could see the girl who went with the voice. She struck me as very young, and far from suicidal in her white sundress and little blue flats. And I'd thought the song was wrong for her too, though for a different reason.

She cocked her head at me and held out her hand. "I'm Kathleen Conarn," she said.

I took her hand, which was wet from the water fountain. "Harry Evans."

Kathleen lifted an eyebrow—yes, just one. It's a trick she's perfected and uses to great effect.

"Harry?"

"It's Harriet. I prefer Harry."

"Hmm. I don't blame you," she said. "I like Harry. It suits you, even though that's silly, because how would I know what suits you, but"—she made a small nervous motion as though she might have been about to touch my hand again, and I thought incredulously that she might actually be flirting with me—"it's different. Sort of a warm name. Trustworthy."

I laughed. "That's better than a lot of things, I guess."

"So," she said. "Come on in while I get my stuff and lock up in here. I'm clearly done for the day. And," she added over her shoulder as I followed her into her practice room, "since I've just declared you trustworthy, why don't you tell me what *you* thought of the aria."

"Me?"

"You do have an opinion, don't you?"

"Just because I have an opinion doesn't mean it's worth hearing," I said. "If you really want to work on a piece—"

"But you don't like it either," she said. "Why not? Same reason as Bella?"

"Well, no. I'm not surprised about what she said, but it wasn't what I was thinking of while I was listening. I was thinking that your voice was wrong for the aria."

"Really?" She didn't appear to be offended. "How?"

"It's a beautiful voice," I said. "You must know that. It's the kind of voice that makes people stop and listen even though they shouldn't, like I just did. I just found myself wishing that I could hear you singing something else, something less . . ."

"Depressing?" Kathleen had turned away to stuff her music into her bag and her hair slipped over her shoulder, hiding her face.

This is another gesture I've come to recognize since. Kathleen's hair is part of her defensive array: sometimes shield, sometimes camouflage. A quick shrug of her shoulders or tilt of her head and she will be hidden from me behind a gleaming red curtain.

"Well." I was upset by her sudden withdrawal. I wanted her to smile at me again. "You have to sing depressing songs. That's what we're all doing here, right, learning how to sing about falling in love with the wrong people and dying at the end? But 'Suicidio!' is just so *bleak*. And you don't have a bleak voice."

As soon as I said it I knew that was precisely the problem, and I felt better for having expressed it that way. It wasn't criticism of either Kathleen's voice or her maturity. But she still didn't face me. She finished packing up and then she leaned over the piano, gave herself a couple of notes, tucked her hair back, and launched into "Si, mi chiamano Mimi." I knew she was mocking me, trying to make a point by singing the most cliché, lovely thing she could think of, but I still could have dropped down on the floor right there and listened to her sing until she ran out of repertoire.

Kathleen's voice is as close to perfect as a voice gets. The sweetness of tone, the clarity, and the flow of sound from her open throat make me think of a fountain in the sun. What's more, even when she was singing the way she was then, completely carelessly, I heard a longing in her voice that was the longing of one note for the next, of each phrase for the following, perfectly suited phrase. It was longing borne out of the act of singing itself and the sense of it did not leave me until she stopped singing, as abruptly as she had earlier, and turned to face me.

"No suicide for me, then, Harry?"

"No," I said. "And if you're going to be a great soprano you have to learn to take compliments."

She inclined her head a moment, as if she was considering that.

"All right," she said. "Thank you. But I think you owe me a drink for convincing me of something that the great Isabella Menotti couldn't convince me of."

I had a German lesson in twenty minutes. I clearly wasn't going. "I think *Bella* owes *me* a drink," I pointed out. "But since she's unlikely to make good, I'll buy you one. Where do you want to go?"

"Anywhere," Kathleen said. "Wherever you want to take me is fine."

WHEN KATHLEEN TOLD me her history, or at least as much of it as I've ever gotten all at once, we were in bed together, just lying there. The pain was so bad that she couldn't even talk for a while, just lay there with tears running down her temples into her hair. She shook her head when I asked if there was anything I could do, but then grabbed my wrist when I tried to get out of the bed. So I stayed. When she could talk she told me more than she'd ever told me before, about her mother having killed herself, about the dreams she had about the ocean and how upset she was when she first saw it in real life, about all the weird pains. When she stopped talking I wiped at the drying tracks of tears on her face.

"So Bella never knew what she was talking about," I said.

"What do you mean?" Kathleen asked.

"When she told you that you couldn't do justice to 'Suicidio!' because you hadn't experienced enough pain in your life. She was wrong."

Kath shrugged against my shoulder. "I guess."

I traced her bruised eyelids with my finger and realized that I believed her completely—I didn't think for a minute that any of this was "in her head"—and I felt furious at the doctors who had failed her. When she was sixty-three, my grandmother tripped and fell shoveling her driveway. For weeks after that her hip hurt. Her doctor said it was just bruised but she insisted on a bone scan and she turned out to have bone cancer that killed her.

"People are always right about their own bodies," I said, and Kathleen made a choked sound that might have been laughter.

"I wish I wasn't."

THIS MORNING, SITTING in the sunshine on the first day of what was supposed to be our perfect vacation, Kathleen practically choked on a swallow of coffee. I could hear the strain in her voice the way I used to be able to feel that a cello string was about to go. She is a very good liar about specifics—about whether she took a pain pill or drank an extra shot or actually did the goddamn dishes—but terrible at concealing the actual truth about anything. I knew last night that she was just saying she'd clean up to give me permission not to do it myself. That's why I let it go, because she was trying to take care of me and it felt lovely. And I knew now that she was keeping something from me.

She wasn't talking to anyone down on the beach. There was no one there. She could well have been talking to herself. But she was angry and she flinched away from the touch of the sea.

"So are you ready to hear my plans for the week?" I asked.

She looked at me over the rim of her coffee cup and I watched her find her balance again, saw the spark of humor come into her eyes.

"Oh God," she said. "Is it color-coded? Or . . . wait, is there a *schedule*?"

"You say that like it's a dirty word."

"Umm, yes. Because it is. Hello, vacation? No schedules allowed."

"But it's a schedule of fun things we're going to do—or can do."

"Do you hear yourself? *Schedule* and *fun* all in the same sentence." She shook her head. "You're not well, Harry. You need help."

"I'll go get it," I said. "You'll see."

I took my empty bowl and cup into the kitchen and

pulled the schedule out of my backpack. In my defense, it wasn't an actual schedule, just a list of all the activities on the resort we might like and the times when they were offered.

"Come on," I said, sliding the door open again, "there's a wine tasting class in the main restaurant every afternoon at four."

She grinned. "Wine tasting? Every day? Sign us up!"

"And there's golf and croquet and mini-golf. I know you love mini-golf, or how about horseback riding—"

I stopped to gauge her reaction to my litany and caught her in the one gesture she made that broke my heart. She lifted her chin, sniffed, and jerked her shoulders back, all in one motion. It was Kathleen bracing herself to get on with it, no matter how much she hurt. Now she was doing it while staring at the sea and I realized suddenly what could be wrong, what it could be that she wasn't telling me.

Don't let her have lost the sea, I thought, not even sure what I meant. *Please, not that.*

*P*oor woman. Poor girl. When we speak of her among ourselves we call her by the name we used for all of the lovers who have come before her in this tale. It means "seeker of one who is lost," for that is what she is, this Harriet. Harry. As they all were, six men and another woman before her, though they did not know it.

And yet the love between these two—Harry and Kathleen—is woven in a pattern we have not seen before, we who have watched the fabric of each love come together and then unravel, strand by strand. It is shaped in part by strength and truth, by the revelations that Kathleen has offered and Harry has accepted. The open heart of the one in pain sings in a voice like sunlight splintering on the water, and the open heart of the one who would die to ease that pain sings like the walls of an ancient sea cave. It is the sound of rock in her voice that interests us particularly.

What will she do when she hears what we tell Kathleen? For that is the other new and subtle cast of the pattern. Always before, the lost ones came to us alone, seeking the answers and the escape that we offer. Carrying the new secret back to their lovers, they played at oysters—encasing their terrible choice in layers of tears and silences until it grew into a pearl that choked them.

But Kathleen does not know. And when she comes

to us, finally, as she must, woven tightly to a woman as steady as a rock, will Harry not come too?

If she does come, there will be no secret to tear these two apart, but the choice will be all the more terrible, shared by two.

The seeker of the one who is lost will know her beloved for a stranger, unknowable.

And she will know herself for what she is.

KATHLEEN

Aria for Soprano

I wake up late on the morning we leave and feel the double deprivation of the sea I've been dreaming about and the sea outside the French doors that won't leave me in peace. I turn my back on it, swing my legs off the bed and go straight to the bathroom to brush my teeth. As soon as I put the brush in my mouth, though, I choke and have to take it back out again.

We are leaving today. We are going back to Boston. I am not staying here and I am not *coming home*. I am not swimming this morning. There's no time for a swim, no time to risk going out too far and being unable or unwilling to come back in. I lean over the sink and recite these certainties, then try again to brush my teeth.

This is the first sign that I'm in trouble. Next comes the panicky need for the water, any water, but ideally the sea itself. I start to feel this way on the drive back across the causeway and I remind myself that I've come back from this stage too, and it should be easier now that the sea is trying to mess with my mind. Outside the shuttle window, the water slips past, the early-morning mist still hovering over it. A heron stands on one leg and dips his head for a fish, splashing drops as he surfaces, empty-beaked. I can recall the feeling of those drops, that water, on my skin, but already it is fading. The car drives on, to the end of the causeway, and then we are on the highway, speeding up, leaving the sea behind.

At the airport, Harry apologizes for being so quiet and I feel only a dull, guilty gratitude that she hasn't pressed me this week. She's tired, worn out from drinking more than she's used to drinking, from a late night in the hot tub last night, and from packing this morning. She leaves me at the gate to go find a cup of coffee. I sit bolt upright in a chair at the end of a row. It's a straight shot from the gate back to the security check-in, then there's an escalator and only a short walk from the bottom of it to the exit doors. If I get up now and go, just bolt out of the airport and hail a cab, I can ask to go to the nearest beach. This is Florida, after all, aren't there beaches everywhere?

A ghostly version of me is already running, unraveling my path to this chair. She is white-faced, gasping as she flies past people and they turn in alarm, wondering what the emergency is. I close my eyes to watch her go. I take deep breaths and press down into the seat with my spine so I can feel how fully I am sitting here, how thoroughly I am *not* moving, *not* running, *not* escaping. I am staying put, dammit, and getting on the plane.

But if I get on the plane I will lose my chance and I can't lose my chance, not when the sea is still so close . . .

"Hey," Harry says. "I got you some tea." She holds out a

paper cup that will be so hot, in my hand, against my thigh, that I will not be able to hold it. I will spill it everywhere, scald myself, or worse, scald Harry.

"Kath?" Harry says. "You okay? Do you want me to put it down next to you?"

I nod. I feel her gaze on my face as she sits down, sets the cup beside me, takes a sip of her coffee. I clench my hands even tighter. *Don't start*, I think. *Don't start.*

She doesn't start.

"I know this is hard for you," she says softly, "having to leave. I don't understand exactly, but—I just—I know it's hard so I'm trying to leave you alone, okay?"

I nod again.

"We'll come back, okay? We'll get a house right on the beach, what do you think?"

Come home.

I am on my feet, fumbling in my carry-on bag for my wallet. Harry stands up too.

"I want to go get some stuff for the plane."

"Do you want me to come with you?"

"No!" Too quickly. She flinches.

"I'll be right back," I say. "Save my tea."

IT HAS TO stop now. It can't go any further, to the point where I believe that I can stay submerged indefinitely, that I can breathe underwater. If it goes further, it ends in the emergency room and a confusion of searing white light and metal until eventually, inevitably, they knock me out. I'll fall into a sleep like sludge then, thick and clammy and hard to shake.

In the ladies' room I let cold water run over my wrists

and hands. I tell myself that it's seawater, just seawater without the salt.

"You too, hmm?"

I turn to the woman beside me at the counter.

"I'm terrified of flying too," she says. "I've heard that works."

She makes a gesture at my hands. "Water on your pulse points. Supposed to calm you down, isn't it?"

She's maybe sixty, small and brown and wiry. She's wearing Florida clothes: turquoise hooded sweatshirt and little matching tennis skirt, sparkly T-shirt and cork-heeled shoes. I bet she's not afraid of anything, not really.

"My husband loves to travel," she says, "wants to treat me by taking me on trips. And now my grandchildren are scattered all over the place. I've done hypnosis, behavioral therapy, good old-fashioned Kentucky therapy—you name it, I've tried it."

"Kentucky therapy?"

She turns off the water at her sink, pulls down some paper towels, and pats at her hands. "Bourbon, honey," she whispers. "Never worked, but I had fun trying."

I laugh. "I like champagne."

"Well, hey, if it works . . ."

I shake my head.

"Listen, I'll tell you the truth," the woman says. She slings her purse over her shoulder, turns back to the mirror to fluff her hair. "Only thing that's ever worked for me for sure? Plain old Dramamine. Take two when I get on the plane and wake me up when I get there."

She pats my arm as she leaves. I look down at my hands in the sink and turn off the water suddenly, decisively. It's not helping and it's stupid to pretend that it is. I can feel the difference between seawater and tap water, for God's sake, and it's not tap water I want.

I meet my own eyes in the mirror and flick water at my reflected self.

"Soprano," I hiss. "Stop it. Stop it now. Drama Queen!"

Two more women come in, look at me strangely before they duck into the stalls. I am blurry now, as if hidden behind a waterfall or a curtain of rain. I splash more water off my hands at the mirror—if I'm going to go crazy, might as well go for broke. *Come home, Drama Queen, Drama Queen, Drama Queen, Dramamine, Dramamine.*

I've never taken Dramamine before; can't remember what it's for exactly. Isn't it for motion sickness? Water runs down the mirror in rivulets, water that I can shake off without a care because it doesn't help, goddammit, it's not even real water, not really real, not straight from the sea. Then I remember and remembering makes me laugh because Dramamine is perfect, Dramamine is exactly what I need, Dramamine is for when you're seasick and isn't that what I am?

My blouse is splotched with water and I shiver in the newsstand as I hunt for the medicine aisle. When I find it, I pick up a box of Dramamine and start to open it right there. But of course I have to pay for it first and I can't take pills dry. I grab a bottle of water, then a box of candy. I'm hysterical now over the idea of Dramamine and how hilarious it is that it's a pill for seasickness, which is what I have, more truly and deeply than anyone I've ever met. But just in case Harry doesn't get it, in case she doesn't see the irony here, I'm getting her a box of sea salt caramels. Get it? You eat salt that's been stripped from the sea and I'll take these pills to strip the sea from my head. And we'll both be fine.

A book. I should get a book to read on the plane. I'm going to sleep on the plane, and when I wake up we'll be in Boston and I won't be seasick anymore, but Harry won't ask questions about what's taken me so long if I come back with something to read. I can't make sense of a single book on the rack, though, so I grab a magazine instead. As soon as the clerk has rung me up, I fish the Dramamine out of the bag and read the dosage: one to two tablets every four to six hours. I gulp three down with water.

They are boarding our plane. Harry stands outside the line trying to pretend she's not nervous. She is holding my tea in one hand.

"Are you all right?" she asks when I reach her. Then, with a narrower look, "Where did you go, the other end of the terminal? You're breathing like you've been running."

"I'm sorry." I sound like I'm talking from far away, but then I don't have to say more because it's our turn to board, sidle into our seats, and stuff our bags beneath us.

"So what did you get?"

The package of pills is in the bottom of the bag and I don't want her to see it. I fumble for the box of caramels, get the ribbon tangled in the handles as I tug it out.

"Here."

"Silly," she says, but she is pleased. "Thank you. But don't think you can hide the rest of your loot—" She reaches for the bag and I try to jerk it away. The magazine slides out onto the floor.

"Aha," Harry says. "Just as I thought. Trashy airplane reading." She picks it up. "*Town and Country*, Kathleen?

Really? Let's see, we've got a cover article about the next
generation of philanthropists, another about the ten most
gorgeous, unspoiled vacation spots in the world. We can
plan our next trip."

She starts paging through and while her head is down I
stuff the plastic bag with the Dramamine box still in it into
the pocket on the seat in front of me. The flight attendant
checks our seat belts and I sit back and let my eyes close.
Behind my eyelids is a buzzing darkness like my head is
full of bees.

"Oh wow—look at this!" Harry elbows me and I open
my eyes.

Come home, Kathleen. Come home.

And there it is in Harry's lap. Home, impossibly so, but
home all the same. The sea, dark green and impenetrable,
seething at the foot of great gray cliffs. There's sun on the
water and the picture is taken from high up, from the top of
the cliffs where green grass is growing thick and soft. But
that water, hundreds of feet straight down and full of rocks
in the shallows, the water frothing up pale and blue-green
against them—I *know* that water. I feel myself free-falling
over it. Any minute now I will hit the water and the waves
will part for me. The water will be cold, rough at the surface, with a slow, dragging current beneath. I push myself
upright but it's too late, the sea has won out, the Dramamine is just another stupid useless pill that will make me
feel woozy and awful for a few hours. If only I hadn't seen
this picture, at this moment, if I could have had an hour to
forget . . .

"Isn't that gorgeous?" Harry asks. "Look where it is,
Kath. It's there, in the caption."

She slides the open magazine into my lap and leans against me to point at the page, her hair brushing my cheek. The pills start to take me under, too late, dammit, too late because now I don't want to go, now I'm fighting it, longing to open my heavy eyes and see the picture again. I don't need to read the caption. I know where it is, where it must be, the only possible place that could make the voices I've been hearing swell like the last mournful lament of an operatic chorus before the curtain falls.

"Ireland," Harry says. "It's the Cliffs of Moher in County Clare. Isn't that near where you were born?"

*C*eara, mother of Caolinn and grandmother of Deirdre, loved the Cliffs of Moher. There were those of us who murmured that she might one day choose to dive from those cliffs, might send her body arrowing into the sea, torn tufts of grass from the clifftop still clenched in her toes. We do not trust prolepsis, but we thought that such a dive might cleave through the uncertainty of things that have yet to come to pass. We sought to know Ceara's end. We swept a table clear and cast across it the vertebrae of a shark—female works better, pregnant best—killed with a single spear thrust between the eyes. The tumbled pattern that emerged was of Ceara balanced between fire and water, dying from either one.

She did not dive from the cliffs, but she fled to them throughout her life, clambered across the dusty path to the grassy stretch at the top and sat there, feet dangling, feeling the distance between herself and the sea. As a child she picked the improbable flowers that grew in clumps near the cliff's edge and took them back to her father. He worked in one of the great houses many miles inland, rode there and back every day and changed into a fine black suit in an empty stable stall, wiping his hands and face with lavender water to wash away the smell of horse. When Ceara brought him flowers, half-wilted already and shivering on their stems as if unsure how to stand straight without the wind to batter them, he smiled gently and stroked her hair.

Ceara had red, red hair that fell past her waist and against which sunlight splintered and dazzled, as it does off the waves of the sea. She was thin and taut, sharp-featured and sharp-tongued, with none of her father's gentleness. When she learned what we had to tell her, she laughed and said that she was safe from love, at least, for who would ever fall in love with her? Who would dare?

She fought the man who did, fought him with the sharpest words she could hone and then fled from him to the cliffs, where she lay on her belly and crawled right up to the edge to curse at us, the words spattering into the water like hard-flung, stinging pebbles. She swore she did not love him and then with her next breath belied herself, swearing that she would never give in to him. When he followed her one day and dropped down into the grass beside her, we thought then to see her dive. But the fire that the bones had shown us was not merely the fire of her hair—it was the flame of the longing that licked at Ceara for this man, for the touch of his big hands, scarred with the marks of hooks and rope burns and the knives used to gut fish.

Ceara was drowned, so her grieving lover told her father, in a fishing boat during a storm. He returned home to their baby girl, Caolinn, and would speak of Ceara no more. Theirs was a passion stronger than either of them and it made sense of the pattern we had seen. Ceara believed that she was choosing water over fire, knowing one or the other would kill her. There was a storm, and *there was a boat, and she wrenched herself from her true love's arms and threw herself overboard just as they hit a swell. He called for her until he was hoarse, but she never surfaced. The ragged echoes of her name drifted around her as she sank, swift as an arrow after all.*

She knew no moderation, that one, not in hatred nor in love. The fire was still in her eyes when we found her caught in an old shipwreck by a nail in the hem of her dress. We freed her to sink down into the black quiet of the old ship, but we took that fire, bottled it up securely. It burns even now with a clear red light like the sparks from a hearth fire flaring too hot.

Muirin, mother to Ceara and daughter of Victoria, was named in defiance, but her mother died long before she could instill in the little girl any of her own strength—of will or body. Muirin means "born of the sea" and Muirin could feel nothing all her life that was not dulled and blunted by that loss and her awareness of it.

She was thrice-exiled—from the sea, from Ireland, and from her own blood—for she was raised in England by her mother's husband, who was not her father. She grew like certain small plants both Above and Below, thin and stunted and unbeautiful, bowed forever against wind or current and seeming to huddle close to the ground. Of all the women who have borne the curse, only Muirin and Victoria had brown hair. And while Victoria's hair was glossy as a seal's pelt, Muirin's seemed to swallow the light. It made her white face seem whiter, her large eyes larger. She had extraordinary eyes, neither wholly blue nor green nor gold nor gray, but they were the eyes of an exile, dimmed and clouded by hopelessness.

Muirin fell in love with the servant of a man who wished to marry her for money. The would-be husband was English, red-faced and sweaty, with a falsely simpering voice that plucked at her until she had to clench her hands into fists to keep from covering her ears. When this man's servant, who dressed him and knelt to polish his boots, found Muirin weeping in a hallway one day, he lifted her like a child and crooned to her in a tongue she had never heard before but which made her faint against him, gasping, as dizzy as though he had already kissed her. She had not known how she longed for the very cadence of Irish speech, almost as much as she longed for the rhythm of the surf in her ears. Muirin lifted her lovely eyes to the sound of that voice and the man holding her saw beneath the veil of her despair. He held her no less gently then, but also no longer as he might hold a child, for that one glimpse of her sea-colored eyes had been enough for him, as one murmured phrase in his voice had been enough for her.

But there are plants that know only how to cringe and refuse to bloom. We have kept such plants in our own garden and learned to coax them along carefully, but not to expect full flower. When they finally die, the stems and leaves can be hung a long while and brewed into a tea that numbs pain. So it was with Muirin who, when she fell in love and then bore her lover's child, discovered only that she had been right to despair.

Muirin waited for the tide to find her in the shallow

pool of a sea cave. She did not bind herself, as she might have done, or lull herself with drugs or weight her pockets with stones. She needed no artificial aids, for she was half-drowned in her own misery already. The weight of it in her lungs made her sink so fast that we could hardly keep up with her plummeting form. We took the shining moment of happiness she had felt when she first knew herself capable of love—it is a fragile thing, like a bauble of silver filigree, best strung on a chain and worn close to the heart. When we let her body go, she sank so deep that we could not follow, nor indeed, even see where she lay.

ROBIN

Composer's Notes

Robin Conarn had learned never to reveal the relief he felt when his phone blared the crashing chords of the "Ride of the Valkyries." Instead, he pretended annoyance as he picked up.

"I have *got* to reprogram that ringtone."

Kathleen laughed. "Maybe you can't. Maybe I put a special fail-safe in your phone so that will always be my special ringtone."

"You're lucky you're too old for an allowance," Robin said, "or it would be officially revoked. Why aren't you in bed?"

"It's only eleven, Daddy," she said. "Why aren't *you* in bed?"

"I was working."

He had been sitting at the piano in the big sunken living room that was also, by virtue of being the only room in the house big enough for the baby grand, his studio. He got up from the bench to stand before the wall of windows that framed a sheer drop down a wooded incline, with more forest beyond. This late at night, with light behind him, his own reflection stood between him and any clear view of the world outside.

"How was Sanibel?"

"Did you get the pictures I sent?"

"I got a lot of photos of you with seafood and what appeared to be alcoholic beverages in the background, yes."

"Oh, those were all Shirley Temples," Kathleen said. "I should have sent more pictures from outside, but I kept forgetting to take my phone to the beach with me. It was *so* beautiful. Harry said she felt like she'd never seen real flowers before. And the water is so clear, and the sand is *white*—well, you've been down there. You know what it looks like."

Robin, listening with a composer's ear for a note gone sharp, heard the insistence in her voice. Something was wrong.

"How is Boston then, after all that white sand and seafood?"

"Boston's fine," she said, "which is to say still cold and wet and miserable, as you can very well imagine. Daddy, I'm okay."

"Glad to hear it," he said lightly. "How many more weeks in the semester?"

"Eight," she said. And then added, "Do you remember the Cliffs of Moher?"

The words came like a blow, the cliffs themselves conjured into the room with their naming. Looking out over darkness, he could almost feel the scouring wind at the top tearing at his hair, hear the keening of seagulls overhead.

"I saw a picture of the Cliffs of Moher on the plane,"

Kathleen rushed on when Robin didn't answer her, "and I realized that I can't remember seeing pictures of them before. But they're right there, aren't they? Near where you and Moira grew up."

"Yes." Robin focused deliberately on his reflected image, saw a tall, lean, handsome man, his blond hair cut short, his gray eyes wary.

"It's so beautiful," Kathleen said. There was a plaintive, longing note to her voice. "More beautiful than Sanibel, even."

Robin shut his eyes. "It is. There's a beach too, though not at the base of the cliffs. Over in Doolin, in the cove. We used to play there all the time as kids. And we took you there when you were a baby."

The memory was abruptly sharp and clear, of coming home one afternoon and finding the house empty, of pushing through the long grass that encroached on the path to the shore and finding Moira there, sitting on the sand with her back to him. When he'd first approached her he'd felt a spasm of fear—where was the baby? But Kathleen was sitting in the triangle Moira had made between her outstretched legs, chuckling and chuckling, shrieking with laughter when the water lapped over her little round feet, leaning forward to pat it and try to hold a handful before it slipped away.

"You were an astonishingly fat baby," he said. "And so white-skinned, with a bunch of red hair that stuck straight up in the air. My mother used to say you looked like a scoop of ice cream with a cherry on top."

"You never told me that!"

"Didn't I?"

Robin could still see them, the quiet girl and the ecstatic baby she was sheltering—from what? Even then he'd wondered. He tried to see more of it but couldn't shake the image of Moira and Kathleen and his own bare feet in the sand near Moira's slender leg. He could smell it though. He let his voice go soft and his words rise and fall as though half-sung.

"Well, and sure, Kathleen, it's greener there, God's own green, you know. It's because of all the rain, that washes color into everything, and freshness; so that even the sea and the sand of the shore smell more like new things growing than of fish or salt."

Kathleen drew a sharp breath, as if his words had struck her as strongly as her abrupt question about the cliffs had struck him. "Why haven't we ever gone back?" she burst out. "Why haven't you ever wanted to go home?"

Another word, another blow.

"Home?" Robin said. "Kathleen, you had to learn to sing without a Boston accent."

"I . . ." She faltered. "That's not what I mean. Haven't you ever missed it, or felt homesick for the cliffs and for the things you just said, the greenness and the freshness?"

"Of course," he said, "but none of that makes it home, for either of us."

"But you *do* miss it?"

"I don't think about it very often," Robin said. He could hear his responses coming up dull and flat against her urgency. "Why all the questions about Ireland all of a sudden?"

"I told you," she said, "I saw a picture of the Cliffs of Moher and . . . I felt homesick."

"That's proof you're Irish then, if one picture can send you reeling."

"Is that why we've never gone back? Because one picture can send *you* reeling?"

Robin laughed shortly. "I suppose that is why, or partly why."

"And the rest is because of Moira?"

"Kathleen—" Robin began, but she cut him off.

"Oh no, Daddy, that's my other line and I have to get it. I'll call you later, okay?"

And she was gone, the phone abruptly quiet in Robin's hand, while he wondered whether he was more alarmed at her obviously invented reason to end a conversation she had started in the first place or relieved that he hadn't had to answer her question. *Because of Moira?*

YES, BECAUSE OF Moira. And because he couldn't explain how thoroughly she haunted Ireland for him. Even when he tried to picture the cliffs or the sweep of the whole cove from the bluffs above it, or the narrow lane to their house edged on both sides by hedges that brushed the sides of the car as you drove past—even those images were disrupted by the curve of a freckled shoulder in one corner, or half-obscured by a curtain of curly red hair. It was as if Moira kept stepping accidentally into the frame of a photo he was taking and then refusing to move, Moira at every age: fifteen years old when he first kissed her, sixteen when they fumbled their way into the act that symbolized—for both of them—eternal love, eighteen when they were married, twenty when Kathleen was born. Twenty-one when she heaped rocks into the pockets of her dress and walked into the sea.

The more time passed, the more uncomfortable Robin was thinking about her. He could bring her image completely to life even after all these years, from the head-to-toe freckles that had so embarrassed her and so delighted him to the cloud of waist-length hair that had been her one unabashed vanity. But she remained eternally a girl in his mind, while he grew older, so that remembering her, caressing her mental image, had begun to feel almost impure. He'd outgrown her, literally, and the memory of that transcendent love felt like some lewd fantasy. Until he'd met Tae five years ago, Robin had maintained a casual dating life and his waking and sleeping sexual fantasies had always featured Moira. He could still bring the taste of her to his lips if he concentrated, a taste like fermented honey and salt water. But what would she feel like now, slipping out of the darkness of the room behind him to wrap her arms around his waist? Would she have gained weight? Gone gray? Lost her hunger for him or her allure? But of course, if Moira were alive, would any of them ever have left Ireland at all? Would it still be home, as it had not been for him for so many years now, as he had never wanted it to be for Kathleen?

Damn Ireland, he thought wearily, retreating to the piano bench. Damn the rain that fell like a silver veil and landed on an upturned face like a benediction. Damn the green that was greener than anywhere else, tumbling at every turn right into the dark green, dangerous sea. He'd lived with its siren song all his life but he'd never thought to hear the longing for it in his daughter's voice. He thought he'd taken her far enough away.

ROBIN HAD LEFT Ireland only months after Moira died. He was twenty years old and had a scholarship offer to study at the New England Conservatory, just as Kathleen was doing now. His memories of his decision-making process then—the determination to leave, to go all the way to the U.S. instead of just studying in Dublin or even London, to take his baby girl with him rather than leave her in a relative's care—were clear and oddly uncolored by emotion. He supposed he had been fleeing. He'd lived in the same village all his life. Moira was everywhere: Moira as a child, Moira as a girl, as his lover, as his wife, Moira pregnant and pensive, singing softly as she walked along the shore, her hand on her belly. And Moira was in the water, the same water where, if he'd stayed—if *they'd* stayed—his daughter would have learned to swim and to fish.

Moira's father was a fisherman, as half the village had once been. He received the news of his daughter's suicide without any apparent surprise and only a shading of his eyes with his hand that might have indicated grief. Later, when Robin told his father-in-law that he was taking Kathleen across the Atlantic, the older man again seemed unsurprised. He was holding Kathleen, stroking her comical shock of red hair.

"'Course you're takin' her," he said. "I would've taken her mother away from here if I could've. Take her far away as you can. It'll come out the same in the end. Grandmother, mother, daughter, granddaughter. It won't matter where she is, lad. It'll come out the same in the end."

Moira's own mother had also killed herself when Moira was a baby. And her grandmother—the one people spoke of with pinched, disapproving faces—she'd drowned herself, and only her father's tearful pleas to the priest had gotten her a Christian burial. Robin opened his mouth to ask his father-in-law what he meant—*It'll come out the same in the end*.

But he did not ask. Or if he did—years later, though he remembered having that conversation, he could not remember how it had ended—he did not get an answer.

Robin's own parents wanted to keep the baby while Robin finished his degree. But while he was gone his mother, who had never been able to have children after he was born, would have made Kathleen *her* daughter, not his and Moira's. He packed up both his own things and Kathleen's and brought her with him.

In his first composition class at the conservatory, Robin discovered that his musical talent was bigger and stranger than he'd imagined it to be. It was not that his pieces were immediately good, but he had an instinct for melody and he could hear in his head how other instruments might support that melody, or play against it to interesting effect. By the time he finished his undergraduate program, he had a fellowship to continue on at the NEC, focusing on orchestral composition.

Robin paid their bills by playing piano and singing in clubs around Boston. From the time Kathleen was four or five years old she was going with him, sitting in the corner on the floor and coloring one of her endless pictures of underwater palaces, with a free hamburger from the kitchen staff congealing on a plate next to her. Later in the evening she would curl up on his coat and fall asleep. But for as long as she was awake, and even as she carefully constructed her edifices of seashell and coral on the page, she would sing along with whatever he played. She had such perfect pitch that her child's voice seemed to weave itself into the piano notes such that the casual, half-drunk listeners in the bar didn't even hear her.

Robin arranged voice lessons for Kathleen with a classmate: he taught the woman's son to play the piano while she taught Kathleen the fundamentals of singing: how to breathe, how to count, how to listen. When the two adults stood together in his friend's kitchen after the lessons, listening to her son pound out scales in the other room, she would shake her head and tell him that she had gotten the far better end of the deal. Kathleen was both gifted and disciplined. When she was ten, she stated her desire to be a singer, with a touch of amazement that such a thing counted as a *job*. It remained only to be seen what would happen with her voice in adolescence. She sang in the choir in middle school and high school, her voice soaring in the occasional solo moment, suspended above the massed choir in a delicate, shining arc that Kathleen herself seemed able to see as she held the notes.

Robin came to every concert and never tired of seeing in his daughter's face when she sang the joy that he had been afraid she would never feel. She had bouts of wrenching tears, whispered complaints of pain in her feet—*whenever I walk, Daddy, it hurts like someone is stabbing me*—and on her fair skin. Moira had suffered this way, Robin remembered, though she had never talked about it so clearly. He remembered the sweaters that his mother knitted for her, all good rough Irish wool, which she never wore. And he remembered a moment when Moira had caught him tucking a wool blanket around baby Kathleen and had snatched it away.

"Don't!" she had whispered—the more upset Moira was, the quieter she spoke. "Oh, don't, you'll hurt her." And she wrapped the baby instead in a linen tablecloth that had been a wedding gift, so heavy and slippery and oversized that it spilled out of the cradle and dragged on the floor.

Robin feared that these strange things were inherited markers on Kathleen of her mother's depression. But though he had known Moira when they were both children, he had never really talked to her until she was a teenager. For a while, he recalled with a wry smile, they had not done much talking. And by the time the urgency of their physical connection had cooled, Moira had begun to retreat from him. There was so much about her that he never knew, so much that she did not want him to know.

Moira had never sung like Kathleen sang, though. She'd had a lovely voice, but not a voice that silenced people with longing or awe. Sometimes when he watched Kathleen sing or held her while she cried from the pain, Robin thought of Moira, who should have been there. It seemed to him that she had become a shadow of her daughter in more ways than one. She lingered, always, in the background, her absence, her death, her *suicide*, put forth by therapists and doctors as the likely root of Kathleen's "problems." And for Robin, the only one left who knew—had known—them both, Moira also began to seem like a paler version of Kathleen. He found himself comparing the two women: their voices, their pain, the color of their hair. And he repeated to himself the word that he had settled on for his daughter: *stronger*. She was stronger than Moira had ever been and that would save her.

MONDAY MORNING, AFTER the unsettling call with Kathleen, Robin was so distracted that Tae had to ask him three times what kind of tea he wanted.

"I'm sorry," he said. "I'm concentrating on not calling her back."

"Why?"

"Well, for one thing I very much doubt she's awake this early," Robin said, "and beyond that, I want to call her back because I'm worried, which will make her mad. But she sounded agitated, the way she gets sometimes before she—" He hesitated.

Tae lifted the tea bag from his cup, pressed the liquid out with slim, deft fingers, and deposited it on a saucer.

"Before she has one of her bad spells? It's been a while now, hasn't it?"

Robin nodded, still staring at his phone screen. If there had just been a message, something flip and typical—*Sorry! Tom drama! No worrying! Hi to Tae!*—he could have relaxed a little.

"Rob?"

Lifting his head, he caught the expression on Tae's face before she hid it behind her tea. She was hurt. Robin could have smacked himself. Tae was first violin with the philharmonic and a technically brilliant violinist, her playing exquisitely clean and precise. Robin had always found her musicianship to be a perfect reflection of her personal and inner life. There was no suicide in *her* past, no messy and inexplicable syndrome. They'd been living together for two years now, and he believed that one of the reasons they were still happy was their mutual acceptance and appreciation of distance. But on a few occasions she had said something, offhand and quietly, that suggested that maybe the only one who needed or appreciated distance was him. When it came to his daughter, especially, Robin couldn't sort out whether he was protecting Kathleen's privacy by not letting Tae in or whether he just didn't want to risk seeing distaste on Tae's face in the midst of a crisis.

"I'm sorry," he said again. He slid his phone away from his plate. "Yes, it's been a while now, since before she and Harry started dating. I could be overreacting of course, because she was asking questions that took me so off guard."

"So call her later and leave a message," Tae said. "Invite them down some weekend. That gives her a reason to call you back without feeling like you're just checking up on her. And we haven't seen them since Christmas."

"That's a good idea."

"What about today?" she asked. "What are you working on?"

Robin made such a face that Tae laughed, her bell of black hair swinging around her face as she shook her head at him. "Let me guess. You have to tackle vocal music? Where are you starting? Hester?"

He groaned and Tae's smiled widened. "I've never seen you get nerves about composing before. It's cute."

"It won't be cute when I don't have a single aria to show anyone in a few months," Robin said.

"You've just got to start, isn't that what I'm supposed to say? The blank page is your enemy. Write something down. Is Hester a soprano?"

"I don't know!" Robin managed not to glare across the table by frowning at his tea instead.

"So write a song for Kathleen," Tae said.

"What?"

"Leave Kathleen a message, then let it go until she calls back—which she will—and write a song for her instead of staring at your phone."

"She'd love it," Robin murmured, "but I have to focus on this project."

"Oh bull," Tae said. She kicked him lightly on the ankle with her bare foot. "That *is* nerves talking."

"Did you ever guess when I took this commission that you'd have to turn therapist?"

"No," Tae said promptly, "and I'll only do it so long before I lose patience with you. I've played your music in performance. I know exactly how good you are and how good this opera will be. But writing a song for Kathleen is exactly what a good therapist would suggest right now, like the exercise people do when they're grieving or recovering from trauma, write it all out and then delete it. Write this out and put it aside and then see if you can get back to Hester and—what's his name?—the hunchback."

"Chillingworth," Robin said absently. As Tae had talked, the measured cadence of her persuasion, the elegant rhythm that was Tae, had given way to, not music, exactly, but something else in his head. It was too soon to grasp at it; all he could do was listen. Tae got up to clear her dishes, her silk robe falling like water around her thighs.

"I'm going to dress," she said. "I've got a section meeting at nine."

THE SOUND HE'D been hearing was not music. It was the sound of Kathleen screaming. Robin supposed it was Tae's reference to "trauma" that triggered that memory, though he couldn't say who had been more traumatized by that terrible morning, him or Kathleen. The scream had been a rising note that went on and on, perfectly in pitch—*My God*, Robin had thought even as he plunged down the hall to her room. *My God, how does she sustain it?*

Kathleen was sitting up in bed, scrabbling at her mouth with her fingers and still screaming. Robin knelt on the bed and grabbed her wrists. Her eyes were black and frantic, and though she saw him and knew him, she seemed to think that she couldn't speak. She was soaked with sweat, he could smell it in her hair and feel it slick on the skin of her arms, and she kept trying to put her hands in her mouth. Robin fought her, using his greater strength to keep her hands imprisoned. He struggled with the urge to hit her to make her stop screaming. Talking to her—*Calm down, Kath, calm down, it's all right, you're all right, drink this, just drink this, breathe, breathe, swallow*—he felt a bizarre disconnect as he heard the soothing, crooning sound of his voice and felt the barely suppressed violence in his body as he restrained her. He did not identify his own emotion as fear until later, when he sat beside the hospital bed and watched her sleep. She had been sedated by then, and her face was so bleached of its normal high color that he could see a scattering of pale gold freckles across her nose that he had never noticed before. That he could fail to know something about his daughter so obvious as the fact that she had freckles on her nose; that he could have reacted so poorly when she needed help that he had hurt her—her wrists were circled with bruises from the pressure of his grip.

Now he sat at the piano and tried to modulate the scream into something else. If it just slid down, *down* into a high E, then a melody was possible, a melody that would begin with faltering words and grow stronger as the vocalist sang herself away from the scream.

Tae brought him a second cup of tea before she left that morning, but he only discovered it when he stood up from the piano hours later and nearly knocked it over. He was exhausted, exhilarated, stunned by the revelation of his daughter's voice as an instrument. He knew its texture, its tonal quality, its range and power, knew that it would flow over a piano accompaniment like a river over rounded stones. He didn't let the piano into the song until halfway through, because she was singing of pain. Instead he wrote a cello line underneath the voice. The sound would be darker, heavier, and occasionally flawed by moments of strong bowing—he notated them, uneven ground for Kath to sing over instead of a smooth path.

The words to this song had come easily, though Robin knew he was no librettist. He'd simply used Kathleen's own words, or versions of the words he had heard her use to talk about the pain in her mouth—*my tongue cut out, my voice cut off*. And in her feet—*when I dance, I dance on knives*. Clumsy, but he could fix them later. He felt a telltale vertigo, a sense of almost appalled awareness of the quality of what was taking shape on the page. The aria filled the room, then receded as he notated the final, tentatively hopeful phrase of the song—*and perhaps the water will wash it away*—just as

Kathleen would sing it, on a fragile, fading note that none-theless was not final, that left breath and melody open to begin another song. This one would be about the water, of course, about the sea.

Robin smiled as he gathered the score sheets together. Tae would never say "I told you so," but she'd be pleased with herself when he told her how he'd spent his day. Making room on the top of the piano for the new pages, he glanced at the much-scribbled-over page from several days ago on which he'd tried to start an aria for Hester Prynne, then reached for his pencil. Tae would really be hard-pressed not to gloat over *this*. He drew a bold line over all of the cramped, frustrated notations, and at the top of the page made one note, underlined for emphasis: "Hester—not so-prano. Mezzo."

THE NEXT DAY, when Kathleen hadn't responded to his voice mail, Robin sent her a text suggesting a visit. He even had a specific weekend to suggest, when the string quar-tet that Tae played with was doing Brahms, one of Har-ry's favorites. Then he started working on the second song for Kathleen that he had begun to hear, faintly, the night before. He knew better than to question the luxurious ease of this particular composition process. Eventually, and usu-ally without warning, it would get hard again. He was still not sure what story he was telling. This one was once again for voice and piano and cello, but with a flute to play the lonely sound of the sea itself, of the singer's longing, or both.

Tae came to the doorway that evening and stood waiting for him to finish the phrase he was marking.

"Come eat dinner," she said. "If you ate lunch while I was gone it must have been the special invisible food we keep here."

"On an invisible plate," Robin acknowledged. Tae moved into the room and he drew her down onto the bench next to him.

"How was your day?"

She made a face. "Several hundred sixth graders there to hear the *1812 Overture*. I don't know why they don't just bring them in, give them the cannon fire and the fireworks, and send them home."

Robin laughed. "And the cymbals. Don't forget the cymbals. Very important."

"I'll take your word for it," Tae said. She leaned over the music, then stopped herself and glanced at him.

"I'm sorry, I just caught a glimpse—don't give it to me if you're not ready."

"It's fine," he said. "Nearly finished, I think."

Tae scanned the music in silence for a few minutes.

"It's lovely," she said. "Where is it going?"

"You mean the whole cycle?" Robin stood up and stretched, pulling her with him. "Don't know yet. Any ideas?"

"Well, they're both very literal," Tae said. "The one you showed me last night is about pain and this one is about missing the sea. Maybe one way to go with the next song is more abstract." She moved to the door and then turned back, seeing that he had not followed her.

"Robin," she said. "Not until after you've eaten dinner, please."

"MAYBE IT'S ME," Robin said on Thursday morning. They were in the bedroom, while Tae dressed for work and Robin packed his gym bag so he could work out before his lunch appointment.

"Maybe what's you?"

"The not calling back," he said. "I just realized that Kathleen's not the only one who hasn't gotten in touch with me. I also haven't heard from Allan Charpentier since I sent him the overture—what, almost two weeks ago now?"

"But aren't you having lunch with him today?"

"Him and Jim, yes."

"So he knew when you sent it to him that he'd be seeing you and could give you feedback today," Tae said. "That means that he liked it."

Robin checked the weather on his phone—still nothing from Kathleen—and switched from a cashmere sweater to a thinner merino one. "Why does the fact that he hasn't followed up mean he likes it?"

"Because if he didn't—especially if he was actively worried about the quality of the music or the direction it was taking—he wouldn't want to talk to you about that in front of Jim," Tae said. She slipped her earrings in and tapped them lightly. They were pearls that Robin had bought her, set on a small dangle and with an unusual gold creaminess to them. For a long time he had assumed that Tae's minimalist approach to dressing was entirely a choice, and it was, but it was more an expression of her consummate professionalism than her personal style. She didn't wear perfume in case it bothered other players, didn't wear rings or bracelets because they cluttered her hands and arms while she played, and of course lived in black and white. When

Robin had gotten her those earrings and a coral-colored silk dress for her birthday last year, the expression on her face had been almost greedy.

"We're having dinner with Jim and Lorraine this week-end too, aren't we?" she asked.

"Unless Allan did hate the overture and I'm actually being fired over a steak salad."

Tae came over and slipped her arms around his waist.

"You're not seriously worried that Allan doesn't like the overture, are you?"

He shrugged.

"I suppose I should be grateful you're anxious. You could have gone the other way, developed a raging ego, and decided to refer to yourself in the third person."

"First-person plural," Robin said. "We would prefer to adopt the royal *we* when we become that arrogant."

THE ORCHESTRAL MUSIC of *The Scarlet Letter* would tell the story of the religion that overshadowed the story. Robin was using the organ both to echo the stately chords of old Protestant hymns and to thunder over the rest of the instruments like the voice of the people's merciless God.

Allan's enthusiastic praise of the direction Robin was taking the music had left Jim Dolan, the donor underwriting the commission, practically bouncing in his seat. He'd wrung Robin's hand and asked to hear an aria as soon as Robin had one finished. Maybe one of the opera company members could be prevailed on to learn just an excerpt from the new piece and let Jim hear how it would sound?

Of course they would, Robin thought, just as he himself would offer up the pages of his score before the proverbial ink was even dry, despite his general reluctance to share work before it was complete. Jim had seven figures committed to the creation of this opera. In a clear and concrete way, he owned it. Even more persuasive in some ways was the fact that Jim himself didn't see it that way. He was just such a passionate fan of opera that he got excited over any new work that might energize the genre and bring in a new audience. To hear Allan tell it, the only way Opera Philadelphia had gotten in the door with Jim, who could clearly afford to donate many millions, was by throwing out plans to talk building renovations or naming opportunities and instead pitching the idea of a new opera with an American novel as the libretto and Robin as the composer.

As for writing an aria for Jim and Allan to hear—Robin flipped through the stacks of paper he'd accumulated since he'd started the project. He had found the complete text of *The Scarlet Letter* online and excerpted and printed out nearly every moment that he suspected needed to be included. He had more than a hundred pages, including speeches by individual characters, dialogue between characters, and narrative insights about characters—of which there was a great deal and all of it overwritten, or whatever it was Hawthorne had done to his prose to evoke a Puritan sensibility.

He still wasn't ready to deal with Hester, though at least now he had her vocal range right. He stopped on a speech made by the tenor, Dimmesdale, the father of Hester's baby who was too cowardly to admit his sin. Robin didn't have any trouble hearing this voice, a young man's voice, with some of the physical wavering of a voice that had not matured fully any more than had its owner. And yet it was a beautiful voice, as it had to be to capture the sympathies of the other characters and of the audience, a voice with the lushness of a woman's, with moments of occasional roughness and enough power in the lower notes to create an impression of restrained sensuality. Robin took the sheet over to the piano. *The challenge here*, he thought, *is that the organ must play behind him whenever he sings, even if only softly or sparely. The organ is the voice of God for this man, the voice of the Church. It has to be there behind him, haunting him, sometimes even drowning him out.*

By the time Tae called to say that rehearsal was running long, the text that would become the lyrics of Dimmesdale's aria was heavily marked up, with words moved and extraneous lines slashed. The music itself, scored for orchestra with the organ as anchor and the violins underscoring the singer's melodic line, was sketched out so boldly that the pencil was smudged in places, dark as an ink pen in others.

There was, Robin saw now, a striking contrast between his music and the voice for which he had just been writing. The music that gave texture to both the Puritan community and their God was measured, powerful, sometimes implacable in its repetition of themes and phrasings. The character of Dimmesdale was entirely the opposite: weak, both physically and morally, prone to fits of passion. But he had such a compelling voice, a voice in which neediness was not strident but supplicating, insistent as the plucking of a harp.

What would that voice sound like against Kathleen's?

Robin pulled a fresh sheet of paper out, already imagining the framework for the duet, with the tenor voice pursuing the soprano. He was intrigued by the idea of making this light, young, male voice into a force of sexual power, even of sexual threat. Perhaps the unexpected richness of the tenor's lower range might burst out and overwhelm the higher voice . . . He scribbled the notes down.

HE FINISHED THE tenor aria for *The Scarlet Letter* the next afternoon, beating back the strains of the duet that kept trying to start up in his head until after dinner, when he handed Tae the draft of the piece for Dimmesdale and went back to the piano. Writing "Desire," a duet for tenor and soprano, felt less like creating music than trying to keep up with it. The two voices blended and twined around one another, never dissonant but always and increasingly unsettling together, hard to listen to and just as hard to write. Robin felt so physically restless that he wrote most of it standing up, stopping when it grew dark to switch on a lamp and the overhead light.

"So did you finish the song?" Tae asked the next morning. She was leaning against the kitchen counter, blowing on her tea. "I didn't even hear you come to bed."

"I'm glad I didn't wake you," Robin said. "I don't think I had any choice but to finish it once I got started."

"Do you like it?"

"I think so. I wasn't sure if it would just be an exercise, putting another voice opposite Kath's, especially without any context except what I gave it. But I think I'm distanced enough now that it was mostly—not all, but largely—about the way the voices played off each other."

"When do I get to see it?"

Robin shrugged, a gesture he knew to be telltale to her,

meaning that he wanted her feedback as soon as possible but didn't want to say so.

"I need to get out the door pretty quick this morning," she said. "I'll look at it as soon as I get back tonight. What are you going to work on today?"

"Don't know yet. Maybe I'll take a break today, leave the house for a change, that sort of thing."

"You know," Tae said, "if you're writing duets for Kathleen now, there's another voice that's sort of an obvious pairing, don't you think?"

WELL, ROBIN THOUGHT later, yes, there was. Harry's. Kathleen liked to say that Harry had a "Puritan" voice; he smiled now, recalling that description. He would write her into the *Scarlet Letter* opera, but for the fact that the novel was singularly lacking in compassionate, self-effacing female characters. Whatever she was, Harry was no Hester Prynne.

But her voice, that cool voice that spoke of open spaces high up inside arched ceilings, rather than outside in the sun, her voice was marvelous. Robin flipped through the pages of "Desire" as he considered the shape the next piece might take. He had found himself floundering early on in this last composition for lack of lyrics, but couldn't even begin to write them himself, not words of desire, either felt or repelled, by or for his daughter. Instead, he had stopped briefly to pace and try to think of the most intense and obvious poetic expression of desire he knew. The words of the duet now were St. Augustine's, of all things: *I fell headlong then into the love wherein I longed to be ensnared . . . What is this but a miserable madness?*

For Harry and Kathleen, he would give in to the temptation to call the duet simply "Love." Robin could hear the beginning strains of the piece: cello, violin, piano, and a harp, an instrument he rarely used because it bored him. But here a harp might serve two purposes: to emphasize with occasional rippling, lush scales the ascetic texture of Harry's voice, and to suggest a loss of something idyllic. It would play at the beginning of the song, but then be cut off, abruptly, when the mezzo started to sing.

And speaking of something serving two purposes—he pulled out his phone and texted Kathleen: *Have you had a chance to check your schedule? And do you have a favorite love poem?*

This time, finally, she texted back almost immediately. *Don't know about that wknd yt, and i think wrong person. Can I ask Harry?* And then before Robin could even reply, she sent another text. *Told you Harry would know. She says bearet browning and also saffo. Probly spelled wrong. Im ok, pls stop worrying.*

Robin wrote back, *Trying,* and got no reply. He wasn't sure if he felt better or not for having at least heard from her. He texted again asking her to call in the next few days, then deliberately put his phone on the coffee table and did a search for Sappho on his computer. Her poetry struck him as an odd blend of elevated classical language, full of references to gods and winged chariots, and startlingly visceral expressions of love and longing. Scrolling through a four-stanza love poem, he found lines that he couldn't *not* use:

> *Then in my bosom my heart wildly flutters,*
> *And, when on thee I gaze never so little,*
> *Bereft am I of all power of utterance,*
> *My tongue is useless.*

SUNDAY NIGHT, LORRAINE Dolan greeted them at the door and said that she'd made her husband promise not to ask any questions about *The Scarlet Letter*.

"I can't stop the man from talking about opera, short of taping his mouth shut," she said, "but this is a social evening. So if he starts asking you for a progress report, you have my permission to throw a breadstick at him."

Instead, at dinner Lorraine asked about Kathleen.

"She was down in Sanibel with her girlfriend last week," Robin said. "I've only talked to her a little since they got back but, to quote directly, it was 'fabulous, amazing, and fantastic.'"

Jim Dolan chuckled. "Sounds like our eldest," he said. "That girl experiences everything in all capitals. I tell her she needs to consider a career as an opera singer."

"Singing isn't exactly Carnie's strong suit," Lorraine said. "But your daughter is a singer, isn't she, Robin?"

"She is," Robin said. "But she's promised never to throw anything at the orchestra. She knows that'll get her disowned."

"So she's a soprano?" Jim asked. "What's her dream role now at, what, twenty-four? I always think that's an interesting question, you know, to hear how a young singer's understanding of their craft changes just by hearing the roles they long to do. There was that one young man I talked to at the conservatory here when he was just starting out—stunning baritone voice, just stunning, and so exciting to hear it at, you know, twenty-two, twenty-three, and think what that voice would sound like ten years down the road."

"And what did he aspire to sing at twenty-three?" Tae asked.

Jim snorted. "Giovanni, of course. The pinnacle of success in his mind was Giovanni."

"Jim," Lorraine said dryly, "you've lost track of your question."

"No I haven't! I wanted to know what Kathleen's ideal role was."

As Robin opened his mouth to answer, he registered the fact that his own music for Kathleen was playing in his head.

"I don't know, honestly," he said. "She's suited for both lyric and coloratura roles"—and how could he say *that* without some pride creeping in?—"but a lot of what I hear is frustration with soprano parts."

"You mean how she has to either die or go crazy?" Lorraine asked.

"Or first go crazy and then die," Tae said. "There's always that option."

They all laughed. "Yes, exactly," Robin said. "She's probably going to confound your experiment, Jim, about judging the maturity of a singer, because she claims that she's never going to sing some of the classic roles: no Violetta, no Butterfly, no Lucia—"

"My God, stop!" Jim cut in. "She'll be out of roles completely at that rate." Then he grinned. "You'll just have to write them for her, Robin. Have you asked her about Hester?"

"Hester's a mezzo," Robin said, and then flushed. He had decided it of course, but hadn't said it out loud yet. But the news, if it could be called that, seemed to go over well with his hosts. Jim said nothing for a moment, then nodded his head decisively.

"Yes. Yes, you're right."

Lorraine, meanwhile, smiled.

"Good!" she said. "And not just because I love the mezzo voice. It's been years since I read the book, of course. I've been meaning to reread it ever since you and Jim started planning the opera, but anyway, I seem to remember Hester as a striking woman, isn't she? Tall, dark-haired, deep-bosomed, and all that."

"She has to be," Tae put in, "to hold the letter in place."

"And Pearl, the little girl, she'll be your soprano then, hmm?" Jim said.

Robin hadn't even thought of Pearl yet, but of course that was the only thing that made sense. She would be a high soprano, pure, unearthly.

"Well then . . ." Jim didn't wait for his answer. "Kathleen can sing Pearl."

Robin shook his head. "I don't think I'd even want her to," he said, "much as I'd love to hear her singing music I wrote. There's something so confining about the world of this book—all three of these main characters just stuck, unable or unwilling to escape."

"But that's why it will make such a great opera," Jim said. "They might as well be cursed, as so many are. It's the nature of the genre, what makes it so great—that inevitability, that sense of tragedy that the characters can't escape. You don't listen to an opera for the plot."

"*You* don't," Lorraine murmured. "I'm sure some people do."

"Only someone who doesn't know the story could do that," Jim protested. "And then you go to hear how they get there, to their death, their madness"—he waved a hand at Tae in acknowledgment of her earlier point—"or both.

You know it's going to happen, after all, it's just a matter of time once you know the story."

As if on cue, Robin's phone, which was in his pants pocket, began to play the "Ride of the Valkyries." Everyone at the table jumped, and Jim might have been about to make a joke, but Robin was already out of his seat and halfway out of the room, his phone in his hand.

"Excuse me," he managed to say over his shoulder. "It's my daughter."

He stepped out into the foyer. "You did spell Sappho wrong," he said, "but tell Harry the recommendation was a good one."

But it wasn't Kathleen. It was Harry.

"WHAT DID WE tell them?" Robin asked in the car. He was driving, though Tae had been unhappy when he insisted. His hands were steady and tight on the wheel, at ten and two o'clock.

"About why we had to leave?"

"Yes. I can't remember what I said."

"Just that Kathleen was in the hospital. They're parents, Robin. That was enough."

He nodded.

"Will you tell *me* anything?" Tae asked. "Did she have another—"

"Another break, yes. Harry took her in. They got her sedated but they want her admitted for a full stay, ten days or more, and they'll need my consent on that."

"You can fly up in the morning," Tae said.

He nodded again.

"Do you want me to come?"

"No," he said immediately, then tried to soften it with an explanation. "It's just that there won't be anything for you to *do*, it's just a lot of sitting in hallways and waiting rooms and in her room if she's up to it, and I don't think she'd want you—"

She interrupted him. "It's okay. She wouldn't want me to see her like this. I can understand that, Robin. But I could come up for you, you know. I could just stay at the hotel, do some work during the day."

He shook his head. "Thank you."

They drove in silence. Robin thought he could hear music, very faintly, almost but not quite familiar. Finally he realized that the car radio was on, the volume set so low that he could barely hear it. He turned it up loud enough to register a Beethoven adagio, then turned it off all the way. He reached over for Tae's hand.

"I'm sorry," he said. "I always tell myself that this will be the last time, that maybe it won't happen again . . ."

She curled her fingers around his hand and placed her other hand on top. It was an oddly clumsy gesture for Tae, helpless and distracting. He had to extract his hand almost immediately to return it to the wheel.

"Sorry," he said again.

"Stop apologizing, please."

"Sor—"

He grimaced and returned his attention to his driving. The Dolans lived in a neighborhood of old trees and deep lawns, the houses set well back from the street. In the dark, the winding road unfurled like a black ribbon in front of the car.

Victoria, mother to Muirin and daughter to Fand, was so named by her mother in hopes that England would save her where Ireland could not. We watched Victoria avidly, suspecting she was cursed by her mother's choices but not entirely sure. She came to cool her poor feet in the sea, screamed in agony when she turned sixteen. She ran to the shore and rinsed her mouth in the ocean, still retching, and a tiny fish swimming past swallowed some of the pain that leaked from her mouth. We caught it and sliced it open, but we needn't have bothered. The blade of Victoria's pain had already begun to work its way through the poor creature, slitting it in two from the inside out.

Victoria defied love. She married against it and lived against it and turned her face from it even as she strained and sobbed and clutched at the back of the man who offered it to her. After she bore his child and not her husband's, she told her serving women that she was going to bathe in the sea and left them, wearing only her thin shift and with her dark brown hair hanging in braids down her back. She held the knife in plain sight in her hand. None tried to stop her. They thought she was mad. She stood in the small, licking waves of a receding tide and called to us, taunted us with her refusal to come out into the water to die. She opened her arms up with the knife and died in the wet sand dreaming of speaking words of love aloud. Her servants found her and her husband carried her body inland, where it was buried in the dense darkness of rock and soil.

Her lover came to kneel on the fresh-piled dirt, long after the others had gone, and snarled, his hands wrist-deep in wet earth, that she should have left the knife for him to use after her. He was very like her, so strong he knew not how to grieve, only to rage and burn. Had the knife lain where it fell when Victoria fell, this man might indeed have claimed and used it to spill his own blood. But it came back to us, following first the tide and then the deep cold current and finally the pull of the spells we had embedded in it when we poured it into the mold.

After that we were not surprised by what happened to the others, to daughter after daughter after daughter. We felt the weight of the curse settle over us as well, as if some shipwreck from Above had cast a great glass dome into the sea that drifted down to our caves and our gardens and settled over the top, invisible but inescapable.

We have studied, and we have learned, a great deal about the nature of curses since Victoria's time.

A curse spreads through lives like black oil on the surface of the sea, first flowing swiftly out in all directions and gobbling up those it can touch only briefly, shallowly. But eventually even oil will settle into water, stain the heart of every drop with a gleaming black that cannot be filtered out. This man Robin, whose lover was cursed and whose daughter is cursed, can no longer be surprised by the clutch of fear, any more than a fish is surprised, in the end, by the shadow of the circling shark.

He was afraid for Moira, for her black moods and her days of weeping and her insistence that she walk by the water alone. He feared all along that one day she would not turn back to the shore. He has come to know that he could not have saved her, though he does not know why. But he tells himself that he can save Kathleen, that he must save her.

But he cannot. Only she can save herself.

Come home, Kathleen. Come home.

ROBIN

Composer's Notes

The very ordinariness of a psych ward always threw Robin off. The elevator doors slid open onto an immaculate, overlit lobby dominated by the high counters of a nurses' station and several impressively generic flower arrangements. The ambient noise was a murmured humming coming from a patient's room. It rose and fell like a Gregorian chant as Robin approached the nurse on duty.

She took him for a psychiatrist visiting a patient; he could tell instantly from her quick smile and the gesture of accommodation she made, glancing up from writing something in a chart and immediately setting it aside. When they recognized you as just another worried relative, Robin knew, they sometimes looked up only long enough to identify you, and then went right back to whatever it was they were doing, offering the barest minimum of engagement.

"How can I help you?"

"I'm here to see Kathleen Conarn," Robin said.

"Are you her private physician?"

"I'm her father."

"Oh." She shifted modes quickly, turning her back on him to get Kathleen's chart off the rack on the wall and flipping through it with an air of professional detachment.

"Mr. Conarn? Do you have some identification with you?"

"Driver's license all right?"

"Yes, of course. Let me make a copy of it."

Robin waited for her to return his license, then took the clipboard she held out to him and listened to her explanation of why his signature was required to commit Kathleen, what the implications were of committing her, and how such a commitment might be rescinded. Robin did not pick up the pen dangling off the top of the clipboard from frayed string. "I'll need some more information first," he said. "What's her doctor's name?"

"Dr. Biancini is treating her."

"Can you page him and tell him that I'm here and I'm not going to sign anything committing my daughter to a hospital for seven to ten days until I've spoken to him?"

"Well, I-I think he's in meetings all morning, but I can page him."

"Thank you," Robin said. "What room is Kathleen in?"

The nurse tipped her head in the direction of the hallway to her left. "Room 512," she said.

During Kathleen's first hospitalization, she had been heavily sedated for several days and Robin had dozed off in the chair beside her bed, only to wake up, suddenly, to find her racked with choking sobs in her sleep. Tears were coursing down her face and soaking her hair, and her whole body was shuddering and clenching. Robin had tried to wake her up, then pushed the call button for the nurse, and when someone didn't come, had practically run down the hall, where he stood, frightened and increasingly angry, for nearly fifteen minutes. On the wall above the nurses' station, he had watched a light from a long row of numbered lights blink on and off, the signal from the call button he had just pushed. When a nurse finally appeared in the doorway to Kathleen's room, he had turned on her. *My daughter is in trouble. She's crying and she seems like she might be in pain, but she's not responding to me. Why didn't someone come to her room immediately?*

The nurse's face had hardened and gone deliberately blank, even as she bent over Kathleen to check her vital signs.

"We're busy here, sir," she had said. "We have other patients. Sometimes you just have to wait."

Robin knew he was not a forceful man by nature, and the idea of shouting or making threats was distasteful to him. Since that first time he had experienced it himself, he had witnessed enough confrontations between the nurses and furious or desperate family members to know that the more out of control you got, the more scornful and superior the nurse grew. The strategy he had developed for hospital staff was simply to make eye contact whenever he could. He was fairly confident now that Dr. Biancini would at least be paged, though whether or not he would decide to come back up to Kathleen's room before his rounds was another matter entirely.

He saw Harry as soon as he reached the room. She was standing by the bed with her face turned toward the tumble of red hair on the pillow, her arms folded tightly across her chest as if she were cold. As Robin entered, she crossed quickly to the door.

"They just sedated her again a few minutes ago," she whispered.

Robin felt briefly unsteady on his feet, as if the weight of suitcase and coat had suddenly unbalanced. There had never been anyone else here before. He'd always been the one at the bedside, hurrying people away, speaking softly so Kathleen wouldn't hear, keeping her friends in the hallway because she wouldn't want them to see her like this. He set down his bag, shifted his coat to his other arm.

"Why?" he asked. "What happened?"

Harry blinked. She was clearly exhausted, her curly hair rumpled, flatter on one side than the other, the usual rosy undertone missing from her face. There were blue smudges like bruises under her eyes.

"Why what? Oh, the sedation." She pulled her arms in even tighter across her chest. "She woke up just after I got here and started screaming about her skin burning, wanting a shower. They'd put that thing on her wrist—"

"The restraint. Did they do that last night when you brought her in?"

Harry nodded. "She started yanking at it and a nurse came in and gave her another shot. I'm not sure she even registered that I was here." She glanced up at him, then quickly away, but Robin felt a shock of empathy at the sight of her face. She looked punished.

"Harry," he said. "This isn't your fault. She'll come out of it." He did not add details about how long it sometimes took, about the days and weeks of wan listlessness, Kathleen too weak and shaky to dress herself, too drugged to do more than nod when he talked to her, even when he teased her, her usual nimble rejoinders lost in the fog that crept across her eyes and turned them from blue to gray.

Harry hunched her shoulders forward and Robin put a hand out to her. In person, she was smaller and softer than he remembered, perhaps because what he recalled about her was some combination of the strength Kathleen relied on in her and her spacious, resonant voice. He touched her shoulder and she shrugged into his hand, a hesitant acknowledgment of his gesture.

"I should have done something sooner," she said. "There was something wrong in Florida and I knew it right away. I thought at first it was that the seawater didn't feel good—you know how she says it feels good on her skin? I thought it wasn't working or something. She was almost reluctant to swim after the first day."

Definitely something wrong then.

"But you don't think that's what it was?"

Harry shook her head. "Twice when I woke up in the morning she was down on the beach by herself, talking to the water. I did ask her once who she was talking to, but she pretty much shut me down."

Robin went around to the side of Kathleen's bed and dropped into the chair there. Her right wrist, cuffed to the bedrail, was bruised and swollen, her hand drooping from it like a worn-out flower. She had her mother's hands, fine-boned, long-fingered, the skin almost translucent across the backs.

"You think she was hearing voices?" he asked.

Harry shrugged miserably. After a moment she said, "I need to use the bathroom, okay? I didn't know when you'd get here but—"

"Go," he said. "Get some food, a cup of tea."

"Can I get you anything?"

"I'm fine."

He waited for her to leave the room before he leaned over Kathleen. She was so pale that he could see the constellation of freckles on the bridge of her nose. Every hospitalization, every breakdown, when Robin first saw Kathleen, he saw Moira flickering over her, the mother superimposed on the daughter. It was the unexpectedly visible freckles and the stuporous sleep that claimed her. For Moira, those sleeps had come from cold, not drugs, after she'd slipped out of the house in the dead of winter to swim. When she came back, or when he found her struggling into the shallows, her lips would be purple and she would be shivering so hard she could barely walk.

He had a sudden visceral memory of lying in bed with Moira with the fire high and every blanket in the house piled on top of them, her skin so icy cold that he had to force himself to hold her, trying to brace her against the racking, convulsive shudders of cold with the heat and strength of his own body. When she had finally fallen asleep, he'd lain awake beside her a long time, afraid to let her loose.

She'd been pregnant already that night. That had been a piece of his fear when he'd woken and found her gone, that something could happen to the baby. Robin was certain that he had put his hand on Moira's still-flat stomach, that he had tried to warm Kathleen up too. But that memory—of his fingers splayed across her cold skin—could not be trusted.

He might well have invented it to match the protectiveness he felt for Kathleen now.

There was a knock on the open door, an announcement of presence rather than a request for entrance. In this case, they'd been joined by not one but two doctors, a barrel-chested man with curly, graying black hair and a slender Indian man not much taller than Harry. Only the big man wore a white coat. The other man was in a beautifully tailored gray silk suit. The prescription pad protruding from his breast pocket might have been an ostentatious prop, a reassurance that he *was* a doctor, even if he didn't look the part. Robin stood up.

"Mr. Conarn?" the big man said, moving forward to shake Robin's hand. "I'm Dr. Michael Biancini, the attending on call. I've been overseeing your daughter's care." He did not lower his voice or even glance at Kathleen. Robin instantly disliked him.

"I just flew in this morning," Robin said. "I understand that you need my signature to admit her for an extended stay. Why is that necessary?"

Biancini's eyebrows rose above the frames of his glasses. "You don't think it is?"

"I didn't say that," Robin replied. "I just want to know what exactly you can do for her during an extended stay. If you've read her full history, you know that we've been through this before."

"Yes." Biancini glanced quickly over at the other doctor before dropping his head to flip through Kathleen's chart. "I have her records here. Six hospitalizations in eight years, all following acute psychotic breaks, courses of a number of medications, SNRIs, SSRIs, and tricyclics . . . I see a note that a long-term course of Haldol was tried only once, is that true?" He offered the chart to the Indian man as he spoke, pointing at one of the notations with his index finger.

"Yes," Robin said. "It made her a zombie."

Biancini nodded, still focused on the other doctor. His deference was almost comical, given the difference in their physicality—Biancini towered over the other man. But he was clearly waiting for some signal now before he said anything more. The Indian doctor studied the chart without speaking, flipped a page, then another, frowned at a notation, and appeared to reread. Then he flipped back through the pages and handed it back to Biancini, nodding.

"Yes," he said, an answer to some question Robin hadn't been privileged to hear. "Mr. Conarn," he said, looking directly at Robin and speaking with grave courtesy, "was the Haldol effective in controlling the delusions about water, the urge to immerse herself in it, the physical pain she complains of?"

"No." Robin shook his head. "She could barely follow a conversation when she was on it, but she would still go into the bathroom and try to run a bath, then refuse to get out." He hesitated before saying more, reluctant to expose Kathleen to either of these men, but tempted, as always, by the hope that they might help her. "I had to drag her out," he said. "So no, it didn't help at all."

The Indian man nodded again, then extended his hand. "Forgive me," he said, "I'm Dr. Kapoor. Dr. Biancini brought me in as a consult after he reviewed the patient file."

"Dr. Kapoor is head of the neurology program at Harvard," Biancini said.

Robin glanced from one of them to the other. "Neurology?"

Biancini frowned. "Mr. Conarn, your daughter has been administered just about every psychotropic medication we have available for the treatment of persistent somatic delusions and psychosis. Given her history, she seems to be running out of options."

Robin heard a note in the room like a single beat from a bass drum, so low that the listener feels it rather than consciously hearing it, the vibration moving through the body like an intrusive pulse.

"Running out of options," he said. "What exactly does that mean?"

"Please—" Kapoor gestured at the chair Robin had been sitting in when they entered the room. "I'd like to examine your daughter before we speak further."

Robin sat reluctantly and Kapoor went around to the other side of the bed to examine Kathleen. He sat down on the edge of the bed and felt her pulse, rubbing his thumb gently over the bruised wrist.

"This is from the restraints?" he asked, and Robin almost answered him, before realizing that the question was directed at Biancini.

"Yes. She put up a pretty good fight."

"And what is she on now?"

Biancini consulted the chart. "Alprazolam, administered on admission and again this morning, and Haloperidol, just ordered for today." ·

Kapoor nodded.

"Haloperidol . . . Haldol?" Robin asked sharply. "No. You can't give her that. I told you—it made her a zombie. It took her weeks to come back even after they took her off it."

Biancini kept his gaze fixed on the back of Kapoor's head.

"We can wait on the Haldol," Kapoor said. "Tell me—I know you observed the negative behavioral side effects, which are extremely common on that drug, as you must know—and you say she still suffered the delusions. But did it alleviate any of her physical pain?"

Kapoor brushed Kathleen's hair aside very gently and pressed his fingertips down the length of her neck on either side, then pinched her jaw and opened her mouth to peer inside. Kathleen stiffened and tried to turn her head, but the moment Kapoor released his hold on her jaw her lashes fluttered and she went slack again.

Confirming that the sensation of having her tongue cut out is just a phantom pain, Robin thought, and then noted with relief that the neurologist had not bothered to check Kathleen's ears. Of course, there was nothing in the chart about auditory hallucinations. *There might not even have been any voices*, Robin reminded himself, but heard beneath his relief the jangling chord of fear.

"It didn't help with the pain, no," he said, "just seemed to make it harder for her to articulate what hurt and how much."

"And has she ever been given a narcotic pain medication?" Kapoor asked. "OxyContin? Dilaudid, any of those?"

Robin nodded. "The first episode with her mouth, when she was sixteen. They gave her something for the pain then, I think."

Biancini was already flipping through the thick chart. He reached the page he wanted and his thick eyebrows shot up over his glasses. "Percocet on admission, then a later course of morphine," he read. "Patient reported no pain relief. Unable to eat or drink per sensation of pain in the mouth, reported pain consistent with traumatic injury to the tongue."

Kapoor tilted his head in acknowledgment but said nothing. He stood up and slid the bedclothes from under Kathleen's limp arms, folding them down first to her waist, then all the way to her feet. Robin wondered at the elaborate process—why not just pull them off and be done with it?—but then realized that Kapoor had been checking to make sure that Kathleen was covered by her hospital robe before he exposed her below the waist. The gesture of consideration surprised him: usually once Kathleen was sedated this heavily, hospital personnel treated her like a rag doll. He reached out and slid his hand around hers, felt her slender fingers twitch under his. Too late, he turned back to see what the neurologist was doing.

Kapoor had picked up one long white foot to do a standard reflex test, running his pen down the length of the instep.

"No!" Robin said, rising to stop him. "Don't!"

The pen flicked and Kathleen screamed as though she'd been stabbed, arching off the bed and jerking her foot away from the doctor's touch.

"Jesus!" Biancini said.

"Shh, shh, it's okay, it's done." Robin put his hands on her shoulders, leaned in close so she could hear his voice. She'd flung her head about so wildly that her hair fell across her face. Robin pushed it back and saw that her eyes were open, pupils dilated until the black blotted out the blue. She looked right through him and her mouth worked in a way he recognized.

"Basin," he snapped as Kathleen began to retch. Robin sat her up and she vomited clear liquid into her lap, choking and spitting and thrusting her tongue. Behind him, he heard Biancini calling for a nurse and then Kapoor came around the bed and helped him support Kathleen. He had a towel in his hand and used it to gently wipe her chin and neck.

"It's the pain in her mouth," Robin explained. "When it gets this bad she can't keep anything down and she'll retch like this without any provocation." He pushed on the bed rail until it gave, then sat down next to Kathleen and held her up with an arm behind her back.

"Shh," he said, close to her ear. "Shh, it's all right. Try to take a breath." A thick hank of her hair was stuck to her cheek and he pulled it free, tucking it behind her ear. She had started to shudder in the aftermath of the vomiting.

"She needs a blanket—" Robin began, and turned to see if a nurse had arrived yet. A nurse hurried in at just that moment, clicking her beeper off as she approached the bed. She had short, curly blond hair and Robin had a moment's fear that it was Harry before he noted the scrubs, then another wave of relief. This was what Kathleen didn't want Harry to see, her eyes blank and her lips colorless, a puddle of bile on her thighs. Robin shifted his arm to try to pull the blankets away so the nurse could help change Kathleen's gown. He jerked, startled, when the neurologist's fingers touched his own at the nape of Kathleen's neck.

"Excuse me," Kapoor murmured. "I'd like to check her glands and her throat if I could. Please, yes," he continued, turning his head and his attention to the nurse as she hurried to his side. "If you could raise the bed for us. Let me finish here and then you can get her cleaned up."

Robin ceded his place and the nurse elevated the bed, then got a fresh robe and set of sheets and stood waiting.

Kapoor shone his penlight into Kathleen's eyes, pinched her chin again, and tried to get her to open her mouth. She tore her head away, moaning.

"Is she able to speak at all when she's like this?" Biancini asked, coming back to stand behind Kapoor.

"Not clearly."

"And neither the Haldol nor any pain medication has any effect?"

"No," Robin said. "Not on the pain itself. As I said"—he did not attempt to soften the edge of his voice—"the drugs you all give her seem to do a lot in terms of dulling her responsiveness, her general affect as you put it, but inside the haze she's always still in pain."

Kapoor withdrew from the bed and nodded to the nurse.

"Please," he said. "Let's step outside." Biancini was already out the door.

"I'll be right back," Robin said to Kathleen. Her eyes were closed again and she lay limp under the nurse's quick brusque hands, which were already reaching around to unbutton the gown behind her neck. Robin had that flash of Moira again, Kathleen's slender arms recalling Moira's as he peeled her icy, sodden clothes from her. *This is worse*, he thought, *worse than anything Moira ever went through. And even so Moira's pain killed her.*

Out in the hallway, Robin rounded on Kapoor.

"So? What was it he said?" He gestured at Biancini, a quick flick of his hand, a conductor's sign for silence. "She's 'running out of options.' What exactly does that mean?"

Kapoor clasped his hands behind his back. "Mr. Conarn,"

he said. "As Dr. Biancini stated earlier, a review of Kathleen's file indicates that psychotropic medication is simply not effecting a change. Neither, as you say, is pain medication. I observe peripheral neuropathy in the feet without any visible underlying cause. I observe a pain in the mouth consistent with either a delusion or a very, very rare nerve condition called trigeminal neuralgia, the other symptoms of which she does not display. The pain is a fact, you would agree?"

"I would," Robin said tightly.

"The pain is a fact and yet the cause is a mystery." Kapoor actually shrugged. "Sometimes the brain still escapes us. What has been successful when other avenues have failed—to relieve persistent delusions or chronic pain—is electroconvulsive therapy."

"Shock therapy?" Robin asked. He heard a stifled gasp and glimpsed Harry approaching behind Biancini. She was shaking her head.

"There are many common misconceptions about the treatment," Biancini said. "People have seen too many movies, don't understand the science. The treatment today is not your grandmother's ECT . . ."

He trailed off and Robin realized that he himself had taken a step forward. He had the savage urge to shove the man. He met Harry's eyes past Biancini's elbow, and what she saw in his seemed to alarm her more. She took a step toward their little group and Kapoor, noticing her, glanced swiftly at Robin.

"Perhaps we should talk in a private office?"

Robin shook his head. "This is Kathleen's girlfriend. Harry, these are Kathleen's doctors."

He tried to smile at her, but knew he failed utterly. Harry's answering expression was both anguished and grateful as she stepped into the conversation.

"Please," she said. "There's got to be another way."

"There is," Robin said. He turned back to Kapoor. "It's not an option we're willing to consider," he said. "Whether it's my grandmother's or not."

"I would not pursue a course of electroconvulsive therapy for any patient without weighing the risks and benefits and making sure that the patient is well-informed about the treatment," Kapoor said. "But I will tell you, Mr. Conarn, that in this case, having reviewed the file and examined your daughter, it is my only recommendation."

KATHLEEN DID NOT wake up all day, a fact that led Robin back out to the nurses' station to confirm that, as he had begun to suspect, at least one dose of Haldol had already been administered before he protested it and Kapoor agreed to hold off on it.

"She'll be out of it even when she does wake up," Robin said wearily to Harry when he came back in the room. "We need to go get you out of here, get something to eat."

She came meekly enough that Robin, glancing at her face, saw that he should have insisted they leave an hour ago. Harry was putting her coat on in slow motion, looking at Kathleen with no expression at all on her face.

THE IRISH BAR near his hotel had changed so little from when Robin had played there at night that when he followed the waitress to their table he almost bumped into her, automatically continuing past the table to the piano in the back corner. He ordered a gin and tonic. Harry ordered tea and clutched the hot mug, still hunched inside her coat. Her curls hung limp around her wan face.

"It's all right," Robin said. His drink arrived and he took a healthy swallow. He was not used to lying, any more than he was accustomed to having to make conversation after a day spent in the hospital.

"She'll get better," he said. "She always does, after a few days. By the time they discharge her, trust me, we'll all be irritated with her." He tried a joke. "You know no one does prima donna like Kathleen."

"She told me things got bad," Harry said. "She told me about the pills and the pain—everything. I feel stupid that I didn't realize—" She broke off. "Have they ever suggested that before?"

Robin's stomach clenched. He did not ask what "that" was.

"No," he said. "And I don't care if it is Kapoor's 'only recommendation.' I won't consider it."

The waitress arrived to take their order. Neither of them had even glanced at a menu and Harry looked panicky when the waitress asked her what she wanted.

"I'm fine with the tea," she said.

"You need to eat," Robin said, "and their clam chowder used to be the best in Boston."

"What are you getting?"

Robin grimaced, caught. "I'm not hungry."

Harry shook herself and spoke in something close to her usual crisp tone. "If I need to eat so do you." She turned to the waitress. "I'll have whatever he's having."

Despite himself, Robin smiled. He ordered a basket of bread and chowder for both of them.

"Their clam chowder *used* to be the best?" Harry asked when the waitress had left. "When was that?"

"Well, let's see . . ." He did the math in his head. "I worked here for four years when we first got to Boston, and I was twenty-two then, twenty-two to twenty-six, so . . ."

"So it's been almost twenty years since you had their clam chowder?"

Robin grinned at her. "I bet it's the same," he said. "They haven't changed a single other thing. I bet the piano still has a soft left pedal and the same dead keys it had when I was playing it."

Harry peered around at once for the piano and seemed to realize as she did so that she still had her coat on. She took it off and draped it over the back of her chair.

"I dare you to go check," Robin said. Harry smiled slightly, but he could tell by the set of her jaw that she was feeling it too: the sick tightness that had settled in his belly in a way he recognized from Kathleen's previous hospitalizations.

"Was it always just the two of you?" Harry asked abruptly. "I mean"—she flushed—"I know about Kathleen's mother, but what about your family?"

"Moira and I were both only children," he said. "My mother could never get pregnant again after me. They wanted me to leave Kathleen with them when I came to Boston, but I wanted my daughter with me, and anyway, I didn't want them raising her." He took another drink, recalling the avidity of his mother's face when she held baby Kathleen. "My mother died only a few years after we got here, before I was making enough money to afford a trip back, and my father was lost at sea a year later."

"My God," Harry breathed. "I'm so sorry. You couldn't have been very old—they couldn't have been very old."

"They weren't. My mother was forty-five when she died and my father forty-seven." He caught the horror on Harry's face and shook his head. "Harry, it wasn't all that unusual where we grew up. It was a small town, isolated. The nearest hospital was an hour away. People who went to hospital often never came back."

"You weren't planning to go back," Harry said, "when you came to Boston."

She hadn't phrased it as a question, he noticed.

"Do you know how many men there died in fishing accidents every year?" he asked. "At least a dozen, some years twenty or more. There used to be crosses along the shoreline just like you see on the highways here, only more of them. And it hasn't changed much. There's a school bus now, crofter's cottages converted into shops full of sweaters. But most of the men still fish, or they run tourist boats out to see the seals. That's what I would have gone back to."

He drained his drink, thinking that he wanted another and that he shouldn't have had even the one. In the mirrored wall over Harry's shoulder, he saw himself hazily reflected, at once both younger and older than he was, his face softened by memories and alcohol, his blond hair silver in the dim light. The waitress brought their food and Robin leaned back to let her set the bowl in front of him.

"It smells the same as I remember if that's any recommendation," he said. "Now eat."

"Yes, sir," Harry murmured, picking up her spoon. For a moment they were both silent, though the chowder was nearly too hot to eat. Harry tore pieces of bread off and dipped them in her bowl. Some of the color was returning to her face.

"So did your parents understand why you didn't come back?" she asked. "Did they ever come here?"

"They were both gone by the time I would have had enough money to bring them over," Robin said. Harry's family, he recalled, was both large and supportive, with grandparents, cousins, aunts, and uncles all vacationing together and—this was how he'd learned about them— weighing in on Harry's latest girlfriend when Harry brought her to a family picnic.

"My parents and I weren't close," he said, and then added, surprising himself, "they didn't like Moira."

"Why not?"

"They thought she was 'trouble'—that was the word my mother used. They refused to come to our wedding."

"Because you were both so young?"

Robin laughed shortly. "We weren't young to be getting married. A few of the girls we knew were married before they finished high school."

"Then what was it?"

Kathleen had never asked him this question. She'd never asked, he'd never told her. He traced a finger in the wet mark his glass left on the table, marked out a time signature absently, as if he were beginning a composition. *Hardly an original piece, though*, he thought. *Transcribing, that's all this is, transcribing the answers to questions I never wanted to ask, never wanted to answer.*

"Moira's family had some skeletons in the closet," he said. "Her grandmother Caolinn had gotten pregnant—this was back in the forties, when they still sent girls away to convents to hide their pregnancies—and she couldn't name the father."

"Couldn't or wouldn't?" Harry asked. "Was he married, or—"

"Caolinn said she'd been raped." Robin hesitated, realizing belatedly that this piece of the story would be hard for Harry to hear. "Not everyone believed her, or was sympathetic to her, because Caolinn was . . . She had a close friendship with another girl in town—to the point that they were always together, neither one would accept any male callers—"

"She was a lesbian," Harry said.

"The word would never have been used," Robin said, "but yes, in retrospect that seems to have been understood. The upshot was that Caolinn wasn't trusted, then she got pregnant and had a baby girl, Deirdre—Moira's mother, Kathleen's grandmother—and she died. With no father named for the baby there was no one to raise Deirdre. She grew up in the church orphanage."

"Did Caolinn die in childbirth?"

"No." Robin saw from her face that she was trying to follow the thread of the story as though it would lead somewhere useful or important. *It doesn't go anywhere*, he wanted to warn her. *It's like a song cycle, closing in on itself.*

"How did she die, then?"

"She killed herself."

Harry drew in a sharp breath. "How?"

"She took a rotten boat out into open water and drowned."

"And Deirdre, Moira's mother?"

Robin flattened his palm on the tabletop, blotting out the music he'd been scribbling, stopping the flow. "Harry," he said, "this is a terrible story. I've never told Kathleen any of it."

"Did Deirdre kill herself too?"

He nodded. "When Moira was a baby. Her father raised her."

Harry was shaking, he could feel the tremor through the tabletop. "Did she drown herself?"

"No. She slit her wrists in the bathtub. I know that detail—everyone knew that detail and repeated it so that even children heard—because it didn't make any sense."

"What do you mean?"

"I mean that her husband supposedly found her dead in the bathtub with her arms sliced open to the elbow and no knife anywhere."

It was how he'd heard the story as a child, the details about the bloody water and mysterious vanishing knife insisted upon with lurid relish by every ten-year-old boy who commanded the tale—but it was an old story to him. Harry, hearing it for the first time, shuddered.

"Did Moira ever talk about it?" she asked.

"Someone at school said something once, I remember that. When we were teenagers it was our version of an urban legend—don't take a bath alone or a mysterious knife-wielding killer will attack you and make it look like suicide."

"And?"

"When everyone realized that Moira was there—I think we were at the pub; I was playing and she was singing— there was that silence that comes after someone does something inexcusable. Moira walked out. When I followed her, she said that people who thought her mother's death was mysterious were stupid, that her mother had killed herself and 'the knife went back to where it came from.' That's the only time I remember her talking about it."

"What did she mean?"

"I have no idea," he said. "Especially because for a while I thought she had the knife."

"You saw it?"

"I caught her with it. It was in a box in her dresser drawer where she hid presents for me. She slammed it shut and shoved it back in the drawer when I came in the room." He frowned at his half-eaten bowl of chowder. There was a betrayal here, his telling Harry these things that he'd never told Kathleen, never told her doctors, but the story was inexorable now. And Harry sat with that concentrated frown on her face as though she was sure she could make sense of it.

"I can't even remember now why I checked the drawer later, or what I thought she was hiding. I'd like to say I was worried about her but . . . I don't know. She had a box in there that I'd never seen, made of something very smooth and shining, like mother-of-pearl, and there was a knife inside, or not a knife—" He picked up his bread knife and held it up to Harry. "Not like this, with only one edge. It was double-sided, more like a dagger or a letter opener."

"Did you ask her about it?"

"No," Robin said. "I thought about taking it, but I shouldn't have been poking in that drawer to begin with, and I didn't think she'd ever—" He replaced his knife on the table. "Moira was terribly, terribly sad but she was also fragile. I don't think it ever occurred to me that she might use a knife on herself."

"No," Harry said, her tone thoughtful. "No, she drowned herself instead, like her grandmother had. And Deirdre, even though she used a knife, did it in the bathtub. But what happened to the knife that Moira had?"

"I don't know," Robin said. "I think she must have finally

gotten rid of it, maybe even because she was afraid she might use it. For several months, before she died, she sort of slowly broke down. She cried in her sleep, cried when she nursed the baby." His throat felt raw. He picked up his glass and took a sip, though there was nothing left but water from the melting ice. "When I packed up her things after she died I didn't find the knife anywhere."

"So she got rid of it," Harry said. "But you don't know for sure that it was the same knife her mother used, the one that 'went back where it came from.'"

"Unless that's not what she meant," Robin said. "Unless she meant that someone—maybe her father—put the knife back where it belonged when he found his wife's body, and there isn't any mystery at all."

"But there is!" Harry cried. She counted on her fingers. "Caolinn kills herself, that's one, then Deirdre kills herself, that's two, and then Moira, that's three—three suicides of women in the same family line, three generations in a row, all right after they've had babies, all using water."

"Harry," Robin said gently, "as for the 'using water,' it was a coastal village where everyone knew the sea could kill. It doesn't mean anything."

"But Kathleen's obsessed with the sea! Maybe they were too! Was Moira?" She was so frustrated at his obtuseness that Robin began to feel angry in return. Did she really think he had never thought of all this, never tried to make sense of it?

"There's no answer here!" he snapped. "Yes, Moira was obsessed with the sea. Kathleen could tell you that herself, just like she told me when she was a little girl, how she didn't think Mommy wanted to die, just that Mommy wanted to be under the sea where it didn't hurt anymore. Was Deirdre obsessed with the sea? I don't know! Was Caolinn? I've no idea. And I've thought that it must matter, that it must make some kind of sense, but it doesn't except in the obvious way. They were all depressed, suicidally depressed. That's a genetic condition, a documented one, and all it tells us is that they didn't get help. But Kathleen's gotten help and she'll get more, as much as she needs."

"Even ECT?" Harry asked.

He jerked as though she'd slapped him. "Which side are you on here, exactly?"

She drew a sobbing breath and put her face in her hands. "I'm sorry," she said through her fingers.

Robin said nothing. He wished the waitress would come back so he could order another damn drink, but she was probably avoiding their table now, not wanting to get into the middle of whatever this was.

After a moment Harry murmured, "I have to go to the bathroom. Please don't leave."

"I'm not going anywhere," Robin said, surprised, but she was already out of her seat and hurrying to the back of the bar.

The waitress came by to clear their dishes and leave the check.

"Hard, isn't it?" she said, and when Robin glanced up at her blankly she jerked her head at Harry's empty chair. "Kids. My eldest went through a terrible stage when she was that age. How old is your girl there, twenty-five, twenty-six? I thought it'd be a miracle if mine made it to thirty, seriously.

And now"—she leaned across the table to get the bread basket, a reflective smile on her face—"she's got two terrific kids, is married to a sweetheart of a guy, lives out in Beverly, and works with autistic children. And if you'd told me five years ago that'd be *my* daughter I'd have laughed in your face." She turned her smile at Robin. "You want another drink?"

"No," he said, "thank you." He didn't bother to correct her about Harry. He pulled his credit card out absently and slid it into the folder with the bill. *A miracle if she made it to thirty.* Kathleen was twenty-four. Biancini, damn him, seemed to think it was a miracle that she'd made it that far, and why shouldn't he? Biancini didn't even know about Moira, dead at twenty-one, or about Deirdre or Caolinn— how old had they been when they died? Harry thought it mattered; Robin wondered if she could possibly guess how determined he was that it *not* matter, that those deaths didn't have to mean anything to Kathleen.

Harry appeared over his shoulder, put her coat on first, then sat back down. She was shivering again.

"Are you all right?" Robin asked.

"I'm fine," she said. "They had a window open in the bathroom, so I'm cold but . . ." She leaned in across the table, her face tense with contained excitement.

"Robin," she said, "you have to take her to Ireland."

He could only stare at her, but she plunged on as if he'd offered a verbal objection.

"I know it sounds crazy but listen—these women in her family, if it's a small community as you say, well, there might still be something we're missing, some genetic disease, some predisposition. Even if it is just depression, they all killed themselves after they had babies so maybe postpartum blues pushed them over the edge, right? Even that's important for Kathleen to know. She can decide to not have children or to get special treatment if she gets pregnant. The point is that there might be more family history that you don't know, or that you know but you didn't think was important before."

"Harry—"

"And there's another thing too," she said. "I don't know what it means, but I think it would help her to go to Ireland. I get why you didn't want to go back but maybe there are other reasons to go there too. When we were on the plane coming home from Florida, she was having one of those things, you know, where she's just barely keeping it together and everything's hurting, and I showed her a picture of the sea taken from the top of cliffs off the coast of Ireland and she *grabbed* it from me. She kind of conked out for most of the flight"—she faltered for a moment—"I think she took something, Benadryl or Dramamine maybe, because she was *really* out of it for hours, but she wouldn't let go of that picture."

Robin resisted the urge to rub his eyes. He was abruptly exhausted, as much by what was coming as by what had already passed.

"The Cliffs of Moher," he said. "She told me about it."

Harry nodded. "That's near where you're from, isn't it? I thought it was. I asked Kathleen but she couldn't—she wouldn't—say anything. But couldn't you take her there? Take her and let her see the real thing, the cliffs and the town where you grew up, where she was born."

"Ireland's not her home," Robin said, trying to keep his voice even. Hadn't he just had this conversation a week ago?

"It is," Harry said, implacable now. "It's where she's from.

I don't know why she never asked you before why you've never gone back—"

"Yes you do," he said. "She never asked me because she thought she knew the answer—that I couldn't bear to go back because of her mother—and she didn't want to hurt me. And now it seems I've hurt her—possibly put her in the hospital—by not answering the damn question."

"Oh no!" Harry cried. "You didn't, it wasn't that conversation that started this! It started in Florida, I told you—"

Robin cut her off. "When I told my father-in-law that I was taking Kathleen to America, do you know what he said? He said, 'It'll all come out the same in the end.' He was holding her when he said it, holding his granddaughter and matter-of-factly predicting—I don't even know what he was predicting," Robin said, though he could tell from Harry's face that she knew he was lying. Of course he knew. They both knew. Harry knew as much of the story of Kathleen's family history as Robin himself did now. "But I left with no intention of taking her back."

"Of course not," Harry whispered. "Of course you couldn't. But don't you see how all this time you've been protecting Kathleen? And at the same time, she's been trying not to hurt you, not asking you anything about Ireland or about her mother or anyone in her family?"

"And somehow our little unstated pact has stopped working, is that what you're saying?"

Harry flinched, but didn't back down. "I guess that is what I'm saying. I just think, what if you go back and try to find out if there's more to the story of her family. I can't think what it could be, any more than you can, but what if there is something, something so simple and so clear when you're there—" She sat back, trembling with urgency inside her coat. "It could make this whole thing—the ECT—it could open up some other options, that's all. I mean, it probably won't, but it *could*."

"I see what you're saying," he said. "I do see."

Harry drew in a breath as if afraid to hope that she'd made her case. Robin felt himself suddenly inclined to smile at her intensity. It was almost Kathleen-like. He also thought that this was a lover's errand she was proposing, not a father's. Never mind the fact that he didn't want to go back at all, wanted to leave Ireland to the boy who had not yet outlived his young wife, who had never imagined leaving the rocks just off the coast where the seals sunned themselves, groaning and barking, or the sea that was black in some lights and jade green in others but never blue, not even under a blue sky. Never mind, either, that all of his protective energy toward his daughter had been focused, all of her life, on keeping her away from places and knowledge that might cause her pain. The fact was that Harry proposed slaying one monster for Kathleen by forcing her to face another and that was a lover's role.

"I bet you like *Don Quixote*, don't you?" he asked aloud.

Harry blinked. "The novel or the opera—and which opera?"

Robin shook his head. "It doesn't matter," he said. "I can't go anywhere right now. I've got a deadline on this opera commission. You take her. I'll buy the tickets."

Act 2

And so the time has come to untell and tell the tale of Fand, parts of which many of those Below, her own people, have forgotten.

First, to untell, which is delicate work, like picking apart tightly knotted netting . . .

In the story told Above the sea seems a mere wading pool, and desire is leached of its dark power, painted as nothing more than chaste affection.

The Little Mermaid sought out the sea witch. Thus we are diminished from the many to the one and our magic labeled black and evil.

And when the mermaid failed to kill the prince and save herself, she rose into the air, her foolishness and her weakness and her rejection of all the magic offered to her turning her into something called a Daughter of Air, who flitted ghost-like above the human world. One day, the teller promised, the Little Mermaid earned an immortal soul and ascended even higher above the sea, into the ether that those Above call heaven.

That knot opens easily.

She did not ascend anywhere. She lies where she fell, onto the rocks and into the sea, her bones picked clean long ago by the ragged claws of scavengers.

* * *

Her voice was the voice of deep blue-black ocean currents: what a bargain that was, for a mere pair of legs. We wove it into a net to catch shipwrecked sailors in and ease the task of tugging them down to the bottom of the sea. They hear it and they stop their struggles to rise Above. Their blind eyes close and their clenched fists open and they drift down like weary children glad of the chance to rest.

She was called Maeve by the prince who loved her and betrayed her. The name means "fragile" in Gaelic, and it was not poorly chosen for her. But when she proved stronger than she appeared, surviving his betrayal, she discarded both the name and its meaning and instead called herself Fand, after an Irish goddess who married Mannanán Mac Lir, the god of the sea.

She was the eighth daughter, not the seventh, nor the sixth, though some tales would have it so. The Above-lore that sinks this far down is as murky as the waters themselves, but we know that seven is the magic number Above: the seventh son of the seventh son shall find an adventure on the seventh day . . . and so forth. There's much of the lore from Above that wavers and shifts and speaks of the inconsistencies that must be accounted for in a world where the currents of the air can blow the beauty from an orchard full of blossoms in an hour. We've a different world here, and she was the eighth daughter, the loveliest by the standards of any world.

She was taken Above to see the world when she was twice eight years old, sixteen, and about to be wed. Most of us would no sooner explore that dry world than those with two legs would explore ours, but she was entranced by the silken feel of air against her skin, by the light from the sky that splintered into diamonds on the crests of the waves and stung—she had no word for "burned"—her upturned face. Then too there was the boy, riding high in a great ship that bore down on her like a whale and might have cut her in two had one of her sisters not pulled her under, out of the way.

He was a splendid boy, tall and strong, with eyes a bright, glinting shade of blue that is as foreign to us as the colors of bird feathers. We would have been happy to have him when the storm brought so many of his fellows to us, along with all that the ship had held. Some such debris we treasure, like the thick bottles made of glass and the fine small boxes or chains made of silver or gold. Much of it we have no use for: their clothes and books, weapons and foodstuffs. These things float down to the ocean floor and are left alone, save for a few fish that may nudge them curiously. In a few months or years they are gone as if they never existed.

We would have liked the boy, but she had been watching him, even that night, through the driving rain from Above and the rising waves from Below. She caught him almost as soon as he hit the water and swam him to dry land. Who would have guessed she had it in her, that quiet little girl! But there he lay, stretched out on the sand, alive and safe while all his men and possessions swirled around us. And it was not long after his rescue, when more of his people came for him and she had to dive under or be seen, that she sought us out.

We were expecting her. The draught was brewed, cooled, and sealed in one of those same fine bottles that *broken ships spill into the sea. The payment was her voice for her new legs, and she hesitated only a moment before agreeing. She was a fool, of course, but so beautiful that we really did think she had a chance. Hair that had a deep, murky violet gleam to it in our world, but shone like the heart of a fire up Above, long enough to wrap about her exquisite nakedness like a cloak when first they found her. Those big eyes, that white, white skin, her body like supple sea grass that bends and sways and seems to dance when the water flows over it. No girl from Above could move like she did, every tilt of her head sending her heavy hair rippling around her, every step light and graceful as a trickle of water from a silver cup.*

The man who wrote her story into his book of "fairy tales" would have it that the pain was another payment. But he did not understand how magic works. To exact a second, terrible payment for a spell already bought: we would not have done so. The pain was the pain, is all. It was inevitable. We could not have given her legs and feet that did not cause her agony with every step. To do so would have meant changing her essence, making her into something she was not, and that is a great and terrible magic that we cannot work, would not work even if we could. We tried to warn her, to explain to her what the pain would be: Every step you take will feel as if you are treading upon sharp knives, and that the blood must flow.

There is much of the tale told Above that is distorted, misunderstood, poorly told. But that line is true. That is what we told her. Still she put out her tongue to be sliced off, clutched the green glass bottle in her hand, and swam to the surface to drink it.

She was weeping from the pain when they found her washed up on the shore, naked beneath her tangled hair. Her white skin had an iridescence that they could not tear their eyes from, a sheen like the inside of a scallop shell. They were men of the prince's court, several courtiers who counted themselves his friends, with their servants. She cringed away from their hard, hot hands, so they gave her a cloak to wrap herself in and bore her between them on another cloak as befitted the princess that she was, though of course, they did not know that. When they presented her to the prince and she lifted up her head long enough to utter a wordless cry and twine her arms about his neck, he cradled her like a child and took her immediately to his bed. Hours later he sought out those who had found her and demanded to know if they had touched her. She had bled and she had wept, but she had also clung and writhed in his embrace. He was maddened at the thought that he might not have been the first.

The prince carried a dagger in his boot that had been given him by his first sword master. It was a highly ornamental piece but the blade was keen. Feeling its edge at their throats, the prince's men swore that they had only done their duty, only saved the girl's life. They did not confess what their thoughts had been as they had borne her up from the beach, but then, he did not ask them if they had wanted her, only if they had taken her.

The story known Above says nothing of this, nor of the fact that Maeve was the prince's concubine, his favored bed partner from the very first hour she left the sea until an hour before he wed another. But the truth seeps in at the edges: *"The prince said she should remain with him always, and she received permission to sleep at his door, on a velvet cushion."* The tale makes her his pet, and so she was. But she was also his lover, and he was as much in thrall to her—to the strangeness and beauty of her hair and her skin and her long-lashed eyes—as any mortal man has ever been in thrall to a mermaid. She was a fool to go to him, but he was a fool too to think he could ever love another after her.

Perhaps, indeed, the prince did not think at all when, three years after Maeve came to him, he sent a ruby ring to the princess who had been promised to him since they were children. Perhaps he thought that Maeve would recognize the difference between wife and lover and count herself lucky to be the one who made him cry out and bruise her with the ferocity of his grip in the darkness, while his wife slept alone in her chamber across the corridor. Perhaps he saw his wedding as a necessity, a strategic move, not as a betrayal of the woman who loved him.

There is, of course, no way that he could have known that in marrying one woman he was killing another. Maeve could not tell him, however sad and expressive her eyes, however cold her hands, however tremulous her mouth when he kissed her as he rose from their bed on the morning of his wedding and smiled at the sight of his new wedding suit, pressed and waiting for him. He would be dazzling in it and he knew it.

Maeve watched the wedding with the rest of the court, until the heavy, dusty scent of the lilies the bride favored made her gag and she had to slip away. She rose from the chamber pot still shaking with nausea and saw on the windowsill the dagger her sisters had given her. She did not remember leaving it there, to glint in the last red light of the sun. The shadows in its filigreed hilt refused to catch the light and reminded her of all she had lost, of the depths in which she had cultivated her garden, of the beauty of her flowers in the dark water.

She wiped her mouth, pushed back her hair. She took up the dagger. The metal felt cool and liquid, comforting and familiar as the seashells she had collected on the beach ever since she had come Above. It did not feel like she held a murder in her hand.

She waited until moonrise, then slipped into her prince's chamber with only silver light to guide her way. She saw that the sheets—the sheets in which she had lain with him that very morning—had been changed. The prince smiled in his sleep, his cheek against his bride's, his face slack and easy in the aftermath of his release, and his betrayal was the worse for his failure to admit to it. Maeve raised the blade above her head and in an instant would have had him dead, his blood spraying like seawater at the base of a jagged rock, splashing her in an arc from head to toe. The castle was built beside the sea. With a simple turn and a thrust of her arms against the windowsill she could have tumbled back to the water even as she changed, as the frayed and broken edges of her tail knit themselves together, as her scales returned and the searing wound in her mouth sealed itself off and ceased to give her pain.

We waited for her return all through that night. As the

*sun rose and neither Maeve nor the blade that we had
made for her appeared, we wondered: Had we not been
clear? Had her sisters not told her truly? Had the prince
perhaps awakened to stop the knife's descent? It was
many hours before we knew that she had simply turned
away. By then she was gone, too far inland for us to trace
her. Nor could the prince find her, though he tried.*

Aria for Mezzo-Soprano

Taking Kathleen to Ireland initially seemed like a kind of shining solution to something—maybe to everything. But it was the end of March. We'd just gotten back from spring break and had six weeks of classes left before the semester was over. I had voice students to whom I was accountable, we both had performances and exams, and Kathleen wasn't discharged from the hospital until the end of the week. She got a medical excuse for missing those classes, though Professor Menotti, Bella, sniffed over the official paperwork Kathleen handed her, tossed her scarf over her shoulder (Kath did an impression of the gesture), and warned Kathleen "not to confuse ethereal with wan. The one is every lyric soprano's goal. The other just makes the audience nervous."

"Did you tell her you weren't wan on purpose?" I asked. Kathleen shrugged. She'd lost weight she didn't need to lose, color she never had to begin with, and some of the fizzing energy I was used to seeing in her.

Robin had gotten her discharged and off the drugs as soon as he could, against medical advice. He didn't tell the doctors about the planned trip, just said that he'd take their recommendations for Kathleen's care under advisement. It was three more days before she really came back to us, when she sat up, stretched, and wrinkled her nose at how lank her hair had gotten, rather than swallowing convulsively or shifting fretfully against the sheets and the restraints as soon as she was awake. The nurses wouldn't let her shower alone, but for the most part once Robin had announced that he was taking her home, they washed their hands of her. Kapoor never came back to check on her after he spoke with Robin, only Biancini, who asked her to rate her pain level whenever he came in and made a mark on the chart when she answered, wearily, that it was decreasing day by day. I wondered why he bothered.

I spent as much time at the hospital as I could, but I had to go to classes and rehearsals and let repairmen into the apartment. I wasn't there when Robin told her about the electroshock. I came in a few hours later. Robin was sitting by the bed with several sheets of an orchestral score. He'd commandeered the swing table that was attached to Kathleen's bed and was making pencil notes. Kathleen had her eyes shut and her phone in her lap. When I came in she tugged the headphones from her ears.

"What are you listening to?" I asked.

She handed me the headphones and I held them close to listen. "I don't know . . . Tell me—wait. It's not Wagner but that's Birgit Nillson, isn't it?"

Kathleen smiled. She'd gotten so thin that I could see

a tracery of lavender veins along her collarbone. I handed back the headphones and touched her cheek.

"Have you eaten anything?"

She shrugged my hand away. "It's *Fidelio*," she said. "I figured I needed an opera with a happy ending, to remind myself that those things do happen, you know, sometimes. Of course usually everyone dies, but—"

Robin spoke without lifting his head from the score. "Kathleen."

"What do you think?" she asked. "Would I look good with a big white streak in my hair? You know, sort of Bride of Frankenstein after the jolt of electricity?"

I glanced at Robin.

"Kathleen has decided to arm herself with black humor today," he said. "I'm finding it charming, myself, but then I find everything about my daughter charming."

"Especially my tendency to try to drown myself in the bathtub?" Kathleen asked brightly. Robin shook his head and bent over his score again.

"Did he tell you what we thought you might do instead?" I asked. "About Ireland?"

"Yes." She began to carefully wrap her headphone cord around the phone.

"And?"

"I think—" She hesitated, cut her eyes at her father. "I think it's a good idea. I *think*. And not just to avoid the *other* wonderful idea that's been proposed to me by the medical community. I mean, I've never been." She looked at Robin again and this time he met her gaze. He had the same expression on his face that he'd worn when he'd talked to me at the restaurant a few nights before: guarded and slightly alarmed, but also resigned, as if he didn't like what was happening but didn't see any alternative to it. "Some of the things he told me, about my family, my mother, and my grandmother—you said you told Harry all of this already."

"I did."

"Weird, isn't it?" Kathleen said.

"That's one way to think about it," I said. "Maybe it actually all makes sense when you have the whole story."

"It's not like we're going to be able to find *that* just by going," Kathleen said. "That's too easy. But still, I want to see it."

"So we're going," I said. "As soon as the semester's over we're going to Ireland."

BUT OF COURSE the semester took over for both of us for a while. The conservatory puts on a major operatic production each semester, along with concert opera and collections of scenes. Kathleen had sung the lead in *Manon Lescaut* in the fall so she hadn't gotten a major role in the spring production of *Rigoletto*. Amusingly enough—at least to Kathleen—Professor Menotti, who was constantly picking at her in their private lessons, had been incensed when the cast list went up and Kathleen wasn't Gilda. Kathleen had pointed out that there were other talented singers in the program and it was only fair to allow everyone an opportunity. Bella said—famously, now, since either Kathleen or our friend Tom loved to quote the line at parties—that "*fair* has no place in opera."

I'd sung in a concert performance of *Les Contes de Hoffman* in the fall. This spring I was working on a scene from

Vanessa that included one of the saddest, loveliest arias for mezzo: "Must the Winter Come So Soon?" It's a lament for the kind of encroaching, inevitable sense of loss that winter brings and that the singer mourns even as it's happening. I've always loved it and I felt like I was doing it justice in early rehearsals. But the first time I sang it all the way through after Kath had gotten out of the hospital, everyone went quiet when I finished. I wished I was like Kathleen or Tom and could make a joke out of the moment. I also wished that I hadn't sung it better than before—and I knew I had—because I knew why I had. Kathleen was home and singing again and we were going to Ireland in just a few weeks. But still I was frightened. Whenever Kathleen took a shower I stayed in the bedroom where I could hear the water running and make sure she turned it off.

Robin was making all the travel arrangements, so Kathleen and I hardly talked about Ireland at all. But Kathleen would bring it up at odd moments, saying, "I wonder if it will rain as much as everyone says it does," as we walked home from the train station, and "I wonder if they really look like that," as she stood in the kitchen with her spoon raised over her cereal bowl.

"If *what* really look like *what*?"

"The cliffs," she said absently. She set her bowl down untouched in the sink. "The Cliffs of Moher."

And then one night—the first night we'd had sex since she got out of the hospital—she murmured something against my shoulder that I couldn't make out.

"What?" I gathered up the whole long fall of her hair and twisted it off to the side, stroked it smooth on the pillow.

"I wish he'd taken me home before now," she said. "I feel like he still doesn't want me to go."

"Robin, you mean."

"And he won't go himself." She turned to lie half across my breast, resting her chin on her hands. Her mouth shone faintly in the dim light, wet and fragrant of both of us. "You know I want you to go," she said, "but why won't he?"

"Did you ask him?"

She shook her head. I let her hair go and it slithered back down around us with her movement. "We talk about everything except for the things we don't talk about," she said. "And those are things we don't talk about *at all*."

"Do you think it's because of your mother?"

"No. And yes. I think he feels guilty that I know about her, about what she did, that I've always known. Like that's somehow his fault. I knew before anyone could even have told me. But I think he got yelled at a lot by at least one therapist of mine who thought he'd told me about Moira. So maybe that's why he didn't want to tell me any of the rest."

"About Deirdre."

"And the one before." She smiled slightly. "My lesbian great-grandmother."

"I think he's been scared for you," I said. "I think telling you that history would be the last thing he'd want to do. When he told me—it was more than hard for him. It was like he had to force himself not just to tell me but to actually remember it. Like he'd talked himself into forgetting it."

"They're lovely names, aren't they?" she asked. "Moira, Deirdre, Caolinn."

"Kathleen's lovely too."

"Silly." She slid down onto her side, curled up around me. When she spoke again her voice was thickening with sleep.

"Anyway, I hope they'll be satisfied."

"Who?"

"You know. Because we're going to Ireland," she murmured, as if this made perfect sense. "I think that must be what they want me to do. To come home."

THE WEEKEND AFTER classes ended, I had to go to Martha's Vineyard to sing at a wedding. I didn't want Kathleen to come, knowing that we'd have to cross water to get to the island and wondering what on earth I'd do if she had a breakdown an hour before I was supposed to sing a tricky arrangement of the Lord's Prayer and an unaccompanied "Ave Maria" to a hundred and fifty people. But I asked her if she wanted to come, carefully, trying to convey that it wouldn't be a big deal either way. When she said that she was going to stay home and start packing, I didn't question her, even though packing, for Kathleen, usually involved throwing things in her suitcase haphazardly: silk tops totally inappropriate for rainy weather, only one pair of jeans but two different kinds of perfume, the sturdy walking shoes I'd made her buy that hurt her feet, and no socks to wear with them.

The church on the Vineyard was white clapboard outside and unvarnished red wood inside, the vault of the ceiling shaped exactly like the hull of a boat turned upside down. I sang to that ceiling and to the doors and windows left open to the sea air: *"Maria, gratia plena."* There were masses of yellow roses on the altar and the bride was as tall and slender as Kathleen. I thought, *We could get married here. Kathleen would love it.* It was a shock to think it: I'd never imagined our future so clearly before. We could ride the ferry over here together. Kathleen would lean over the railing to watch the white froth the boat left in its wake, laugh at the dazzle of sun on the water. She would love this church. It was built high on a bluff and you could see the glint of the ocean from the windows all around. *Maybe after Ireland* was what I thought next, and knew that the trip had taken on a kind of magic power, not just in Kath's mind but in mine.

I took the last ferry back from the Vineyard on Saturday and got in late. The apartment was a wreck and Kathleen was in a panic because she couldn't remember where she'd put her passport. We eventually found it curled up and stuffed inside a ballet flat in the bottom of her suitcase, which of course meant that her entire bag had to be repacked. Kathleen sat on the floor and burst into tears, trying to flatten her passport out in her hands and crying harder when it insistently rolled back up again. I finally snatched it from her and told her to just go to bed. I was tired—I'd been up early, driven almost three hours, performed, then driven back again, all of which she knew and, typical Kathleen, forgot about in the midst of her meltdown. She came out of the bathroom after brushing her teeth, calm and dry-eyed, and put her arms around me from behind while I knelt over her suitcase.

"I'm sorry," she said. "Inexcusable. How was the wedding? Was it lovely?"

"It was," I said. "It was beautiful. Nothing tacky to report." I didn't tell her about the church built like a boat or the smell of the sea in the air. I didn't tell her about picturing her walking down the little aisle. She kept her arms around me a while, until I stopped packing and covered her hands with mine. Then she rested her cheek on my back for a minute.

"I'm just so scared," she said. "Scared about how much I've got invested in this trip."

"I know."

"I thought about it today," she said. "If this was an audition we were flying off to and putting this kind of pressure on it, you know we'd be jinxing it." She lifted her head. "You remember Tom's story about his friend, the one whose family threw him a huge party before his Juilliard audition and then he walked into the audition room and threw up on the floor?"

"Or Alyce," I said. "Remember my voice teacher in college? Froze up at her Met audition."

"Oh God."

I leaned over to get a stack of clothes.

"You're not going to blow it," I said. "There's nothing to blow, nothing to jinx. Although it might help if you learned how to pack a suitcase."

She laughed, kissed me on the back of the neck, and went to bed.

We were leaving in two days, taking a direct flight from Logan to Shannon Airport, then a bus to a town called Ennis, then another bus all the way to the west coast. Robin had offered to rent us a car, but neither one of us wanted to drive in Ireland. Kathleen was a terrible driver anyway. She was the first to admit it, and she had fears of careening right off the road and over a cliff. I just didn't want to have the added stress of learning to drive on the left while also driving with Kathleen giving directions and possibly dealing with . . . well, with whatever else came up. So we were taking buses.

We weren't going to stay in the village where Robin and Moira had grown up, simply because there was no place where tourists could stay. It was listed in only one of the guidebooks I'd found, as "a charming remnant of an old fishing village, worth driving through on your way to Ballyvaughan, if only to catch a glimpse of a way of life that's vanishing on Ireland's west coast." Alongside this blurb was a photo of a grizzled man standing by a rowboat, a length of net in one hand and a wool cap pulled down over his forehead. He was glaring at the camera.

We were going to a town called Doolin, apparently "the music capital of Ireland." It seemed to be one long main street lined with bed-and-breakfasts, shops, and two famous pubs, one on each end of the street and marking out the town limits. The bus line dead-ended in Doolin, for the simple reason that there was no place else to go except into the ocean. And there was a local Office of Records and Genealogy there, which was where I planned to start. I had a list of angles to try: living relatives, newspapers or other local records like obituaries, even just the correct spellings of names to plug into a Google search. Until Robin wrote the name *Caolinn* down for me, I'd been spelling it in my head the way it sounded: Colleen.

We were staying for four days, booked into a gorgeous inn that was built halfway up a hillside at one end of the town and surrounded by a wide deck of gray slatted wood.

It could have been a house in California overlooking the Pacific, but the website advertised kippers and blood sausage for breakfast and the owner's name was Siobhán, so Kathleen had approved it as "Irish enough." Robin said one of the board members at the symphony had stayed there and recommended it, although not exactly on those grounds.

Before I zipped Kathleen's suitcase up, I checked the local weather forecast in Doolin. It said the same thing it had said every other time I'd checked: partly cloudy, windy, chance of rain. Yet all the photos on the various tourism sites showed sunny skies, sea and sky competing for degrees of blueness, green grass like carpet running right down into the surf. I turned off the computer and went to get another sweater out of Kathleen's drawer, then added "compact collapsible umbrella" to my running list of things we needed to buy. As I bent over the counter, I heard Kath sob once in her sleep, a single deep indrawn breath. Afterward it seemed even quieter in the apartment. I crouched on the floor near her side of the bed. She was breathing through her mouth, shallow breaths, which meant her mouth was hurting. I watched her for a while, thinking that of all the things I was worrying about, packing appropriately for the weather was the least of our problems.

THE DAY BEFORE we left, Tom showed up and announced that we were ordering takeout for dinner.

"And here's my contribution to the meal!" He pulled a bottle far enough out of its brown bag for me to see the foil-wrapped champagne cork. Kathleen was in the bedroom on the phone. I shook my head.

"No?" he said. He usually tried to talk people into things, but this time he immediately slid the bottle back into the bag. "You want to put it away, then?"

"Thanks." I took it and put it in the refrigerator. "Thank you, Tom. It's not like she can't see the bottle or anything. It's just that—she's kind of precarious right now."

He nodded. "I know. I guess I thought that might help. Don't worry about it." He sat on one of the bar stools at our kitchen counter. "How are *you* doing, Harry?"

"Me?"

Tom heaved an exaggerated sigh. "You. I feel like I've hardly seen you all semester, especially since spring break."

"I have five private students right now and I sang a wedding last weekend and now we're packing for this trip."

"Yeah," Tom said. "What's up with that, anyway?"

"What do you mean?"

"Well, you guys went to Florida last minute over break, and now you jet off to Ireland as soon as the curtains fall on spring performances—nice job in the scene, by the way. Your voice made me think of snow."

I flushed. "Thank you."

"But I was giving Kathleen shit about her jet-set lifestyle and she got all prima donna on me, said something about how the trip to Ireland isn't exactly a vacation. So what's going on?"

I wished Kathleen would get off the phone and join us. I wasn't sure how much she wanted Tom to know. I remembered that he was really her friend more than he was mine, and why. It wasn't that I didn't like him, but I always felt like he was interested in other people's drama, like a boy watching bugs on the sidewalk. And if he couldn't find any-thing to be fascinated with, he made something up.

"Nothing's going on," I said. "Kathleen's family is from there and she's never been back."

"And when you get back?" Tom asked. "If Kathleen is still *precarious*?"

"She'll be better."

"I don't know if that's possible," Tom murmured. He caught sight of my face and put his hand on my wrist. "Sorry! That's not what I meant at all. I meant her singing. That's what I meant to talk to you about," he said, "without Kathleen. I wanted to know if you knew."

"Knew what?"

"How she's been singing, since she got back from break and being out of commission for that week. I was in re-hearsals with her for concert opera and for acting tech-niques and— Jesus, I don't know . . ." He made a face. "She's been scaring me."

Join the club, I almost said, but didn't. I sat down and waited.

"The voice itself hasn't changed," Tom said, "not really. But there's something about it now—listening to her, watching her, it seems as if she could literally just go on singing and singing. I'm standing there beside her feeling the strain vocally, physically, and she's just—don't take this wrong—but it's like people I've known doing coke or some-thing. And then when the music stops, she's just *done*. Goes gray, has to sit down, does that weird thing with her mouth where you think she's trying to spit something out. She almost passed out a couple of times."

She hadn't told me any of this. Of course. And why hadn't Tom told me before, or anyone else who was in the damn opera with her?

"She's pushing herself too hard," I said. "That's—it's part of why we're taking this trip."

"Yeah, well . . ." Tom shook his head. "I thought you should know about the singing piece of it. Because if I were *you*, I'd be really worried for her, but if I were Kathleen right now"—he shook his head again—"I don't know."

"What?"

"She's singing better than ever," he said, "which is saying something when you're talking about her. And she knows it; she can feel it. Whatever's going on, that's not easy to give up, you know?"

"She won't have to," I said.

Tom gave me a level look. His face, without the mischief that usually animated it, was fine-boned and full of shadows. An artist's face, like Kathleen's. He knew I was willing it true, wishing it true.

"Magical thinking, Tom," I said. "It's my latest solution to everything."

I'd meant it to be a joke, but it fell flat and instead sounded alarmingly accurate.

KATHLEEN SLEPT SO heavily on the plane ride over that I suspected she'd taken something. When I thought about my conversation with Tom the night before, though, I wondered. I'd defended her to him, said she'd been pushing herself, but how much of that had I even understood myself when I said it? I reclined both our seats, curled up under my sweater beside her and tried to sleep too.

Shannon to Ennis to Doolin, where the answers would be. That was the mantra I dozed off to on the plane. When we actually got to Doolin, though, some twelve hours after we'd left Boston, we were both reeling from exhaustion and jet lag. I left Kathleen sleeping, with the windows open to the sea air, and went to ask at the front desk of the inn for directions to the local offices of the newspaper and of Records and Genealogy. We were here, after all, and only for four days. I felt like there wasn't much time to lose, and I had no illusions about Kathleen coming with me to do anything involving the phrase "archival research." When I came back to shower and to get dinner three hours later, Kath was up, though still drawn and snappish. *She* did *take something*, I thought. I put the notebook and the pen I'd used back into the side pocket of my carry-on, carefully, precisely, like it mattered. I was angry at Kathleen for not helping me, for not even seeming to believe that anything could turn up. I was angry with her for what felt to me like giving in: not eating, sleeping too much, taking the pain out on me. Being used to her doing it didn't make it okay. In fact, I thought, and my hands shook a little as I straightened the pens in the inside compartment of my bag, it felt worse now, felt like I was doing *all* the trying and she wasn't doing any.

"So," Kathleen said, "what did you find?"

I wanted to snap at her for so obviously sounding like she was trying to care. *Come on, Kath, aren't you a better actress than that?* But I wasn't just angry at her. I was frightened too. I hadn't found anything that we didn't already know. And if there weren't any answers here, then I was the one to blame; my false hopes had dragged her all the way here, pushed her past her limits, brought her too close to the sea again. Even the promise of discovering some family connections had evaporated today: there was no one left, as far as I could tell. All these women had had one daughter and then died, and their husbands were either dead too or gone, out of reach of the local records. There weren't any cheerful cousins or aunts or uncles to present to Kathleen as consolation, just obituaries and the locations of graves.

I stood up and went to gather my toiletries for the shower.

"Nothing new," I said. "I found brief mentions of Deirdre's death and Moira's death in the local paper. I didn't find anything about Caolinn, but I don't know exact dates and it looks like even if there was a paper here in the 1940s, it may have stopped printing during the war. So that's a dead end."

"How are the deaths written up?" Kathleen asked.

"What do you mean?"

"I mean, are they written up as suicides? Are the survivors mentioned by name? Do they mention the weird thing with the knife in Deirdre's case? The one that Robin says they never found?"

"Sort of," I said. "At least, that's how I read the piece, knowing what Robin had told me. Moira's—your mother's—is written that she drowned and that you, your father, and her father survived her." I caught her eyes in the mirror, saw the next question coming. "Her father's dead, though. He apparently never remarried after Deirdre, his wife, died and he had a heart attack ten years ago."

Kathleen drew her knees up to her chest and rocked back and forth on the bed. "And Deirdre's death?"

"It's carefully worded. I mean, it was more than forty

years ago and in a small Catholic community, right? So the phrasing I think was 'perhaps, tragically, by her own hand.' And there's a mention of the police still investigating, which is where I read the uncertainty of the knife coming in, that maybe the coroner—if they even had a coroner here, I've no idea—brought that up."

"That must be it," Kathleen said. "I mean, if everyone in the village knew that was how she'd died and knew, when Robin and Moira were older, that the knife had vanished. The police must have gossiped about it."

I nodded. "I'm going to get a shower and we can eat, okay? I don't know about you but I'm starving. I can't even figure out what meal this is supposed to be."

I went into the tiny bathroom, balanced my various travel-size bottles on the soap dish in the shower, and turned the water on. Kathleen opened the door as I was undressing.

"What about Caolinn?"

"I told you," I said, anger winning out for a moment. "There wasn't a regular newspaper or record before then. There would be church records of births and deaths, I guess, but I couldn't figure out where to go for those. The woman at the records office said that she wasn't sure there'd even be anything beyond the headstone in the graveyard, that it might have just been left to the family to record the death if she was really from that tiny little village."

"So you couldn't even confirm that she was one of us, huh?" Kathleen asked. "That's too bad."

She stood holding the doorknob while I got into the shower and tucked the curtain so water wouldn't leak onto the floor.

"Did you check other death notices—is that the word?—or other reports of suicides in the same town?" she asked. "Wasn't that one possibility? That it was more widespread, somehow? This illness or predilection of mine?"

"You know," I said, safe on the other side of the curtain, "you could have come with me and done some of this research yourself."

She didn't answer and I finished showering, quickly, in silence. When I slid the curtain back, though, she was still standing there. She held out a towel.

"It's terrible water, isn't it?" she asked. "Smells funny. It's probably from the pipes, I know. But I could hardly stand it."

"It smells a little like iron or something," I said. "I don't smell it on *you*, though, if that's what you're worried about."

She shook her head. "I thought I would like it here more," she said.

"What? The inn?"

"No, silly." She made a face. "Ireland. I thought I would feel connected to it. But I just feel tired and everything hurts, and now you're mad at me because I'm not helping you and—" She broke off, caught herself on the sob and checked it. I waited, blotting my hair on the towel and resisting the impulse to say it was all right, or alternatively, that right now I was tired too and my head hurt and my feet hurt and I was so hungry that my stomach hurt.

"Can you just tell me, please?" Kathleen said. "Is there any kind of pattern to it? Outside my family, I mean?"

"No," I said. "There isn't. Not that I could see. There aren't that many people in the papers at all, not many people dying certainly, and the others died of old age or illness or were lost at sea."

"Lost at sea," she repeated. "Now there's a phrase." She backed out of the bathroom and shut the door.

O'CONNOR'S PUB WAS dimly lit, smoky, and smelled of fried food and cigarettes. We sat at a table in the back, near the corner where a band was setting up. The process seemed to involve a lot of beer. The waitress took our order without any expression on her face at all, except when Kathleen—trying to get a rise out of her—asked what kind of lettuce was in the salad.

"What kind, then?" she asked, her voice rising a little. "Well, I don't know. Regular lettuce is all it is. What kind were you expecting it to be?"

"Regular is fine," Kathleen said demurely.

"What are you up to now?" I asked when the waitress had gone. "What *did* you expect her to say?"

"I wanted to see how annoyed she'd get," Kathleen said. "She hates us, can't you tell?"

"No," I said. "Hates us? Why?"

"Tourists," she said. "It's like we're a necessary evil to her, to everyone here, probably. I mean, the band's local or at least Irish, and the staff of course, but I challenge you to pick out anyone else here who's not clearly a tourist."

The waitress brought us our water and Kathleen's salad—pretty much lettuce in a bowl, with some shaved carrot on top. I scanned the room. Most of the people here did look like they came from somewhere else. There was a preponderance of backpacks in frames up against the walls and the group of fifty-something women sitting together all wore sensible layers and expensive, sturdy walking shoes. The only immediate exception I saw was an elderly nun sitting at the next table with a burly black-haired man. The nun was tiny, white-haired, and wearing large glasses. She was smiling owlishly up at her companion, and I heard him chuckle in response to something she said. If she hadn't been a nun, I would have pegged the two of them as mother and son.

"Does a nun count?" I asked. Kathleen took a forkful of salad and chewed thoughtfully.

"She could still be a tourist," she said. "I mean, nuns get vacations, don't they? Maybe she's on a pilgrimage."

"To Doolin?"

"Well, it is the music capital of Ireland."

As if on cue, the band started to play. They were good, though Kathleen smirked across the table at me when they opened with The Proclaimers.

"See—tourist music!" she hissed. I shook my head at her and sat back to watch them. They played like they'd been together a while, loose and almost sloppy visually, with sly moments of eye contact that came during the musician-friendly sweet spots of the songs, not necessarily the crowd-pleaser moments. There were two guitarists and a jack-of-all-trades guy on keyboard who also had a harmonica and a tin whistle tucked into his shirt pocket. No drums—it was too small a space for drums and most of the music they were playing didn't need them anyway. One of the guitarists did most of the singing. He had a nasal tenor voice but good pitch and he wasn't indulgent, didn't try to hold notes too long or mess around with vibrato. He kept his phrasings nice and tight for the most part as they moved from "500 Miles" into "Oh, Danny Boy"—Kathleen rolled her eyes—and "The Fields of Athenry."

The waitress brought our fish and chips and Kathleen ordered a beer. I pretended not to notice. The food was greasy but good. I felt my headache receding a bit. I glanced over at Kathleen and saw that she had some color back in her face too. The band was an event here, clearly. We could have talked over them but no one else was. People were there to eat and listen. It wasn't a bad idea for us to be together and not have to talk for a while, to actually listen to music together.

Then the band began the plaintive notes of another song, just the keyboard in the opening bars and Kathleen tensed, then stood up. She was in front of the band before the measure was done, her back to me while all three musicians eyed her curiously. She said something to the singer that made him laugh and step back from his microphone with a grand gesture, guitar pick in his hand. Kathleen turned around behind the microphone and smiled at the audience, but only briefly, because the song was sad and it was about to start. I watched her, the way all the light in the room seemed to catch on her. She was wearing jeans and a white oxford shirt untucked, sleeves rolled up, her long red hair falling all over her shoulders and arms. *Showy*, I thought, but she couldn't help it. I remembered what Tom had told me about her singing lately, how much she seemed to need it. And now, in a moment, she'd gone from fragile to incandescent, the whole bar quiet, people who couldn't see or hear her clearly getting up from their seats to come around, leaning against the bar, murmuring to one another. The band members exchanged another glance behind her back, excited now, unique to artists who know what they've found.

And Kathleen sang:

The water is wide, I can't swim o'er,
And neither have I wings to fly
Build me a boat that can carry two
And both shall row, my love and I.

She sang about being afraid of drowning, willfully, in love if not in the sea, in a love as deep and abiding as the sea. It was a Scottish song I'd heard before, even heard her sing along with it in the car or in the kitchen. Kathleen knew an astonishing number of Celtic folk songs by heart. But hearing Kathleen sing anything full voice is different, and after the second line, when she began, *"Build me a boat,"* she sang to me, her voice splashing across the little distance in the room like a stream tumbling downhill, something joyful in its very nature even though the song was sad. She was wearing dark blue ballet slippers with sequins on them that sparkled when she moved her feet. She was bouncing on her tiptoes so I knew her feet were hurting but no one else would know, no one listening to her sing could possibly know. Her voice dipped low like a swimmer going into the trough of a wave, then came up again, somehow at once teasing and forlorn: *"When cockle shells make Christmas bells, then will I leave my love for thee."* Listening to her sing, I felt the sick surging knot in my belly ease even further. It was going to be okay. It would be okay. Even if we couldn't find out what was wrong exactly, so long as she had this to hang on to, Kathleen would be Kathleen.

She sang three more songs at the crowd's urging, people shouting out requests and Kathleen asking the band, with just a tilt of her eyebrow, if they knew the song in question before nodding and waiting for her cue. I was so focused on her that I didn't notice until the last song that someone was standing at our table, behind Kathleen's chair. It was the elderly nun I'd noticed earlier. She stood perfectly still, her hands clasped in front of her as if she was praying, her eyes fixed on Kathleen. When the set was over, Kathleen relinquished the mike and came back to the table. Behind her, the band members were applauding along with everyone else. The keyboardist even put his fingers in his mouth and whistled shrilly. Kathleen looked over her shoulder at him and laughed as she slid into her seat. The face she turned back toward me was visibly, wickedly delighted.

"Kath—" I began, nodding to the old woman, but before I could say more, the nun actually put out a blue-veined hand and touched Kathleen's hair.

"Deirdre," she said, and then almost immediately, "no. You can't be."

Kathleen twisted around in her chair.

"My grandmother's name was Deirdre," she said.

"Your grandmother," the nun whispered. "Your grandmother, not your mother but your *grandmother*. Am I really that old? She would have been your great-grandmother then."

"My great—" Kathleen swung back toward me and stretched out her hand. "Harry, did you hear that? My great-grandmother!"

I grabbed her hand. I was praying, to no deity in particular, that this woman not turn out to be delusional. *Please let her know something*, I thought. *Please*. But she was so frail. Above her stiff white collar her neck was crimped and colorless.

"Not Deirdre and not Deirdre's daughter either, but of

course not—her daughter didn't favor her. Her daughter had curly hair and freckles. What was her name?"

"Moira," Kathleen said. "My mother."

"Your mother, Deirdre's daughter. And Deirdre was your grandmother."

Kathleen strained toward her. The nun still had her hand on Kathleen's hair. "Did you know her?" Kathleen asked. "Did you know my grandmother?"

"Know her?" The little nun shook her head. "I didn't know her. I watched her grow up but I never spoke to her. I was afraid to."

"Afraid?" Kathleen's fingers tightened in mine. "Why?"

The nun glanced back over her shoulder at the man she'd left behind. He had turned in his seat and was leaning in, frankly observing us but not intervening. Perhaps, I thought—I hoped—that meant that this woman wasn't in need of a keeper, that she knew her own mind. Her gaze traveled next to our clasped hands, mine and Kath's, and her eyes widened. Her hand was still on Kathleen's hair. She seemed to realize it then. She stroked Kathleen's hair once and then drew her fingers back.

"You—what's your name, child?"

"Kathleen. Please—" Kathleen let go of my hand and gestured to the nun. "Would you like to sit down for a minute?"

But the nun had turned to me. "And you, young lady. What's your name?"

"My name is Harriet."

"You love her," she said. "You love her very much."

I had left my hand out on the table. I let it fall into my lap. I felt exposed.

"Yes," I said.

"Please . . ." Kathleen said again.

The nun nodded. "I loved her," she said. "We used to hold hands, but only when we were sure we were alone." She looked at Kathleen and then back at me and seemed to make a decision. She stood up straighter, shifted her shoulders. "I would like to sit down, thank you. I would like that very much. Michael"—she turned and spoke over her shoulder—"I'm going to speak to these young women for a few minutes. I have a story to tell them. I won't be long."

Kathleen had sprung up in that instant and slid over an extra chair. The nun took it. "He's my nephew," she said, "takes me to dinner once a week. He'll be perfectly happy to sit and eat his food without worrying about ordering another beer. I don't care one bit how much he drinks but"—she leaned in and lowered her voice to a whisper—"he's afraid of offending my sensibilities."

"Does your nephew know this story?" I asked.

The old woman smiled. She had a lovely smile. Her mouth tilted up more on one side than the other and her eyes stayed sad.

"No one knows this story, my dear," she said, "not even my confessor."

"About Deirdre?" Kathleen asked.

The nun shook her head. "No, no," she said. "I told you, I never knew Deirdre. I only watched her from afar. This is about her mother, Caolinn." Her smile slipped as she repeated the name. "Caolinn Linnane," she said, "my own true love."

WHEN YOU PERFORM an aria outside the context of its opera, you can choose to tamp down the character and the emotion in favor of sheer musicality. Singing one of Mimi's arias from *La Bohème* in a concert recital, for example, most sopranos choose not to interrupt themselves with the coughing fits that signal Mimi's soon-to-be fatal consumption. They save those for full performances, when they're being asked to *be* Mimi, not merely sing a piece of her. What distinguishes some great singers is their ability to infuse an aria with the entire weight of its surrounding story without resorting to things like coughing or reaching out to a lover who isn't onstage. They can make you hear Manon's faithlessness or Butterfly's naiveté, the coldness that underscores the duke's playfulness in "La Donna è Mobile."

Listening to this woman—her name, she told us, was Marie, Sister Marie of the Convent of Mercy—felt like listening to an aria sung, out of context, by a singer who knew that the whole story mattered. She sat at our table and talked and talked and I thought, *She doesn't know anything. She doesn't know that Deirdre killed herself. She doesn't know that Moira did.* And yet she did know—she knew more than she could tell us. She knew that there were things she didn't understand about her own story, things she'd never forgotten because they were important. Inexplicable to her at the time, even more so now, after all these years, but important.

She'd worn a lock of Caolinn's hair in a locket around her neck for twenty years after she'd gone into the convent. It was ruler straight, she told us, lacking the natural wave and tendency toward ringlets in the damp air that Kathleen's hair had. She'd had to tie string around it to keep it coiled tight enough to hide in the locket. And then one day she'd been on a ferry and the wind had caught the chain and torn it right off her neck. She put her hand to her throat as if she could still feel it there, the slight drag of it at her nape, the sliding of the locket itself against her chest under her clothes.

What did she tell us that we didn't already know? She told us how two girls could fall in love, even in Ireland in the 1940s, long after they should have been married and having babies. How they would walk together on the beach for hours, the one barefoot even in the coldest surf, and talk of running off together, to Shannon, to Dublin, to America. She told us that Caolinn used to sing in the pub in Doolin, sing with her bright red hair tucked behind her ears and her arms and shoulders dusted with gold freckles against the sleeves of her thin summer dresses. She told us that she used to sit in the back—just where we were sitting now, in fact—and watch her lover sing like a greedy child watching sugar spun into candy at a fair. She sat watching and longing and thinking *mine, all mine* while around her men sat thinking the same thing. Until one night one of them made it so, made Caolinn his at least in one way. Caolinn would never say who. Perhaps she didn't know. But then there was a child, or was going to be a child, and somehow this was tangled up in the minds of the village with Caolinn and Marie holding hands on the beach, both of them bareheaded and bare-legged when they shouldn't have been.

She told us Caolinn had loved the sea, had drunk seawater sometimes, scooped it up in icy handfuls and let it run down her legs. She said that even when they talked of running away together, Caolinn was reluctant, that she would tell Marie to leave on her own, to never see her again. "I'm not fit for love," she'd whisper, her face pressed against

Marie's hair as they embraced, furtively, desperately, in empty fishing shacks, behind shocks of tall grass by the sea. "I'm not for you, Marie. I'm not for anyone. At least it will end with me, is all. There's that." And when Marie asked her to explain, she shook her head.

But then there was going to be a child and the light left Caolinn's face, left it, Marie said, like the color drains from the sea just before a storm comes in. Once, going to meet Caolinn in a long-abandoned hut, she found her lover on her hands and knees on the floor, hiding something under the rotting boards. She lingered after Caolinn had left— she confessed this later, her sin of mistrust, she confessed this when she did not confess anything else—and found a knife under the floor, smooth and slippery and half-buried in the sand. She was frightened. She left it where it was. Later, she thought she ought to have thrown it into the sea.

Robin had found a knife too. It was like an aria that plays on a melodic through line, so that, listening, you feel sure you've heard it before: in the overture, in Act 1. Robin had found a knife. Had Deirdre's husband? The same knife? It couldn't be the same knife. And neither Caolinn nor Moira had used it, anyway, to kill themselves. Yet Sister Marie's fingers twitched as she described the knife, recalled herself reaching out for it and shaking the sand from it. She told us the pieces of the story that mattered, the important pieces, the ones she'd held on to all these years.

Caolinn was sent away to have her baby and Marie's father told her it was a convent or marriage. She was sitting outside of the chapel with her face to the sun when an older nun leaned over her and whispered, her breath hot and meaty on Marie's cheek, "Your sins are washed away now, child, and best you say a prayer of Thanksgiving to Our Lady for saving you from damnation. She's gone, that one. Gone down and good riddance to her." Marie knew then that Caolinn had died. She felt hot and cold at once, dizzy and feverish. She did pray. She prayed, *Dear Lord, please let it not be the knife*, because then it would be her fault. If she'd thrown it away . . . But it was not with a knife that Caolinn had killed herself. She'd drowned, was all Marie ever knew, taken a rotten boat out to sea and drifted until the water came in and the boat went down.

"I DIDN'T CRY," Marie whispered. Her voice was fading from talking so much. She took a sip of the glass of water I pushed in front of her. "I didn't cry then. I was afraid to, because I was still a novitiate and the other nuns were watching me. I couldn't let them see me cry for her. Some of them knew about us and didn't care, even sympathized I think. But others who knew, like the one who told me—" She hunched into herself and put her hand again to her throat.

"I didn't cry for her until I lost her hair," she said, "because it seemed like God was really taking her from me then. The chain was under my habit where I always wore it, and the wind, when it came, it ripped it right out and off before I could grab for it. And when it went into the sea, I imagined that the waves were reaching for the last of her, the only bit they hadn't already taken." Her mouth trembled briefly. She looked at us both. I don't know what she saw in our faces. "I hated God for that loss as much as for the loss of her," she said. "Why couldn't he have left me that much?"

I opened my mouth to say something, I had no idea what. But Kathleen spoke first.

"Where were you?" she asked.

"Where was I?" Marie repeated, clearly puzzled.

"When the wind took the locket of Caolinn's hair. You said you were on a ferry. Where were you going?"

"I was going to her grave," Marie said. "For a long time I couldn't even ask where it was. I couldn't ask anyone about her. When so many years had passed that I thought it wouldn't matter anymore, I asked. She was buried on Inis Mór." When we both stared blankly, Marie smiled, briefly shifting from tragic storyteller to contemptuous native. "Inis Mór," she repeated. "The Aran Islands off the coast, where her mother's people came from."

"Did you know Caolinn's mother?" I asked. "When you were younger?"

Marie frowned. "No," she said. "No, her mother was gone. Caolinn's father had brought her over to the mainland when she was just a baby."

"Her mother was gone?" Kathleen asked.

I didn't want to look at her. I made myself do it, certain that she would flick me one of her lightning glances that conveyed both a flash of bitter humor and an "I told you so." But she was focused entirely on the little nun. Her face, in profile, was pale and calm, but the pulse in her neck was beating visibly. So it wasn't "I told you so" at all, I realized. Kathleen wanted it not to be true as much as I did.

But of course it was true.

"Drowned," Marie said. She reached for her water glass again, her hand shaking. "I don't remember. But I think— drowned. When Caolinn was a baby." She sipped again, spilling some water onto the table. "It's been so very long, my dear, I'm sorry. I don't—I don't remember."

"It's all right," Kathleen said. "Thank you for telling us the story. I didn't know anything about my family and that's what we came here to find. So thank you."

Marie regarded Kathleen over the rim of her glass and her eyes welled over.

"You look so like her," she said. "So like them all. I'd have known you were theirs if I'd seen you anywhere in the world."

"Thank you," Kathleen said again, gravely. The nephew, who had sat patiently through the entire recital, only looking curiously over at our table occasionally while he ate his meal and nursed a second beer, now wiped his mouth and rose. Kathleen leaned toward the old woman. "Can I tell you something before you go, Marie? I don't know if you'll believe me—I don't know why you should believe me—but it's true. I know it's true."

Marie nodded.

"God didn't take your necklace from you," Kathleen said. "It was the sea. That's all it was. Like you said, the sea wanted all of her and she wanted to belong to the sea."

Christ, Kath, I thought, *don't scare the poor thing. She doesn't know*. But of course she did. She'd loved Caolinn, who had always wanted to walk barefoot in the surf and who had hidden a knife in the sand but then drowned herself. Marie wasn't the one Kathleen was scaring. Marie pressed Kathleen's hand as she rose and allowed her nephew to help her out of the bar. And Kathleen watched them go while I sat beside her with my hands clenched in my lap and my stomach hurting. I was the one who was scared. *The sea wanted all of her and she wanted to belong to the sea*. Was that it? Was that what we'd come to Ireland to learn?

nd what of the others who loved the Little Mermaid, the ones of whom the familiar tale has so little to say? She left behind the grandmother who had raised her, the father who had been her king, and seven older sisters, as powerless as spectators at a play. For many months they watched their sister walk with her two-legged lover on the beach at sunset. They saw how lightly she moved, how little she leaned upon him even when he drew her close, how stealthily she edged toward the water so that the sea could ease the pain in her feet.

"We did not know," they said to one another, "that she could be so brave. I could not. Could you?"

"Not I."

"And you, sister?"

"Not I, not for a man."

But for her, they began to tell themselves, to tell one another, for her perhaps they could be so brave.

They waited until it was almost too late to come to us. We felt the supple parting of the water at our gates as it moved over the seven tails that hovered there, hesitating, then swimming away. Three times they came to us and turned away, never passing under even the high curving whale bones that mark the entrance to our gardens. Finally they entered, seven in a long, lovely line, their faces set and pale, shining with the force of their fear and their hope, like the little fish that live in perpetual darkness and so must make their own light.

"What will happen to her when he weds another?" they asked, and we answered them as we had answered her.

"Nothing. She will stay as she is, fish out of water, with her pain and her silence and her broken heart."

"And her children, should she have children?"

It was the youngest who asked this, the youngest of all but for the Little Mermaid up Above. Her sisters turned their faces away, but she put out her chin and asked the question again.

"She goes to his bed every night," she said, "every day. She may already be with child."

"She is not."

"But even afterward, if he leaves her and she finds another lover or if she is taken . . ."

"Then her child enters the world Above, breathing air, walking on two legs, whole and healthy or not, as chance may have it."

"And the child will not suffer?" the princess asked. "Not as our sister does?"

A sidelong glance, a shifting, a flick of the fingers from one of us, though we spoke not at all, and the princess cried, "How could you cast a spell like this and not tell her? That it might go on and on, that any child she bears—up there—will suffer this agony, that she will have no choice herself but to die to end her pain!"

"What she did not wish to know, we did not tell her."

The princess cursed us, weeping, her tears turning to black pearls as they slid off her cheeks. They landed *softly in the sands of the chamber and we gathered them later: tears of rage, of hatred, powerful poisons when dissolved in fresh water.*

Then the sisters closed in around the youngest among them, touched their tails to hers, forgave her the horror of the questions she had asked.

"Our littlest sister," they said. "Save her. We will give you anything you ask."

And really, it was not so much. She gave up her living tongue to grasp at love, for such is the price. To craft the means to kill a man, we needed only the hair of the seven royal princesses, though it is true that we sheared their long locks right to their scalps and that the eldest flinched under the blade so that a cloudy puff of blood rose from her head.

They were no longer lovely when it was done. They gazed from one to the other and not one of them lifted a hand to touch her head. We left them rediscovering themselves in one another's stricken gazes, eyes wide, exposed, as they learned the lengths of their necks, the shapes of their ears, the juts of their jaws.

We made the blade, heated it until it glowed blue, then white, cooled it until it hid its fire. We sharpened it on a braid woven of her sisters' hair, a bond so strong now that the knife-edge sparked against it. We bloodied it once, on the severed tongue of the one who was intended to wield it, and we brought it out to the princesses, her sisters, in a pearl case. For love of her they bore it to the surface of the sea, brushed off her cries of dismay at the sight of their poor bare heads, pressed the blade into her hands.

In the story told Above the words are repeated just as they were spoken.

"Plunge the blade into the heart of the prince," they told her. "When the warm blood falls upon your feet they will grow together again and you will once more be a mermaid."

And when she hesitated, from wonder or hope, disbelief or rejection, they crowded in around her, stroking her slender white legs with their wet hands. Nor could she find words to tell them that their fingers felt cold and alien against her skin, even as she sighed with pleasure at the water's caress.

"Come back to us," said the youngest of her sisters. "Oh, little love, come back."

KATHLEEN

Aria for Soprano

Come home, come home, they said, the fucking women in the water, the ones who ruined our vacation and made me think I was crazier than I already knew I was, who got in my head and wouldn't get out and who made me lie to Harry.

When I saw that picture of the Cliffs of Moher, I knew what they meant but I couldn't say anything then. How many Dramamine had I taken? I can't remember. Harry probably knows. But it doesn't matter, because while I was busy being crazy, seasick and crazy, Harry and Robin came up with Ireland all on their own.

I know that Ireland is what they meant, where they wanted me to come. I know I've *come home*. It should feel like home. Instead it's just a place, alien as any other place I've ever been.

I sit at breakfast with Harry and two other women, a mother and daughter doing a walking tour of western Ireland, and push some food around on my plate so Harry will think I'm eating the chunks of rubbery melon, pieces of a grainy Irish sausage. I slice my toast into tinier and tinier triangles on my plate. The girl across from me is watching me like I'm nuts. I put the knife down, balance it on the edge of my plate. My head is pounding, my mouth hurts. When I pick up my water glass, my hand doesn't shake, but only because I am good at hiding it. I think of Marie, the nun. She was so old and still so sad, the story of her lost love like the melodic line of her whole life, even though she's lived now nearly seventy years without her lover, three times as long as Caolinn lived at all. I'd never thought about that before we came here, about the ones left behind. Robin has Tae but I wonder now if Moira haunts their relationship the way she haunts this place for him. And before Robin, there was my grandfather, Deirdre's husband, who never remarried; before him, Marie; before Marie, Caolinn's father, who brought his daughter to the mainland. I bet he never remarried either. There are as many left behind as there are lost at sea. Harry, sitting beside me, is quiet. Last night we both slept badly, not touching, in the unfamiliar bed. Now I want to touch her. I put my fingertips on the back of her hand as she forks up a piece of fruit.

"You can't have a lock of my hair," I tell her. "If I don't give you one you won't have one to lose."

Everyone at the table stares at me.

AFTER BREAKFAST, WE go to Inis Mór. I know that it is a mistake, but Harry needs to do something, and what else is left to do? She shows me pamphlets at breakfast, in full cruise-director mode, suggests that we join one of the bus tours that drive people around the island, browse the sweater shops and cafés in the villages, maybe even walk up to the ancient fortress perched high on a cliff. She does not mention checking records or hunting down family histories, but I know that's what she wants to do. There's a visitor's center on Inis Mór and I'm sure we'll end up there, Harry smiling at whoever is working at the desk and explaining that we're just doing genealogical research and could they help us with some names and dates. She hasn't given up, still thinks there must be some *answer* that we've come all this way to find.

The weather is awful: cold, steady rain that blows suddenly sideways with the gusting of the wind. We walk to the pier after breakfast with our heads down. The woman in the ferry ticket office is giving out rain ponchos to people who don't have them. Boarding the boat, it's all I can do to navigate the slippery metal steps. I can hear the sea, and I want to stay on deck to watch it, but we all get herded into the cabin, which is horrible. It's luxurious for what it is, I suppose, with high-backed cushioned seats and plenty of space between the rows. But the windows are so small that only someone sitting down right beside them would be able to see out. The cabin is filling up with people, including the contents of two tour buses: some German high school students and a group of older Americans who are complaining loudly about the weather. I am blocking the aisle. A woman touches my elbow, indicates the empty seats beside me. She smiles, polite, patient, and I bolt for the open door.

The wind and the sudden surge of the motor as we cast off throw me up against the deck railing, which is slick with rain and sea spray. I grip it and hang on to keep from being swept overboard, or from diving in. It would be simple enough: put one foot up onto the lower rung, then the other up onto the top one, and plunge into the sea.

It is the most beautiful water I've ever seen, a dark, dark green, not black as it appears from far away. It has a dull gleam like rough-cut quartz, across which the ferry is churning up foam that is such a pale green it's nearly white. It seethes beneath us, around us, before it rejoins the rest of the sea a few feet out, the paler color submerging itself eagerly in the darker depths.

Harry has come out with me. She stands under the shelter of the upper deck, her hands tucked in her pockets, her hood cinched tight around her face. One curl has escaped and keeps slapping against her cheek, resisting her efforts to tuck it back.

"Go inside, silly," I shout over the noise of the motor. "There's no sense in you getting soaked just because I want to be out here."

"I suspect we'll both be soaked before the day is over," she says. "We may have to break down and buy sweaters. Makes me think this weather is just a tourist trap."

I try to laugh and then turn away, partly because I can't fake it convincingly, partly because my hair is in my mouth, plastered to my cheeks, wrapped around my neck like a choker.

I can taste the sea from the spray, thick and salty and cold, and I can hear the surging, liquid slamming of the waves against the sides of the boat. I grip the wet railing tighter, so tight it hurts my hands. Two quick steps up, it wouldn't matter if I tripped, fell sideways, didn't make a clean dive. I'd be in the ice-green foam and then away, beneath the waves and the wind and the grinding sound of the boat's motor, and I could dive again and swim down, down toward home.

I pull all my hair back from my face with one hand, tuck it down into my jacket. Water runs into the waist of my jeans, seeps through my shirt where my hair is lying against it. Harry comes up beside me, puts her hand over mine on the railing. I want to shake it off, but I don't. This is not her fault.

Is this how Moira felt, then? And Deirdre and Caolinn? Like they would die without the touch of this water? It washes over my feet, soaks right through my boots and heavy socks, and it does not say a word to me. This is enough of a relief that it takes me a moment to realize that for a few minutes after each fresh wave my feet don't hurt at all. Not at all. At first it just feels strange; it takes me a while to even identify the sensation as the cessation of pain. I put out my tongue to lick my lips and the water is like a balm.

But my mouth, my tongue, wasn't hurting this morning, hasn't been bothering me since I got out of the hospital. And now, as soon as the seawater is gone, my tongue burns in my mouth, the pain as bad as it's ever been. My feet throb too, worse and worse in between each new wash of water. It is hard to stand up; they haven't hurt so much in years, not since I was a teenager. The water comes again—ah, God, that's better—and recedes again, and the pain is like knives through my skin, right up into the bone.

I sit down, fall down, on the deck, catch myself a bit on the railings. Harry bends over me, murmuring something that I can't make out. A great wash of water breaks over me and I am wet from head to toe, soaked with this sea—

As you were meant to be. You drink it in the way they drink in air Above. When you return to yourself you will breathe too, just as they breathe their air.

And there they are after all, the voices again, close as if they were speaking in my ear, their words clear even as the wind tosses Harry's away. Telling me that I have nothing to be worried about, that I won't drown after all—

You will. You must listen carefully, Kathleen. You will drown. You must use the blade first or you will sink into these depths as another corpse and we cannot help you.

I don't understand. I swallow and the taste of the sea begins to leave my mouth, the pain like a slow-moving blade seeping in to replace it. The women murmur of death and drowning and breathing water like air, and I think that perhaps what they mean—what I mean—is that I can't fight this, this water or this pain.

The pain is the pain, that's all. So we told her, so we told them all. You were not meant to live like this. You must come to us soon. He will tell you how.

Another wave, delicious feel of the icy water on my skin, running through my hair. I clamp my mouth shut against the urge to open it and drink more water. The pain is growing, bad enough that I can barely concentrate, barely listen. I cannot *be* these voices then, they cannot be me, even though they are in my head.

Must come to them? Come to who? Who will show me? Show me what?

There's a hand on my back too heavy to be Harry's, and an Irish voice asking if I'm ill. It's probably one of the crew members on the ferry, though I don't lift my head to be sure.

"You'll be all right with a bit of ground beneath your

feet, then," he shouts, and briefly, his hand moves to the top of my head, caresses my wet hair. "We're almost there now, just a few more minutes."

Seasick. He thinks I'm seasick. If I could laugh—I shake with it anyway, with something that's longing and laughter and incredulity all together. Because he's wrong, of course, but also right, more right than I knew back in the airport in Florida. A whole packet of Dramamine wouldn't ease this, because I am finally, literally, sick *for* the sea—my throat clenches against the pain in my mouth because I've been refusing to open it, refusing to let the water in again. If I don't taste it again soon I *will* throw up.

I lift my head, open my mouth on a gasp, swallow a gulp of water flung up over the side of the boat. The pain vanishes. There is a gap here, between the deck and the first rung of the deck railing, wide enough for me to fit. I grope blindly for Harry, not lifting my head from my knees, and find her hand. I grip it so tightly that I can feel the small bones moving at the base of her fingers. I am hurting her, I know I must be hurting her, but it's either that or drown. I don't know if she knows this or not, but she doesn't make a sound, at least not one I can hear above the waves and the motor, and she doesn't let go.

WHEN WE DOCK, Harry and the crewman pick me up, help me off the ferry past murmurs of sympathy for me, poor seasick girl. The sodden red curtains of my hair hide my face, drip water on the ground as I walk between the supporting arms. I am dimly aware of being embarrassed, glad to hide behind Harry and behind my hair. But only a few yards onto dry land I am starting to shake with pain as the sea leaves me, and it is hard to think of anything beyond that.

A round-cobbled street, the smooth stones mocking my feet because they hurt to walk on as much as if they were made of shards of glass. Then a step up and a straight-backed chair, just inside the door of a craft shop.

"Thank you," Harry says to the ferryman. "Thank you for your help."

"Are you making the trip back today, then?" he asks.

"Yes, I think so."

"Well, get some solid food into her stomach before then. Just some brown bread, maybe a bit of soup. Nanny O'Meara's makes a lovely bowl. And we'll see to her, get her back all right."

"Thank you," Harry says again. Then she is crouching in front of me, rubbing my hands.

"Are you all right?"

I shake my head.

"Stop—" My voice feels like sharp pebbles in my mouth, the sound just as broken and uneven. "Stop rubbing my hands, please."

She does. My skin feels like it might split open and bleed as soon as the water dries on my clothes. I make Harry buy me new socks and a heavy sweater, and she helps me first into the public restroom, then into the new, dry clothes.

"Kath, this wool"—she holds out the sweater to me— "won't it bother you? It's awfully rough."

Yes, and usually I'd flinch away from it. But it works the way it needs to now. It itches, chafes my skin like sand-paper, but I am used to that. And after she has tugged the socks onto my clenched feet, my feet still hurt, but in the way my feet always hurt. It's bearable, maybe even more bearable than usual because it's dwindling. Now I know how much worse it can be. I try not to think about how much better it could be.

She is kneeling in front of me again, her hands still clasped warm around my foot.

"Better?" she asks.

Of course I cannot explain my shuddering sigh of relief. I just nod. We are a set piece, she and I, the hysterical soprano and her faithful friend in the mezzo role. For God's sake—

"Harry, get up," I snap, and her face tightens, that expression again like I've just hit her.

I try to fix it. "I just— I don't want you kneeling in front of me, for God's sake, on this dirty floor. You're not my servant."

"I never thought I was." She stands up, puts her hands into her pockets. I keep my head down. The silence between us stretches out long enough that two women enter the bathroom and leave again.

Harry sighs. "Are you going to tell me what's going on?"

No. "Let's just go back to the shops, okay?" I lean over to put my shoes on, gritting my teeth as water from my wet sneakers soaks through my socks. "Maybe we can find that restaurant the man from the ferry was telling us about."

"It's in the next village," Harry says. "You have to get on one of the tour buses to get there."

"Well"—I can talk like a cruise director too—"that's what we were planning to do anyway, right? So let's do that then, before all the good buses are taken by the tour groups."

I stand up and turn to leave the bathroom and Harry, *Harry* of all people, grabs my arm and yanks me back. "Damn you, Kath! Don't you shut me out, don't you dare shut me out now."

She is so angry, finally angry at me, and really, who can blame her? I don't. She has her hand locked around my wrist, the hand that kept me out of the water back there on the boat.

She thinks I'm not going to respond; she jostles my arm a bit. "Kathleen!"

What can I say? What can I tell her? She is here, she hasn't shied away once, and she is saving my life. I know that. She deserves to be treated like my lover, not my nurse. But if I tell her—what? That the Irish water really does make me think of drowning myself? That when it touched me I felt completely pain-free, but when it left me the pain made me want to scream? That I heard voices in the water, voices I've heard before?

If I tell her all of this, she will be so frightened. And she will be right to be.

I keep my eyes on her hand on my arm while I lie to her a little more.

"I'm sorry," I say—better to start with something true. "I don't know how to explain it. I just hadn't even been near water since we were in Florida, and the water here is so different."

I have my story now, and I'm sticking to it. I can even embellish, watch me.

"It's as if we're in another world now, you know? With this awful black water and the rain and the terrible food and—I just keep thinking about Sanibel and how far we've gone from there, from everything that was there, including how happy we were . . ."

I take a stumbling step forward to hold her tight against me. I press my face into her neck, kiss her wet skin, then turn my head and find her mouth with mine. She moves her hands to my hair and holds my head, kissing me back so desperately that I know that she knows I'm lying to her.

The door opens again and we pull apart as a group of teenage girls tumbles in, their hair plastered on their cheeks, eye makeup running. They are laughing, jostling, teasing one another in German. There is not room in here for all of us.

"It's okay," I say quickly. "We were just leaving."

INIS MÓR IS the largest of the three Aran Islands. The children are taught only Irish in school, no English until high school, and there's a year-round population of nine hundred people. So we're told by the charming Sean, who bullies us genially into his tour bus as soon as we step outside the bathroom. For only ten euros per person he'll drive us all the way around the island, let us off for an hour or so for lunch, show us the medieval graveyards and the ruined churches and the thatched cottages that people still live in. There are eight of us on the bus, just a van really, all of us very wet and getting wetter sitting so close together with our windbreakers on.

Harry has the middle seat on a row of three. I sit beside her, reach out after a minute and hold her hand. It is much warmer than mine, and feels drier, though I don't know how that could be true.

"Ugh," the woman on Harry's other side says, "I'm wet through and we've only just gotten here. I don't know how these people stand it." She raises her voice to address Sean in the driver's seat in front of her.

"Do the Irish get depressed from the weather sometimes, from all this rain?"

"Depressed, is it?" Sean steers us sharply to the left to let a slatted truck full of sheep go by. "No. No, we don't get depressed by the rain. Bit moldy, maybe, around the edges, but not depressed." He darts a glance over his shoulder and winks at me. I realize too late that he is flirting with me in the harmless way that old and oldish men have always flirted with me. I try to smile at him, but he has already turned back to the road.

"Now then," he says. "We'll be coming up into Kilmurvey in a few minutes now, where you can get a bit of lunch, walk up to the ruins if you've a mind to."

Harry leans forward. "Isn't there a visitor's center there?" she asks.

Sean shakes his head. "There is," he says, "but it's closed this week and next. They're installing an 'interactive exhibit hall' is what they're calling it, with computer touch screens and videos and the like."

"Oh." Harry sits back. Even I—queen of the self-centered—can't help but notice how pale and bedraggled she is, only buoyed up by her need to take care of me and her certainty that there was going to be something to find on Inis Mór, or maybe even just something to try. She bites her lip and turns to the window. So now it's officially been a wasted trip—worse than wasted, since we've discovered that the suicides probably go back further even than Robin thought they did.

And though I know why, I can't tell anyone because it's not an explanation, not the kind Harry was hoping for, not the kind Robin sent us here for. Not the kind that's going to get the doctors back in Boston to change their minds: *Oh, so it's the sea in Ireland that's the problem? It actually calls to you—called to all these women, you say—and makes you want to drown yourself in it? Let's try that electroshock therapy we recommended, shall we? That and staying away from Ireland. We recommend that too.*

"Ah," Sean says from the front, "here's a true Irish sight for you . . . Do you see?"

He brakes gently as he steers off onto the grass alongside the road and gestures up yet another steep, rocky hill to a house just being built, all shining sheets of glass and long white beams, in stark contrast to the closely piled rocks of the fences around it. There are horses grazing in the pasture in front of the house, several brown ones and one white, off to himself. He swings his head in our direction as Sean points him out.

"There's a good bit of new construction going on here," Sean says. "But this house always brings to my mind the old Irish proverb"—he swings around in his seat—"maybe you know it then? About the three unluckiest things in the world?"

No one does. From the corner of my eye I can see Harry shaking her head.

"Well then, you'll see what I mean here." Sean gestures to the house once more. "The three unluckiest things in the world are a house on a hill, a *bàn capall*—a white horse, that is—and a good-looking woman. So I'm thinking that here we sit in clear view of all three things at once—I'm hoping none of you is superstitious then."

His eyes have flicked to me again just long enough to include me in his proverb, compliment and curse all in the same breath.

"Well now," says a man from the backseat of the van, "I don't know that we all need to be worried for ourselves, do we? Who are these things unlucky for is what I'd want to know—for those who have them or for the things themselves?"

"Ah!" Sean grins back at the man. "You'd have to ask them yourself, wouldn't you?"

"Well, that poor horse certainly seems unlucky," says the woman beside us, "out in that rain every day."

"There you go then," says Sean. He turns back to the wheel and maneuvers the van onto the road.

Unlucky. There's one word for it. I choke back a laugh as I think about telling Harry that this is the answer we've come all this way to find: that I'm just one of the three unluckiest things in the world, according to an old Irish proverb, and so were all the other women in my family. Can we go home now?

I glance over my shoulder to see the man who spoke earlier. He is staring at me, was clearly staring at me already before I turned my head. He's redheaded and lean in jeans and a sleek brown pony-skin jacket. The dense hairs on his coat are beaded with rain, making him gleam faintly in the gray light inside the van, but there is nothing striking about the man himself except for his eyes. They are too big for his face, the way children's eyes sometimes are. They are thickly lashed and a very deep brown without any visible whites at all, more like an animal's eyes than a man's. I turn away.

Kilmurvey is a group of houses and a slate courtyard surrounded by shops. I drink more tea and crumble a piece of brown bread in my fingers while Harry eats.

"The soup is really good, Kath," she says. "Have a spoonful."

I shake my head. Harry frowns as she puts her spoon in her mouth and for a minute I'm afraid she's going to argue with me again about how much weight I need to gain back and how hard that is to do when you don't eat anything, dammit.

But her eyes shift to something over my shoulder.

"That man is staring at you," she says.

"The guy from the bus?"

"Yes. Sort of a smallish guy with red hair."

I glance back and try to smile at him, a nice neutral, non-inviting smile. My face doesn't feel like it's shaped itself into a smile properly, but after a moment he smiles back, only one side of his mouth lifting, and his eyes flicker over my head and then back to me. It's the signal you give someone when you are trying to tell them something private or potentially embarrassing without attracting attention. I automatically look in the direction he has indicated, but all I see is the mural on the café wall at my back. It's clearly labeled as the work of the high school art class here on the island. I twist in my seat to see it more clearly.

"What are you doing?" Harry asks.

"Checking out the mural. I didn't notice it before."

Harry turns around to see. "Nice mermaid," she says. "Especially those breasts. I'm betting the boys in the art class were fighting over who got to paint those."

It is an awful mermaid, blond and perky as a cheerleader

who just happens to have forgotten to put on a shirt or a bra. Clearly she got distracted braiding all those seashells and flowers and—yes, even a seahorse—into her hair. And her tail is ridiculous, too small for the rest of her body, curving up like a smile, green with little sparkles in it. Ugh.

NEXT SEAN TAKES us to a graveyard so old the slabs are crumbling, inscriptions obliterated by wind and lichen. Other slabs are new and smooth, the words that have been carved into them still chalk-white against the gray stone.

We read about Patrick Hernon and Nora Kelly and Seamus Durrane who was only nine years old when he died. Harry draws in her breath sharply at that one.

It is raining again, but it's as if we are all just resigned to being wet now. All around us people from our van are climbing over the slick wet stones, bending to take pictures of the inscriptions. Several people have made their way over to the ruins of the old church and one man has gone up the road a ways to take a picture that will capture the whole scene all at once. No one has even bothered to put their hood up against the rain. It runs through my hair and down my face, cool and soothing as water always is to me, but not what it could be. Not like a drug. Through a hole in the stone wall of the church, where a window might once have been—though maybe it was only ever a hole and never a stained-glass window as I imagine—I can see the sea.

"This is unbelievably morbid," I say, "not to mention depressing. I'm going back to the van to wait until everyone's ready to leave."

I don't wait for Harry. I wade through unmown grass and clamber over a sloping flat slab on my way out of the cemetery. Close to the gate the dark-eyed man stands with his hands in his pockets in front of an upright granite marker.

"Come see this one," he says, no inflection in his voice.

I do, almost without meaning to, but then the name on the bottom registers and I read the whole thing.

> PRAY FOR THE SOUL OF MUIRIN BRUICH
> DIED AGED 22.
> ERECTED BY HER HUSBAND, EAMON.
> PRAY FOR THE SOUL OF CEARA LINNANE,
> HER DAUGHTER, DIED AGED 24.
> PRAY FOR THE SOUL OF CAOLINN LINNANE,
> HER DAUGHTER, DIED AGED 23.

"You see, what they did was, the first one to die in a family, they'd raise a marker here, like this one," the man says. "Then when the others died they'd simply add their names as they could, so long as there was room on the stone and family left on the island to remember. That's why they didn't bother with dates, to save space for names." He takes one hand from his pocket and gestures at the stone. "Caolinn didn't even live here by the time she died, but her grandfather was still alive and he had her name put on."

He looks over at me, pinning me with those deep soft eyes.

"Her daughter, Deirdre, is buried over on the mainland, I'm thinking," he says. "And Moira too."

He turns his head sharply then, as if he's heard a sudden noise. Harry has come up to stand beside me. The man nods at her and walks away.

"What was that about?" Harry asks.

"This."

She reads the marker.

"He stopped me to show it to me."

"He was probably just in the pub the other night," Harry says, though she has stiffened and glanced around for him, angry and suspicious now. "He probably saw the names and made the connection."

No, he knew already. But I don't care about that right now.

"Harry, do you notice how old they are—were? All of them. Twenty-two, twenty-three years old, all of them, and Deirdre and Moira too." I can feel the shifting of panic inside my stomach. I'm older than most of them were when they died. When they killed themselves, which, of course, they did. All of them. Five of them before me, and maybe more before them.

Harry is still staring at the stone. Her face is set, as though she is trying to push the ages, the repetition, away with the force of her will.

"They didn't all kill themselves," she says. "They couldn't have. They wouldn't have been buried here if they had, not in a Catholic cemetery, not, what, a hundred years ago? You couldn't be buried in a Catholic cemetery if you killed yourself."

I let her lead me back to the tour bus, to Sean leaning against the open door and ushering us all in with a sweep of his hand.

"Back there in the cemetery," Harry says to him, not yet ducking her head to climb in, "we noticed the gravestones and I was wondering about them. This island has always been Catholic, hasn't it?"

"What do you mean, lass?"

"A lot of the people died so young . . ."

"That they did." Sean looks like he feels sorry for her. I bet he's used to this, to the American tourists exclaiming over all the babies and children in that graveyard. "There were a lot of illnesses that took the little ones first, especially in the wet and cold, and before we had the health clinic here or an air strip, just a doctor as likely to be short of supplies from the mainland as anyone else."

"Yes, I know," Harry says, "I know that. But what about suicide?"

"What?"

"Well, they wouldn't have buried someone in a church graveyard who had committed suicide. They would have buried those people somewhere else, wouldn't they?"

Sean has bright blue eyes, vivid against his white hair and wind-reddened cheeks. He has been using his eyes to charm us all, but now he doesn't meet Harry's gaze.

"Well now," he says. "We know a good deal here of *déine an tsaoil*, of how hard the world can be. It's a different life, don't you know, different from being back on the mainland. In the winter sometimes, especially years back, we'd not see a single soul from the mainland for a month or more. Lost three of our teachers at sea just last year, all of them on a boat coming back from their Christmas vacations they were, from seeing their families for a bit. My own brother was lost at sea, don't you know, just a few years back."

His voice rises at the end of his sentences, just an inflection, a trick of his accent, I know, but all the same it sounds like he's asking for something. Understanding maybe. Still, he hasn't answered the question.

"But the Church . . ." Harry says.

Sean adjusts his cap. "It's a hard life here," he says again. "It's easier now, but there were times it were a hard, bleak life, and harder even for some who lost a child of fever or a man to the sea. I don't know that we've ever had a priest here who didn't know that, who didn't see how it was here, how it could be."

He turns back to Harry then, offers her his winningest smile.

"Come on then, *a amadáin*," he says, "and watch your head. We'll be needing to get you all back to the pier before the ferry comes, now won't we?"

She climbs into the van and I follow her, while Sean goes around the front to get back into the driver's seat. The man in the leather jacket leans forward and touches Harry on the shoulder.

"You might be wanting to know what he called you just now," he says softly. "Though I don't think he meant any meanness by it. *A amadáin*, wasn't it?"

Harry doesn't acknowledge him.

"He called you a fool," the man says. "Just so you know."

We take a road along the coast back to the pier where we'll pick up the ferry. Sean points out the beach, which is lovely, an almost perfect semicircle scooped out of the cliffs and sprinkled with white sand. Then farther down, at another spot where the land seems to go down gracefully to meet the sea rather than plunging into it, he stops and gestures at a cluster of black blobs a few hundred yards out.

"There's our seal colony, now, you see it? We've got about thirty, maybe thirty-five seals."

The woman sitting against the window on the opposite

side of the van, past Harry, puts her hand on our backs to push us forward as she snaps a picture.

"You got it then, love?" Sean asks, ever solicitous of photo-ops, before he puts the car in gear again and pulls away. "That's a fine sign, seeing the seals," he says, "for all that you've not had good weather to be touring the island today. And of course you know that some of our seals are Selkies, can't say how many, but a few, always a few." He turns back to give us all his most mischievous smile, his most twinkling glance. "Inis Mór has always been home to the Selkies, along with the coast of Connemara 'cross the water."

"What are you saying?" asks a man sitting up front with his wife. He's an older man, hard-of-hearing. He's had to ask Sean to repeat himself a number of times already. "Selkies?" he echoes now.

"That's right!" Sean nods. "Selkies, the seal-people."

"Oh." The man sits back. "Of course. A myth."

WE ARE AMONG the first back on the ferry. A lot of people are still milling in and out of the shops that line the pier. I can't think of anything I'd want to buy right now, and Harry doesn't even suggest it. She fishes our return ticket out of her jacket and smooths it out. It is sodden and starting to tear.

"I feel like I'll never be dry again," she says as we board. Several people behind us chuckle in agreement. If anything, the weather is even worse than before, the wind so strong that the boat is already bucking in the water as if impatient to be away. Or maybe it's the sea that's impatient, to have us all to itself, small and unmoored on the sweeping dark waves.

I manage to keep my feet dry on our way onto the boat. I follow Harry into the cabin and let her take the window seat. From the middle seat in the row I have to lean forward to see the small window. My damp clothes are heavy and clammy against my skin.

"I'm sorry I made us do this," Harry says. "It wasn't exactly a fun trip."

"You didn't make it rain all day, silly."

"But the trip over was so hard for you. I should have thought—"

"You couldn't possibly have had any idea I was going to react that way, Harry." I can hear a warning edge creeping into my voice. What do I even mean "that way"? The way I did react or the way she thinks I reacted? The only way not to think about the water or about my lie is to not talk about it.

At least she takes the hint. "I guess it will make for a good vacation story when we get back," she says, "between this awful weather and the tour guide straight out of central casting."

"I kept expecting him to claim leprechaun ancestry," I say, and she laughs, but not for long. She is too full of the wrongs she's done me to let herself off the hook that easily. I hate that I know this about her and that right now it only makes me irritated. I am struggling not to ask to switch places so I can press my face against the window to see the water. I sit rigid and cold in my chair, my hands flat under my thighs as though by imprisoning some part of my body

I can control the rest of it. I don't have the energy to assuage Harry's guilt.

"Kath, that grave marker on the island . . . seeing that—all those poor women—it changes things, don't you think?"

No, because it doesn't change anything for me. I'm not even sure how surprised I really was when I saw the new names to add to the tally: five that we know of now, dead before they were twenty-five. They must have all left babies behind in cradles, and grieving husbands, grieving lovers.

I think of the man in the graveyard. His eyes were dark with a kind of pity that I recognize now. You see it on the faces in the audience when they realize that the heroine is going to have to kill herself at the end. Pity and compassion, but no surprise.

Harry plunges on into my silence. "We could do more research into your family, still. The Aran Islands must have a historical society, since they're interested in reviving Gaelic language and culture there. There might be records that they've kept that might have some clues in them, even personal records: diaries, letters, newspaper stories."

I laugh; I can't help it. What she's envisioning is so futile and so ridiculous in the face of what I know, the inexorable pull of this sea that can't possibly be explained by a disease or a trick of the genes, and that no one would have written down.

"My love," I say, "give it up. Please. It's not Act 5, not yet. But it's Act 4, for sure."

"What the hell does that mean?"

"It means the mad scene has happened already, the heroine has been betrayed—whatever. We've done our research, Harry, and come up on the inevitable." I rock forward in my seat, still sitting on my hands. The round window over Harry's shoulder is awash with rain.

"The inevitable?" She turns in her seat and grabs me by the shoulders to jerk me around to face her. "Kathleen!"

I catch a glimpse of her face and it's enough to know that I've got to stop this conversation, got to get a grip, just long enough for us to get off this boat, back on land, away from the sea. I should have told her what was happening to me on the ferry ride over.

"I was just joking," I say. "I'm sorry. It was stupid. But you have to admit, part of the reason you want to keep poking through records and stuff is that it's fun for you."

"*Fun* for me?"

I shrug. "It's the English major in you rearing her lovely head. It's okay."

She lets go of me then, sits back, and turns her head away.

"You think that's what's motivating me?" she whispers.

No. I should feel guilty for saying these things, but I just feel trapped. Why won't the goddamn ferry move?

"Not deliberately," I say. "Just—maybe you have a fantasy in which there's some answer for me that only you, with your love of books, can find." I sit back, shut my eyes, swallow hard. Beside me, Harry is quiet for so long that I begin to think that I've gone too far this time. I blindly put out my hand toward her and she catches my fingers in hers.

"Maybe," she says in a low voice. "You may be right. I'm sorry."

The boat leaves the dock with a lurch then and I can't help it—I look at the window again to see the first eager waves splash up against it as we head out into open sea.

The sound the sea makes against the glass is like a voice: liquid calling to solid, the water teasing the hull, which offers only a flat, dull sound of impact in answer.

I have to go back out. Beside me, Harry's head is back against her seat, her eyes closed.

"Tired?" I ask softly. She doesn't answer. Stupid. Of course she's tired. I lean over to kiss her forehead and then maneuver down the center aisle, catching myself on either side as the ferry dips and sways. And then I am out again, finally, standing in the mingled rain and sea spray, water sluicing over the deck with every wave. Within seconds I am soaked to the knees. There are only a few other people out here, a miserable couple—probably trying to avoid throwing up—and one big man by himself who is visibly enjoying the thrill of being on an open deck in the middle of a storm at sea.

The ferry heaves to the side, dipping me so close to the surface of the water that I can touch it with my fingertips. As I do, a wave leaps onto the deck and falls on me like a triumphant predator. When the boat rights itself I am wet from head to foot and dizzy again from the shock of the feeling of this sea against my skin. I hang on to the railing, lean over it as far as I dare, gasping for a gulp of water. And the sea obliges me, sending another wave crashing over the deck from so high that I am able to tip my head back and drink it in before it plays itself out around my feet.

"Funny," says a voice beside me, quite close. "You don't look seasick."

It's the man from the bus, from the graveyard. He's standing next to me, not bracing himself at all against the plunging of the boat, but keeping his footing just the same. His red hair is plastered against his skull, his absurdly thick eyelashes beaded with water. Close up, I realize how slight he is, shorter than I am.

I should ignore him. There are no wrinkles around his eyes, no gray in his hair, so I don't know how he could possibly know anything. He can't be much older than Robin. But even when Harry was grilling Robin, he didn't mention any women before Caolinn, who'd also died too young. This man knew not only where to find my family's gravestone, but also that the names on it would mean something to me. I can't ignore that.

"I never said I was seasick," I say.

"No, that's true, I'm sure. But you let them believe it, didn't you? You let her believe it. She's worried about you," he says. He's so close that his elbow is touching mine, so he does not need to shout. "Does she know of your *andùil*?"

"My what?"

"Your need," he says. "How much you long to dive into the sea and never come back?"

The ferry heaves again, water drenching us from first one side and then the other. From inside the cabin comes a collective shriek. I hang on to the wet railing.

"She knows."

For a moment his next question hangs unasked in the stillness that we two seem enclosed in, within the crashing sounds of the water and the boat. If he asks it then it means that he knows—something—more than I know.

"Does she know why?"

"I don't even know why! Do you think I wouldn't tell her or change it if I could?"

"But you can't," he says. "It is your nature."

My hair is in my mouth and I pluck it out, my fingers numb and shaking. "What could you possibly know about my nature?"

"What I was trying to show you earlier, in the graveyard. That it is inescapable, as it was for all the women who have come before you."

"What is? Wanting to kill yourself?"

He actually laughs, very lightly and quickly. "No, *a amadáin*. Wanting to return to the sea. To go home."

He jerks his chin at the green-black water. "If your kind could be like mine, this would not have happened, not to you, not to your mother, not to the one who began it all. But you are not so changeable as we are. I have always thought that you—your kind anyway—ought to be grateful for that. It is uncomfortable, surely, to slide between two worlds. But you . . ." He turns back to me. His face is full of pity again, his liquid eyes very sad. "You would slide between the worlds if you could, but I think also now you would just wish to go home, would you not?"

I brace myself against another roll of the boat, curl my toes into the water that rushes into my shoes. I remember the café where we ate lunch and how he gestured at the mural on the wall.

"There's no such thing," I whisper. "No such thing—"

"As mermaids?" He shakes his head. When he speaks again, his Irish accent is thicker.

"You are a mermaid, lass," he says. "Like your mother before you and her mother before her, exiled all of you, but mermaids nonetheless."

"The . . . the pain—"

"I don't know much about it. I'm only the messenger. But

the pain, yes, in your legs and your feet is from the split-
ting of your tail, and the abrasion of cloth or wind on your
skin." He leans even closer to me so that he can murmur
under the wind. "Do you see the sense of it?" His coat, that
stylish pony-hair jacket he is wearing, is unaccountably
warm against my arm, even through layers of sleeves.

And I let it go on, this strange conversation, even as I
turn my face into the wind to catch the full force of the
spray and the waves. Already I want to ask him to show
me how it can be done, how I can dive deep and feel the
pain leave me, feel my body change. Already I believe him,
although of course I don't.

"And my mouth? What about the pain in my mouth?" I
laugh, then, bitterly. "Don't mermaids have tongues?"

He shakes his head. "Most do. There are some questions
I can't answer."

"Who can?"

"The ones who sent me to you. They are—" He hesitates.
"You would call them witches, I think."

"Are they the ones who did this to me?" And yes, yes, I
am slipping from my world into his. I am angry at these
witches. I must believe in them to be angry at them.

"You must go to them. They want to see you. Will you let
me tell you how it can be done?"

I hold on to the railing, keep my eyes on the sea, which
is lashed by rain as if under some futile attack. A few yards
away from our boat, the dark swells swallow up the rain
and rise up again, hungry for more.

"There is a cave," he says, "in the cliffs near the town.
It is not hard to get to, when this weather dies down. Go
down to the pier and turn to the right, walk on the rocks.

You will see it before you pass it, an opening in the rock, nothing more."

"And then?" I try to laugh him off one more time. "Do I turn around thrice, touch the surface of the water and recite an incantation in Mermish?"

He ignores me. His voice has the cadence of song now: this must be his message, the message he was sent to deliver.

"Something of yourself," he says, "something of the sea returned to it, and something gifted to the sea from Above."

And at that I feel a new shifting, dizzying level of panic because those words—oh, not the words themselves, but the insistent cadence of them—remind me of the voices that I've been hearing in the sea.

"What—" There has been no wave recently for me to wet my lips on. My mouth throbs with the beginning of pain. "What if I bring the wrong things?"

"I don't know, lass," he says, in his own voice again. "I assume they won't come."

I nod. Simple enough.

"I don't believe any of this, you know," I say, just to say it out loud. The sea shoulders up under the ferry just then, lifting it right out of the water and letting it drop down with a smack. From inside the cabin, people scream again, though they sound more excited than frightened, like riders on a roller coaster. I gasp with relief as I choke on the water filling my mouth.

Beside me, the man lets out a sudden bark of laughter.

"You can believe or not believe," he says, "but you are a *mhaighdean mhara* all the same. And you want to be under the water right now." His hand closes around my wrist as the boat tips and we dip down close to the seething surface of the sea again. "Shall I prove it to you?" he asks, shouting now over a drumroll of thunder and the raised voices behind us—the boat is nearly on its side. "It's been a long time since I've swum with one of your kind."

And he pulls me in, like falling, or sliding, really, just the tug of his hand on my arm and my other hand releasing the railing to reach for the sea, for the icy cold bubbling of the froth around my arm and on my face and then the colder, colder black depths below.

I cannot see a thing, can hear the shriek of the wind even under the water and the protesting, answering shriek in my head that is telling me my lungs need air. I come to the surface spluttering, thrashing—as anyone would who has just gone over the railing of a boat in a storm. The rain is coming down in curtains and I use one hand to sweep my hair off my face, stroking automatically with the other to keep afloat. As I kick with my legs I feel how heavy and cumbersome my shoes are, and my jeans. If I could take them off—

Something bumps against me under the water and I look down to see his head break the waves at my shoulder, a glossy brown head beaded with water, turned toward me and close enough that I can see the amusement in his huge dark liquid eyes, count the whiskers on his muzzle.

The wind cuffs me sideways so that I swallow water midbreath and choke. I need both my hands to tread water and turn to face him fully. I am not going to drown, not on purpose, certainly, and not by accident, not now. I am not afraid, for one thing, and the ferry is still so close. I can hear shouts and screams from the deck. In a minute they will have a life preserver in the water, ready to haul me in.

For now, though, for a moment, I swim with the Selkie in a sea that has turned the color of salt in the rain. I duck my head under and come up again and he is still there. He dives in his turn, butts his head against my thigh, insinuates himself between my legs, his whole strong body pushing against my knees so that I can *feel* the way he swims, the effortless, undulating movement he makes.

Before he can come up again, behind me, I dive down and follow him, brush his tail with my hands, pat my way along his back until I find his neck and we are side by side. I cannot move the way he does, but I could. If I had my body back I could. And so I know that I do believe—of course I do.

Mhaighdean mhara, he called me. Mermaid.

While the prince lay with his bride for the first time, Maeve became Fand and fled from her prince and from the sea, and for many years we knew only that she was alive. After she fell into the sea and the blade made its way back to us, released into the water from her broken hand, we saw that she must have confronted her prince again, and failed, again, to kill him to free herself. We were curious enough then to call on the magic that let us see what happened between them.

Fand's prince still lived in his palace, with a beautiful wife at his side and two heirs safely grown. But he could not sleep in the bed with his wife, for he reached for her in the dark, already sweating with lust, and tried to bend her body to his in unspeakable ways and called her by another name. He kept no more lovely girls at the palace, though the queen would have been glad to relinquish her claims upon him, and he grew fierce and unyielding in dictating the morality of his court. He came to believe in the power of that Hell that those Above speak of with such delighted horror, and in the seductive charm of the demons and witches who are said to be its servants. If ever a man deserved to lose his life's blood, it was this man, and yet Fand could not take his life to save her own, nor even when his one life could have saved two. Fand would have returned to the sea and her daughter with her, both of them free of the pain of their lives Above.

When Fand returned to him, she was forty years old and more beautiful than even his most fevered dreams of her. What kindled in his eyes when he saw her again was the lust he had always felt for her, quick and eager as an adder's tongue. He rose from his chair to reach for her, she held the blade in the folds of her skirts, and still she could not set it against his throat. She did not convey to him by any means that she had a child. She did not ask him, with her enormous stormy eyes, to show her by word or action that her years of pain and exile had not been in vain, that he loved her after all, that he had made a terrible mistake. Nor did he say so unasked. He only grasped at her, tore her dress, set his hot hands on her white skin.

She stepped from his elegant patio straight off the cliff and into the sea. The rocks of the shallows were un-yielding, as she had known they would be. Her body was broken when we found her, her lovely face crumpled, washed clean of the impetuous passion that had ruled her life. We searched her heart carefully for what we knew must be there. She had hidden it well, but we found it at last, and plucked it out.

Left uneased, regrets sharpen and crystallize like the diamonds so prized Above. Fand's was black and many-faceted and heavy as a stone. It gleams with a sullen, reluctant light when shaken from its wrappings into the palm of a hand. And it grows heavier every year.

HARRY

Aria for Mezzo-Soprano

I dozed uneasily when Kathleen left me, drifting off for minutes at a time and then coming back to an awareness that I was wet and cold. The lights inside the cabin were flickering. I was so tired. I leaned my head against the wall just above the porthole and shut my eyes. Then the ferry leapt out of the water and smacked back down so hard and at such an angle that my head slammed into the wall. Several people screamed, a little boy started to cry—and then out on deck there was a chorus of shouting, screaming, a crew member roaring, "Man overboard, starboard, to starboard, dammit!"

"Lights," someone else shouted. "Get the light on the water!"

Feet pounded down the metal steps that lead from the wheelhouse, like thunder in the ceiling. I sat up, rubbing the bump on my head. Through the porthole the water suddenly lit up in the white glare of a searchlight.

"Oh my Lord," murmured the woman behind me. "Oh my Lord."

Out on deck a man called, "It's a girl! She's keeping her head up!"

Then I was on my feet and stumbling through the cabin, clutching the backs of the seats to steady myself and half-falling with every step. By the time I made it to the deck they were hauling Kathleen in on a life preserver, two crew members braced at the railing with their feet planted far apart, one man ducking under the rail to catch her under the arms and lift her up. Another man stood by and swaddled her in a blanket as soon as she was on board.

"There, miss, there, we got you, you're all right."

The ferry lurched and I fell, caught myself on the rail, went down on my knees in front of her. One of the men who had pulled her in bent over us.

"Was there someone else went over?" He had to bellow over the wind and his voice was urgent. "There's a fellow was standing near you said he thought he saw a man in the water too."

Kathleen stared at him. "A man?"

"There wasn't a man with you?"

Incredibly, bizarrely, Kathleen smiled. "No. No man." She raised her voice so we could hear her. "It was just me. Maybe it was a seal he saw." She turned to watch the water, still smiling, though she was shivering so hard that she couldn't keep the blanket up and it kept slipping off her shoulders.

"Not likely to see seals out in this," the crew member shouted. "Are you sure no one else went in with you?"

"I'm sure," Kathleen cried. The wind whipped a length of

her hair across her face so she had to spit it out. "Look!" she said. "Out there, you see?"

The circle of spot-lit water was dark green and frothing under the driving rain. Two pinpoints of red caught the light, vanished, then reappeared. Eyes. They were eyes in a sleek dark head that you might mistake for human unless you knew it wasn't. The seal lingered a minute in the light, as if he was letting us see him, then ducked under a wave and disappeared.

"I'll be damned," the man said beside us. He straightened up and cupped his hands over his mouth to call up to the wheelhouse.

"Seal! It's a seal!"

The spotlight went out and the crew member turned back. "You sit tight here now," he said, clapping Kathleen on the shoulder, "and let us get you back safe."

She nodded, still watching the sea.

"Thank you," I called after him. He put up a hand as he bounded up the steps. I grabbed Kathleen by the shoulders and turned her to face me. I was shaking all over, my teeth were chattering, and my head hurt. I shook her. "What did you do? You didn't—did you do that on purpose?"

She'd been clutching the blanket around her with her hands tucked tight in the folds. She let it go and cupped my face in her fingers.

"No," she said. She leaned in close so we wouldn't have to shout. "No. I promise." She kissed me. Her mouth as wet and cold as mine, but it struck me how calm she was. And Kathleen had never kissed me like that before, never been the one offering reassurance, her holding *me* up.

"It's all right," she said. She rubbed her nose against mine, brushed her spiky wet lashes against my cheek. "It's going to be all right. Here—" She leaned back and retrieved the blanket from the deck, pulled me down to sit beside her against the wall of the cabin, where we were sheltered a little from the wind. She wrapped the blanket around us both.

"Better?"

"I'm so wet I'm not sure anything would make a difference," I said. She laughed and laced our fingers together under the blanket. I wanted to grab hold of her harder than that, wrap her hair around my wrist, my arms around her waist—something to keep her there. She'd put herself on the outside, nearest the water, and she held her free hand out under the railing, letting the bigger waves wash over her hand and wrist.

"Stop it," I said. "Please." I didn't say, *You're scaring me.* I didn't say, *You almost drowned. For once can't you leave it alone?*

She turned toward me and again I had a feeling of strangeness at the expression on her face. There was something of the sureness that she had when she was singing, and something of the same joy.

"Don't worry," she said. "I'm not about to throw myself into the sea. Not now."

"Not *now*?" I snapped. I gripped her hand. "You said you didn't do it on purpose."

"I didn't. I told you I didn't."

"So what, you fell?"

Again, she smiled.

"You think this is funny? After today you think it's funny that you went into the sea?"

She shook her head. "There's the dock," she said. "We made it in. Let's go get you dry."

She helped me up, helped me off the boat, turned back to the crew members with a dazzling smile as she handed back the blanket, held on to me as we made our way down the dock, fished our room key out of my pocket and opened the door. She turned on the shower, peeled my wet clothes off, and put me under the spray. I pushed my hair off my face and caught her hand when she tried to close the curtain.

"You need a hot shower too, more than I do after being in that water."

"You know that's not true," she said, and now, in better light, I saw that the smile still lurked in her eyes and at the corners of her mouth, like a secret she was savoring, something wonderful and astonishing. Amusing too, or perhaps the keeping of the secret was what was amusing. I was reminded of times when I came into the room while she was talking to Tom to find them both laughing at some joke too perfect or too subtle to share.

"Kathleen, *what is it*? What happened?"

She shook her head. "You won't believe me, not yet. Just take your shower, okay? You're getting water all over the floor."

I took my shower, came out still shivering, and heard her talking out in the bedroom. I peeked through the crack in the door. There was no one else there, only Kathleen pacing back and forth in her wet clothes, the frayed bottoms of her pants making tracks like seaweed trails on the floor.

"It all makes sense," she was saying, "it's crazy but it all makes sense, it actually makes *more* sense than anything else. The voices—it wasn't me, it was them all along. It sounds crazy but it really means I'm not crazy, don't you see? I'm not crazy and Moira wasn't crazy, none of us were."

She was gripping her elbows with her hands, arms crossed under her breasts, facing the bed as if she were talking to someone sitting there. *Me*, I thought, *she's practicing making an argument to me. And here I am spying on her.* But I didn't stop. I watched her suddenly bolt for my carry-on and get out a notebook and pen.

"What did he say," she muttered. "I should have written it down right away. Dammit! What was it? Something of myself, something of the sea . . ."

She scribbled furiously. Her wet hair fell across the paper and she pushed it back. I finished drying off, wrapped myself in the towel and tucked the end in between my breasts. I didn't open the door. I turned back into the bathroom and rubbed lotion on my face, finger-combed my hair, brushed my teeth. I'd never thought Kathleen might really be mentally ill. Not once. If I'd considered it as a possibility, would I know what to do now any better than I did?

I spit toothpaste in the sink, cupped one hand to rinse my mouth. I could call Robin and tell him that Kathleen was acting strange, but what could he do? The only thing to do was to get through the next day, our last full day here, and fly her home. And what exactly was so strange now that was any stranger than anything that had come already? Kathleen seemed to have had some kind of revelation in the sea, she seemed to know exactly what was wrong with her, and whatever it was that she thought, it had energized her, excited her. These were all good things. This revelation and the change in her—they meant that the trip to Ireland had been worthwhile, when only a few hours ago we'd thought it a waste. I'd never doubted her before, so why was I doubting her now? Because she'd come out of the sea smiling in the middle of a storm? Because she had a secret from me, something she had to work out how to tell me? Because she hadn't explained how she'd ended up in the damn water in the first place?

The mirror revealed a purpling bruise on my temple where I'd hit my head. I didn't want to go out to Kathleen. She'd been . . . transfigured by something, while I just felt hungry and tired and scared.

But when I came out, Kathleen didn't say anything more about what had happened. She seemed to be feeling the cold, finally, and the chill of having been wet for so long. She went into the bathroom and called out to me: "We should see if we can use the laundry facilities here tonight. These clothes are never going to dry otherwise and we don't want to pack them wet."

"That's a good idea," I said. "We can ask when we go down to dinner."

I heard her turn the water on. I slipped into my underwear, then a shirt and jeans and a cardigan sweater. I hadn't packed for weather this cold. I sat down on the bed to put on my socks. I didn't see the pad Kathleen had been writing on. There was a drawer in the nightstand, or it could have been under her pillow or tucked into her suitcase somewhere. I sat there a moment and decided that I couldn't go hunting for it. She was planning to tell me whatever it was anyway.

We paid five dollars to do a load of laundry and then, rather than brave the rain again, ate dinner in the dining room of the inn. Afterward we sat together in front of the big fireplace in the library, where guests could drink complimentary port or coffee and help themselves to the books.

I drank a glass of port and stared at the flames and waited for Kathleen to say something. I felt dizzy from the port or the wine at dinner or just fatigue or worry. I went over the words she'd used upstairs in the room: *it's crazy but it all makes sense.* And the other thing she'd said, that she'd been hearing voices that weren't in her head, were *them all along.* Who were *they*? I couldn't imagine an answer that didn't frighten me.

"Your hair is so curly from the damp," Kathleen said. "It's curlier than I've ever seen it." I felt her hand on my head, again the new and alarming tenderness in her touch. She tapped the bruise.

"What's this from?"

"I hit my head on the ferry," I said. "With one of the swells."

"Poor love," she murmured. She leaned in and kissed my head. I smelled the salt water in her hair and shuddered.

"What's wrong?" she asked.

"You still smell like the ocean."

"I just rinsed my hair out, I didn't wash it," she said. "I wanted to smell the sea awhile longer."

"It doesn't . . . upset you? This morning you were miserable from it." And the rest, unspoken, as if countering her in the conversation we hadn't had yet: *How does that make sense?*

"Let's talk about it in the morning, okay?" she said. "It's late and we're both tired."

"You're not acting tired." I sounded petulant. I sounded like Kathleen did when her pain was getting bad.

"I am tired though," she said. "And we have all day tomorrow. Come on, let's go to bed." Her hand slipped up to the back of my neck, under my hair. She brushed her fingertips against my skin, traced circles on my nape. I closed my eyes. I did want her. The way she was touching me was so new between us that it felt like—almost like we were role-playing, with Kathleen as nursemaid and me as the passive invalid. I could picture us in the bed upstairs, picture myself lying as if cocooned between the feather mattress and the down comforter and Kathleen bending over me, long and white and supple, not feeling the cold as much as I seemed to be, pulling back the comforter only a little at a time and covering the exposed part of my body with some part of her own, until I gave in and flung the covers off, needing her instead.

But even as I turned my head into her caress I breathed in the smell of the sea that still clung to her. It smelled like dead things and scouring wind and reminded me of staggering out onto the deck of the ferry, how certain I had been that she had drowned.

"I am tired," I said. I leaned away to put my glass down on the tray before the fire. "You're right. We should go to bed."

WHEN I WOKE up, she was waiting for me. She'd dressed and braided her hair. Kathleen never braided her hair, except when she had to do something sweaty or dirty, both of which she avoided as much as possible. She was sitting in the rocking chair that faced the bed. When I met her eyes, she put one foot down to stop the movement of the chair and sat forward, gripping the armrests.

"All you have to promise," she said, "is to hear me out. Then you can tell me how crazy I am, okay?"

I sat up in bed and pushed my hair off my face. "Okay."

"You were right," she said, "you didn't know it but you

were right! There was an answer here. He told me some of it, not all of it, but—"

"Who told you?"

"The Sel—" She bit her lip and started over. "The man, the one from the bus who was staring at me, you remember? He came out and talked to me on the ferry deck while you were asleep."

"And told you what, exactly?"

"He said he couldn't tell me everything, but he told me how to find out. You're not going to believe it, I know. I didn't think I believed it until I knew I did, until I realized that it's the only thing that makes sense, really, the only possible explanation for everything."

"What is?"

When she said it, the sensation I had was not the icy fear I'd been feeling the day before. Then I'd been questioning her sanity and my own ability to handle her, to stay with her, to help her. But the moment she said, "I'm a mermaid," I felt my stomach tighten with a terrible, helpless sense of loss, a feeling more like grief than fear. I wanted her to unsay it, wanted her to take it back. It was as if she'd said, "I don't love you anymore," because it meant the same thing. It meant she was gone, she had left me. I stared down at my hands, clenched around the edge of the comforter, and watched as they obeyed my silent command to unclench, to relax.

"Go ahead," Kathleen said. "Say it. It's all right."

"Say what?"

"Say that I'm crazy."

But I could only have said it aloud if I hadn't believed it, if I'd been willing to throw it out as a point of argument. I didn't tell her that she had red hair, did I? Or that mine was curly and blond? I didn't tell her things that were obvious and irrefutable and so I couldn't tell her that. That she was crazy.

I lifted my gaze from my lap. "Kathleen," I said carefully, trying not to sound like I was talking carefully, "how does this man claim to know this about you? Why would he tell you?"

"They sent him," she said, and the rest of it came tumbling out. Her whole face was flushed, her pupils dilated so that her eyes were nearly black. She looked beautiful. She sat there, setting the chair rocking again as she talked to me about witches who spoke to her in the waves and a cave in the cliffs along the shore where she planned to go today to make an offering of some kind.

"Something of myself, something of the sea returned to it, and something gifted to the sea from—well, he said, 'from above,' which I think now means simply from on land, or from the air. But I think something from the natural world." She tugged on her braid. "A flower, maybe, or a bird's feather. It shouldn't be too hard to find something."

"And what are you supposed to do with these things?"

"Take them to the cave."

"And then what?"

Her face clouded a little. "I don't know. He said they wanted to see me. I think they can tell me how to fix it, how to go back."

"You mean turn you back into a mermaid?"

She must have heard me, finally, though it had taken

her longer than it should have. Kathleen had perfect pitch but she'd missed the flatness in my voice until then. She stopped rocking again.

"You don't believe me."

"You didn't expect me to, did you? You said yourself that you couldn't expect me to."

She didn't say anything. I felt cold and exposed sitting up in the bed in just a T-shirt. I got up and pulled on some jeans, turned my back, and pulled off my shirt, put on a bra and a clean shirt. I turned back around to face her as I folded up the shirt I'd slept in.

"I think in my head I told myself that I *couldn't* expect you to believe me," she said slowly, "but all the same I *did* expect you to. You've—" She hesitated. "I don't know what to do if you don't believe me."

I put the folded shirt on my pillow and started making the bed. I was angry now, angry and sad. I felt like we were breaking up and even though it was because of what she'd told me, because I couldn't possibly believe her, the breaking up felt more important and more real.

"So these sea witches," I said, smacking a pillow, "there's a whole group of them?"

"Yes," Kathleen said miserably. "Yes, that's what he said. And as soon as he said it, I knew they had to be the ones I heard in the water in Florida. They kept telling me to 'come home' over and over again. Then when I saw the picture of the cliffs—remember, when we were on the plane?—I knew they meant Ireland, that this is home."

"What are they like, I wonder? Did he tell you that? Are they half lady, half octopus?" I sat down on the bed, saw her shrinking into herself with every nasty word I threw.

"Why would they look like that?" she asked.

"Well, you're the perfect Ariel, aren't you? So all you need is an Ursula. Too bad I'm no handsome prince. Maybe that's the problem."

"Stop it!" she cried. I stopped. I lowered my head and felt the painful pressure of tears behind my eyes.

"I always hated that movie," she murmured after a minute. "I couldn't understand why she'd want to leave the sea and go live on land, or why she'd ever give up her voice."

"It's not the way the original story goes, you know," I said. "In the original story the witch cuts out her tongue."

Kathleen made a choked sound.

No, I thought. *No. It can't be.*

But more pieces of the story unfolded in my head. I'd had a collection of Andersen stories when I was little, with "The Little Mermaid" as the centerpiece. There had been a picture of her as a mermaid in an underwater garden, embracing a statue. A picture of her lying on the sand, slender white legs splayed beneath her at an odd, helpless angle, like a broken pair of scissors. A picture of her throwing herself into the sea while the prince and his bride slept peacefully.

"The witch cuts out her tongue," I said, "and also tells her that even though she will be beautiful and graceful on land, walking will be painful, excruciating even, like walking on knives."

"How does it end?" Kathleen asked.

"It's a terrible ending. She gets a knife and she's supposed to kill the prince, but she can't so she throws herself back into the sea instead and turns into sea foam or something."

She got out of the chair and sat down on the bed with me, laced her fingers in mine.

"Harry," she said.

I shook my head. What I was feeling couldn't be hope. I didn't believe her, for God's sake. She was mentally ill.

But she hadn't known the story until I told it to her.

"How can you not have heard that story before?" I demanded.

"A lot of people probably haven't heard that story," she said. There was warmth and humor back in her voice. "You know that perfectly well. I didn't know the detail about Cinderella's stepsisters cutting off parts of their feet to fit the glass slipper until you told me, remember? I'd only ever seen the movie."

"But, Kathleen"—I made a helpless gesture with our clasped hands—"it's a *fairy tale*."

She leaned in and kissed me, pushed me backward onto the bed and kept kissing me gently. I closed my eyes, felt the tears that had threatened before leaking out. Kathleen kissed them away.

"You believe in fairy tales, Harry," she said softly. "It's why I love you."

AND AFTER THAT, we had the loveliest day together. The sun was out and everything was so wet from the storm of the day before that the colors of the sky and the grass and even the whitewashed houses and tumbled stone walls gleamed like they were poured from fresh cans of paint. Kathleen wolfed down slabs of brown bread with butter and honey at breakfast and asked the owner of the inn which shops in Doolin were the best.

"We've been out to Inis Mór and to the pub, but we

haven't bought anything yet," she said. "We've got to be good little tourists today."

I listened to her chatting about whose sweaters were fairly priced and which jewelers really made their own pieces. In my head I began a conversation with someone else. Robin, maybe, or a doctor. Not the one we hadn't liked, Biancini. The other one, the neurologist who'd delivered the ECT news.

She came out of the sea with this new delusion—of course I know it's a delusion. But the weird thing was that once she fixed on this idea she cheered up, her appetite came back, her mood—she hasn't been this happy since . . . I couldn't think of when. *Oh, and her sex drive came back too.* Who would I report *that* to? Not Dr. Kapoor, certainly, and not Robin either. But as the day went on I kept it up, offering a jumbled defense of Kathleen's clarity and my own complicity in her madness. Because she couldn't be crazy after all—*just look at her*—drifting down the street, stopping to scratch a sway-backed horse on the nose, grabbing my hand to pull me into yet another shop with Celtic knot sun catchers sparkling in the windows. And if she was crazy (she had to be crazy to believe this thing) then I couldn't do anything but go along, could I? What if I tried to force her out of this delusion and she ran off, or had another breakdown?

We found a shop that sold only Irish music and talked to the proprietor for an hour, listening to his favorites while Kathleen teased him about his anti-opera prejudice. She bought a half dozen CDs for Robin and made the man promise to listen to Patrick Cassidy's *Deirdre*, which has both an Irish composer and Irish story. In a tiny jewelry

shop painted white inside and out, Kathleen bought a slippery silver bracelet of interlocking knots for Tae and a
necklace for herself. It was unlike her to wear jewelry at
all, and I wouldn't have picked that necklace for her. It was
a pendant made from a cone-shaped seashell. The chain
was threaded through the narrow end and at the opening
was a pale green bead that the girl in the store said was an
amethyst.

Kathleen slipped it over her head as we left the shop. Her
braid began to unravel when she lifted it over the chain and
she shook it out and left her hair loose.

"This bead is pretty," she said. "Maybe I'll save it."

"What are you talking about?"

"Well," she said, "I'll have to break it apart to give them
the shell." She held the pendant up so she could examine it
closely. "Yes, it shouldn't be too hard. And that's one thing
I need. Something of the sea returned to it."

We had a bit of a walk to the next shop, which was beside
the only non-pub restaurant in Doolin.

"Shall we eat lunch there?" Kathleen asked. "It's beautiful. All those windows facing the sea."

"Sounds perfect," I said. And then—*and how can I jus-
tify this question? I'm encouraging her, for God's sake*—I asked,
"What are you going to do for the gift from above?"

She had clearly been thinking about this already. "I don't
know yet. I suppose I could just pick some flowers or grass,
but I don't want to do that. I want it to be a gift, something
special. I'm sure I'll find something."

I followed her down the path that led to the restaurant. The wind lifted Kathleen's hair up like a tournament
banner and whistled through the tall grasses that grew

along the path. Kathleen put her hands out on either side to let the grass brush her palms. I almost asked her what she was going to offer of herself, but I could see the answer in the streamers of hair whipping back toward me. One long lock that normally lay hidden at the nape of her neck was noticeably shorter than the rest. She must have cut it just that morning while I was in the shower.

I thought of Marie, the nun who'd saved Caolinn's hair in a locket all those years. What was it she had said about her locket? *When it went into the sea I imagined that the waves were reaching for the last of her, the only bit they hadn't already taken.*

I stopped walking. I felt like I was grasping at something that was slipping away, the same dizzying sense of hope or understanding just out of reach that I'd had this morning when I'd remembered the fairy tale. It wasn't a physical sensation so much as an intellectual one, the way I felt trying to grapple with *The Waste Land* or with a passage of tricky literary theory.

In "The Little Mermaid," the mermaid was supposed to kill the prince with a knife. Where had she gotten it?

The sea witch again, of course.

Caolinn had had a knife. Marie had seen it, had held it briefly in her hands. Deirdre had slit her wrists, and then—according to Moira, her daughter—the knife "went back to where it came from." And Moira had had a knife, double-edged, Robin had said, in a case that might have been made of pearl.

I was standing in the middle of the narrow lane leading to the restaurant. Kathleen was waiting for me at the entrance.

"Come on, slowpoke," she called. "I'm starved."

So what's worse? I thought. *If it's not true, then she's crazy and I'm crazy for helping her. And if it is true—which it can't be, but if it is—why did they all still kill themselves? Just because they had no prince to kill?*

THE RESTAURANT WAS as beautiful inside as out, all blond wood and sheer white curtains, no colors to distract from the food or the view. We ate celery root soup and shrimp salad on crusty white bread and drank a bottle of Riesling. We agreed that Tae would like the bracelet and that Robin would be pleased to know that Doolin was still flourishing as a musical center. I suggested that Tom would have thought the music shop owner was cute and Kathleen snorted.

"Can you imagine what would happen to that poor man if they hooked up and then Tom found out he didn't like opera?"

"Tom wouldn't hook up with him until he'd changed his mind," I pointed out.

"No, you're right." She grinned wickedly. "He'd get double duty of tying his partner up and making him listen to *Les Contes de Hoffman* while he couldn't get away."

"Please! I'm eating!"

She giggled and forked up some shrimp that had fallen out of her sandwich.

"We'll go down to the cave before dinner," she said. "We'll want to go back to our room to put our bags down and get some warmer clothes. And I think I saw a flashlight in one of the dresser drawers. We'll want to get that. We should have boots, but of course who would have thought to pack those?"

I sipped my wine and nodded.

A few shops later she found a decorative saucer on which butterfly wings had been delicately arranged to cover the whole surface, then covered in clear glaze.

"It's a little creepy," Kathleen said, holding the plate up so the wings caught the light. The glaze made them iridescent, like beetle wings or the inside of a shell. "I mean, I hope no butterflies were harmed in the making of this plate."

The shop owner assured her that the artist simply collected dead butterflies from her garden and used their wings. She wrapped the plate in several layers of tissue and Kathleen pronounced our shopping done. Back in the room, she pulled the necklace over her head, slid the shell from the chain, and snapped off the amethyst bead. She retrieved the length of her hair, wrapped in a ponytail holder, from her toiletry kit, and put everything in the bag with the plate.

"Ready?"

I didn't know what to say. I'd let it go too long, let it go all day. We were going to call on some sea witches in a cave along the shore. If I tried to stop her now, she'd just go alone.

I settled for banality. "Did you check the batteries in the flashlight?"

She turned out the light in the room and shone the flashlight on the wall.

"Come on, silly," she said.

I followed her downstairs and out onto the path that led to the pier.

"Why the rush all of a sudden? The man who told you all this didn't say there was a set time for a meeting, did he?"

She was scanning the cliff face off to the right. It was black and pitted. From where we were, there could have been dozens of caves, or none—just shadows on the rock. "He didn't say anything about when, just told me where," she said. She jumped lightly off the side of the pier onto the narrow ledge that hugged the cliff and started to pick her way along it. "I just didn't think we'd want to be doing this in the dark, that's all."

There it was again, Kathleen being practical. In the midst of this madness she was thinking about the wisdom of trying to explore a cave in the dark. I caught up with her but stayed a step behind. There wasn't room for us to walk side by side.

"This man," I said, "the one who followed you all day yesterday, did he tell you what his connection to the witches was, why he was the messenger they sent?"

Kathleen laughed. "He didn't *tell* me his connection to them," she said. "He *showed* me. He showed you too, but you didn't get it."

"He showed me? He didn't show me anything."

"Yes he did."

He'd worn a glossy leather jacket. I remembered that because it had been far nicer than the rest of his clothes. He'd seemed amused by us, had translated Sean's Irish so I'd be sure to know that I was being foolish. And his eyes had been so weird, too big not only for his face but—just too big, and oddly shaped. They'd reminded me of an animal's eyes, of the shock of seeing eyelashes on a deer up close, or a seal.

I grabbed for Kathleen, caught her arm just above the elbow.

"That was him in the water? Is that what you mean?"

She turned back and nodded at me. She wasn't laughing now, but her face was radiant again with the wonder of her belief. "That was him. He pushed me over and went in with me."

"He was a Selkie."

"Yes."

"Kathleen, I can't!" I pulled on her arm, spun her toward me. "I can't do this, I can't believe this. It's got to stop."

"Harry," she said. She pulled her arm free. "It doesn't matter if you believe me or not. I know it seems crazy. I told you this morning that I knew that. But you'll know soon enough." She gestured with the hand holding the flashlight. "See? We're here." And then she turned her back on me and ducked into a dark crevice in the rock.

I hadn't even noticed it. I plunged in after her, but she didn't wait. She'd realized by then that we weren't on the same side. She kept several steps ahead of me, playing the light back and forth so that we could both see where our feet needed to be, but not letting me catch up. It was all I could do once we were inside to keep up with her, because the ledge continued along the wall of what I realized was a tunnel and the sea ran beside it in a channel right up to the other wall. One wrong foot and you'd be in the water in the dark. I could hear the little slaps of the water against the rock at our feet and Kathleen's breathing, but except for the small yellow beam of the flashlight it was pitch-black.

Kathleen swung the flashlight back for me one more time and I caught sight of a rock just before I tripped over it. Then she stopped and shone it in front of us instead. I nearly ran into her back.

"Goddammit, Kathleen!"

"Shh!" she hissed.

She played the light around slowly so we could see the cave. The ledge had ended and in front of us the sea pooled into a dead end. There was nothing but water below and rock around and above us, no sign that people had ever been in here, no writing on the walls, no trash or debris. No animal traces either, no sounds of crabs scuttling away, no discarded shells or skeletons, not even any smell of animals. It just smelled of salt water and of darkness. It was colder in here than it had been outside, with a chill that felt settled and old.

"Here," Kathleen said. "Hold this."

She pushed the flashlight into my hand. I played it along the water's edge, checking for tide marks. That would be all we needed, to get trapped in here when the tide came in. But I didn't even know what I was looking for, how I would tell.

"Stop that," Kathleen said. "I need the light over here so I can see. Shine it on the water."

Her hands shook as she pulled the things she'd brought from her pockets and placed them on the surface of the water. I thought, *For God's sake, just drop them in.* But I crouched down beside her and kept the light trained on the water as she made her offering. I even put my hand on her back as she leaned forward.

"Calm down," I whispered. "The last thing we need right now is for you to fall in."

She hushed me again, sat back with a breathless giggle and groped for my hand.

"Look," she whispered.

She'd laid the things on the water in a kind reverent order that I supposed must have matched her instructions.

First her hair, then the shell, then the plate. They all floated in our weak little circle of light, not drifting apart or sinking, but floating on the surface of the water right in front of us. Then they all vanished, abruptly, as if they'd been snatched under. And the flashlight winked out.

I gasped. "Shit!" Kathleen squealed and jumped, pulling me backward with her. The wall of the cave was like ice against my back. I fumbled with the light, clicking it on and off. Nothing.

"Kath— Christ, I can't see a thing," I whispered. "We're going to have to feel our way out. Dammit."

"Shh!" She was still clutching my hand but she clawed at me with her free hand, first at my arm then my shoulder and finally my face and throat. I realized that she was trying to put her hand over my mouth, to get me to stop talking. Her fingers were frantic, trembling against my lips. I shut my eyes and drew a deep breath, trying to think of what I could say to get her out of here, to get us both out of here. We were going to have to crawl to be safe, to crawl along the ledge, hugging the cave wall . . .

A woman spoke, so close to my ear that it sounded like she was sitting right beside me. I opened my eyes, put my hand up to push her away. But there was no one there. I strained to see something, anything, but the darkness was unrelieved.

"Kathleen, did you hear—"

"She heard."

Another woman, from the other side of the cave, her voice low and pitched to carry.

"Who's there?" I sat up straighter, flexed my fingers just to feel that Kathleen's were still there.

"But we must be paid also," said the first voice, still so close that I should have been able to feel breath on my cheek. No one there.

"And it is not a trifle we ask." Another voice, that made three, this one coming from the water at our feet.

"Thank you for the gifts, Kathleen." Close by again, on Kathleen's other side. She jumped and shrank against me. There was a long moment of silence. I could feel them waiting, feel them listening.

"You're welcome," Kathleen whispered finally. "I-I didn't know what to bring."

"How could you?" Yet another—five voices now, or was it six? I'd lost count. This one came from somewhere over our heads. All women, some young, some old. This one sounded . . . amused. "You couldn't possibly be expected to know."

"And Harry helped you. That's never happened before." This came from another place in the cave. I kept turning my head to try to see the speakers. My eyes ached. Then I realized what she'd said.

"Me—how do you know my name? How do you know Kathleen's name?"

And at the same moment Kathleen sat up straighter against the wall and asked, "Did my mother come to you?"

Another pause. "Yes," said the one in the water. "She came. She brought a braid of her hair plaited with seaweed and feathers, all three gifts in one."

"But then—" Kath's breath caught on a sob. "Why didn't you help her?"

They sighed, all of them, each voice we'd heard already

and others we hadn't. The sound swept around the cave like a wind.

"We tried to help her," one of them said softly.

"We tried to help them all," said another.

"You are the eighth, Kathleen."

"We tried to reach you sooner—"

"But you'd gone too far away."

It was impossible to keep track of the voices, of which one was speaking.

"Do you mean when she went to Boston?" I asked. "How was that too far away?" I felt angry but my voice wouldn't cooperate. It just sounded confused and frightened. I tried again.

"How many of you are there? Why won't you let us see you?"

There was another murmur, communal like the sigh but somehow amused again. They were laughing at us.

"You can't see us," they said, "because we aren't here. We live in deeper waters than this."

"We are bottom dwellers."

"Scavengers, they call us," said one. She sounded bitter.

"We are what we are," said another, as if in reproof.

"And we have sea lilies in our garden," murmured the one by my ear. "They only grow for us."

"She wants to see," said the one at our feet. She sounded exasperated. "Humans aren't used to the dark. She feels blind."

"Ohhhh." A little ripple of sound went round the cave and lights came up in its wake, little blurry green lights, like fireflies except that they didn't move. There were lights in the walls and in the water and on the ceiling, but they didn't correspond to the voices. There were too many— more lights than voices—and they revealed nothing but the cave itself, and Kathleen and me sitting on a ledge. I could see my own hand in front of me, gripping the useless flashlight. Kathleen put her hand over mine and said "Harry?" in a small voice. I glanced up at her face. I think I screamed.

"What?" She fastened her hand on my wrist. I dropped the flashlight and it rolled into the water.

The light was just barely enough to see by, but still for a moment I really thought it had turned Kathleen into . . . into something else. I had to look down to register her clothes, her jeans and her feet still there, sneakers smeared with mud and sand. But her face was appalling. The greenish glow was not reflected on her skin; it shone like it was *in* her skin. The shadows under her cheekbones were dark green and her eyes were long and black and alien. I'd never noticed how oddly her eyes were set in her face. Then she moved her head a little and it was gone. She was Kathleen again.

"Harry, what is it?" she whispered.

I shook my head. "Nothing," I said. "I'm sure we both look ghastly in this light."

The listening voices made a collective sound of disbelief in their throats. Kathleen didn't seem to hear. But they knew what I'd seen in her.

She smiled at me tremulously. "Can I ask—do you believe me now?"

"I believe you." I tried to smile back. "No 'I told you so' later, though, okay?"

"Okay."

Kath let go of one of my hands, the one that had held the light, and we both turned back to face the water. I think we had some vague sense that we needed to talk *to* the water to talk to them—to the sea witches.

"So," Kathleen said, "you tried to help my mother. You tried to help all the women in my family but—what—you couldn't? Or is suicide your idea of a happy ending?"

The water smacked against the ledge and surged up a little over our feet.

"We will tell you the whole story," they said. "We will tell you what you need to know. Will you listen?"

"We are listening," Kath said.

"Both of you—" They hesitated.

"Have we ever told the tale to them both?" asked one.

"Never," said another.

"We would remember that."

"'Them both'?" Kathleen asked. "What do you mean, 'them both'? You mean me and Harry?"

"We mean the mermaid and her lover," they said. "'The seeker of one who is lost,' that is our name for him."

"Or her," said one. "Remember Caolinn."

"Or her," they agreed.

"You're talking in riddles," I said. I could feel the bones in Kath's hand from how tightly I was holding her, or she was holding me. "Just tell us."

So they did. They told us about Maeve, who had re-named herself Fand, who had fled from the end of her own story, who had met a storyteller in Italy and let him reshape her tale into something he called his own. They stopped talking when I made a noise of disbelief. *It's just a story! He made it up! Like "The Ugly Duckling" and "The Red Shoes" and "The Steadfast Tin Soldier."* I didn't say anything, though, and after a moment they went on. They told us how Fand had lived so long in Italy—nearly twenty years before she took a young lover and conceived a child—that the witches themselves lost track of her, lost sight of the curse stretching like a trip wire across her path. They told us about Victoria and Muirin and Ceara and Caolinn. We didn't tell them that we'd already heard that part. They told us about Deirdre and Moira. Kathleen began to cry when they said her father's name. She came up out of a sitting position and knelt forward on the wet shelf, crying silently as they told her how her mother had died. The story went on, lyrical and relentless. They told us about the limits of their power and how they had tried to contact Kathleen before now but hadn't been able to reach so far, not until they discovered a way to use a shell as a kind of receptor down in Sanibel. They explained all her symptoms. The pain in her feet and in her legs. The phantom pain in her mouth. The sensitivity of her skin. The longing for water, for the sea.

They told Kathleen what she had to do to end it all. By the time they got to that part, I knew what it had to be. I shut my eyes as they said the words "and let her blood run over your feet" and thought, *This means I am her true love. That's something.*

A small, dry voice in my head muttered back, *Couldn't it have been a kiss then to break the spell?* But of course it couldn't have been a kiss. It had to be the knife and the blood, the fatal pull of the story toward its ending.

The witches didn't say anything about a *happy* ending. They talked singly and together and over and under one another in rivers and currents of story that washed over us and only broke with an audible splash when they had finished their tale. Something bobbed and shone on the surface of the water in front of us.

They were silent, then, waiting. Kathleen was still crying, shaking her head and choking on her tears.

"No," she said. "No. I won't take it. You can't make me. Just take it back now. If I won't use it, what difference does it make if you take it now or later?"

"We cannot take it," they said. They sounded sad, finally, or maybe just tired. "It will return to us when it has been used for its purpose, or when you are dead, Kathleen. That is how it was made."

Kathleen started wildly to her feet, straining away from my hand. I held on. I knew where she was headed.

"What if I just come now?" she asked. She swiped at her nose with her free hand. "Can't I just come with you now, and then you can take whatever it is you want from me, my hair or my tongue or"—she gagged and had to swallow hard before she could go on—"my voice, whatever that means. Harry can go back to Boston and tell my father—tell him what you did to his wife and daughter and it'll all be over, isn't that right?"

A shiver ran across the surface of the water.

"That's right."

"Because I'm not going to kill Harry!" she screamed. "I'm not going to kill her—oh my God!" She tugged violently to free her hand again and went down on her knees, retching.

I didn't let go. I tried to imagine Kathleen stabbing me with a knife, but all I could conjure up was a stage scene, like the climax of *Tosca*, where the knife goes in and the character crumples, still singing, and you know it's not real. The idea was—it was fantastical, more impossible to believe than the green glow and the voices of this cave. But the image of Kathleen in the water, sinking as Moira had, with her hair mushrooming up around her—that I could picture. I could even picture the look she'd have on her face, the defiant set of her jaw as she refused to take my outstretched hand . . .

"No," I said aloud. I got to my feet and pulled Kathleen up with me. The case with the knife in it caught the light and winked at us. Robin had said it seemed decorative, more like a letter opener than a knife. What would he have done if he'd known the whole story? I felt my brain start to work again. What had the witches called me? *The seeker of one who is lost.* But I wasn't the same as Robin or Marie or even the damn prince. They hadn't known anything. They couldn't have *done* anything because they hadn't *known* anything.

"If we don't take the knife now," I said, "it'll just follow us, right? It'll show up on her bed someday, or in a drawer?"

"Yes." The voices sounded almost apologetic. "That is how it was made."

"Kathleen," I said. "Get up, love. We'll figure it out. But we've got to get out of here first." I turned back to the water and raised my voice to address the witches again.

"We dropped our light," I said. "We can't see to get out of—"

The flashlight popped out of the water and rolled against my feet. I reached down, picked it up, and turned it on. It worked. Kath had gotten sick, either from the pain in her mouth that the story had triggered or in reaction to what the witches had told her. She was limp now, hardly conscious.

"At least you're not fighting me," I muttered to her. I stuck the light in my pocket so I could reach into the water and pick up the box. It was an unusual shape, like a flattened oval, striated in bands of white. The pearl from which it had been carved would have had to have been as large as a basketball. I didn't open it.

"Will you die for her, then?" murmured the voice closest to my ear. "Is that your answer?"

"What if it is?" I asked. It sounded like a taunt. Maybe it was. I felt like I had a secret from them now, like I understood something they didn't. They were inside this curse as much as Kathleen. But I was only here because I wanted to be, because I loved her. And now I knew everything.

"If I turned the knife on myself, what would happen?" I asked. Behind me Kathleen made a choking sound of protest and put her hands on my shoulders.

"Harry—"

"Shh," I said.

There was a silence. Then the voice in the water sighed. "She must be the one to wield the blade."

"I thought so," I said. I stood up. Kathleen clutched at me, pulling me toward the tunnel.

"You think we are cruel," said a voice from the wall, and the others chimed in.

"We are only what we are."

"We were paid for magic and we did as we were bidden."

"The spells we wove for Fand were intricate, beautiful things."

"As was the blade we made for her sisters when they gave us their hair."

"And yet—" They hesitated. "We would gladly see them undone now and their power drained away."

"Then do it!" Kathleen whispered. "Cast a new spell to end it some other way, or call the old spell back. You said you needed payment. Isn't there some way we could pay you?" She crouched over the water again. Her hair tumbled over her shoulder and into the pool. "My hair, my voice . . ."

"Use the blade," they said. "Come home."

Kathleen hit the surface of the pool with her open hand. Water sprayed back at her and slopped over my feet. "Damn you," she snarled.

The green lights began to go out, one by one. I tugged Kathleen up again.

"They can't do anything more," I said.

"Can't or won't?" she demanded.

The cave continued to dim. The witches did not speak again. I tucked the box with the knife in it under my arm and gripped the flashlight, then turned us both around and began to pick my way along the ledge. Kathleen straightened up and pushed away a little to walk on her own. We navigated side by side until we emerged from the tunnel, where it got too narrow to walk any way but single file again.

"You go first," I said.

Kathleen sighed. "I'm not going to do anything stupid."

"Good."

When we reached the pier, she turned back to help me up.

"Besides," she said, "once I made myself sick on the whole grand 'Fuck you' gesture I realized I didn't want to even give them the satisfaction, you know?"

"I don't think they would have been satisfied," I said. "I mean, they want the curse to end but they don't *want* you to kill yourself. Or me."

She shuddered and didn't answer.

"They're just as trapped by it as you are, as we are," I said. I shifted the box under my arm. It was so smooth and curved that it was hard to hold. "I think they'd love a way out, but they can't find one, any more than anyone else has."

"There isn't a way out," Kathleen said bitterly. "It's like we're back to square one only now I *know* I'm eventually going to kill myself."

"There's got to be something," I said. "There does. Fand was much older than the others when she killed herself. They said it was because she was stronger and that you're strong like she was, but there might be something else. We just have to think. I want to write the whole story down and try to figure it out."

"My God," she said, "listen to you. You find out that the only way I can avoid my inevitable suicide is to kill you, and instead of bolting you're planning a literary analysis of the whole thing."

I reached for her hand. "I'm sorry."

"And you thought *I* was crazy!" she said, but she let me lace my cold fingers with hers as we scrambled up onto the pier.

"I felt worse when I thought you might be," I said.

Kathleen made an incredulous sound. "Worse than you do now?"

"Yes." My throat closed around the words that would convey to her the wrenching loss I'd felt this morning, the hopelessness. It didn't make any sense to feel less hopeless now, but I did.

"And what about my father? Will hearing all this make him feel better than thinking I have some sickness I inherited from Moira? Can I even tell him any of it?"

I stopped walking and tugged Kathleen to a stop with me.

"You'll tell him all of it," I said. "Or we will. He'll believe us."

"Harry—"

I cut her off, shrugging my shoulder to call attention to the slippery case under my arm. "We've got proof, remember?"

Kathleen flinched. "Why did you take that thing? How can you even stand to hold it?"

"I didn't want it to just show up mysteriously."

"No." She shuddered. "That would be worse."

"And Robin has seen this knife before. Your mother had it."

"Oh God. She showed it to him?"

"No. He caught her looking at it one day."

"Just like Marie caught Caolinn," she murmured.

"In that way, yes. But the witches said they'd never told one of the mermaid's lovers the story before. Yet now they've told me, and we're going to tell Robin."

"Why?" Kathleen asked.

We'd reached the lighted streets of Doolin by then and stopped under a streetlamp near O'Connor's. Whenever the doors opened, the sounds of ragged music poured out, a male singer fronting a guitar-heavy band. I felt like we were in a bubble of strangeness, with the ordinary world pressing in.

"Because it's a fairy tale, love," I said. "Isn't that what you reminded me of this morning? It's a fairy tale come real, and anyone who knows fairy tales knows there's always a way to break the spell."

"Really?" She glanced down at the box I held and then jerked her head away.

"Really," I said. "There's got to be."

Act 3

ROBIN

Composer's Notes on Duet Between Soprano and Mezzo-Soprano

Kathleen had texted as promised when she and Harry had landed at the Shannon airport. Then Harry had sent several pictures of Doolin, tourist pictures: a plate of Irish breakfast, complete with blood pudding and real oatmeal; the view out a bus window down a narrow, hedge-choked lane; a placid gray horse nosing around a tumbled stone wall at the edge of a field. From Kathleen, Robin heard nothing more about the trip until he got another longer text saying that they'd touched down in Boston and wanted to tell him about the trip. Could they come visit for a few days?

Robin had said of course without even checking with Tae, who shook her head when he apologized for that and said of course it was fine. The bed in Kathleen's room had clean sheets on it; there were fresh towels in the bathroom. Robin had gone to the grocery store this morning and gotten shrimp for dinner, checked that there was white wine in the refrigerator.

And yet he knew that he was unprepared for this visit, because it wasn't just a visit. What had happened in Doolin that Kathleen couldn't tell him over the phone or that couldn't wait a few weeks? Robin felt the kind of pointless urgency that he often felt in the hospital thrumming through him as he sat at the piano late that afternoon and tried to attack the next scene of *The Scarlet Letter*, which introduced little Pearl as an uncanny, changeable child. After less than an hour, he pushed the bench back and the sheet music aside and gave this effort up as a bad job. It was going to be difficult to capture Pearl's strangeness without resorting to the kind of music-box melody that would make her seem just mad. Today Robin feared he'd write his own edginess and anxiety into the music.

He gathered up the pages of Hester's scene with the other women of the town. The ease with which he set Hester's voice up in contrast and conflict with other women's voices made him think suddenly about doing the same for Kathleen. Almost absently, setting down the finished scene, Robin reached for a fresh score sheet and scribbled notes. Singing against a lower chorus, Kathleen would escape vocally. But backed by other sopranos, she ran the risk of pushing the whole song higher and higher until there was nowhere to go. Above the struck-out words ~~Male Chorus~~ and ~~Mixed Voices?~~ he wrote, *Women's voices, perhaps discordant or atonal? Reference Gregorian chant?* He set the otherwise blank sheet down on top of the piano and stared at it awhile, hearing Kathleen's voice laid over the tightly woven texture of the music of that tradition, in which the vocal sacrifice of the one into the many produced a sound somehow all the more potent for its restraint and containment.

"Daddy?" Kathleen's voice, Kathleen's light, quick steps in the hall. Then she appeared in the doorway.

"We're all here," she said. "Tae pulled in right behind us."

Robin crossed the room and drew her close. She felt strange in his arms, like she was made of wire instead of bone, humming with both tension and a new and unfamiliar energy.

"Are you all right?"

She shook her head once against his shoulder, then pushed away.

"Kathleen—"

"Ro*bin*," she returned, a mocking lilt to her voice. "I'm fine." She turned to give Tae a hug. "Hi, Tae. You've let your hair grow. It looks beautiful."

"Thank you," Tae said. She was always careful not to act maternal with Kathleen, but this time when they drew apart she put her hand on Kathleen's cheek and held her still a moment. "We're glad to have you here," she said. Then she smiled and withdrew her hand. "Your father is so dull I can barely stand to be in the same room with him."

Kathleen laughed and Harry, appearing in the doorway of the kitchen with a tote bag over her shoulder, smiled slightly.

"Harry," Robin said, "come in, silly, put your bag down, have a glass of wine. Here—" He reached for the tote and she gripped the handles and took a quick step back.

"No," she said. She flushed and glanced at Kathleen. "No, sorry, I-I'll hang on to this. It's—it's not heavy."

Kathleen made a sound that wasn't a laugh. "It's quite light, actually."

"Kath—" Harry began, but Kathleen cut her off.

"Listen, Daddy, Tae . . ." She turned to face them both and again Robin thought there was something different about her, some new awareness of her body. It reminded him of the difference you might observe in a young singer who'd been taught how to breathe properly, or in a young musician who had finally learned how to hold his instrument so he wouldn't grow tired.

"We've got a story to tell you," Kathleen said. "And we're going to tell it to you. We found some answers in Ireland. But they're—it's not simple and it's not—" She broke off, crossed her arms, and tried again. "You'll understand everything when we tell you. And in the meantime I'm going to do what Harry's been asking me to do ever since we found things out and that is to lay off the black humor, which is, at the very least, confusing right now."

"At the very least," Robin said dryly.

"Well," Tae said, "should we start dinner and talk afterward?"

"That would be great," Harry said. "I'm starving. Can you help me with our bags, Kath?"

When they'd left the room, Tae turned to Robin. "Hello."

"Hello yourself." He smiled at her. "We've been invaded. How was your day?"

"It was fine. Are *you* all right?"

"I have no idea," Robin said. "I know neither what's happening nor what's happened."

"Kathleen seems . . ." Tae frowned. "I don't know. I haven't seen her since Christmas. It could just be that she's so thin and clearly tired."

"But it's not," Robin said. "It's something else. She warned us just now, I believe. You heard her: they've 'got a story to tell us.'"

THEY ATE THE shrimp with rice and a salad. They drank white wine, but only a bottle between the four of them and Harry didn't touch her glass. As soon as Tae rose to clear the table, Harry jumped to her feet and offered to do the dishes.

"They can wait," Tae said. She turned to Robin. "I have some scheduling work to do in my office—"

"Please," Kathleen said. "We want to tell you both, Tae."

Tae nodded. "Should we move to some more comfortable chairs?"

Some of the tightness in Harry's face visibly softened, as if the mere approach of the conversation was a relief. In the living room, she sat at one end of the sofa and Robin and Tae both waited for Kathleen to sit beside her. But Kathleen dropped onto the rug at Harry's feet, so Robin took the chair closest to Harry's seat and Tae settled in at the other end of the sofa, legs tucked up and her hands quiet in her lap.

"Now you have to promise not to say anything until we've finished," Kathleen said. "No interrupting to tell us we're crazy, okay?" She tossed her hair down her back and shook a finger at her father as if she were teasing him, but both words and gestures hung sharp and staccato in the air.

"Kathleen," Robin said. "Just tell us what happened."

They must have consciously orchestrated their telling of the story, they told it so well. They even switched parts, mimicking the push-pull of their experience in Ireland, first Kathleen foregrounding her skepticism and her despair against the backdrop of Harry's hopeful, eager search for answers in county records and the local pub. Harry began the tale of their encounter with the old nun, but Kathleen finished it, confirming that there had indeed been another pair of female lovers in her family. Then after the trip to Inis Mór and the boat ride, Kathleen was the hopeful, eager one, her voice rising and shaking, while Harry sketched out her growing fear and confusion as she followed Kathleen around Doolin and then into the cave. They never quite interrupted one another but they told the story in insistent, propulsive cadences, speaking sometimes by turn and sometimes together, not letting the narrative thread drop even for a minute.

They're afraid to stop telling *the story*, Robin thought. *They haven't thought past that, past telling it to me, to us.* He glanced at Tae, who was watching the girls. Her expression was akin to the one she wore when she was hearing a particularly difficult piece of music for the first time.

Robin himself felt trapped in the story and in their telling of it. When they reached the part in the cave and crossed into the impossible, he caught hold of the only dissonance they had not smoothed out—they clearly disagreed about when and how to show him the knife. Kathleen would have had it appear at the moment in the story when it did appear, bobbing in the water at her feet, while Harry had held off, perhaps wanting to wait and show it to him as proof after he had voiced his inevitable disbelief.

"Enough," he said. "Stop." He leaned forward and put his head in his hands. "Let me see it now, please."

"I'll get it," Harry said. She got up and left the room.

"I—she keeps it," Kathleen said into the silence that followed. "We figured that was the best way. I didn't want it. But the witches said—they made it seem like if I didn't take it from them, it would just appear in my suitcase or something. So Harry took it."

Harry came back carrying the tote she'd refused to part with earlier. She hesitated in front of Robin, torn between the impulse to remain standing and formally present him with the knife and the wariness that his abrupt demand for it had awakened in her. Finally she slipped past Kathleen and sat back down on the sofa, then fished the case out of the bag. Robin took it and rested it on his knees, the weight registering as familiar when it should not have. He'd never lifted it, that day he'd found it in Moira's drawer, he'd only opened it. He realized that the box felt like a laptop on his knees; it was just as heavy and nearly as large. The bizarre similarity nearly made him laugh and he thought of Kathleen's remark earlier about how she'd try to lay off the black humor. Clearly, the impulse was genetic.

"It opens . . ." Harry began, leaning forward to show him. But he remembered the catch on the underside. When he pressed it the lid rose smoothly, like the top of a great shell, and he saw the knife inside, fitted into brackets so cunningly made that they might have been part of the box itself.

Robin looked up. They were all watching him, Kathleen with desperate focus, her eyes fixed on his face so that they would not waver downward to the box. Harry was tense

and expectant and Tae—he could not read the expression
on Tae's face.

"Do you want to see it?" he asked her.

She got up and came around to sit on the arm of his
chair. Robin held the box up and Tae took it, balancing it
on her own lap and closing the lid, then feeling for the catch
and opening it again.

"It's hard to believe that this is as old as they told you
it was," she said. "And I can't think what it's made of, the
materials—this box—it's just like it was sliced off a pearl.
The striations along the lid here, if you think of it as a cross
section, that's exactly how a pearl develops, in secreted
layers like this." She ran one of her hands across the surface, shaping her palm to the curve. "And it feels very or-
ganic, the way it responds to the warmth of my hand—it's
like a violin that way."

Robin did laugh then. Tae looked up at the girls and
back to him.

"I'm sorry," she said.

Robin shook his head. "Don't be. You're demystifying it.
It's just an object to you, not a threat or a memory." He set
the case carefully on the coffee table.

"So you *do* remember it!" Harry said.

He gave her a level look. "I do."

"But why didn't you say so!" Kathleen cried, rising to her
knees. "You just sat there just now. And then you asked Tae
what she thought as if it was just an ordinary *thing* instead
of admitting right away—"

"Admitting!" Robin surged to his feet, Tae bending to the
side to let him out of the chair. He walked to the window
and spoke from there, his hands thrust into his pockets.

"You came in here, sat us down, told that story—you *wanted* me to say that it was impossible, that I didn't believe you. And then you could bring out that knife, knowing I'd seen it before—"

"*I* didn't know," Kathleen murmured. Robin shook his head.

"Harry did," he said. "And don't go down that path, Kathleen, not now. Was I supposed to tell you that your mother had hidden a knife in her lingerie drawer? You already knew she'd taken her own life, you'd known it since before I was ready to tell you. Why would I have told you about the knife? What could that possibly have done but cause you more pain, knowing that she was suicidal long before she died?"

"But that's not what the knife is for," Kathleen said, still speaking softly, her head down now, demure and passive but for the occasional cutting flash of her eyes. "So it didn't necessarily mean she was suicidal, having it there. If you'd told me—"

"Goddammit, Kathleen," Robin roared. She flinched. "I didn't know this story. I only knew there was a knife and then it was gone. Have you thought of what it means to me to know it now? What it means that my wife had that knife *in our bedroom*?"

Kathleen began to cry. No one else moved and for a moment her sobs were the only sound in the room. Robin turned back to the window. He remembered Moira saying to him once, fondly, *You're just not very good at being angry, Robin. It's not a bad thing, not to me, surely.* He couldn't remember ever being angry at Moira. She had been right. He wasn't terribly good at it.

A hand on his shoulder, very lightly. Tae had come up to stand behind him. He could not do anything to convey to her that he was glad she was there. He could only stand rigid, clenching and unclenching his fists. After another moment, she rested her hand briefly against the nape of his neck, then withdrew it.

"I'm going to get a glass of water," she said. "Would you like one, Rob?"

He nodded. His throat felt like it was lined with gravel. "Thank you."

"Anyone else?" Tae asked. No answer from the girls. Perhaps they nodded, or shook their heads. Tae left the room and Robin heard the refrigerator open, the clattering sound of the ice maker.

"We didn't think," Harry whispered. "We didn't—what you said earlier was right. We didn't think you'd believe us."

"I know," he said.

He swung around slowly. Kathleen had her head buried in Harry's lap, her shoulders heaving. Harry was stroking her hair, but her eyes were on Robin. Her face was stricken.

"You forget," he said, "that I grew up there."

"I—" Harry bit her lip. "I think I know what you mean, but—"

"I've seen the seals, heard them calling out across the water. I've walked to the edge of those cliffs. I've been out in the sea in a far smaller boat than the one you were in."

Kathleen picked up her head and pushed her hair out of her face, listening.

"It's not to say that kids grow up like this in Dublin," Robin said. "The Aran Islands are different, the islands and the coast around them. It's not a question of belief. You grow up knowing a white horse is unlucky, never mind why or how you know it. You see things wavering in the rain out on the water—a figure high on the cliffs that could be a woman or a bird. When you look again it's—she's—gone. You hear screaming in the wind and who's to say what it is?" He could hear his voice changing in his head before it emerged from his lips, the lilting, accented rhythm underscoring the words.

"You tell your father or your grandfather that it's just the wind and they stare at you like you're daft and suggest you get your hearing checked. But they don't say what *they* think it is, that screaming that sounds like a man in pain, or a wild creature. You don't speak the name of anyone who's gone to sea until they're safely home again. You leave a bowl of fresh milk under the eaves of the house when you want good luck in the morning, and when it's gone you wonder if the cat got any of it. You don't look too closely at the seals when you glimpse them in the sea near your boat. Yes, one of them looked almost like a man or a woman, but what's the use of knowing for sure? What difference will it make to you? Better just to leave well enough alone."

He paused. Tae brought him a glass of water then went back to her seat on the sofa and tucked up her feet again. Robin took a drink, felt himself adrift in the middle of the room. Kathleen got up, stumbled over Harry's feet, and came to him.

"I'm so sorry," she said. "I— You're right. I couldn't possibly have understood before. Now that I've been there, I do understand. I can't"—she swiped at her cheeks—"I can't imagine how she stood it. That water so close all the time! Daddy, she—she loved you very much, to have resisted it for so long."

He nodded. Kathleen reached for him and he held her hard with one arm, his water glass in the other hand. He felt his daughter holding herself stiff against him, the sheer force of her will even when she broke down. Moira used to melt into him, a succumbing that Kathleen would never allow. Robin pressed his lips briefly to her hair, then let go. Kathleen pushed herself away from him and crossed her arms.

"So if you do believe us," she said, "then—"

Robin cut her off. "I didn't say I believed you," he said. "I can't *not* believe it. And I *won't* believe it either, can you understand that, Kathleen? I left Doolin, took you away, so I wouldn't have to make those distinctions, and now here we are all the same. It's come home to us. You and Harry"—he glanced over to the sofa—"are fixated on the wrong thing. You think it makes a difference if I believe you? Or if Tae believes you? Or if we believe halfway? It doesn't matter."

"No," Harry said, "no. I see what you're saying. We still have to figure out what to do."

"You mean like, for example, I could go get ECT and hope it erases my memory of the whole trip," Kathleen said.

Robin lifted an eyebrow at her. She shrugged.

"Just outlining options," she said. "Your point is that the options haven't necessarily changed the way we thought they had."

"The point is you—we—still have options," Robin said. "Choices to make. Now you may make some different choices, because of what you learned—or *think* you learned—in Ireland. But that's why you went, isn't it?"

Harry nodded. "Yes. And I'm still glad we went. I think we did establish that Kath's not crazy, or if she is then so am I and so is the nun we met and"—she ran a hand through her curls—"you know what I mean. Which means that she can say no to ECT. She doesn't need it. The doctors were wrong."

"I wonder," Kathleen said, "if it'll be any better having that"—she pointed to the knife on the table—"hanging over my head instead of the idea of ECT."

Tae spoke quietly from her seat, her hands cupped around her water glass.

"There is a difference, I think," she said. "No one—not even the witches who gave you that knife—is telling you that using it in some way is a *good* idea, or that you'd be foolish *not* to use it. They've said that it's the only way, but they did seem—from what you told us—to understand why you wouldn't choose to take that way."

"As none of the others ever did," Kathleen said. A note of pride crept into her voice. "Seven women before me and not one of them has used that thing. I'm certainly not going to be the first. I think they knew that even when they gave it to me."

"So put it out of your mind," Robin said. "It's not a choice, not even the way we felt like ECT had to be a choice you considered—or we considered. It's not and we all know that. Let Harry keep it or"—he hesitated only a fraction of a second, hoped she didn't notice—"let me keep it."

Kathleen nodded, then smiled faintly. "This is terrible," she said, "but I have to pee."

She slipped out of the room. After a moment Harry got up and went to the kitchen for more water. Robin came over to the sofa and sat down beside Tae.

"Thank you," he said. "Thank you for being here. I'm afraid to even ask what you thought of all that."

Tae had her right hand tucked inside the napkin she'd wrapped around her water glass. She set the glass down on the table and slowly opened the napkin from around her index finger. A vivid bloodstain bloomed inside the folds and Robin saw a clean deep cut across the tip of her finger. It bled again freely as soon as she took the pressure off it.

"What—"

"The knife," Tae said. She nodded to it. "I was trying to make sense of it, just how it was made, while you were talking. I can't see a seam of any kind between the hilt and the blade. It's remarkable. And then I touched the tip of the blade, just touched it."

She looked up at Robin. The serenity he was used to finding in the depths of her dark eyes was not there. "I've no idea what it's made of, or how," she said, "but it's certainly sharp."

LATE THAT NIGHT, unsurprised to find himself unable to sleep, Robin sat at the piano in the dark. He struck a chord, then another, modulated up, down, into deliberate dissonance. He imagined the whole house straining to hear what he would play to vent his emotions after this evening, the windowed walls of his studio withholding even reflection while they waited. And the three women in the upstairs rooms—what might they expect to hear?

He read over the first scene of Act 2 again. It was still good. Robin felt a guilty impulse to pick up his pencil again and keep going, to work and not think about Kathleen at all. He rose from the piano bench and found his pencil, his highlighter, the photocopied packet of the pages of *The Scarlet Letter*. He could highlight lines of dialogue and think of other things, like how he was going to take his own advice to Harry and Kathleen and figure out what to do in the face of—or in spite of—this new possibility. That his daughter was a mermaid.

It would be frighteningly easy to believe. He didn't want to go to sleep just yet because he did not want to dream of Moira. She'd felt like a rare, slippery creature even when he'd known her. Why shouldn't she have been from some other world? And if she'd been—what she'd been meant to be—all along and he'd seen her in the water one day, who's to say he wouldn't have loved her all the same, with her fair freckled skin and her soft, tremulous mouth?

But I wouldn't have kept her, he thought. *I would have known better.*

He'd drawn a long, curling tail in the margin of the pages. He made a move to strike through it, but instead flipped the pencil over and erased the image. *I don't have to believe any of it*, he reminded himself. *I just have to decide what to do.* And really, what he was going to do was simple. He was not going to let his daughter die, whether that meant getting her psychiatric help or keeping her from giving in to despair because she couldn't live underwater. Moira, though she'd tried, had never found joy in anything. Kathleen had—Kathleen *did*. She could laugh at things, even laugh at the ridiculousness of saying, out loud, "Actually, I'm a mermaid." She had Harry, who knew everything and believed her, and she had him. She had friends, a career ahead of her, and her singing—no one could tell him that Kathleen didn't find joy in her singing.

But is it enough?

"It can be," he said aloud. "It has to be."

A sound behind him of someone drawing in a startled breath. Robin turned and saw Harry in the doorway.

"Sorry!" she said. "I didn't—I wasn't trying to sneak up on you."

She was in pajama bottoms and a T-shirt and she held a fat notebook against her chest. Robin thought of the night they'd had dinner in Boston, the fire in Harry's face as she'd begged him to take Kathleen to Ireland. *If she'd known Kathleen was a mermaid all along, she'd have loved her even more,* he thought. *She's in the middle of one of her beloved stories now, half fairy tale, half operatic tragedy.* Not kind of him, not at all, but he wasn't feeling kind. He was tired and drained and he could tell from the way Harry was holding her notebook that she had something else to show him.

He put down his pencil and gestured her into the room. "Come, sit," he said. "Do you want a drink?"

Harry shook her head. "I'm sorry to interrupt you," she said. "But I want to show you something—it's something I haven't even shown Kathleen yet, something I've been working on to try to figure out"—she sank onto the sofa and balanced the book on her lap—"if there's any way to *use* what we learned from the witches."

"I don't understand."

"Well, it's about the women, the ones who came before. I knew there had to be patterns and breaks in patterns so I wrote down everything we knew, everything I could remember from what the witches told us, and then I started trying to make dates match up, corroborate the details with the graveyard records and with internet research."

She opened the book and leaned forward to show him, flipping pages as she talked. Robin saw the names flutter past again and again, sometimes in a single list and sometimes each with a page to herself: Deirdre, Caolinn, Ceara, Muirin . . . There were printouts folded and tucked into the pages: articles on Irish uprisings, Selkies, mermaid lore. But Harry flipped through quickly, all of this just evidence of the work she'd already done, he didn't have to see it, certainly shouldn't question it, the important thing was—here.

Halfway through the book Harry had constructed another timeline. But when Robin tried to read it—he needed to take the book from her to do so—she stopped him.

"Read this first."

Another printout, a thick sheaf of pages, the top one a picture of a man dressed—and surely there was some irony here—rather like Nathaniel Hawthorne in the pictures Robin had seen of him, in black waistcoat and frock coat, high-collared white shirt and somber tie. But where Hawthorne was ruddy and handsome, this man was long-nosed and sunken-eyed. Robin turned to the next page and saw the title: "The Little Mermaid" and the first line: "Far out in the ocean, where the water is as blue as the prettiest cornflower, and as clear as crystal, it is very, very deep . . ."

"That's Hans Christian Andersen," Harry said, leaning in even more and tapping the picture. "I printed it out because of course she couldn't love him—I mean, I've read a lot about him in the past couple of days and it all fits. He was terribly ugly and awkward, sexually repressed or confused or both. He was in love with Jenny Lind for years, just from hearing her sing. Imagine if he'd heard Kathleen!"

Robin was skimming the story. "Harry," he said. "I don't

see what you're getting at. Even if it is true, that Andersen met—what was her name?"

"Fand," Harry said. "Well, according to the witches, first it was Maeve—that's what the prince called her—but then after she left him she changed it. I looked up the origins for the name 'Fand' and the choice makes so much sense." Her words tumbled over one another as she flipped through her notebook again. "Here it is. Fand was the 'wife of Manannán Mac Lir, the king of the great sea.' And she was both beautiful and powerful."

"And you think *this* Fand—Kathleen's ancestor—met Hans Christian Andersen and he wrote 'The Little Mermaid' about her."

"Yes." Harry nodded. "I could show you all the proof I found if you want. There are entries in Andersen's journal about a woman whom biographers have never identified, and letters that were found in Andersen's papers when he died that may have been from the same woman. But that's not the point. The point is this!" She turned the notebook around, finally, so Robin could scan the timeline she'd sketched across two pages, this one neat and unmarked by cross-outs or notations, just the women's names, birth and death dates—some with question marks by them—and the ages at which they died.

"What do you notice?" Harry asked. "Look at the ages. Do you see?"

He did see. "Fand was much older than any of the others when she died."

Robin ran his finger down the pages and despite himself felt some of Harry's desperate hope infecting him. That discrepancy couldn't be just a coincidence. They had all died before they were twenty-five, all but Fand. Fand had been forty. *Not exactly old*, Robin thought, feeling a twinge of wry amusement at Harry's—and his own—excitement that someone should have lived to be *forty*! And yet . . .

"I see it," he said. "But I don't see why. Harry, we know almost nothing about these women's lives. We can do nothing but speculate about why Fand lived so long. Maybe— and I hope this is true—she was just strong, she found some joys in her life. Kathleen can do that, especially with our help."

"Yes." Harry nodded. "Yes, that's true. I agree with you. But I have a theory about why Fand lived so long—" She drew in a deep breath, taking the plunge. "It means doing something for Kathleen, you doing something for her, but it's nothing bad or weird and it can't hurt anything. It can't hurt to try it."

Robin gave in to his amusement. "It's like trying to say no to a puppy," he said. He laughed when she flushed. "Go ahead. Tell me your 'theory.'"

"I think it was the story that kept her alive," Harry said. "If you consider the dates: she met Andersen when she was twenty-two—that's the winter he spent in Naples, going to the opera. He must have met her there. Then he writes this story and publishes it when she's twenty-three. It's a huge success right away, makes him famous, is read all over, translated into other languages. Everyone loves it. Not only children read his fairy tales, adults did too, and loved them. They called him a genius. And it was her story, Fand's story, that did it."

"And you think," Robin said, "that being a muse, of sorts, kept Fand going, kept her alive."

"I do," Harry said. "I think it's the *only* explanation. Like I said, I can show you other things I found that support it—and then she would have finally killed herself when Victoria, that's her daughter, was born."

"When she realized she'd passed the curse on," Robin said. He felt the sureness of this knowledge like swallowing a stone. He knew this truth in a way Harry could not. If Fand had not known—what if she hadn't known that her daughter would suffer the curse?—and then the baby wailed when she had to learn to walk . . .

"Yes," he said. "I can see why she might have killed herself then."

"Anyway," Harry said impatiently, "the point now, for us, is that being a muse, like you said, kept Fand going. Well, Kath can do more than that. She can sing her own story. And you can write it for her."

Robin opened his mouth to protest and couldn't, remembering suddenly the note he'd made this morning for the next song for Kathleen: *Women's voices, perhaps discordant or atonal?*

The sea witches, of course. And you'd stage them loosely encircling her, with some in the balcony seats as well, so that they wove their voices around her like a net she had to sing through. As for the other songs he'd written already, the songs that had emerged almost against his will, there were the three for Kathleen alone, in which she sang of pain and longing for the sea; there was the duet with the tenor who longed to possess her, the prince, of course; and the duet with the mezzo who loved and missed her, her sister mermaid.

"It doesn't hold up to a full five-act treatment," he said thoughtfully.

"What?"

"It might be just two acts." Robin got his own notebook from the piano and jotted down the titles of the songs he already had. "I think we can figure out structure later, actually."

"Wait." Harry looked bemused. "Does this mean you think it's a good idea?"

Robin stopped writing. "What you mean is 'Is it going to help Kathleen?'" he said, "and that I don't know. I understand why you think it might. She loves singing almost as much as she loves the sea—*needs* it almost as much. But whether singing an opera version of her story will literally save her life?" He shook his head. "I think that's one thing I've heard tonight that I wish I *did* believe, Harry."

"But you're making notes already."

"I'm making notes because I've already been writing songs for Kathleen," Robin said, "and you're right about us needing to do something to help her, something that—as you say—can't hurt. We need to do it for ourselves, so that we know we are doing something, no matter what we believe."

"You've been writing songs for her?" Harry asked. She cocked her head to one side. "Can I see one?"

She was suddenly a singer and not a desperate lover. Then Robin thought of something else and burst out laughing in earnest.

"You don't know what you've gotten yourself into, Harry," he said. "Because I'm a terrible librettist. So if I'm going to do this—if *we're* going to do this—that's your job." He took the pages of "The Little Mermaid" that he had set aside on the piano bench and handed them back to her.

"There," he said. "Work from that. If it's any help, with *The Scarlet Letter* I started by just highlighting the lines in the original text that I wanted to keep."

Aria for Soprano with Tenor Intrusion

I suppose time just *flies* when you're writing an opera. You're inspired, you're excited, you're doing something creative and productive and working with this wonderful, talented collaborator . . . you stay up far too late working on it, you mutter to yourself about "balancing lyricism with clarity" or "letting the dissonance prevail in this passage," you pick up conversations from the day before exactly where you left off and expect everyone else around you to understand what the hell you're talking about. You ignore your girlfriend. Or your daughter.

In Robin's case, as I point out to Tae, he's been doing both. But Tae's no help. She shakes her head, says he's always like this when he's composing and he's always composing. Because, you know, he's a composer, Kathleen. This is his job. And she gives me a look that makes me wonder what things would have been like if she'd started dating my father when I was still a teenager. As in, how much of my shit would this woman have put up with?

Not a lot, is my guess. And now poor Tae is basically my keeper for the summer. She works, of course, but she keeps semi-regular hours, unlike Harry and Robin, who are now holed up in the studio for long stretches of the day writing. They check in on me, eat meals with me. (Well, they eat and I push things around, different piles every meal. Sometimes I color code, sometimes I do it by texture.) But they're far too absorbed to pay me much attention. They don't even notice the food pushing. Tae is the one who takes hold of my wrist one morning, circles it easily with her slim strong fingers. She catches me as I put my cereal bowl in the sink and we stand there a minute. I have the urge to fight her, but I don't. Her hand is wet.

"If you don't start eating soon," she says, "you'll have to go to the hospital."

I shrug. See, I can be a sulky five-year-old in *every* way!

"Your father wanted to say something to you," Tae goes on. "And Harry's been fretting for days. She thinks if she says something it'll only make things worse."

This is probably true. I don't say anything. "I don't care if you don't want to be in that studio with them, Kathleen," Tae says, "but"—this is said very gently—"you're not going to starve yourself in my house."

"I could leave," I say. "That would solve the problem for everyone."

Harry would flare up here and I'd get a good fight; Robin would get very rigid and sarcastic and push me further. Tae doesn't let go of my wrist, though she's holding it so loosely her clasp is like a bangle bracelet I could easily shrug off.

"You could," she says, "but I wish you wouldn't. I'd miss your cheerful company."

I laugh, which hurts because I've been holding myself so stiff for so long, stomach muscles in and diaphragm contracted, throat tight against the horrible things I want to say, fists clenched around the terrible things I want to do.

It is June. I've been a mermaid for a month, give or take a few days. Of course that's not right—I've been a mermaid my whole life. But before I knew what I was, I only felt sick and strange and frightened a lot of the time. The rest of the time I was singing or in love with Harry or buying a pretty dress or saying outrageous things to make people laugh. Now I'm a mermaid and everything is wrong *all the time*. Food tastes funny, feels funny in my mouth; wine makes my head hurt and my stomach roil; clothes feel more abrasive than ever, every tag or rough seam dragging like teeth across my skin. The sun is too hot and too bright, the ground too hard and dry, and people, even the people I love, look as clumsy as clay figures if I stare at them too long.

Harry has this idea that "Art" with a capital *A* can save me. She thinks that my singing is at least as important to me as the water is and that if I can sing my story—or some version of a part of the first mermaid's story—I'll feel better. Live longer.

SHE TOLD ME this the day after we got here, while I was still waking up from a dream—one of my new recurring dreams of swimming underwater in which my movement through the water makes sense, in which I can almost catch a glimpse, when I turn my head, of something fanning out behind me. I kept my eyes shut while she talked; I was still trying to reconcile the physical sensations of my body in the dream with my body lying in the bed. I suppose I was not what anyone would call receptive to Harry's proposal.

"Your father's already written all these songs for you," she said. "I think that's what actually sold him on the idea, that he already had songs written, and they're beautiful."

"You've heard them?"

"Not all of them," she said. "Just a snippet, late last night. But it's beautiful. It's— I can't explain it. You need to hear it, Kath. And if we all work together—I'm going to work on the libretto and Robin just needs to find a musical through line for the pieces he's already done—"

"So what do you need me for?"

"To sing, silly. To listen to it and offer suggestions. Kathleen, come on, get up."

"No," I said. I pulled the pillow over my head. "Wake me up when the opera's done."

So I HAVE only myself to blame for being ignored now. I said I didn't want any part of the opera. Well, I don't. It's stupid. And it's not just that it's a stupid idea that makes no sense. It's also so transparent, on both their parts, that I feel this kind of molten rage whenever I see them working on it. I'm supposed to forgive them already, before they've failed, for trying to help, for putting their love and their talents into this desperate gesture. My father has postponed his commission for *The Scarlet Letter* to work on this instead, which is this great professional and personal sacrifice. Except it's not. When he told his big donor about this new project, he apparently also played him some music from it, stuff he'd already written, and the guy liked it so much he's underwriting this opera too. And Harry pulled out of her contract with Central City, which was supposed to take up most of her summer, then flew back up to Boston and met with her advisor, who got excited too, so now writing and directing this opera is going to be part of her senior performance thesis. She gets to write and do research, which she certainly loves at least as much as she loves singing, and they both—she and my father—are just doing it because they love me so much and they want to save me. Screw them. They can't save me from this.

Some things I try, to save myself or not.

I TRY TO conquer the knife.

I do not take it out of the box, but I do everything else I can think to do. Just counting the layered striations on the box takes forever. I count them and lose count and start again. I open and shut the lid. I touch the handle with my fingertip, tilt the box up so I can see the angle and sharpness of the blade, the almost invisible serrations running down its inside edge. I imagine holding it, lifting it, plunging it—I put it away. I walk around the house, shaking all over, my feet throbbing.

Some of the women drowned themselves. But drowning would be either giving up or madness, the kind of madness we've now apparently decided I don't suffer. It would be nice to think that if I just walked out into the sea and waited for my lungs to fill, that some magic might take pity on me. But it won't. Too easy, doesn't work that way.

Others used the knife. I think they must have been the stronger ones. When I can't stand it anymore, I'm going to use the knife too. I don't want anyone—Harry, my father, the witches—to think that I didn't know what I was doing, that I died hoping for anything but death.

I TRY TO run away.

Florida again? California? Europe? I have a dozen itineraries stored on travel websites. I slip out of bed in the middle of the night and pull one up—a resort in Bali where the rooms are built over the water so tropical fish swim right under your feet—and click through picture after picture, the colors as vivid and false as a backdrop.

Some nights I stare until my eyes burn. Behind me, Harry is a small huddled lump in the bed. We bounce off each other all day, barely speaking, me glaring when I catch a worried look, getting her back with a snide comment about "her" opera. I have to go as far away as I can—all the way to Bali—to come back to her, to crave the warm, flowery smell of her body, to put my arms around her and feel relief at rediscovering her. In bed, in the abrupt darkness that falls when I turn off the computer, Harry is softer and lighter than I remember or expect. I pretend that she is still asleep, though I know she isn't. I just want our dream selves to find each other.

One night, she kisses me, pulls back.

"Are you all right?" she asks.

And I ask in return, my hands in her hair, "Where is the knife?"

I just want to know. I want to know where it is, so I can

picture it there, safely shut in its box. But now of course, instead of wherever it *was*, it is here, in the bed, between us.

"My God, Kathleen," Harry says. Her voice breaks. She fumbles in the darkness, pulling on her clothes. I know she can't sleep with me now and I start to cry. I cry until my throat hurts, until I gag, until Harry has to turn on the light and sit and rock me. I cry until we are both so exhausted that we fall asleep, but when I wake up in the morning she is gone.

I TRY TO think about things I will miss.

I watch my father at the piano, a single off-center frown line appearing between his eyes. I will miss his hands, the sureness in them and the grace. The first time I saw a professional concert pianist I was startled by how ugly her hands were, the knuckles swollen and the backs of her hands seething with veins. I thought every pianist had beautiful hands, because Robin does.

I will miss his frown line. I used to stand on his lap and order him to frown so I could run my finger down that line. I will miss his trick of raising only one eyebrow, a trick I inherited from him. Does that make me human after all?

I walk through the house and make lists of things. I will miss my blue washed silk dress, which is so soft it almost doesn't hurt to wear. It was the first thing I paid for with money I earned singing. I will miss the view from Robin's studio in the fall, when the birch trees turn red. I will miss Tae's spicy scallops with orange peel.

I lie on my bed and think of more: I will miss Puccini and Mozart and Offenbach. I will miss Tom and Carianne.

I will miss hearing Harry sing. I will miss singing. I will miss applause and the smell of roses, the cold fresh scent of them when they are first thrust into my arms.

I TRY TO go without water. And while I am doing this last idiotic experiment, I am finally saved, from myself anyway.

I plan the no-water thing carefully. I go a whole day without showering or drinking water or washing my hands. I use hand sanitizer in the bathroom instead of soap. It's the kind that has little antibiotic "beads" in it and as it dries I can feel these like grains of sand on my palms. I have trouble sleeping that night. My feet hurt and my scalp itches and the skin on my hands feels too tight. The next morning I braid my hair and pin it up so it won't rub on my neck, put on an old sundress, nothing else. I stay in my room until I know Tae has left for rehearsal, so I don't have to eat breakfast or go near the sink. I go out to the living room and turn on the TV. From downstairs I can hear the piano, a fragment of melody that sounds like water running, and I turn the TV up. There's nothing on that I want to watch, but I watch all morning. I pace the room, kneading the soles of my feet into the carpet and inviting the pain, then flopping down on the sofa and pointing my toes in the air to feel the stabbing change to a throb when my weight is off my feet.

When I can't stand the TV anymore, I turn it off and hear Harry singing something with the rhythm of a prayer or a plea, an incantatory melodic line that starts in her bottom register and rises to the top. She sounds like a swimmer surfacing from deep water, her voice breaking on the last words, which I think are *little sister*. But I am covering my ears, one hand still holding the TV remote, so I can't be sure.

I flee back to my room, put the first disc of *Tristan and Isolde* in the CD player. I don't even have to go to the bathroom. My mouth hurts horribly and it feels as if I'd bled into it and the blood had somehow dried on my teeth and tongue.

Harry has her suitcase out, half-filled because classes start next week. I can't think about anything but water. Even Wagner isn't drowning out the music I heard this morning, which, now that it is playing in my head, is not just water running but water receding, or maybe water being left behind. The Little Mermaid leaves the sea behind, doesn't she, when she staggers out onto the beach on her new legs? I wonder if that's what my father was playing, that moment in the opera. If so, it was good. He got it right. I should tell him.

But I don't. I pull out my suitcase and start throwing things into it, then just at it. I think about ransacking Harry's suitcase just to mess up her neat piles, but she'll think I was searching for the knife. Maybe I am. I put my hands over my face. My fingers are cold and I feel dirty.

When Harry opens the door, I jerk my hands away, grab for something to fold so I'll seem busy. But she isn't coming to check on me. She holds out her cell phone.

"Tom," she says. "He says if you think you can get away from him by just not returning his calls, you should try harder." She makes her "Tom is so annoying" face, but she's trying not to smile and without thinking I smile back at her. Trust Tom—and the familiarity of our responses to him—to ease the sharp edges between us.

I take the phone and talk to Tom. He has been singing all summer and his voice fizzes in my ear. We set up a dinner date back in Boston. I walk into the bathroom while we talk and catch sight of myself in the mirror. I am hollowed out, my hair several shades darker than usual because it's dirty and pulled back so tight.

"I saw our master class diva at a fund-raiser a few weeks ago," Tom is saying. "As soon as I introduced myself as a conservatory student she asked about you."

"Shut up."

"She did! Wanted to know if you'd died lately, stabbed yourself, been burned alive, you know, the usual cheerful soprano bullshit."

"Fuck you," I say, but I am smiling. "What did you tell her?"

"I said you were committed to singing only roles with happy endings, that you weren't into all that heavy shit."

"Tom," I say warningly. My reflection is trying not to laugh. If only he knew.

He sighs. "I may have suggested that you were auditioning to sing voice-over for an upcoming Disney movie."

"You know this means you're buying dinner."

He is gleeful. "It will be worth it. You should have seen the expression on her face."

I close Harry's phone carefully, go look for her to give it back. I stop halfway down the stairs to my father's studio and sit on the step. The staircase is open and I can see the two of them, Robin standing by the window while Harry types something furiously on her laptop.

"Can you play the prince's part again?" she asks, without looking up from the screen.

Robin goes to the piano and plays. "But it wouldn't be the piano," he says. "It would be the string section there."

"I know," Harry says. "That's okay. I just needed to hear it."

I almost ask him to play it again. The sound is yearning, though it doesn't make me think of water at all. It makes me miss Robin and Harry, though they're sitting right there, makes me miss them back weeks and weeks, all the days I spent shutting them out.

I think about Tom's mockery of the diva, about the difference between choosing a tragic ending and choosing not to choose one. There is a difference, isn't there? For a moment, talking to Tom, I knew—remembered—that there is a difference. I don't believe there's a happy ending here, and I've been so angry at Harry and my father for trying to make me believe that there is. But maybe they haven't. The music they're writing—the mermaid leaving the sea behind, the prince longing for her, her sisters pleading with the witches to help her—maybe Robin and Harry are just choosing someone else's tragic ending over mine. Watching them through the stair railings, I can feel how hard it will be to come back to them, like struggling to shore after swimming out as far as I can go. I've forgotten to conserve my strength for the way back. I am tired just contemplating it, and also abruptly too dizzy to move. Whose stupid idea was it to go without water for two days? That's not tragic, that's just pathetic. I get up, holding on to the banister, and my father hears me and comes quickly to the foot of the stairs.

"Are you all right?"

I nod. "I brought Harry her phone."

Robin comes up a few steps to take it from me and I back away.

"I'm smelly," I say. "I need to take a shower."

He takes me in, nods gravely. "Are you going to?"

"Yes."

He starts to say "Good" and then stops. "Well," he says, "enjoy it. We'll be wrapping up here in a little while."

I want to say that it sounds beautiful so far, from what I've heard. I want to say I'm sorry, that I think I understand now what he's trying to do. But it hurts to talk, I'm so thirsty, and I can't get the words out. I go up the stairs to the kitchen, drink three glasses of cold water in a row, gasping in relief between swallows, then take a fourth glass to my bathroom and start the shower. I step under the spray and start to cry as the water pours over me, tearless sobs of relief that I don't even try to stifle as I soak my hair and shampoo it, lather soap to wash my poor feet. I tip my head back and let more water trickle into my mouth, even though my stomach hurts from having drunk so much water so fast.

I know what I can do to try to tell Robin and Harry that I'm going to be okay, that I've gotten over myself. I'll ask if we can go out to dinner. Someplace ridiculous, with a big list of flavored margaritas and food that's terrible for you, like breaded zucchini and coconut fried shrimp. There's nothing tragic about going out to dinner at a restaurant like that, and you can't give up on life and eat something called a zucchini zircle all in the same night.

SO WE GO to dinner, my clean hair soft and damp across my shoulders, and I tell them that I've heard a little of what they're working on. I expect Harry to jump on this, insist that I listen to everything, but she seems flustered.

"You heard the music, is all," she says. "It's gorgeous! The lyrics are . . ." She shrugs, more self-conscious than I've ever seen her. "It's really hard to get it right."

"Harry," I ask, "have you ever *listened* to operatic lyrics?"

"I know, I know, most of them are better off not translated. But I can't just deliberately write something that sounds stupid."

"For the record," Robin puts in from behind his menu, "I keep trying to tell Harry how much of an improvement she is on my previous librettist, but she won't listen."

"That's because his previous librettist was Nathaniel Hawthorne." Harry snorts, though she is amused. "And among other things, he's dead. I certainly hope I'm an improvement over him."

"But you love Hawthorne," I say.

"True," she says. "But I'm not going to write your—this— story in language like that, so formal and removed. I want it to feel more . . ."

More what? I want to ask. But our appetizers have arrived, in big baskets lined with grease-splotched paper. We are all starving, which is my fault; it's as though no one else has been allowing themselves the things I've been scorning: food, drink, laughter, touch. I find Harry's hand under the table and run my fingertips across her palm, making her shiver.

"Stop that," she murmurs, then she reverses the gesture and I shiver too. I can't remember the last time that happened, when I felt, in a touch, the same thing Harry felt.

I do not have to choose the tragic ending. I am choosing not to choose it.

When we go to bed that night, I reach for Harry right

away. We both cry, silently, having to kiss away tears, but we do not talk about the crying or stop making love, not even when Harry fumbles for a Kleenex from the box on the nightstand. I keep moving beneath her, my hands on her hips and my mouth on the cord in her neck, a touch that always makes her shudder. She blows her nose and then tips her head back, gasping, grips my shoulders tight. Later, she sinks down beside me and wipes my wet face with the edge of the sheet.

"Go to sleep," she murmurs. "You're so tired."

"I have to start packing tomorrow," I say.

"That's true."

I feel her waiting in the darkness. I nestle closer, glad that I can, that I want to.

"I hate packing," I say.

"I know."

"And I'm so bad at it."

"You are. You're the worst packer I've ever met."

"Could you help me?"

I can feel her mouth shaping a smile against my shoulder. "Go to sleep."

"But I can't now. I'm worried about packing."

She bites me gently. "I'll pack for you."

"Really?"

"Really. Now shut up and go to sleep."

IT IS THE first night in weeks when I do not dream of the sea or, if I do, I don't remember it. It is all sweetness and light for a while after that, long enough to get us packed and back to Boston. Robin tries hard for casual as he sees us off. He is, after all, coming up in only a few weeks to keep working with Harry. Then he'll make several trips up this semester while they finish the opera. He may even rent a place in Boston next semester when it goes into rehearsals and performances. So there is nothing to worry about. He'll see us both often enough to keep an eye on me. Still he hugs me hard before I get into the car, cups one hand across the back of my head and kisses my hair lightly before he lets me go. It's how he used to send me off when I was little, when it was just the two of us against the world.

I pull back, smile brightly at him. He gives me a little shake, his hand on the back of my neck.

"Quit it, Kathleen," he says. "I know you're hanging by a thread."

"It's a strong thread, though," I say. "More like a thin rope, how's that?"

"I love you," he says. "Can you use that to strengthen the rope?"

I fling myself back against him. He used to hold my feet under the water for hours even when he didn't know why it helped. Now he's writing an opera for me and I know that he doesn't think that will help either. It's just all he can think of to do.

"I love you too, Daddy," I whisper. "That doubles the rope, triples it even."

I slide into the passenger seat and watch Robin as Harry backs down the driveway. Tae goes to stand beside him and he puts his arm around her, but he does not take his eyes off the car. Just before we turn the corner out of sight, he raises his hand to wave goodbye and I wave back, though I'm not sure he sees.

Harry and I listen to terrible music in the car because I

insist on controlling the playlist and only playing one-hit wonders. By the time we hit Connecticut she is threatening to pull over and make me walk the rest of the way.

There is a bad moment back in the apartment in Boston. I am in the bathroom putting things away when I hear Harry in the bedroom, an indrawn breath as if she's cut herself and tried not to cry out. I stick my head around the door.

"What's wrong?"

"Nothing." She turns quickly, throws a T-shirt over the suitcase, but I still catch sight of the knife box.

"Did you cut yourself on it?"

"No." She shakes her head. "No, it's fine. It's closed. I'll put it away."

But she is white. She goes back to unpacking, unpacks around the huddle of cloth hiding the box. I watch her a minute before I guess.

"Did you try to leave it with Robin?"

"I did leave it with him," she says. "We agreed that I would. I put it on the table in the studio this morning."

"They said it would follow me."

"I know!" she snaps. "I'm the one who asked, remember? I hoped that maybe Robin, since he'd had a connection to your mother and to you—I thought it might work to leave it with him." She snatches the shirt off and glares defiantly at the box. "And I guess I wasn't quite prepared for the whole 'mysterious box popping up where you least expect it' routine."

I don't want to think about the implications of the knife migrating from Robin's studio to Harry's suitcase—my suitcase, actually, those are my clothes she's unpacking. All my attempts to fend off tragedy fall a little flat in the face of such magic. If the knife can follow me, then there's really no escape.

But, I remind myself, they *told* us that this would happen. Nothing's changed, no new threat has appeared. Same knife, same curse, different day.

"You know where you should put it," I say, "if you really don't want me to find it?"

"Where?"

"In with the cookbooks. I'll *never* check there."

Harry doesn't laugh, but her face relaxes fractionally. "Very funny."

Score one for those of us hanging on by threads.

"So," Tom says, "Harry tells me *not*, on pain of death or dismemberment, to ask about your trip to Ireland. But how was the rest of your summer?"

We are having dinner at a tiny French restaurant so layered in toile—curtains, tablecloths, overlays on top of tablecloths, napkins on top of overlays—that I feel irresistible giggles rising, the kind of delicious silliness I haven't felt capable of in months. I lean over the table and whisper conspiratorially, so that Tom has to lean in to hear me.

"I'll tell you about my summer if you answer one really important question for me," I say.

"What?"

"Is the food here toile too?"

The waiter chooses that moment to slip the bread basket onto the table, covered in a toile napkin of course. We hold out until he's gone and then cackle with laughter.

"You're terrible," Tom says finally, taking a drink of his

water. "God, I missed you this summer. There were some talented singers, great connections and all that, but they were all so deadly *dull*."

"All of them?" I ask, arching a brow at him. "How was the bass-baritone contingent?"

Tom does his best impression of blasé. The deeper the man's voice, the harder Tom falls for him, with a hairy barrel chest a highly desirable secondary allure.

"Well, we were in rep with *Boris Gudenov*," he says, "but Boris was ancient, of course."

"And this stopped you?"

Tom considers this. "I never said that." And then, as I dissolve into giggles again, "Shall we get a bottle or go by the glass?"

I shake my head regretfully. "I'm off wine, I'm afraid."

"Harry's orders?" Tom asks.

"No! It just—it's not agreeing with me lately."

"Neither is food, apparently," he says. "You are planning to eat, I hope? After all that about how I had to buy tonight, I'd feel stupid if I ended up only paying for one meal."

"I'm planning to eat," I say. "It's just—it was a long summer."

"You're killing me," Tom says. "Honest to God, Kathleen, between Harry using her 'this is serious, Tom' voice and you looking, frankly, like shit—beautiful as ever, don't get me wrong, but still like shit—I'm dying to know what the hell is going on." He picks up his glass of water, puts it down without drinking anything. "Don't look at me like that," he says, and suddenly, alarmingly, he *is* serious, his eyes softening under the silky blond bangs that fall so artfully over his forehead.

"You don't have to tell me," he says. "Make something up. Harry's having an identity crisis, wants to grow her hair out and start singing Wagner in a breastplate and horned helmet. Something like that."

Even as I laugh, choking on a bite of bread, my throat tightens on the awareness that Tom loves me, that I love him, that he'll be another casualty of this story before it's over, one way or another. How much do I want him to know?

"Harry hasn't gone over to Wagner," I say. "She's writing a libretto with my father, did she tell you that?"

Tom nods, cautiously intrigued again. "She wants me to sing the male lead, which I have absolutely no time for this year, not if I'm going to graduate in May, but I said I'd come by later this week and run through a few of the arias with them."

"You'll be singing the prince, then. You'll be very good."

"Kath, I'm not doing it, I told you, there's no way in hell I can take on a lead role in a student production on top of everything else. Harry just needs to hear the part sung to get a sense of how it's working, that's all." He cocks his head. "Are *you* singing in it?"

The waiter comes to take our order, so I'm saved for a moment. I ask for sea scallops and another glass of water. When I turn back to Tom, he's still waiting for me to answer.

"I don't know," I say. "I— They haven't asked me to yet. It's complicated. I-I think I'm going to have to but—"

"You're going to *have* to? Why? Because it's Harry's project? Or your father's?"

"No, silly. Because they're writing it for me."

Tom contemplates me a long moment. "So you're the

Little Mermaid," he says, so matter-of-factly that I start visibly, feel the pulse beating in my throat. But of course, he didn't mean it like that.

"Harry told me what the story was," he says, "how they're retelling 'The Little Mermaid.' What's the catch at the end, that the mermaid can either kill the prince and be a mermaid again or let him live and then she dies?"

"Something like that."

"Only Harry's changed the story—très, très operatic, from the sound of it. I mean, here the mermaid is like Medea or Salome or—who's the one whose husband sacrifices their daughter to get good winds for sailing?"

"Clytemnestra."

"Right. Lots of righteous, vengeful female power here."

I put my napkin in my lap, unfolding it carefully. She changed the story. Of course she did. But it had never occurred to me. "How did she—how is the story different, do you know?"

Tom shakes his head at me. "You don't know any of this already, seriously?"

"Long summer, remember?"

"Well, in Harry's version—Harry and Robin's version, I guess—the mermaid *does* kill the prince, lets his blood run all over her legs, sings this triumphant aria about returning to the sea, changes back into a mermaid and dives out the window, or maybe vice versa." Tom makes a flipping motion with his hand, like a fish leaping up out of the water and then back in. "You know, maybe she dives out the window first *then* turns back into a mermaid. I don't remember. But that's how it ends. Poor prince—me, if I wanted it to be—

dead on his wedding night and the mermaid back where she belongs."

I keep my hands in my lap so he won't see them shaking. "So is that a happy ending or a tragic one?"

He considers this. "Happier than the original, certainly. Much more surprising. And more satisfying too, don't you think? I mean, I kind of like the idea of the girl who's sacrificed everything for love finally taking it back, don't you?"

"You would," I say, more snidely than I intend, but that's because I'm deflecting madly here. I'm shaking everywhere, fine tremors running even along the soles of my feet. *She's changed the ending.* So if I sing this role, I sing a different ending. I sing the ending that would circumvent the curse.

"Kathleen?" Tom waves a hand before my face. "Earth to Kathleen? First you get snarky and then you go all vacant on me."

"Sorry," I say. I focus on him again, his fine-boned face as familiar as Harry's, his voice as lithe and glimmering as he is, whether he's singing or tossing off sarcastic gibes. He won't believe it, I know, but he won't think I'm crazy either. He'll cast what I tell him into a kind of net of the impossible, along with his own dreams of finding a man he desires who will love him back, nailing an audition at the Met, seeing his parents on their feet in the audience some night, clapping until their hands ache.

The waiter sets down our plates, cautions Tom that the edge of his is still hot.

"He'll have a glass of wine," I say. And when Tom raises an eyebrow, I nod, toss my hair back from my shoulders.

"You're going to need it," I say as the waiter walks away.

"And then maybe another one, after I tell you the whole story."

"Do we have to wait until the wine is actually in my hand before you start?"

"Not unless you want to."

We smile at each other. Tom carves petals from a butter rosette and spreads them on his bread. I watch him. I don't know how to begin.

"Talk, Kathleen," he says, "or so help me I'll stab you with my butter knife." He does an abbreviated fencing thrust across the table.

"So," I say, "I'm a mermaid."

Tom looks at me, down at his butter knife. He chews, swallows.

"A mermaid," he says. "As in, fish tail, breathes water, sings sailors to their deaths?"

"I don't know about the last part."

"But the rest."

"Yes."

"And you know this how?"

"Well," I say, suddenly feeling bubbles of laughter rising again, a hilarity to the telling of the story. "A seal told me," I say, "but I didn't fully believe him. It was the sea witches who convinced me, and Harry."

"The sea witches." Tom puts his knife down, just so, on the edge of his bread plate. "On second thought," he says, "let me wait for my wine, okay?"

SO I TELL him everything. He takes it all in so calmly that assuring him at the end—as I had planned to do—that he doesn't have to believe me seems unnecessary. His only odd comment, as we are waiting for the waiter to bring Tom's credit card back, is about the way that Harry and Robin have changed the ending of Fand's story.

"So in the opera they're writing, you—if you agree to do it—would be playing the original mermaid, right? Only onstage you do it, you kill the prince."

A lurch in my stomach at the thought, like opening-night nerves.

"You know more than I do about the plot," I remind him.

"But what exactly is supposed to happen if it works? Will you suddenly not be in pain anymore?"

I shake my head. "I don't know." I've never thought beyond the curse.

"I wonder," Tom says, "what Harry and Robin are hoping for."

I DO NOT ask Harry what she's hoping for. I do not ask Robin, either, when he comes up a few weeks into September. It's enough that I'm being stitched back into the world every day, waking up in our apartment, hearing the obnoxious morning radio show that's the only thing that wakes me up, smelling the Turkish coffee that our upstairs neighbor brews, so strong it smells more like licorice than coffee. As I walk to class, people I know wave me down, tell me excitedly about their summer at Glimmerglass while I shift from one foot to the other and listen as hard as I can to block out the pain.

I fall on my classes like I've been starving for music, which I have. I did less singing this summer than I think I've ever done in my life. For a moment at the start of each private lesson, I'm afraid I will open my mouth and nothing will come out, my voice severed by my new knowledge like Fand's tongue by the witches' blade. It never happens, but the fear never abates either.

Tomorrow is Halloween. Robin is coming in again today and staying for a couple of weeks. Carianne is having a Halloween party, only scary costumes allowed. I have been threatening to go as Bella Menotti, my voice professor, who is glaring at me right now over the glasses that she deeply resents needing. She's compensated for their diminishing effect on her persona by dying her hair jet-black and wearing it swept up in red jeweled combs on either side of her face. She looks like a drag queen doing Maria Callas doing Carmen, which makes me giggle.

"Yes? Kathleen? This song is funny?"

God, I hate her. I shouldn't; she's an amazing teacher. But she's definitely of the tough-love school of coaching. I don't know that I've ever heard her say anything purely complimentary to me. Harry thinks all voice teachers must hate their students, because if they're training us then it means their own career is over or fading. And Bella had a brilliant career, cut short by nodules that wouldn't go away. But the things she snarls at me for are so particular to *me* that it's hard to imagine that she says them out of envy. Bella says my voice is too clear, too fluid, unmarred by roughness or a tremor or audible break. And apparently this makes me unfit for the great tragic roles, because it's those breaks in the voice that the audience is really listening for, the moments when the singer stumbles that make her real and lovable to them.

Ha. If only actual stumbling counted. Right now my feet

burn so much I'm curling them up and trying to stand just on the sides of them.

"Stand up straight!" Bella snaps. "Weight evenly on both feet, for God's sake. You'd think no one had ever taught you anything. Now, milady"—she sweeps me a deep, ironic bow, red silk scarf trailing to the floor, from her seat at the piano—"whenever you're ready."

So I sing a Handel aria that's part of my repertoire and as I sing I sink back into myself. I feel the song in my belly and in my throat, in my ears and behind my eyes—and then Bella is smacking the top of the piano to get my attention.

"Your voice has changed." I didn't think it was possible for her to glare at me any more fiercely. "Sing 'the balmy ease of sleep' again."

I do.

"Again."

I know what she's going to say before she says it, because by the third time I sing the line, I can hear the difference. It's a delicate song, meant to be delivered with silvery clarity, which I have, and tremendous vocal control, which I have also always had. But now I sound like I'm reining it in. It has the effect of making the song sound not merely gentle but faded, as if the listener's awareness of how much more my voice *could be doing* ruins the experience of what it *is* doing.

Bella is frowning. "Your voice has opened up, gotten too big for anything so small as this. Can you feel it?"

I nod.

"I can feel your voice in the back of my head, in my neck muscles, when you are singing," she says. "That's how the listener can hear you holding back. It comes out, no matter how you try to hide it."

"Do you want me to try it again?"

"No." She shakes her head, still frowning, riffles through the music on the stand in front of her. Secretly, she is pleased by this development, because it means I need her more.

"Try something else," she says. "Do the one I'm not supposed to know about, the one you've been working on for a year now."

"'Suicidio!'? You said—"

"I know what I said." Bella waves a dismissive hand, erasing the past. "Find your music."

I find it, slightly crumpled from having spent months shoved into the back of my portfolio. I scan the pages as I spread them out in front of me—*Piombo esausta fra le tenèbre!*—and recall the cave where the witches met us, the darkness into which they spoke to us at first, then the lights coming up everywhere and nowhere, lights that illuminated nothing.

"Well?" Bella is a study in impatience. I shift my stance—*Weight evenly on both feet, for God's sake!*—and nod for her to play the opening bars. La Gioconda doesn't have to *want* to kill herself, I realize suddenly. She can simply be contemplating it as a reasonable option, or an inevitable end. No one's liked to hear me sing this aria because it's always so bitter, so harsh. But if I sing the longing in it—the longing for darkness, the longing for release—even the word itself, *suicidio*, is a beautiful word if sung correctly, open-throated and with a caress of the soft *c* in the middle—if I sing it like that, like this . . .

Yes. And the long *i* sound of the third syllable—most so-pranos reach up for it, deliberately let us hear them reach-ing, to strike it desperately, strenuously, like ringing a bell. I drop down onto it from the *c* and let it unfurl like a wave cresting out of deep water. I do the same thing when I come to the mournful words lower in my register—*Fra le tenèbre! Tocca alla mèta.*—casting the consonant sounds out lightly, the way I laid my offerings on the surface of the water in the cave, and letting the vowel sounds carry them away.

It is not the aria I remember. It is something else now. It is mine.

WHEN I FINISH and dare to peek at Bella, her eye makeup is running. I don't know what to do. We are both saved by the sound of someone clapping vigorously from the door-way. I spin around and see Tom.

"Bravo," he says gravely. "Bravo."

"Tom," Bella says. She takes off her glasses and dabs her eyes. "You are interrupting a lesson, as you know perfectly well. What do you want?"

"I need Kathleen," he says. He could be all of about twelve talking to Bella, with his charm tamped down and his body language that of a supplicant. He's practically bowing and scraping for God's sake. "She's late for an audition."

"An audition? For what?"

I start to say I have no idea but Tom cuts his eyes at me and I close my mouth.

"Student production," he says, "and I wouldn't pull her out of a lesson, but if she doesn't come now the whole sched-ule's thrown off and there are already thirty people sitting in the hallway, Professor Menotti. You know how these things go."

Bella sighs. "At least she's warmed up." I think she is relieved to see me go today.

I gather up my music. I'm stupid, but not totally. My father got in today. I'm having dinner with him tonight. But I didn't ask beyond that, so he could have been here all day, auditioning singers right down the hall from my practice room, and I wouldn't have known it.

"I didn't even know they were finished with the opera."

"They're not," Tom says, practically dragging me down the hall. "But after what I just heard in there, I don't feel even a little bit bad about stretching the truth. Since when is 'Suicidio!' so fucking beautiful, Kathleen? It's supposed to sound torn and despairing, or haven't you ever translated the lyrics? And did you notice you made Bella cry?"

"I hardly had time to notice," I snap back, "though I did notice you were clapping."

He stops abruptly and turns to face me. We're of a height, since I always wear flat shoes, and I have the urge to brush his hair out of his eyes so I can see his expression more clearly.

"I told you," he says, "it was fucking beautiful. Let's talk about something more important. Haven't you noticed I've been avoiding you?"

"You have?" Of course he has. I haven't seen him or talked to him for more than a few minutes since we had dinner together back in September, since I told him the whole story.

Tom stares at me in bemused frustration. "I can't tell if

that means I was doing a good or bad job of it," he says, "if you didn't even notice."

"Why were you avoiding me? Or are you still avoiding me?"

"No," he says, "and I should think you would have guessed by now."

We stare at each other a minute in the hallway. "Well, it's not that you think my crazy is contagious," I say, "because you've had a death grip on my arm for the last five minutes. And you know Robin is here, which means"—I feel a smile tugging at my mouth—"they got you. You're singing the prince's part after all and you've been too embarrassed to tell me that you gave in."

He grins back at me. "Guilty. Though it wasn't entirely embarrassment. As soon as I heard what they've written so far I wanted you to hear it too, but Harry wouldn't let me. I think she's determined to present it to you all finished and perfect. But this afternoon"—he is delighted with himself—"she's in class. And it's high time you heard this, so you can stop messing around ruining *La Gioconda*."

"Ruining?" I shriek, but Tom turns me around by the shoulders and propels me into a practice room.

My father is sitting at the piano. He looks abashed when he sees me and he doesn't get up from the bench. I think he's hiding.

"Hi, honey."

"Hi, yourself." I'm not letting him off easy, even if this was Tom's idea and not his. I've sung with my father at the piano hundreds of times. But this feels awkward and stiff, like an audition. And I'm not even sure I want the part.

Tom swivels his head theatrically from one of us to the other. "So, umm, Robin, this is Kathleen. She's a second-year student here and—"

"Tom," my father says, "please don't take this wrong, but would you—"

"Get the hell out?" Tom asks. "Gladly. Between the two of you and your preperformance jitters or whatever the hell you've got, I feel like *I'm* going to throw up." He gives me a smacking kiss on the cheek. "Break a leg."

"Go away, Tom."

"By the way," he says, "if you don't do this—open yourself up to this, for whatever the hell reason you want—I *will* think you're crazy. And not just regular crazy either. Full-on batshit."

"Go away!"

It is silent for a moment after he does.

"Well," Robin says finally, "I can see why you and he are such good friends. He's nearly as good at making people want to throttle him as you are."

We are smiling at one another now, but neither of us moves. We can't. He's got to stay behind the piano because if he gets up then he's my father, not The Composer, and he can't ask me to sing the lead role in the opera he's writing. And I've got to stay here because if I get up and go over to him, put my arms around him, sit down on the bench beside him and bump him with my hip until he slides over, then I'm his daughter, not a singer about to do the first run-through of music written especially for her.

But I can't sing yet either because I haven't even read the damn score. I go over to the music stand and try to take in the pages spread out on it.

"Is this for full orchestra?" I ask, a question I should have asked months ago. Only that was back when I was pretending no one in my father's house was actually writing an opera. For me.

"It is," Robin says.

"Who's—do you have an orchestra lined up?"

He flushes slightly and adjusts the score in front of him. "Well, Jim—you remember Jim Dolan, don't you? He's underwriting *The Scarlet Letter* and now this piece as well? He suggested we pitch it to Opera Boston, not for a full run of course, but it fits their mission statement of producing contemporary opera and it's not a long piece. So they're tentatively on board."

"Tentatively." He is not getting off the hook this easily. "Have they heard it?"

"They've heard the music." My father looks even more chagrined, plunges a hand through his hair in a gesture of frustration so familiar that I feel dizzy, because nothing else about this moment feels familiar at all.

"But not the vocals."

"No."

It really is an audition then, for Opera Boston if not for Robin. How funny. I try to read the music in front of me again, but all my training seems to have deserted me— Menotti would have a field day with this scenario—and I'm having trouble sorting notes from words. I can tell, however, that this is a really difficult piece to sing.

"This is your first aria," Robin says. "You've seen the prince from afar and fallen instantly in love with him, but you love the sea too. You're trying to reconcile the two loves. You imagine swimming with him, embracing him, showing him the beautiful garden that you tend on the ocean floor, but then you realize that he would die if you dragged him under."

"Play the lead-in first," I say, "then play it all the way through."

He plays it and I follow along in the score. Then I make him play it again and I follow again. The words are lovely, written with an ear for how they'll sound when sung and not spoken. The music is something else entirely.

"Play it again."

I close my eyes and listen. Even without the words I can feel the mermaid's voice shaping the sea. At first, she out-races the waves that the prince's ship leaves in its wake, her voice leading, the strings following, cresting, receding. Then she plunges into the water and dives deep, her voice spiraling and softening. She sings of her garden, darting from one melodic line to the next as she describes the gorgeous undulating plants that grow there.

"Stop." I open my eyes. "It's strange-sounding but I like it, sort of like making the listener play a game of hide-and-seek, or catch-me-if-you-can. Play that section again."

He does. I stop him again—from nervous auditioner to peremptory diva in ten minutes flat—and shake my head at him.

"Daddy," I say, "there's no way to sing this without losing the effect. It just—the breath control it requires . . ."

He frowns in concentration, eyes on his score. "Try it."

"Start at the beginning then."

So we begin again and I chase a man I've glimpsed only once and long to see again. I leap through and ahead of the waves, feeling the water that his ship cleaved return to itself, the waves retaining no memory of his presence or his absence. But I cannot return to myself. I am changed by that glimpse of him and for a moment the music leaves me stranded, my voice without accompaniment. I sing recklessly, higher and higher, like flinging myself out of the sea and knowing I will only be airborne for a few seconds before I drop back in. Robin's hands hover over the keys, his eyes on me reflecting the same terrified exhilaration that I feel in my throat as the song pours out. How did he know I could sing like this? How did I not?

Now comes the tricky descending section. I sink down into my voice as I sink into the sea, down to my garden on the ocean floor. *"Flowers like flames, red and blue, and in the heart of them all, a statue of a handsome man, blank eyes blind to the beauty around him. His body, once white, is now streaked with green and black, the colors of the sea itself at its depths."* The words are as familiar as if I have sung them before and it is not, after all, difficult at all to sing as if giving a breathless, excited tour. I sing as if I have what I have always dreamed of—Harry underwater beside me, both of us breathing easily as we swim—and because she wrote the descriptions, I can almost believe that she *can* see it, and that she finds it beautiful too. Robin nods as he plays, lifting his fingers from the keys for a moment at the end of each fragmentary line. His hands move as if over the surface of rough water. When the section ends on a plaintive, repeated phrasing— *Never him, never here*—we keep going. The woodwinds will come in here, flutes taking over for the clarinets as the melody goes higher, rising from the bottom of the sea to the surface again. I sing a fantasy: since I cannot live on land and my beloved cannot live in the sea, we must both

learn to fly and then we can soar away like birds. I do not
so much swim up from the depths as fly from them, breaking the surface of the water with a sound that splinters in
the air like water droplets in sunlight, flash and dazzle that
cannot last, but that sinks back and vanishes and was only
an illusion after all.

I come back to myself, standing at the music stand in a
practice room. My feet, astonishingly, do not hurt. I should
be out of breath, anyone would be out of breath after singing that, but I am not.

"How did you know?" I ask.

My father's hands are shaking. He removes them from
the keys, puts them carefully over his knees. "How did I
know what?"

"That I could sing that. It's ridiculous to expect anyone
to sing that. Those runs, the range it calls for, the push in
the last lines and the crescendo at the very top . . ." I am
shaking too, the all-over shakes I get sometimes when the
pain is really bad. But nothing hurts. At this moment, nothing hurts, not my feet, not my tongue. I feel like I've been
underwater and am still emerging.

"You sound like you're angry," Robin says. Abruptly, he
laughs. "If you think about it, this may be the most cliché
father-daughter fight we've ever had."

"What do you mean?"

"I know you, Kathleen," he says gently. "I knew you
could sing this when I wrote it. I could hear you singing it
in my head. So are you going to be angry at me for knowing you too well? Because I'd rather that than—well, than
what you've been angry at me for."

"Which is what?"

"For wanting to save you. For trying to save you"—he gestures at the music in front of him—"with this. I know you don't think it's possible. I didn't think it was either."

"But now you do?"

I cannot fail to see that there is joy lurking in his eyes, cautious and newly kindled, but there all the same.

"You didn't hear what I heard," he says. "You didn't see yourself as you were singing that. I could *see* your feet stop hurting."

I jump. "How?"

"You shifted your weight on them and I could tell. Maybe Harry was right after all."

I don't have a response to that. I look down at the music again. I want to ask him if we can do it again. I want to do another aria. It won't matter, I know. They'll all feel like this one did, maybe even better. The pain is lapping back in around the edges of my feet. What will it feel like to sing the moment when she kills him? I shiver.

"What's wrong?" Robin asks.

I cast around for something else to think about.

"You said Opera Boston was 'tentatively' on board with the production but hadn't heard any vocals."

"Yes."

"They were worried about the lead role? They weren't sure it was doable?"

"Well." My father is suddenly very nonchalant, and very pleased with himself. "What was said was that the role was unsingable—I'm fairly sure that was the term used—as written and that I needed to make the demands realistic, especially for a young singer. So they were waiting for me to do that and deliver them a singer, which I promised to do."

"Liar! You never had any intention of rewriting the music."

He arches an eyebrow at me. "Should I have? Because if you don't think you're up to it, I could rein it in a bit, I mean, if it really is 'unsingable.'"

I giggle. "They really thought it was?"

"They did."

"So can you imagine the expressions on their faces when they hear me?"

Robin grins. "I can."

I can't hold out anymore. It's like the music lurking in the score and in the piano keys is a current tugging at me, as strongly as the sea ever has.

"Can we go through it again, Daddy, just one more time?"

HARRY

Director's Notes

By March, only weeks away from opening night, I had narrowed my list of things I hated about writing and directing an opera down to three: doing interviews, dealing with the lighting designer, and lists.

I had a clipboard of lists that I carried with me everywhere. I'd used my iPad at first, but there was something so satisfying about being able to throw away a piece of paper when the list was all checked off that I switched. I had a list of the cast, their entrances and exits, and the state of completion of their costumes. I had a list of scenes, a list of arias, a list of duets, all marked with the system of check marks and abbreviations I'd come up with to indicate how well-rehearsed they were, who needed to be where when, what props and costumes went with—or on—which actor when.

Kathleen said I'd clearly found my calling in directing and producing, a way to channel my knack for details and organization into art. When we were getting ready for bed at night, she'd steal lists from my bag and quiz me on them, laughing and shaking her head when I remembered even the nonsense notes I'd made in the margins, scribbled phrases like *nt wh or rd or bl dress—yell?*

"Yell? Somebody is going to yell? Is that a stage direction, Harry? And are we going to yell *at* a dress or *in* a dress?"

"That's just an abbreviation. It's yellow, yellow not white or red or blue because I've ruled out all those colors for the wedding dress. The prince's bride can't be wearing red because then the blood won't show up—even though we're just doing it with lighting, it has to be a vivid effect. And not blue because that's a water color, so the costume designer suggested yellow." I rubbed my forehead, reached for the toothpaste. It wasn't that any one detail like this was too much. It was just that there were one hundred of them to think about. One thousand.

"But not a white dress either?" Kathleen asked. "I assume that's what 'nt wh' means? Why not? It's a wedding dress, isn't it? Seems obvious it should be white."

I brushed my teeth instead of answering. I had immediately pictured the prince and his bride in white, the Little Mermaid in blue as she stabbed them. The effect of the red light would then turn her dress purple, a deep water color. But it would also heighten the brutality of the scene.

Kathleen waited for me to spit.

"You know," she said, "I am—she is—murdering them. You're the one who made that decision with the script in the first place. Kind of late to back off it now, don't you think?"

"But if the bride is in white—if they're both in white—it's

something else that I don't know if I like. It's lambs to the slaughter, it's a virgin sacrifice—"

Kathleen burst out laughing. Her color was high these days, the flags of red along her cheekbones vivid as if she were in constant stage makeup.

"But, Harry, that makes it better, doesn't it? I mean, listen to you, Madam English Major, shying away from a chance to double the metaphor, or the symbolism, or whatever it is. They *are* sacrifices, just like her tail was a sacrifice, or her pain or her sisters' hair. The whole story is one sacrifice after another."

I shook my head.

"I'm so tired I can't even think straight," I said. "I'll worry about it tomorrow." But mentally I crossed out the note and scribbled *wh for pr and prs* over it. I hadn't wanted to make *Kathleen* a murderess, even though I knew that the Little Mermaid had to be, to save herself. There were moments, as the performances drew near, when this whole production felt not just out of control but beyond control, inevitable, inexorable. Thus, my many lists.

"Go to bed," Kathleen said. "I'll be there as soon as I've dried off."

She was soaking her feet in the tub, her skirt tucked up around her knees. During rehearsals, her pain eased visibly—you could see it in both the way she placed her feet and in her increased ability to be still for long moments, listening to another singer. When she sang the music Robin had written for her, her pain went away altogether. The only problem was that it always came back.

I worried that in some ways it was worse to have those

reprieves. I remembered how she'd been on Inis Mór, when she'd started to dry off after being drenched in seawater, like a junkie coming down from a high. But she seemed okay. I saw her wince or bite her lip more often than before, as if it was harder to hide the pain when it wasn't constant. Well, it probably was. But she was also more willing to try to do something about the pain. She soaked her feet a lot, drank water without my having to remind her. Once when I heard water running in the bathroom and couldn't resist peeking in, she was sitting on the edge of the tub with her feet under the faucet murmuring "please, please, please." But when she saw me, she smiled and pulled me over to stand behind her. She rested her head against my stomach while the water ran over her feet.

"It'll be okay," she murmured when she turned the water off. "They'll feel better again tomorrow when I sing."

I should have thought about that, about what would happen when the opera run was over. We were only doing two weeks of performances, after all. What was Kathleen going to do if—when—the pain came back for good? But I couldn't think past opening night, couldn't see past my piles of lists and my clipboard, couldn't be anything but grateful for the small miracle that this music was working on Kathleen. Because there were times when I wasn't sure we were going to get this thing to the stage.

ROBIN DIDN'T SEEM to share any of my anxieties. In interviews, he fielded even the worst questions—*So, given that this is a vehicle for your daughter, would you characterize this as a vanity project?*—with a faint smile. There were a surprising number of press interviews, because Robin was the composer and because Opera Boston was involved. Robin charmed every reporter, handsome and relaxed, legs crossed at the ankles, nursing endless cups of tea.

"How do you do this over and over again?" I complained. "I'm scared to drink anything because then I have to go to the bathroom halfway through the interview."

Robin grinned. "Just go," he said. "They'll wait for you to come back. Can't do the interviews without us, Harry."

"They could do it without *me*," I said. "You're the genius. I'm just an MFA student with Post-it flags stuck to her shirt."

We were waiting for the *Boston Globe* reporter today and I was in a bad mood. I'd been onstage with a couple of lighting techs all morning, trying to light the underwater scenes without turning the singers' faces blue. They'd used me as the dummy singer, so I stood center stage with my hands out at my sides while a girl with a headset on stood with one foot on each of two armrests in the orchestra and bellowed instructions to her partner up in the lighting booth. My hands went blue, dark blue, pale blue, then yellow, and my head started to hurt. In the end it was agreed that the only solution was to "Get George."

"He'll figure it out," the girl assured me as she texted him. "George could make a dead body look alive with a couple of well-placed filters."

George texted back and said he'd meet me at the theater the next morning at nine, but that was the only opening he had for the rest of the week, which meant I then had to get in touch with Tom and ask him to come to the theater instead of the coffee shop where we'd been planning to meet at nine-thirty. Tom apparently had to talk to me urgently.

And although I knew that this could mean his costume didn't match his eyes, I still felt a pang when I thought about the meeting. I didn't have time for a casual coffee, which Tom knew perfectly well. I was half-afraid we would get together and he'd give me a lecture about how stressed out I was and half-afraid he really did have something serious to tell me. God forbid he drop out of the show.

I went from the theater to the costume department at the conservatory to check on the sea witches' robes, which had accidentally been ordered in bright red, then ran to meet Robin and the *Globe* reporter for lunch.

"Headache?" Robin asked as soon as he saw me.

"Why?"

"You're squinting. I know that squint. You've been working for too long and you've forgotten to eat. Order an appetizer now. We can order entrées when Lindsey gets here."

"Yes, Dad," I muttered, and Robin smacked me with his menu. The waitress laughed at us as she took my order for a cup of chowder, extra oyster crackers on the side.

"You better believe it," Robin said when she'd gone. "Speaking of—how's my other daughter doing?"

I fished some Advil out of my bag and gulped it down with water. "She's doing great, I think. She's singing so much that it's sort of like she never really has a chance to crash, you know? So even when her feet hurt, she seems almost philosophical about it."

"Kathleen?" Robin asked. "Are you sure you don't have her mixed up with someone else?"

"I know. It's remarkably drama-free at our place these days. I barely know what to do with myself."

The waitress brought my soup and I crushed some crackers and sprinkled them on top. There it was again, the fear half-spoken by both of us, hidden in our assurances of how well Kathleen was doing. What would happen to her when the opera was over?

The chowder was hot. I swirled my spoon in it and then nearly tipped the cup over when a woman skidded to a stop at our table.

"Robin? Harriet? My gosh, I'm sorry I'm late! This is terrible. Have you been here long?"

"You're not late, Lindsey," Robin said. "Harry's eating because I forced her to." He stood up and pulled a chair out. The woman slid into it and smiled across the table at me.

"Harry. Sorry. I called you Harriet. I'm Lindsey Percival. *Boston Globe*."

"Nice to meet you," I said. I shook her hand, which was larger than mine. She was tall, with short spiky blond hair and silver tassel earrings that brushed her shoulders. She was built like a swimmer: broad-shouldered, with visible muscles in her long arms and in her legs, which were bare despite the fact that it was March in Boston.

"So has Robin told you that we know each other?" Lindsey asked.

I glanced at Robin, who was smiling at his menu, shaking his head. "No."

"My parents own Danny Boy's," she said. "It's one of the bars where Robin used to play. I would bug him to let me sit on the piano bench with him, try to make him play my favorite songs. I babysat Kathleen a couple of times, didn't I? I took her upstairs to our apartment and braided her hair. She'd come down with these crazy hairstyles, poor kid, but I thought it was awesome, like I had my own personal redheaded Barbie."

Robin laughed. "And yet you cut all your own hair off."

Lindsey ran a hand smugly over her choppy hair. "Got tired of washing it. I row crew," she added to me. "Started in college and got hooked. Besides, I didn't like doing my *own* hair, I liked doing other girls' hair. And Kathleen never complained. She must have a high pain threshold."

I carefully didn't glance at Robin.

"So how's she doing?" Lindsey asked. "I can't believe how old she is—and how gorgeous! I saw the photo up on the Opera Boston site. Tell her I say hello and that I want the first interview after opening night."

"I'll tell her," Robin said. He had that expression of private amusement on his face again. I wished he'd let me in on the joke. I also wished my headache would go away. Lindsey Percival's eyes were shockingly blue, like some of the lights we'd been working with this morning.

We ordered our food and Lindsey brought out paper, pencil, and her iPad. She tested the microphone, turning the iPad on the table to angle it more toward us than herself. "Backup, just backup," she murmured. "And to save me from figuring out my own spelling. I'm the world's worst speller."

She asked Robin about the development of the score, what the shift was like from orchestral and instrumental music to opera, why he thought audiences were so resistant to new operas, why this one would be different. Everyone asked these same questions. I ate my club sandwich, feeling my headache recede. I liked hearing Robin talk about the opera. His answers felt familiar by now, but not boring. I was frankly happy to have an excuse to just listen to something besides my own anxious litany of things that I hadn't done yet, or things that could go wrong.

"Harry?"

Lindsey had her pencil poised. I'd missed a question directed at me.

"Sorry. Can you repeat that?"

"What was the experience of writing a libretto like?"

"Hard," I said.

Lindsey laughed. "Can you be more specific?"

"It was like trying to do anything you've never done before and aren't sure you're any good at, only harder." When she laughed again I realized that I was trying to make her laugh. I wasn't sure why.

"So any ideas for the next one?" she asked.

I stared at her blankly. "The next what?"

"The next libretto," Lindsey said. "Robin says this one is brilliant, the director of Opera Boston says it's brilliant—"

I flushed. "He did not!"

Lindsey flipped through her pad. "No, you're right," she said. "He said the libretto was 'tremendously exciting, clearly the work of a singer for singers. People are going to be really blown away.'"

I opened my mouth, closed it again. The next one? No one had asked me this question before. The previous interviews had focused far more on Robin, the known quantity. They'd asked me about the writing of *The Little Mermaid* libretto but not about whether I might write another one.

And I certainly hadn't had any effusive praise read back to me before.

"I haven't really thought about anything past opening night," I said, "since I'm also directing."

"But would you like to do more work as a librettist?" Lindsey asked. "What would your dream project be?"

"Oh, Robin's already doing that," I said. "I love *The Scarlet Letter*. But then most of the things I'd love to see or sing in are probably texts already. They don't need a librettist, just a kind of script doctor, someone to stitch things together."

"And you did more than that with *The Little Mermaid*?"

"Yes, well, there's very little actual dialogue in the story, so—yes, I guess I did a lot of writing."

"A *lot* of writing," Robin put in quietly. "And all of it, as I said, brilliant."

Lindsey was giving me her jock's grin again.

"I've stumped you," she said. "I love it when I leave my interview subjects speechless."

"I just haven't thought about it."

But now I was. And the disconcerting thing wasn't that I suddenly found myself thinking about writing another libretto. It was how many ideas I had.

"I'd love to do more Andersen stories," I said, "though I'm sure they've probably been done before, some of them. 'The Snow Queen,' 'The Little Match Girl,' 'The Red Shoes.'" I looked at Robin. "Have all of those been done?"

He shrugged. "Doesn't mean you couldn't do them again, Harry, your own way."

"But I'm not a composer. You'd have to do the music!"

"Now I'm going to sound like you," Robin said. "Not until *Mermaid* is over. And *The Scarlet Letter* is done. Besides"—he raised an eyebrow—"I'm hardly the only composer in the world."

"But—"

"Sooooo," Lindsey cut in, "is now a good time to ask if you two enjoyed working together?"

Robin laughed. "It was a joy."

"*Tam Lin*," I said abruptly. They both stared at me. "As an opera," I clarified.

Lindsey shook her head, making her earrings dance against her neck. "I don't know that one."

Robin looked thoughtful. I could practically hear him recalling the old ballad, evaluating it for dramatic potential, melodic possibilities. He nodded slowly. "I like it," he said. We grinned at each other. Then he suddenly slapped his blazer pocket and extracted his phone. "It's Jim Dolan. Excuse me. I'll take this outside."

I schooled my face out of what must have been an expression of panic. Whenever Robin's phone or my phone rang, I still expected Kathleen on the other end, her voice constricted with pain.

"You all right?" Lindsey asked. She touched the back of my hand. "I can ask easier questions if you want. Let's see, who's your favorite composer? What role do you dream of playing? What's your favorite ice cream flavor?"

Up close, the blue of her eyes was even more startling. She had a cleft in her chin. "I can't even come up with an interesting flavor," I said. "I like chocolate."

She wrinkled her nose. "Is that an Italian composer? I've never heard of him."

I started to laugh and realized that she was still touching my hand, just with the tips of her fingers.

"I'm sorry," I said. "I honestly just don't think of myself as a librettist. I mean, not the way Robin is a composer. I'm a singer, and a decent one, but not like Kathleen. And this opera, I was halfway through writing it before I realized I'd started, if you know what I mean."

Lindsey raised her eyebrows. "That's how most of the best writing happens, in my experience."

"Maybe. But I'm not a writer. I mean, I wrote this opera, but I was doing it for Kathleen."

I flushed when I said it—no one had asked about our relationship in any of the interviews and I hadn't brought it up either. Of course, I realized, Lindsey hadn't asked about it either.

"Ah," she said after a moment. She withdrew her hand and sat back in her chair. "Well, at least my radar was working." She pulled a rueful face and I flushed more. I hadn't even realized until that moment that she was flirting with me.

"I'm sorry," I said.

She shrugged. "For what?" She took a sip of her iced tea. "How long have you been together?"

"Almost two years."

Robin slid back into his seat at that moment. I gave him what must have been an inappropriately big smile, grateful for his presence.

"Speaking of contemporary operas—we were speaking of contemporary operas, weren't we?" he asked. "Jim just saw *Nixon in China* while he was *in China* and had to call and tell me about it. Apparently, it was a rather surreal experience, but the singing was astonishing, he said." Robin winked at me. "He also said to tell you and Kathleen both that he and Lorraine are excited about next weekend."

"No nagging you about *The Scarlet Letter*?" I asked.

"We-ell," Robin said, "he did mention something about not wanting to lose track of our other project."

Lindsey was packing up her shoulder bag.

"I've got everything I need from you two," she said. "Thank you. And, Robin, it was amazing to see you again. Mom and Dad are going to be so excited when I tell them I not only saw you, but interviewed you, that you're a celebrity now."

"Oh God," Robin said. "Please don't tell them that. If I ever want to just pop into Danny Boy's for a drink, your dad will never let me live it down."

Lindsey chuckled. "Never." She turned to me and held out her hand.

"Harry, it was nice to meet you. Good luck with the opera, and good luck with any future operas," she said. "Singing or writing."

She swung her bag over her shoulder and left. She walked with a slight swagger that her heels exaggerated.

"What did I miss?" Robin asked. "Any more hard questions?"

I shook my head. "Thank God she didn't know *Tam Lin*, though, or I don't think she'd have let her 'what's next?' query drop so easily."

Robin chuckled. "Or thank Jim for the timing of his phone call. But you know, I was thinking while I was hanging up—*Tam Lin* is practically opera-ready. Another short one, like *Mermaid* is, only two acts, plenty of Celtic references in the music. And you'd have to have a tremendous duet between Janet and the Fairy Queen when she pulls him from the horse."

"To sort of narrate what's happening to Tam Lin," I said.
"Yes."

"Soprano and contralto?" Robin wondered. "Which
would be which?"

I frowned. "I don't know. Soprano for the Queen, I
think."

We both nodded, and then our eyes met and Robin's expression turned sheepish. I'm sure mine did too.

"Come on, Harry." He laughed. "Let's get out of here.
We're dangerous together."

KATHLEEN COULDN'T DECIDE which delighted her more:
that Robin and I wanted to write another opera or that her
old babysitter had hit on me and I hadn't noticed.

"I love it!" she said, twirling linguini around her fork.
"I used to have a picture book of *Tam Lin*. There was a
page for every transformation he undergoes, with Janet—
though I think it was Jenny in this book—hanging on
grimly in every one. What are they again? A bear, a swan,
a snake . . ."

"Well, I think it's a 'serpent,'" I said, "which could be a
sort of dragon, not a snake."

"Oooh," Kathleen said. "That is better. And then he turns
into fire and she has to jump into the water to put it out.
I remember that." She paused, chewing. "I can't imagine
where I got that book," she said. "I mean, I even remember
Jenny being visibly pregnant and that's not exactly a plot
point for the picture book audience."

"What about the end?" I asked.

"What do you mean?"

"Well, how did your book end?"

"Oh. Well, the Fairy Queen rides off in a huff and then on the last page, across from 'The End,' there's a picture of Tam Lin and Jenny holding their baby in the rose arbor he used to haunt when he was under his enchantment."

"Ah," I said. "It was a kid's book, then, despite pregnant Jenny."

"Why?" Kathleen asked. "How does the ballad end?"

"The Fairy Queen has the last word. She says something to him that sounds like she's cursing him, but really all she does is remind him of everything he had in Faërie. He may have escaped from her, but now he's mortal, not covered in fairy glamour, which could be a bit of a disappointment to both him and Jenny. Or Janet. Or whatever her name is."

Kathleen shook her head. "How unromantic you are." Then she poked me in the back of the hand with her fork. "I still think you should write it. When you mentioned the part about the Fairy Queen and her curse—imagine if you did it that way, if she did have the last word and the rest of the staging was just pantomime, just the two lovers picking themselves up out of the water and going home." She shivered. "Gives me goose bumps, that does."

"Can we just get through next weekend? Please?"

"If you insist. Now, tell me more about Lindsey—did she actually ask you out? In front of my dad?"

"No!"

"Did she play footsie under the table?" Kathleen's eyes were dancing. "Or put her hand on your knee?"

"Quit teasing me," I snapped. I felt annoyed and wished I hadn't even told her. I'd been so thrown off by the flirtation that I'd felt a need to confess it, but now I felt stupid.

"Harry—"

"Just because I don't get hit on often enough to recognize it—"

Kathleen grabbed my hand hard enough to hurt. "Stop it. You don't get hit on because everyone we know knows we're together and also because you're oblivious."

"Is that a bad thing?"

She loosened her grip, enough so I could turn my hand in hers, but she didn't let go. She tugged on my hand until she could hold it to her mouth, brushing my fingertips across her lips while she talked. There was tenderness, in her eyes and in her lips and in her hands, as she pulled me up from the table.

"It's not a bad thing," she whispered later, stringing kisses like a necklace across my throat. "I'm glad you're oblivious."

"What about you?" I whispered back.

She tilted her head to smile at me, her breasts pressed against mine.

"I'm not oblivious, Harry," she said softly. "But I'm immune."

"To flirtation?"

"To flirtation from anyone else," she corrected, kissing me again. "Silly girl," she murmured. "Stop worrying. Put your hands on me."

I WOKE ABRUPTLY in the middle of the night and jerked up on one elbow, my heart pounding. Kathleen was lying curled into me and I'd had the impression that her eyes were open and she was staring at me. But her eyes were closed, her face white and set in the moonlight. Her breath smelled funny, or maybe her hair did. Not a bad smell, but odd, and strong. I leaned over her and breathed it in.

Seawater. More precisely, it was the smell of the cave where we'd encountered the witches. Cold, old, deep water, wet rock. I sat up fully and pulled my knees to my chest, shivering. I reached over and opened the drawer in my bedside table, pressed the latch on the knife case inside. As soon as it was open wide enough for me to see the knife inside I slapped it shut, closed the drawer, and lay back down. I made myself turn on my side toward Kathleen and put my hand on her hair, stroke it until I could convince myself that it wasn't damp or sticky with saltwater. After a long time, the smell of the sea receded. Kathleen sighed and turned her back to me.

"It'll be all right," I whispered, as if she was awake with me and needed soothing. "It'll be all right."

I thought of Kathleen's idea for *Tam Lin*, of the Fairy Queen getting the last word and how that sounded, how it felt, to have the last word, to be the one echoing into a listening silence. What would the words be that couldn't be answered? I let myself think about words on a stage, about the Fairy Queen's curse of Tam Lin, because I was tired and I had too much to do. I couldn't afford a sleepless night. I had to talk to Tom in the morning, meet with George the lighting designer . . .

GEORGE WAS YOUNGER than I'd expected him to be, probably my age, only about a foot taller and with terrible skin. He wore his frizzy brown hair in a ponytail, and a T-shirt that read INTERNATIONAL SARCASM SOCIETY: LIKE WE NEED YOUR SUPPORT. He was also, thank God, a genius.

"We need to light the back wall," he said. "And maybe layer it with green on top of blue—I've got some ideas. Go stand center stage."

He vaulted over the seat he'd been lounging in and disappeared up into the lighting booth. I climbed onstage and did as I was told. I stood there a few minutes, itching for a list to write on, then gave in to the impulse and went back and got my pad. I was absurdly afraid of displeasing George, so I hurried back into position. Still nothing happened. I checked a satisfyingly long list of things off from the day before, then ruined it by adding as many new things for today and tomorrow. There was at least one thing I was forgetting too—there was always one thing. I shut my eyes to try to remember, but I just felt tired.

When I opened my eyes, I was underwater. I blinked and took a step backward as if I could step out of the water that wasn't there. I turned in a circle and the illusion held, dark blue, nearly purple near the floor, shifting to blue and then blue-green above my head.

"How's that?" George called.

"It's amazing," I said, "but am I blue?" I dropped my pad and held my hands out, palms up. They didn't look blue. I didn't feel blue-green light on my face either, just that I was standing in the colors.

"Nope," George said cheerfully. "Well, your pants legs are—that can't be helped—but I rather like that effect, don't you?"

I glanced down. My khaki pants looked like I'd dipped them in a wash of indigo dye that deepened from my knees to the floor. George was right (of course). It was a good effect. It would turn the mermaids' pale green chiffon a darker, wetter green and the sea witches' purple into black.

"Need any tinkering before I write down the specs?" George called. I realized I hadn't answered his last question.

"I don't think so," I said, "but I would like to see it from the audience."

"I'll step in," said a new voice. I looked over to see Tom coming down the side aisle. I glanced at my watch. He was early, which was not a good sign. Tom wasn't on time for anything, much less early. But he seemed fine, as far as I could tell looking from forty feet away. Maybe it was just going to be that he didn't like the color of the prince's tunic in the shipwreck scene.

"How's the effect?" I asked.

Tom didn't even stop walking, just kept on going right up the side steps onto the stage and across to where I stood.

"It looks like you're standing—like we're standing underwater," he said when he got close. He raised his voice to carry. "It's like I always say, 'We all owe our careers to the lighting designers. We'd be nothing without them.'"

This got no response from the booth; George didn't even bother to laugh. Tom made a face of mock distress.

"Have I offended?"

I smiled as I went to stand in the center aisle. "I think you merely stated the obvious as far as George is concerned."

But then I saw the way the lighting effect was working on Tom, who was suspended—stranded even, because he was so slight and so incongruous in street clothes that seemed suddenly wet and strange—in water. It really was amazing. Kathleen was going to love it.

"Do people tell you that you're a genius often?" I yelled up to George.

"Yes," he called back. "Can I assume we're done here?"

"Yes, thank you!"

The stage surfaced gradually as George hit various lights. Tom came downstage.

"Coffee?"

"I've been drinking too much coffee these days," I said. "Let me just get my stuff."

"I'll bring it," he said. He joined me in the aisle and handed me the pad and pen. For a moment we stood there awkwardly while I flipped the pages shut and slid the pen into the spiral along the side.

"We can go get some coffee if you want to," I said.

Tom shook his head. "No. I don't need any either." He hesitated a moment. "It's brilliant, Harry, do you get that? Singing it, listening to it—I don't think you know how good it is."

I sank down onto the arm of the nearest seat. "That's not what you wanted to talk about, Tom."

He kept on as if I hadn't spoken. "And she's more than brilliant," he said. "Christ, even in rehearsals when I know she's holding back, not singing full voice, not reaching—it's going to knock people for a loop in performance."

"That's not what you wanted to talk about either."

He let out a noisy breath that stirred the hair over his eyes. "Carianne is freaking out a little," he said.

This was such a non sequitur that I didn't know what to say. Carianne was playing the princess, the prince's chosen human bride, for whom he betrays the Little Mermaid.

"She's freaking out?" I managed. "Why? She's doing fine."

"Not about the singing," Tom said. "About Kathleen. About the way this part has hold of her, the way she's singing it, acting it, everything. She's scared about the death scene."

"Carianne is?"

"Yeah."

"Why?"

"Jesus, Harry!" Tom snapped. I jumped and knocked my pad off the armrest I'd balanced it on. "Try to think about someone else for one fucking minute, will you?"

"About someone else—"

"Besides Kathleen!"

"But—"

"Harry," he said, "I *know*. She told me. I know. And I thought this was a good idea. Stupid, maybe, in terms of actually solving anything, but a gorgeous gesture and then just a gorgeous fucking piece of music and a singing opportunity that I, Carianne, and the rest of us are unbelievably lucky to get as students. And I know it's helping her, I see that, but it's not fair to the rest of us, especially not to Carianne."

"Why *especially* not to Carianne?"

"Because she doesn't *know*!" he said. "I know what's going on, what you're trying to do by having her kill them—kill us, Carianne and me—and I'm taking the risk lying there that Kathleen is going to stay Kathleen and not turn into the Little Mermaid because . . . because I trust her to *try*, at least, because I trust you and I trust Robin, but Carianne doesn't even *know*, she's just freaked out and doesn't know why and what the fuck am I supposed to tell her, Harry? 'Hey, you're imagining things'? 'It's not like there's any chance that Kathleen will get confused and actually kill us with a real knife during the show'?"

I felt like he'd hit me—and been right to do it. I was the director. This was my show; these were my singers. I should have at least noticed Carianne's anxiety.

Try to think about someone else for one fucking minute.

"I kept telling myself you were just going to complain about your costume," I said. I reached down to pick up my pad. "I'm sorry, Tom. Can we—can we sit?"

He nodded. I slid over and sat down and he sank down next to me.

"I didn't know you knew," I said. "Kathleen didn't tell me she'd told you—she told you everything?"

"Well," he said, "I suppose I don't know if she told me *everything*."

"But you know about the knife."

"I know about the knife."

"Do *you* think the performance is—" I hesitated. "Dangerous, then? For you and Carianne?"

Tom sighed. "No. I'd have to believe that Kathleen was actually losing touch with reality and I don't think that. It's more that it's so good, Harry, so easy to believe in when you're singing it, that it gets to you. It's gotten to both of us, me and Carianne, just lying there in rehearsal with her over us, miming stabbing and singing that aria, just the notes she has to hit over and over and then sliding down off them the way she does . . ." He shivered. "It's unreal to listen to her do it and just lie there." He put his elbows on his knees, his head in his hands. "I'm not making much sense, am I?"

"I think you are," I said, because I did see, now, what he meant, and what he needed. "You need to know that I've thought of it too, of how to control the moment. It's my job, after all, Tom. And even though I didn't know that you knew the whole story, I should still have known how much that scene demands of you both. I should have said something and done something about it."

"Yeah, well . . ." Tom scrubbed his hands over his face then lifted his head.

"It's a prop knife," I said. "You'll see it. You'll see it before every performance, right before you go on for that scene. I promise."

"You know, now that we're actually having this conversation," he said, "I feel like a complete ass. Of course it's a fucking prop knife."

"We can do without a knife entirely if you want," I said. "Just have Kathleen mime the motion like she's been doing. We have the red light coming up on you both—that would be enough to convey the stabbing. It's not a realist production, for God's sake."

Tom shook his head. "Won't work," he said. "Her sisters give her that big shiny knife on a platter."

"It's a scallop shell."

He snorted. "Whatever. They give it to her and she holds it up and sings to it—she's got to use it when the time comes."

"You can think about it," I said. "And either way—no matter what—I'll talk to Carianne. She's singing really well, I noticed."

"She's got an audition out in Houston coming up," Tom said.

"You're kidding! That's amazing!"

"Yeah." He nodded. "And this show's giving her confidence, that's the thing. Singing this music, just going into it thinking you'll try to hold your own, that's all, and then realizing that you're doing better than that." He turned toward me for the first time since he'd sat down. "It's exhilarating, to tell the truth. None of us wants to back out of this. Not for anything."

"But you shouldn't be scared, Tom," I said. "Not for-real scared."

"I won't be if you promise me you'll take care of it."

I remembered waking to the smell of the sea in our room, in our bed, the momentary fear of Kathleen's eyes on me in the dark. But the knife had still been safely in its drawer.

"I promise you I'll take care of it," I said.

"All right then," he said. "But now I will let you buy me some coffee."

So we went to get coffee and cinnamon rolls and I found out he was up for an Adler Fellowship in San Francisco. I watched his face light up with hope and terror when he talked about the audition process and chided myself again for taking Tom for granted—for taking all our friends for granted. We'd throw him a huge party when he got the fellowship—or even if he didn't. A champagne-only party. Kathleen could plan it.

When Tom went to the men's room I pulled out my pad and made a note to tell Kathleen and Robin about both the Adler audition and Carianne's audition in Houston. Then I added an item to my to-do list for opening night: "*Chk prop knife frequently. Bring real 1 with u on night of and put someplace safe.*"

THE QUESTION WAS: where? The case was too big to carry with me and the knife was too sharp to carry safely without the case. Two days before opening night I had no solution. I sat on the edge of our bed and took the case out of the drawer. In our production, the mermaid's sisters presented her the knife they'd bartered their hair for on what was supposed to look like a half of an enormous shell. (Or a platter, according to Tom, but if amateurish props were our biggest problem, I could live with that.) But the real knife case couldn't be a shell. It was too flawless, too symmetrical. I ran my finger over the nacreous striations. Whatever it was, it had been polished—or manipulated—somehow coaxed into this particular shape.

The apartment door opened and I jerked open the drawer to the bedside table and tried to jam the case back in. It caught on something in the back of the drawer and wouldn't fit. I glanced at the clock—after ten. Tae had arrived in town for performance weekend and she and Robin and Kathleen had gone to dinner. I'd still been rehearsing the scene with the sisters and the sea witches so I hadn't been able to go. I hadn't even noticed how late it was.

"Harry?" came a voice from the kitchen, and I stopped fighting the knife case. It was Tae, not Kathleen.

"In here," I said, and she appeared in the doorway, slim and chic in cropped navy pants and an ivory sweater.

"We brought you some food," she said.

"Thank you."

"Kathleen and Robin are on their way up," she said. "They *may* have stopped at the convenience store around the corner for ice cream. Kathleen was dropping veiled hints."

I smiled. "I'm sure she was very subtle." I let go of the box and it stayed, wedged half in and half out of the drawer. I felt stupid and awkward sitting with my back to Tae, trying to hide the thing. I fumbled in the drawer for something to drape over the knife case.

"Are you all right?" Tae asked. She took a few steps into the room, then stopped. "Oh."

I gestured vaguely at the case. "It's not really stuck. I mean, it fits, it's just tight . . ."

"You keep it there, right by the bed?"

"It's on my side," I said, and then didn't know what to say.

There was silence for a moment, then Tae said, "But you had it out. Why?"

"I need to put it somewhere during the performances."

"What's wrong with where it is?"

"Nothing, I just—" I stopped, seeing her puzzling it out.

"Will it not stay there?" she asked.

"It has," I said. "It has stayed there since I put it there, but I tried to leave it with you and Robin."

"So you did," she said, nodding. "I thought you had, but then I asked Rob where it was and he said you must have changed your mind and taken it. I didn't want to press him and"—she came over and sat on the bed beside me—"I think he didn't ask because he didn't want to talk about the thing at all."

"Yes, well, it's here," I said, "and it's stayed here, in this drawer. But it's making me nervous and I thought during the performances I'd like to—"

"Keep it a little closer?" Tae asked.

"Something like that."

"But you can't keep it on you," she said. "It's too big and

too obvious. And you can't leave it backstage, there'd be no way to keep track of it there."

"No, I know," I said.

Tae leaned across me and took the case out of the drawer, held it cupped in both hands.

"It's beautiful, isn't it?" she said. "It's got to be made of pearl—but can you imagine a pearl this large?"

I half-laughed. "We should have asked the sea witches to show us one when we had the chance."

"You can't just leave it somewhere," she said again, thoughtfully this time. "It's so lovely someone might actually take it, or at least not be able to resist opening it and—" She felt my involuntary shudder.

"I can take it," she said.

"Tae, no, that's—"

"I know what it is," she said, "so I'll be careful with it—and careful of it—and I've no obligations during the performances, just to sit in the audience and enjoy."

"But where will you keep it?"

She smoothed one hand over the top, as if measuring it. "It will fit in my shoulder bag, I think," she said. "It's not heavy, just awkwardly shaped."

I watched her holding it, feeling as I had when we'd first shown it to her, that the very way she handled the thing, with the same matter-of-fact reverence for its power that she might hold a violin, made it less frightening, less strange.

"I'd hate for you to have to carry it around all weekend," I tried, but Tae stood up.

"Your food's getting cold," she said, "and I need to get this put away." She did not say *before Robin and Kathleen come in*. I followed her out into the kitchen, feeling mingled guilt at having literally passed the burden of the knife to her and relief at being so briskly managed.

"Tae," I said, "has anyone ever told you that you'd be a natural director?"

She laughed.

When the case was stowed away in her quilted patent leather bag, her coat slung casually on top, I relaxed enough to realize that I was starving. The pad thai they'd brought me was indeed cold, but I didn't care. Robin and Kathleen came in a few minutes later with a quart of gelato that Kathleen had insisted on because it was called Orange You Glad You Picked This Flavor? She scrounged some chocolate sauce from our fridge and we all had a bowl. Then Robin and Tae left and we went to bed.

It's not here, I thought as I fell asleep. And I slept better than I had in months.

ROBIN

Composer's Notes

The night before dress rehearsal, Robin woke abruptly from a dream he hadn't had in years, in which he carried his baby daughter on a puzzled and then panicked search of their tiny house, looking for Moira. He got out of the bed and made his way to the bathroom, nearly tripping on Tae's tote bag beside the sofa. He'd come in for the tech and dress rehearsals, plus final meetings with the orchestra and the conductor and a composing master class that the conservatory had asked him to do. It was too long a stay for a hotel to make sense, so he'd rented a short-stay apartment. Tae had gotten in last night. The apartment was attractive, open-concept, and high-ceilinged. In the dark, though, it was as disconcerting as any unfamiliar space.

Robin ran water into a glass and drank it, reminding the shadowy figure in the mirror that an anxiety dream at this moment hardly needed analysis. Naturally he was nervous about how the show would go, how it would be received, as well as worried about Kathleen, who was clearly doing so well, flying so high, that it felt like both an imperative and a betrayal to wonder what would happen to her when the show was done. These present anxieties had simply gotten tangled up with his old fear for Moira, which had haunted him long before and after he'd actually lost her.

He got back into bed, where memories insinuated themselves around the fragments of the already-fading dream. He had carried Kathleen with him that morning, from the bedroom as soon as she woke screaming for Mama, out to the main room and the little kitchen, then outside and around back, still no sign of Moira until he saw her footprints on the beach. Even then he hadn't been worried enough, because Moira went down to the beach every day, every chance she had. But that morning he'd stood there, holding the wailing baby, and stared at the footsteps that didn't make sense. How could they go in the direction they went, up into the rocks and then out toward the sea again, the impressions deeper in the soft wet sand of the last few yards, as if she were weighted down? How could her footsteps go out right into the water and not come back?

Robin turned onto his side, putting a hand in the indentation of Tae's waist to feel her breathe. He used to hold Moira this way. After she'd had a bad spell and had drifted into an exhausted sleep, it had comforted him to feel her breath rising and falling under his palm. But she'd slipped away from him easily enough that last time. He hadn't even known she'd left the bed. The feeling that threatened with that recollection—of waking to Kathleen screaming and feeling the bed empty beside him, long empty, no warmth or smell of Moira lingering—was a black, howling fear that made sleep impossible, because Robin couldn't tell himself to stop being irrational. Tae might not slip away or stop breathing beneath his hand in the night, but it could happen. It had happened to his wife. It could happen to his daughter. She seemed to have slipped free from the curse for now but she had not really escaped it. Believing she *had* was not rational. You didn't just slip away from a curse that drove a young mother out before dawn to fill her pockets with stones and walk into the sea.

THE NEXT MORNING, nerves jangling from little sleep and too much coffee, Robin walked over to the girls' apartment. Harry let him in, a half-eaten bowl of cereal in her hand.

"Kathleen's getting dressed," she said. "And before I forget, I have your tickets for tomorrow—you and Tae, Mr. Charpentier, and the Dolans." She gestured to five tickets fanned out on the kitchen counter. Robin picked them up.

"I tried out a couple of different rows when we started rehearsals in the space," Harry said, "to see which one had the best sightlines. I got you row five. And the ticket office keeps trying to get them back, so I must have been right about those being good seats."

"Why do they want them back?" Robin asked. He slid the tickets into his wallet.

"Because we're sold out," Harry said, "and as director I'm only allowed two myself. So they keep trying to tell me I've reserved too many—my parents are coming, of course, and they'll be sitting next to you. And I have to remind them, again, that these are for the composer and the under-

writer and—what's Allan's job again?—the artistic director of a major opera company that might want to stage the
production."

Robin eyed her as she ate the last of her cereal. "You're
doing an excellent job of sounding aggrieved about this
situation," he said.

"Aren't I?" She grinned at him. "Sold out! All of opening
weekend! It's so inconvenient."

Robin laughed. "It certainly is."

Harry put her cereal bowl in the sink. "Also I got you aisle
seats, not center row, in case you and Jim have to get up."

"Why would we have to get up?"

Harry raised her eyebrows. "To take a bow? To come up
on stage and let people clap for you?"

"We can just stand up where we are," Robin protested.
"Jim and I don't need to come up onstage."

"No way," Harry said. "First of all, it's an opera, for
God's sake. You wrote *all the music*. You don't get off with
discreet recognition."

"Hear, hear!" Kathleen added from the bedroom.

"And second of all?" Robin asked.

"Second of all," Harry said, smiling slightly, "Jim Dolan
is too short."

"Too short? For what?"

Kathleen popped her head and shoulders around the
door frame, her braid swinging. "Daddy! Don't be dense!"
She vanished again.

"How am I being dense?"

Harry laughed. "Kathleen has pointed out that in the
event of a standing ovation—"

"*When* there is a standing ovation!" Kathleen called.

"The audience wouldn't be able to see Jim. So," she said, shrugging, "you and Jim have to sit on the aisle so you can easily get up to the stage."

Robin shook his head. "I'm glad to see *someone* is confident about tomorrow night."

BUT AS HE and Tae sat in the dark later that morning during the dress (he took the seat Harry had selected for him because she was right—it was very good) he remembered Kathleen's fizzing assurances about a standing ovation and could not argue with her. This thing they'd made together, the three of them—it was hard to believe that they had made it, that he had written those notes, those phrases. It wasn't just that it was good, better than good; it seemed to unfold inevitably, such that every choice on the stage, every line sung or movement made, seemed to be the right choice, the only choice. And seeing the opera unfold was very strange after having only heard it, but heard it so deeply and so much. The choreography brought out dark undercurrents that were at once mesmerizing and difficult to watch. Finding the Mermaid washed up on the sand, the prince removed his cloak and tenderly lifted her onto it, singing, *"You poor thing, you beautiful girl. You'll catch cold out here, the sand will rub your white skin raw. Take my cloak, wrap up in that. It's velvet, feel it, how soft it is, how warm?"* Robin remembered writing those lines, fitting the music to words Harry composed. He had wanted to capture both tenderness and powerful attraction, but also a certain pat quality to echo the shallow reassurances the prince was offering, so inadequate to the agony the mermaid was experiencing in her new human body. He had thought he'd succeeded, but now onstage it went further, into a frightening dissonance between word and action as, instead of wrapping the mermaid in his cloak, the prince unbuttoned his pants and lowered himself onto her as the lights went down.

Robin flinched. Onstage Tom helped Kathleen to her feet and they slipped into the wings. Several black-clad techies crept out to shift the scene from the beach to the prince's castle.

"Staging not working for you?" Tae asked quietly.

"I wouldn't say that. What did you think?"

"I'm not sure it would have worked any other way," she said. "I've wondered how you were going to get us to the point of knowing that she has to kill him, of siding with her when she does."

"Well, I'm not sure *I* had anything to do with it."

Robin was glad when the lights came back up on the castle, airy drapery and piled cushions signifying decadent royalty. He knew all about how a piece could slip away from you, for good or for bad. When he'd been a pianist, there had been nights when he'd lost himself in a song, forgotten the audience entirely, only to look up and find people listening with eyes shut and tears on their cheeks. When he'd begun composing, he'd known he was good when the professor had played a piece for the class and Robin hadn't recognized his own work at first.

With this opera, though, had he done that essential stepping outside of himself that made the piece more than the sum of its parts, or was that all Harry's contribution, or the singers' gifts? He wished it didn't matter, but he sat tense and coiled in his seat as the mermaid acclimated to life at the castle and accepted the prince as her lover. The mermaid sang of the terrible pain in her feet and in her mouth, her voice made to sound in danger of fraying by the trick of a taut, minor scale that would have been impossible for many vocalists. Into her silences and sometimes overtop her— he couldn't hear her, after all; to him she was mute—the prince sang of his feeling of protectiveness for her, and of the sexual obsession that he justified as part of that protection. His voice was occasionally impassioned, but grew only more beautiful in those moments, sung in the sweet spot of the tenor range and never flawed by uncertainty or pain.

Watching the two of them face off on the stage, he chasing her, often looming over her (and that was a neat trick, considering that Tom was barely Kathleen's height), was so unsettling that after a few minutes, Robin shut his eyes and just listened. Yes, the tension was there in the music, not just in the words or the dance of seduction taking place onstage. He was ashamed of his relief, and then abruptly, remembering his dream, ashamed of what might have subconsciously informed the music he wrote for these two. He had held Moira as she cried from the pain, or simply lay in bed shivering from it, and had wanted her. His tenderness for her had always been tangled up with desire for her. He thought he'd forgotten that part of life with Moira, the endless, guilty longing for her even as she unraveled and slipped away.

Robin opened his eyes to watch the prince telling the mermaid he was going to marry a foreign princess. The liquid quality of Tom's voice, the ease of it, made his blithe assurances nearly plausible, sung along a melodic line that was almost sprightly, almost a pop tune, but less interesting than it could have been, a little repetitive, a little cold.

The prince sang, *"You mustn't worry, this doesn't mean anything for you, you'll always be my little love."* He stroked the mermaid's hair as she crouched at his feet. It was like he was petting his favorite dog. As the brief aria ended with her still huddled beside him, he crooned the last line—*"Do your feet hurt, my dear? Shall I take you to bed?"*—and leaned over, not to lift her, but to sweep her hair aside to kiss the back of her neck. The lights went down on him crouched over her, predatory, with a spotlight on the triangle of the mermaid's exposed white skin. As the prince's notes faded, the cellos were set briefly adrift from the rest of the orchestra to heighten the strange richness of their sound. The music of the deep sea that had opened the first act washed over the tableau.

Robin was on his feet before the house lights were up, turning restlessly in place and unable to look at Tae. He wanted to hit something, to hide his face, to shout or curse or run—somewhere. Away. Tae grabbed his wrist.

"Rob."

He ran his hand through his hair, still not looking at her, not even facing her.

"Robin," she said. "Do you want to go?"

He shook his head. Yes. No. "What is wrong with me?"

"You're brilliant," Tae said, and when he whipped his head to glare at her, to shake her off, he froze at the expression on her face. She was not crying, not Tae, but her eyes were warm and very bright with what he recognized at once as mingled tenderness and desire.

"Did you think I was making fun?" she asked softly. "I've worked with brilliant, remember? I've played beside it, played for it. I've even been brilliant once or twice. I know what it does to a conductor or a musician when they come off the stage after pulling off something like that." She waved her free hand at the stage. "And you've had to sit and *watch* it after it's done. It must feel . . . strange."

He leaned down and kissed her, too hard, they didn't do this in public for God's sake, but she went up on her tiptoes and gave as good as she got, tipped her head back when he moved his mouth to her jaw and her throat. By the time she pushed gently on his forearms to ease away from him, he felt saner, even if he did want to grab her again.

"You should go see Kathleen," she said, "and Harry."

Robin grinned at her, feeling himself loosening into his body as he did. "Not right now I shouldn't," he said. "I might need a minute."

Tae laughed but then peeked over his shoulder and stopped.

"Harry's coming," she murmured. She stepped in front of him, which would have made him grin more, given the reason he needed Tae as a shield, but then he saw Harry's face and felt his hilarity and arousal drain away.

"It's fine," Harry said, hurrying up to them. "Everything's fine. Kathleen's fine. She just can't breathe."

KATHLEEN WAS PACING her dressing room. She'd changed into the blue dress she'd wear for the rest of the opera, for the wedding and then the murder. The little room smelled of sweat and perfume and also unmistakably of salt water, so much that Robin looked at Harry and Tae. Could they smell it too? Harry caught his eye as he sniffed again and nodded slightly, her face still strained. Yes, she could. Whatever that meant.

"No, no, I can breathe fine," Kathleen was saying. "I can. And it's going away already."

"What's going away?" Robin asked. He reminded himself that what appeared to be the hectic flush of fever along her cheeks was just stage makeup. Nonetheless, she was clearly breathing funny, drawing in deep, audible breaths with the visible effort of someone having an asthma attack.

"The pain," Kathleen said. She made a face. "I was so mad, that's all, or I wouldn't even have said anything." She shot an almost resentful glance at Harry. "It's been so much better, the pain going away completely the whole time I'm onstage, but then today, for the dress, it decides to come back."

"The pain in your feet?" Robin asked.

"Yes," Kathleen said, "only—" She hesitated. "It felt different. It went up my whole legs for a while there."

Robin remembered Tom helping her to her feet. He hadn't thought anything of it. "But it's going away now?"

She nodded. "Gone, see?" She held her skirt away from her body and took several dramatic strides toward him. "Fine."

He nodded. "And the breathing?"

"No, I told you," she said, "I can breathe fine. I could always breathe fine. Didn't I sound like I was breathing fine?" The frown on her face was such pure frustrated diva that Robin smiled.

"You know you did," he said. "But you *look* like you're having trouble breathing."

"It's hard to explain," Kathleen said. "It did start to hurt while I was singing, but almost as if I was breathing *too* well, as if my ribs were going to crack or—" She broke off and shuddered slightly. "It felt weird. That's why I told Harry. It just felt . . ." She turned to Harry, who was standing clutching her clipboard to her chest, and seemed to finally register Harry's pale, set face.

"Oh no," Kathleen said, her voice softening. "No, no, it's all right. It's fine," she said, moving to Harry and putting her arms around her. "I shouldn't have gotten mad at you," she crooned. "I'm fine now, really."

Harry burst into tears, dropped her clipboard, and hid her face on Kathleen's shoulder.

Tae put a hand on Robin's arm. "Four's a crowd," she murmured.

He followed her out into the hall and turned to shut the door, even as the stage manager came striding past, slapping her hand on dressing room doors and bellowing, "Five minutes, people! This is five! Curtain up in five." She skirted around Robin and Tae to roar her warning into Kathleen's dressing room, but Kathleen herself stuck her head out.

"Got it, Abby," she said. "Thanks."

Abby nodded and kept going. Kathleen turned to Robin and Tae. "She's got a future as a drill sergeant, don't you think?"

"I think she's got a future as a stage manager," Tae said.

"Kathleen—" Robin began. She held up a hand.

"Hey, my hands hurt too!" she said brightly, then shook her head when Robin took a step forward. "Daddy," she said, "I'm fine. I think now everything's starting to hurt from sheer nerves. It's hard to sustain this level of brilliance in one body, you know?" She gave him her best preening smile and he laughed despite himself.

"I'm sure it must be very taxing," he agreed. And now he'd have to wait until later to ask if she was joking about her hands hurting, or if, despite all her assurances, he should go back to being frightened for her, and about what. He heard Harry blowing her nose behind the door. Someone, anyway, had never stopped worrying.

"I've got to go talk to her a little more, or she's not going to make the five-minute call," Kathleen said.

Robin nodded. "We'll be in our seats," he said. "You know, row five, on the aisle."

"Go practice getting up and taking your bow," Kathleen said as she closed the door.

"I DON'T KNOW who to be more worried about," Robin said as they sat back down, "Kathleen or Harry."

"Harry is stretched thin," Tae said. "We talked about it a little last night." She slid her tote bag under the seat in front of her. "She was worried about the knife."

"The knife?"

"I think," Tae said carefully, "she wanted to make sure it didn't make its way into the performance. Remember when they left our house and we thought she'd left it there, with us? Apparently she thought she had too."

"She—" Robin checked himself. He didn't need Tae to spell out the implications. "Where is it?" he asked instead.

Tae nodded her head toward her bag.

"Is that—are you comfortable with that? It cut you."

"I've no intention of even opening the case."

"We could leave it in our room, even see if our building has a safe for guests to use. Don't hotels and condos have that sort of thing sometimes?"

"I'm not sure that's good enough for Harry," Tae said. "I'm fine keeping it here." She smiled. "We can call this my contribution to the opera."

Robin opened his mouth, then shut it again as the lights went down for the second act. He couldn't even picture the knife clearly, could only recall the shape and luster of the case and the shock he'd felt both times he'd opened it and identified its contents. First in Moira's drawer, tucked behind her nightgowns, when he'd drawn it out and pressed the catch—not meaning to pry, just curious, nothing more— and recoiled from the knife inside. Then so many years later, when he had opened it again, willing it not to be what he knew it was. It had sat on a table in his studio the rest of the visit, while he and Harry plunged into the work on the opera. When they left, it hadn't even occurred to him to check that the knife was still there, because why wouldn't it be? Why would they want it with them in Boston? It was safer with him and Tae.

He remembered looking over one day, registering that the case *wasn't* there and thinking—what?—nothing. Willfully, nothing. Feeling relief at its absence but deliberately not wondering where it could be. Robin thought of Kathleen unpacking, which for her involved throwing clothes from the suitcase haphazardly into drawers and closets, and uncovering the case. He shook his head sharply to dislodge the image. He had told Harry and Kathleen he believed them, not least because they'd had the knife as proof. But recognizing the knife wasn't the same as *believing in* the knife. Even now, he felt a twisting unease knowing it was in Tae's shoulder bag and couldn't explain why. Was it the knowledge that the knife had been meant—made, even—to kill him, or to kill Moira's poor father? That it was meant to kill Harry now? He believed that much. Yet the idea that the knife might have a say in its wielding, might will itself into action, tempt or taunt the woman it belonged to by refusing to be discarded or destroyed—did he believe that? Did he need to?

The knife appeared in the very first scene of Act 2—or rather, a stage prop version of it appeared, given to the mermaid's sisters by the sea witches in exchange for their hair. The sisters took a proffered shell reverently, passed it from one to the next, then the oldest sister lifted the knife out and held it up so the audience could see it. It was much larger than the real knife, and far showier too, nearly a foot long and gleaming silver when the spotlight hit it. The sisters passed the knife back and forth, singing of its power. *"So light a thing to bring our sister back to us, but its blade is sharp"*—and here one sister holding it made a show of cutting herself on the blade and cradling her hand—*"sharp as the betrayal of a feckless man."*

When the mermaid's sisters passed the knife to her, she refused to open the case and at first attempted to give it back to them, pushing the shell away while her sisters juggled it between them, mimicking the bobbing movement of an object on the surface of the sea. The oldest sister finally caught it and thrust it into the mermaid's lap, scolding her fiercely. *"You say you love this man! He does not love you. You are a pet, a plaything, a pretty bauble to be tossed away."* The mermaid, frozen, clutched the knife case to her chest and shrank from her sister as the bitter aria cut off abruptly. Then the orchestra resumed, softly, as the sisters reminded the mermaid of the world she had left behind, its warm currents and deep-sea gardens, their father's castle and the schools of bright fish that swept through the windows in the morning. The scene ended with them sinking back into the water—Robin noted admiringly that this was conveyed entirely by rising blue and green light on the backdrop—and the mermaid reaching out a desperate hand to them, before sinking back on her heels and slowly picking up the knife.

Robin leaned forward to watch Kathleen during the scene change. She rose easily to her feet and handed the knife and the shell it rested on off to a waiting tech. The fake knife, at least, seemed to hold no talismanic power over her.

"She looks fine," he murmured.

"She does," Tae agreed.

Robin reached for her hand. "Thank you for taking it," he said. He jerked his head toward the bag at her feet.

"You're welcome," she said gravely.

"It doesn't bother you?"

"No." Tae shook her head. "No. You said it yourself. I've touched it, I know how sharp it is. I'm just keeping it safe, and away."

"But you don't really think—"

"I think it's a distraction they don't need on opening night," Tae said. "Beyond that?" She shrugged and a ripple of discomfort crossed her face, like the passing reaction to an unpleasant odor or a grating sound. "Beyond that I don't know what to think."

ON OPENING NIGHT they went to dinner with Allan Charpentier and Jim and Lorraine Dolan. Jim was in high spirits and inclined to tweak Robin about the press he'd been reading.

"You'll have our *Scarlet Letter* sold out too!" he crowed. "I don't think there was a single interview where it wasn't mentioned—but you've got to finish it now, Robin!" He waved a breadstick across the table. "No more side projects until that one's done."

"No indeed," Lorraine put in, laughing. "You certainly weren't excited about the *Tam Lin* idea the *Globe* article mentioned, were you, Jim?"

Jim laughed. "I think I jumped and spilled coffee across the table," he said. "That's why Lorraine remembers. Of course I think *Tam Lin*'s an exceptional idea too—but for the next one, please, not instead of the one that's half in the bag!"

Robin smiled. "I think *Tam Lin* was Harry's idea for a next project, not mine."

Tae sighed. "He doesn't read any of his own press, won't even let me read it to him."

Robin looked around the table. "What?"

"The *Globe* article, Rob," Tae said. "It does quote Harry as saying that *Tam Lin* might be a good idea for a short opera, but then it describes the two of you exchanging a— what was the phrase?"

"A conspiratorial glance," Allan joined in, "with the clear implication that the two of you are already thinking about how to write it together."

"We made a good team," Robin said mildly. "And Harry loves *The Scarlet Letter*—the book, I mean, she hasn't heard any of the opera. But she's got a real gift with a libretto. I might ask her to do some work on that one too." He hadn't thought of it before, for the obvious reason that they'd both been too consumed with *The Little Mermaid*, but it was a very good idea, actually. Harry might well know what to do with some of the passages and sections where Robin had found Hawthorne's text difficult to work with.

"Aha," Jim chuckled. "I bet that's the very expression you got on your face during the *Globe* interview, Robin. Like you just left us all sitting here at the table and went back to your piano and picked up a pen."

Robin grinned and didn't argue, not even to say that he used pencil to compose, not pen.

WHEN THEY ARRIVED at the theater, Robin left the others to find their way to their seats and went backstage. Kathleen flung open the door at his knock and he jerked back at the sight of her before he realized that it was only the stage makeup being used to make her a mermaid. Her eyes were thickly elongated with dark blue on both top and bottom and lined on the insides of the lash lines in silver. They looked like a swan's eyes, or a snake's. Something had been done to the planes of her face too, bringing out long curving hollows along Kathleen's cheeks and up the sides of her neck.

"Creepy, huh?" Kathleen said, grabbing his wrist and tugging him into the room. "Harry and I talked about it with Shan, the makeup artist, when we first got started. The whole thing is that the mermaid, when she's a mermaid, maybe doesn't even need to conform to our ideal of beauty. I mean, why would she? It's a whole different world underwater. So we came up with this—Shan said it works really well on the shape of my face, actually, and then there's a super-quick wipe-off and reapplication between scenes."

"Before the prince finds you on the beach?" Robin asked. The weird angles and shadows did seem to fit her. On someone with a fuller face, rounder eyes, a shorter neck, the makeup would have been clownish.

"Exactly," Kathleen said. She turned back to the mirror and sprayed her hair, pinned back with a thicket of bobby pins and then curled and rippling halfway down her back. "Harry was even more control-freaky about this makeup than she was about everything else," she said. "I think she wanted me to look like I did in the cave where we talked to the witches. We had a flashlight, remember, that fell in the water? And there was this light that came up at one point, when Harry complained about not being able to see, but it was sort of bluish and hitting us from below. Not, I gather, very flattering."

She grinned at her reflection in the mirror, which was disconcerting. Her teeth gleamed white even against the matte pallor of her skin, and the exaggerated tilt of her eyes and brows made her smile feral.

There was a terrific pounding on the door and the shout, "Five minutes! Five minutes to curtain, people." The voice didn't pause for acknowledgment, but continued down the hallway.

"Abby?" Robin asked.

"Of course," Kathleen said. "It's her show now. We're all just here to do her bidding."

Robin realized that he had to leave and that he hadn't reassured her, asked her how she was, wished her luck. It was hard to imagine this creature needing luck, though, or reassurance. He watched her slip into her green satin flats—her costume was nothing so obvious as a mermaid tail, thank God, but a flowing dress that was pale, pale green, almost silver, at her shoulders and then gradually darkened all the way to the floor, where it puddled around her feet in a color as much black as green.

"Are you warmed up?"

"Daddy," Kathleen said, "go sit down. Watch the opera. I love you."

"I love you too," he said. He put out a hand and touched her hair lightly, feeling the hairspray crackling under his fingers.

"Don't mess it up!" She flashed, but she stood still facing him. Head-on her eyes, at least, became her own again.

"You look—extraordinary," he said. "And you'll be extraordinary. You know that."

She rushed him and hugged him swiftly, then stepped back before he could close his arms about her. He could smell the mingled scents of hairspray and stage makeup on her and something else, something almost unpleasant.

"Go on," she said. "Go. It's time."

Robin was halfway down the hall before he identified the odd smell—the smell of the sea, of deep salt water, with a tang in it of vegetative rot almost, but not quite, like mulch. It's because the plants are different down below, he thought. They grow without sunlight so of course they smell different. He kept walking, out the backstage door and around to the lobby, then down the aisle to his seat. The house lights were flashing and went down for good just as he sat down. Robin shut his eyes briefly as the overture began. A part of his brain saw him spin around and run back to Kathleen's dressing room, grab hold of her and tell her not to go onstage, to stop, to wipe the makeup off and come back to herself, to send the sea away, not call it to her as she must have done.

Too late now. He opened his eyes as lights went up on
the bottom of the ocean, green and blue and purple, and the
mermaids appeared, all long white arms and sinuous movement. Robin drew in a deep breath. The sea was re-created
in front of him, but the smell of it was gone.

IT WAS THE Little Mermaid's sixteenth birthday, the occasion for her first trip to the surface of the water. In the
Andersen story, the finery for this occasion included live
oysters that gripped her tail, but onstage, the Little Mermaid's sisters clipped shells into her hair and twined ropes
of pearls around her arms from wrist to elbow. When they
were done, they stepped away, giggling with the excitement
of the celebratory ritual, while the Little Mermaid lifted
her arms, shook her head to feel the shells clatter.

"*So heavy,*" she sang. "*It hurts a bit. I feel like I'm wearing
chains.*"

"*That's the price of beauty, love,*" her sisters sang back. "*You
want to catch the eye of a lover someday; you'll need to bear a little
pain.*"

"*Love won't hurt me,*" the Little Mermaid retorted. "*Love
isn't chains. Love is like rising through the sea and breaking the
surface for the very first time, feeling the air on your face, a caress
you dreamed of but could never have imagined.*"

As she sang these lines, all the sisters lifted their arms
over their heads and the lights changed color slowly, growing paler and paler until the mermaids all burst into open air
and the approximation of sunlight. Kathleen's coloring was
so startling in this moment that she hardly needed the spotlight on her. She spun around and around, eagerly taking
in all the sights she'd never seen before while her sisters

watched indulgently, until she caught sight of the prince on the deck of his ship. Tom was spot-lit too, and dressed like a Byronic hero in a white linen shirt, black pants, and a black velvet vest. His stark clothes cast the richness of his coloring into such relief that he really did appear to be a different species than the creatures who had appeared on stage so far. His hair was a warm gold unimaginable underwater, his skin tanned, his cheeks ruddy. When she saw him, the Little Mermaid broke off in a delighted catalog of new sights—*"Oh, the sky! The sky! And those things in it that look so soft, like puffs of spilled wine, are those clouds?"*—and then fell silent. She seemed even to fade a bit, to grow muted herself until the prince was the only bright spot on stage and the audience saw him through the mermaid's eyes.

The sparse, light-dependent staging ensured that there were no fake rocks for the mermaid to recline on while she sang her first lovesick aria, chasing the prince's ship through the water until it finally outpaced her. Instead she stayed where she was while the light flowed over and past her, suggesting her movement through the water. When the first staccato section of the aria was done, Robin heard Jim draw in his breath sharply. He resisted the urge to lean over and murmur, "That was nothing. Just wait." Kathleen's voice descended, her phrasing languorous as she sang of her deep-sea garden. Then she began the impossible climb, higher and higher, up and out, her hands in the folds of her skirts at first and then rising as she sang of climbing, surfacing, soaring. The aria ended with her arms flung out like wings and the final note shimmering, almost visible, in the air above her.

There was a moment of complete silence in the theater as

the conductor held the musicians off for the applause that would otherwise drown out the segue into the shipwreck scene and the audience seemed to be holding a collective breath. Robin wondered if Jim had breathed at all for the whole second part of the aria. The conductor hesitated— perhaps there wasn't going to be any applause after all?— and lifted his baton, and the audience erupted. Onstage, the mermaid lowered her arms and her head in one grace- ful gesture of submersion that encompassed the sketch of a bow, then lightning crackled, thunder answered, and a storm arose to destroy the prince's ship.

WHEN THE LIGHTS came up for intermission, Robin and Tae stood up and stepped into the aisle to let the others out. Jim had his cell phone in his hand and was thumbing the screen to life as he walked. He stopped in front of Robin.

"Thank you," he said.

Robin didn't pretend to misunderstand. Jim's expression was one of almost agonized excitement and Lorraine was mopping at her eyes. Allan had remained in his seat, his head down. He looked as if he was praying.

"Thank *you*," Robin said. "You're a part of this too, Jim, both of you. How many underwriters would have balked when the composer called and basically asked for a leave of absence from a commission, plus by the way more money to underwrite the thing that's taking him away from that commission?"

"I'll gladly take credit for being a part of this," Jim said. "And I'll even take credit for believing in you, Robin, before tonight. But Kathleen—" He shook his head as if to clear it. "Listen, I'm going out into the lobby," he said. "I need some

champagne—I think Allan may need something stronger—
and I'd like to get in touch with a few people in case they
hadn't planned to come up for the opera. Are there still
tickets left?"

"I think so," Robin said.

"Not for long," Jim said. "Come meet us out in the lobby
and we'll have a toast to that."

"We'll be along," Robin said.

Tae touched his hand as Jim and Lorraine wended their
way up the aisle. "She seemed fine," she said. "By which I
mean that she *sounded* astonishing and *looked* beautiful."

"She was having trouble walking," Robin said. "Did you
notice? When she first had to get up after the prince found
her on the beach she almost collapsed."

"Was that Kathleen or the mermaid, though?" Tae asked.

"I don't know."

"They'd let us know if anything was wrong," Tae said.
"Harry would send someone out to get you."

"I know."

"Well, I'm going to join the line for the ladies' room," Tae
said, "and then maybe join Jim and Lorraine in the lobby."
She hitched her shoulder bag up and slipped past him.
Allan got up and followed her, shaking his head at Robin
as he passed.

"Astonishing," he said. "I—you know everything I want
to say. Just—Jim's right. I need that drink."

Robin stepped back into the row to get out of the way of
the people surging back and forth in the aisle. Harry's parents, sitting on Allan's other side, were still in their seats.
Her father was intent on the program, sucking on the stem
of his eyeglasses. He was compact and balding and didn't

resemble Harry at all, but the expression on his face was somehow precisely the same one Harry got while she wrote.

Robin made eye contact with Harry's mother, realized he couldn't remember her name.

"Are you enjoying it so far?" he asked.

"Oh yes!" She stood and flashed a shy smile.

"I could sit," Robin protested.

"Oh no, I should stand up at least, stretch my legs, though the first act didn't feel long at all." She held out her hand. "I'm Jane, by the way. Harry promised she'd introduce us after the show but I'm sure we can manage."

Robin took her hand. "And I'm Robin. It was good of you two to drive in. Harry was excited you were coming."

Jane smiled again, looking absently around the theater. She didn't obviously resemble Harry either, except for the way her smile changed her eyes and an unexpectedly girlish roundness to her face. She had light brown hair cut in a bob and wore thin gold-rimmed glasses and a blue silk shirt-dress that was at once elegant and no-nonsense.

"You teach, don't you? At a college out in Worcester?"

"Yes, we both do," Jane said. "Scott teaches history and I'm chair of women's studies."

"Ah," Robin said, "so a librettist in the family isn't too far off the mark."

Jane frowned thoughtfully. "Well, no, I suppose not. And yet it's still a shock, isn't it? I mean, Kathleen—" She gestured toward the currently empty stage. "I don't know opera well but I know she's quite . . . exceptional. Isn't that a shock to you?"

"It is. And Kathleen would be delighted to hear me admit it."

"I mean to you as her parent especially," Jane went on, almost as if he hadn't spoken. "Or maybe it's never been like that for you. You're an artist yourself, so . . .

"Did you have that moment?" she asked. "That moment of realizing that the encouragement you've been used to giving them isn't just not adequate, it's actually misplaced? I remember feeling just utterly bewildered during Harry's first recital. She didn't start singing seriously until college, you know, so none of us had any idea, and we're not exactly a musical family. I mean, we were far more likely to have NPR on, and to expect the children to listen to *All Things Considered* right along with us."

Robin chuckled. "This explains a lot about Harry, actually."

Jane laughed too. "Well, yes, she is ours, no doubt about it. But that first recital, you know, I realized only a little way into it that I'd been planning to say these dreadful things, *pat* things, about how wonderful she was, how lovely she sounded—and yet I had no idea how to respond to her actual singing. I felt, well . . ." She cast Robin a sly glance. "I felt at sea, if you'll pardon the reference.

"And now tonight I feel that same way again. Just when I'd gotten used to her singing and learned—or sort of learned—how to respond to that, she writes an opera! I—" Her eyes glittered with tears. "It's rather terrifying, don't you think? I mean, how can you ever tell them how proud you are, how humbled that you made sure they brushed their teeth and did their homework and somehow they went from there to here?"

"I don't know," Robin said. "I think it has been easier for Kathleen and me, since it's always been just the two of us and she grew up literally falling asleep in bars under my piano."

Jane nodded, dashing at her eyes with her fingers under her glasses.

Robin felt that they understood one another perfectly, that they were the only two people responding to the opera in precisely this way, and each equally unable to express their response.

"I think you must have done far more for Harry than just make her brush her teeth at night," he said. "She knows who she is, and she'd never have been able to just plunge in and write this libretto if she didn't have that sureness. To change the source story the way she did—" He broke off. "Uh-oh. Was that a spoiler?"

But Jane's reply was cut off by the dimming of the lights that signaled the end of intermission, and by Tae and the others returning to their seats.

Jane put her hand on Robin's sleeve before he could turn away. "I didn't read the program," she murmured. "I wanted to be surprised as much as possible—though I do know the original story. But Harry's always liked a happy ending."

THE SECOND ACT opened at the wedding reception for the prince and princess. The prince asked the Little Mermaid to dance for him and his new bride and afterward, nearly fainting from the pain in her feet, she slipped out of the party and onto a balcony overlooking the sea. The reception went on in pantomime as Kathleen sank into a heap on the balcony and pillowed her head in her arms. Gradually the lights dimmed on the interior of the palace and came up in blue and green on the sea, where the mermaid's sisters were rising to the surface to offer her the knife. Robin glanced at Tae's tote bag, tucked under the seat in front of her. The knife case was just visible peeking out the top, while onstage the sisters forced Kathleen to take the prop knife. She staggered with it into the bedroom she had shared with the prince—now the bridal chamber—and stowed it in a chest at the foot of the bed. Then she slammed the lid and stood staring at the bed. *"Someone has strewn flower petals on the sheets,"* she sang. *"They smell sweet but they are dying even now. The first time he took me upon the sand, no one scattered flowers where I lay."* And she reached down in a sudden fury and swept the petals from the bed, then fled back out to the balcony as the newlyweds entered the room.

The consummation of the marriage happened in near blackness, with the mermaid spot-lit, her rigid back to the room, her hands clenched on the railing of the balcony. The luxurious string melody that the mermaid had danced to during the reception sped up and grew discordant, then slowed and faded as the light came up on the couple, the bride asleep and the prince propped on one arm beside her.

"My bride," he sang. *"My virgin bride no longer. I wonder where my little one is. Dangling her feet in the sea again? I am hungry for her even now, even here, but tomorrow will be soon enough for her."* He kissed the princess on the cheek—a strangely chaste kiss, as though in taking her once he had quenched all his desire for her—and lay down to sleep.

The mermaid entered the chamber in silence. The drums that had underlaid the sea witches began to beat slowly and the percussion made intermittent shivering sounds as Kathleen walked slowly up to the bed and around it, bending over the sleepers. She stopped in front of the chest and opened it, then stumbled back. Robin flinched from the realism of the fall. Kathleen really looked as though her legs would barely support her.

She crawled back to the chest as the strings rose, an insistent, ugly sawing sound that resolved itself into a plaintive moan as it descended and the cellos took it up. She snatched out the knife and Robin lurched forward in his seat and grabbed Tae's hand, both of them looking at her bag, where the knife box still winked at them.

Onstage, impossibly, Kathleen had the knife in her hand—the real knife, too small for a staged murder but gleaming somehow far more persuasively than the silver foil one had. That was why she'd fallen back so realistically, Robin thought. She'd opened the chest, expecting the prop knife.

It was too late to do anything. Where was Harry? In the wings, surely. She must see it, but what could she do? Rush on stage to stop it? Was she close enough, wherever she was?

Robin got to his feet and was hissed at from behind, stepped out of the row and then stood frozen in the aisle, feeling himself stupidly trapped in the audience—literally trapped, with no way to reach the stage save for vaulting the orchestra pit. Trapped, as well, in thrall to his own music, to the story he and Harry had insisted was true, the story that had the mermaid rising from her crouch at the foot of the bed to lunge at the prince and plunge the knife into his chest as blood arced out in a great wash of—

Red light. Staged blood. Red light and feathers from the deliberately torn pillow, Tom jerking on the bed in terrible rhythm as she stabbed him again and again, clear red light washing over the bed and over the mermaid's dress, turning it purple as she sang, clutching one of the bedposts for support. *"His blood is cool as water on my legs, my feet—I had forgotten what it was not to feel pain like a blade, like a knife going through me. Now as it eases I can barely stand."*

She made for the balcony, calling to her sisters, *"I have killed him! I have killed him!"*

The mermaids rose again from the sea and caught her as she plunged—ungainly, ungraceful for Kathleen, a tumble over the railing of the balcony and roll across the rocks to the bare stage lit like water. Her sisters knelt around her as she raised herself up on her arms, her legs curled behind her so that in her long dress they could have indeed become a tail.

"I have killed him," she sang, half-sobbing. *"I have killed him!"* She held the knife over her head before flinging it across the stage. It made no sound when it landed but skittered into the shadows behind the balcony. There was blood, real blood, running down the side of Kathleen's neck.

"I tried to fly like a bird, my sisters," the mermaid sang, *"to walk on land, to love a faithless man. All impossible things. I am free now. Take me home."*

And the stage went black.

HARRY

Aria for Mezzo-Soprano and Duet with Soprano

Her face was what held me still in the wings. From where I stood I could see her face as she lunged at the bed with the knife raised and I couldn't move, couldn't rush out to stop her or bring her to her senses.

I'd known what had happened as soon as Kathleen had looked into the trunk, before she fell back from the sight of the knife. The expression on her face then was familiar—Kathleen in despair, and in terrible pain too, from the way she was moving to the bloodlessness of her lips beneath the lipstick. It seemed impossible that the opera could go on—that was my first thought. That was why I didn't move to stop her at first. I thought that in the aftermath of the impossible happening, there must be a bubble of stillness.

There wasn't, of course. The music urged her on even as I stood there, wondering how to get to her. But she was no longer Kathleen. Her lips were drawn back and her eyes were black and the cords stood out along her neck and the back of her upraised hand and even as she sprang forward her neck began to bleed. She didn't seem to feel it, didn't stop stabbing over and over, while Tom jerked up in response.

I couldn't see his face, or Carianne's, turned away from me in feigned sleep. I could only see hers. Tears poured down her cheeks and blood ran down the side of her neck and over her collarbone. She was not Kathleen. She was the mermaid. I don't know how else to explain it. I couldn't stop her because she wasn't mine to stop, I suppose. Also, she was doing what she had to do, what *I had made her do* with my libretto, and because it was already written it was already done.

And of course, she wasn't really stabbing Tom. The mermaid stabbed the prince, just like we'd rehearsed, while a red spotlight came up on the white bed and bathed it in the illusion of gore. Feathers from the pillow beside Tom's head, which was overstuffed and designed to burst and spray feathers when she stabbed it, flew into the shafts of red light and came down red. The mermaid killed the prince and his blood washed over her feet. But Kathleen did not stab Tom. Even as I watched and saw the two things happening simultaneously—the stabbing and the not stabbing—I almost couldn't believe it.

When she dropped her arm and began to sing, she was Kathleen—enough so that I was frightened for her. She seemed to be having trouble walking, more than I'd ever seen her have. She clutched at things as she made her way across the room. Then she half-fell over the balcony wall and I couldn't see her anymore from where I stood. I could hear her triumphant final notes, but already I was wondering if she would need help standing for applause.

The stage went black and the audience erupted. I stepped back farther into the hallway and looked to see if Abby or anyone else was around to help me with Kathleen if need be. Then I heard crying and someone murmuring, "It's okay. It's okay, honey. Come on." I turned back to the stage exit. Tom was helping Carianne offstage. She had her hands over her face.

"What happened? Carianne, are you all right?"

"Fuck you, Harry!" Tom snarled. He was shaking with rage, his face flushed with it under his makeup. "You promised, goddammit. You fucking promised."

Carianne gasped. "I-I'm sorry. I don't know why I freaked out. It's just . . . there was a different knife than the one we rehearsed with and Kathleen was bleeding. I think she must have cut herself on it or something—and the look on her face . . ." She swiped at her cheeks. "Tom's overreacting."

"The fuck I am."

"It was just so much more real than in rehearsal," Carianne said. "I'm sorry. I've got to get it together." She noticed her hands and whimpered in distress at the sight of the makeup all over her fingers. "It's going to get all over my dress!"

"It's okay," I said. "You do need to get it together, so you can go take a bow, because you were wonderful. Here." I fished tissues from my pocket and dabbed the worst of the black smears off her face, then handed the tissues to her to clean her hands. I could feel Tom glaring at me and didn't look at him. I felt close to tears myself.

"She would never—" I began.

He cut me off. "Do you have any idea what that was like out there? Any idea? I thought she was really going to fucking kill us."

I met his gaze. His eyes were wild. "Jesus, Harry," he said. "You got in—you got all of us in—so far over our heads."

Carianne looked up from her hands. "What are you talking about, Tom?"

Neither Tom nor I answered her. Behind us the applause continued, interrupted by shouts of "Bravo." Then Abby came tearing down the hall.

"Harry," she said. "Come quick." And to Tom and Carianne, she impatiently added, "Why aren't you two on stage? Come on, all of you."

She practically shoved us all onstage, where we made a less than dignified entrance through the empty bedroom and around the mock balcony where Tom and Carianne joined the rest of the cast. Robin had found a way onstage and picked Kathleen up, managing to bow with her in his arms, taking her bows for her while also clearly—to me anyway—trying to surreptitiously back them both out of the spotlights.

Tom's arrival prompted a new surge in applause. He took Carianne's hand and they took a bow together. Then Jim Dolan stepped forward and motioned for quiet. The audience stopped clapping to listen, while a techie handed Jim a mike. He thanked everyone for coming and said something

about how when he'd agreed to release his favorite composer from his commitment to one opera to write another
one with and for student singers, he hadn't had high expectations. There was laughter and more applause. Someone
thrust a bunch of roses into my arms and I clutched them
as I threaded my way through the cast.

Kathleen was bleeding down both sides of her neck,
rivulets streaming over already drying streaks. There was
blood on Robin's sleeve and the shoulder of his suit. And
she was breathing in wrenching gasps, clutching Robin's
wrist and trying to pull herself up in his arms as if she
wanted to expand her lungs to take in enough air.

"Kath," I said. I dropped the flowers to free up my hands.
"Kathleen, what do you need?"

She shook her head, but I couldn't tell if that was because it was too hard to talk or she didn't have an answer.

"Let's get her out of here," Robin murmured. He shoul-
dered his way to the wings, then kept going, not toward the
dressing rooms but down the hall toward the back door of
the theater, which led to the lot where the singers and orchestra members parked.

"Robin! Where are you taking her?"

He swung around to wait for me. "I don't know," he said.
"I thought at first the hospital—" Kathleen moaned and
shook her head, practically clawing at him to get him to acknowledge her objection. "I know, darling," he said gently.
"Be still."

The outside door opened and Tae stepped in. "I pulled
the car around. Are you ready to go?"

"The hospital may be the only option, Kath," I said.
"You're bleeding, you can't breathe—"

"And can't walk," Robin said grimly. "She can't even put weight on her legs."

"Kathleen . . ." I tried to get her to look at me. I could tell her mouth was hurting too, from the way she was holding her jaw and the convulsive way she was swallowing in between those terrible breaths. "Sweetie, we just need to—"

But Kathleen suddenly pulled herself up again in Robin's arms and with a visible effort made her throat work well enough to call out, "Tom!"

He'd been lurking just at the entrance to the hallway, his own triumphal spray of roses dangling half-forgotten at his side. Kathleen stretched out her hand and he came, his expression set. Then he got close enough to get a good look at her and his face crumpled. He cupped her cheek and kissed her.

"Tom, I'm sorry!" she whispered. "I didn't—I promise that I didn't—I could feel it happening and that I was her and you were him but I knew we were also ourselves. I swear that if I'd stopped feeling us both, I wouldn't have kept going. I would have thrown the knife away, Tom." She began to cry weakly, pressing her face into his hand. "I would have."

"I know," he said. "I know you would have. I just—I thought I'd get a little more warning about when it was time to believe before I had to."

"I'm sorry," she said again, and he shushed her. He slid his hand down from her cheek and then stopped, brushed her hair away, and peered closely at where her neck still bled.

"Have you seen this?" he asked Robin.

Robin shook his head. "I can't put her down," he said. "She can't walk."

"Well, that's not surprising," Tom said, "seeing as how she's growing gills."

So INSTEAD OF going to the hospital, we went to the sea. Tom held the door for us while Tae ran ahead to unlock the car. I slid into the backseat and Robin ducked down and deposited Kathleen half in my lap. I had to support her upper body or she would have slid prone across the seat. Her long skirt was so tightly tangled around her lower body that I couldn't see her legs. She was shuddering and twitching in pain, clutching the arm I had braced around her waist and making strangled sounds. I held her tight and sat as straight as I could, bracing my left arm against the door frame to make it easier to hold her head up. Tae threw the car into gear and took us out of the lot fast enough to throw me back against the seat.

In the front, Robin turned to look at us.

"All right?"

"I guess," I said. My voice betrayed me, though. I sounded terrified.

"Tom's going to make our excuses," Robin said.

"What's he going to say?"

Robin didn't bother to answer me.

What we were doing—the composer and librettist fleeing from opening night through a back door, taking the incapacitated soprano with them—was so bizarre that I don't think either of us could imagine any "excuses" that might account for it, not even from Tom. God, poor Tom. Poor Carianne. And my poor parents—I hadn't done more than hug them before the show. I could picture, all too clearly, the scenes unfolding in our wake: our friends huddling in groups backstage, the Dolans and Robin's other friends huddling in the lobby, fear and confusion dampening the pride and excitement that all of them ought to be feeling.

As if on cue, my cell phone vibrated in the pocket of my blazer. I managed to extract it one-handed and sat staring as it jumped in my hand again and again. My mother. Abby. Abby. Three different singers in the cast one after the other. Jim Dolan—I'd forgotten he even had my number. Abby. My mother.

"Give it to me," Robin said.

I looked up from the screen to see him half-turned in his seat and holding out his hand.

"Mine too," he said. "I'll put them both in the glove box for now."

Mutely, I handed over my phone, feeling another message come in even as I let go. Other people's panic seemed impossible not only to answer but to even acknowledge, intruding as it did on the terrifying realization that we might have done magic together, Robin and I, but done it too soon or too well. *Idiot!* I thought. *You were so sure this opera was going to* work. *What the hell did you imagine that might mean?*

Kathleen jerked again and moaned as I tightened my arm to keep her from sliding onto the floor. It was like trying to gather a wild animal onto my lap. Whatever I might have imagined, it wasn't this.

"Tae, where are we going?" Robin asked.

"Pleasure Bay is open access all night," she said, "and there certainly won't be anyone swimming there at this time of year."

"How far?"

"Ten minutes, no more."

I bent my head over Kathleen. "Ten minutes, Kath, just hang on ten minutes and we'll have you in the sea."

Kathleen tried to nod, I could feel her head moving against my forearm, but she didn't say anything. Her breathing grew so labored and loud that after a few minutes we would have had to raise our voices to be heard over the sound. Tae took us through the dark streets, traffic thinning out as we left downtown and approached the harbor area. She turned at the sign for Pleasure Bay/Castle Island and drove along a black lane without passing a single other car, then pulled into a parking lot and stopped under a light. Robin opened the passenger door of the backseat and leaned in.

"Kathleen," he said, "can you sit up a little so I can get you? There, yes, that's good." He slid his hand under her neck and lifted her head off my arm, then gently pulled her toward him.

"Sweetie, you have to let go of my arm," I said. I tried to extricate my other arm from around her so I could press myself back against the seat and make it easier for Robin to take her, but her grip stayed locked.

"Loosen her fingers, Harry," Robin said. "She may not be able to." I followed his gaze to Kathleen's hands. Her fingers had elongated until they nearly wrapped around my arm and they were *webbed*, with taut, translucent skin extending between the fingers all the way up to the first knuckle. I remembered her complaining during dress rehearsal that her hands had started to hurt.

I had to slide my fingers under hers to pry them off my arm, and then she flailed her hands as if she didn't know how to move them or where to put them. Robin eased her out of the car, shifted her in his arms, and began to walk along the path from the parking lot to the beach. I scrambled out and ran to catch up with them, stumbling a little when we reached the sand. Tae caught my arm to steady me and we crossed the short expanse of beach to the ocean. There was little surf here, because of the way the bay was sheltered. The sea lapped delicately at the sand and then retreated just as softly. Robin waded in and Tae and I followed, then both staggered back from the shock of the icy water. I gritted my teeth and kept going. Robin and Kathleen were visible as a single figure up ahead, her hair spilling over his arm on one side and the trailing skirt spilling over on the other.

"If I ever talk to her again," I said, "I am so going to make fun of her for how ridiculously perfect she looks being carried into the sea."

Tae didn't laugh. "You'll talk to her again."

We were up to our knees in the water but Robin was well ahead of us. He hadn't stopped to get accustomed and he was in up to his waist. He put his head down and murmured something to Kathleen, then cried out when she suddenly wriggled and flipped out of his grasp and splashed into the water. I screamed as Robin went in after her, surfaced briefly, and spun in a circle where he was, looking wildly toward us for a moment.

"She's gone. She went in and I felt her for a moment and now she's gone, goddammit. It's so dark I can't—" He spun again and dove into the water, surfaced several yards out.

"Kathleen!" he roared. "Kathleen!"

Tae plunged in up to her shoulders. "Robin, be careful, please!"

"But what if she's— What if she needs help?" Robin asked hoarsely. He was out beyond his depth, treading water, still turning in a slow ring even as he talked, scanning the water for any sign of her. I was doing it too, my eyes aching from trying to see movement on the black surface of the water. I pushed forward until I was next to Tae, the water lapping at my chin.

"Just wait," Tae said.

We were all shivering convulsively. I started to cry, ugly wrenching sobs, my nose running.

"Did you see her after she went in?"

"I told you, I felt her," Robin snarled. "The water surged around me like someone pushing off, that way." He gestured out to where the bay met the open sea, then suddenly slapped the water. "Kathleen!"

A head broke the surface. Then another, and another. Soon there were seven of them, sleek wet heads shining in the moonlight and ringed loosely in a semicircle, perhaps twenty yards away. I couldn't have said what they were from that distance and in the dark. Mermaids? Selkies? They did not acknowledge us. They seemed, like us, to be waiting.

When the eighth head broke the surface in their midst, they surged forward as if in greeting and welcome. But she held them off with an imperious turn of her head and a look. I couldn't see her face but it didn't matter. I *knew* that look. I burst out laughing, choking through my tears from sheer incredulousness, that the first thing she would do when I was expecting her to be so utterly changed would instead be so familiar. Then she plunged toward us and fanned her tail, pure silver in the moonlight.

"My God," Robin said. Tears were streaming down his cheeks. Kathleen came up out of the water and flung herself at her father. He grabbed her and held her tight, his face in her hair, then suddenly set her away from him and tried to disentangle her arms from around his neck.

"Kathleen," he said. "The water. Don't you need to breathe?"

"Oh, Daddy," she said, and her voice was hers and not hers, amused and sobbing and singing all at once, in just two words.

"I can breathe air for a little bit," she said. "Long enough to thank you, long enough to tell you what you've done, all of you . . ." She turned to me and I started to cry again at the sight of her face, which was hers and not hers, just like her voice. Her eyes glittered with black light but there was no hectic flush in her white cheeks, no urgency to her gestures, no desperation in her voice. The hysteria we'd grown used to calming in her was gone.

"Daddy," she said, "it's done. It's broken." She put her hands on either side of Robin's face. "You saved me, Daddy. You saved me and you ended it, you and Harry. Please—oh please don't be sad."

Her voice had water in it, a liquid undercurrent that made it difficult to understand her without listening hard. I felt like I was eavesdropping but I couldn't stop straining to follow her words.

"I'm not sad, baby," Robin said.

"Liar," she crooned. "Liar." And she flung herself upward again to wrap him in her long arms, both of them seeming unaware of her nakedness as he pulled her close. She murmured for a long minute in his ear and he stiffened

and pulled back to look at her. Then he nodded. She pulled
his head down to hers and murmured something else that
made him laugh and hug her tighter for a moment, his eyes
shut and tears seeping out under the lids. At last he set her
away from him.

"I love you," he said. "Little mermaid. Now go on. Those
of us without fins and tails are freezing out here."

He swam back to take Tae's hand and tug her toward
the shore, while Kathleen splashed his back. "You take that
back! I haven't got any fins!"

"But you've a tail now, don't you?" Robin turned once
more to smile at her and spoke in lilting Irish cadences,
making his words a blessing. "And if I never see you again,
my darling"—his voice broke—"it's glad I am that I got to
see you as your own true self."

KATHLEEN SWAM TO me, looped her arms around my neck,
and pulled my face down to hers. Her lips were cold and
wet and when she slid her tongue into my mouth I tasted
the sea, felt it rushing in my ears. I couldn't kiss her back.
I didn't even put my arms around her, afraid to feel this
sinuous wet creature instead of Kathleen. I was already so
wet and cold.

When I felt her tugging harder, pulling me under the
water with her, I tried to pull away, but she was too strong.
She pulled us both under and the one-sided kiss filled with
water—and then I was kissing Kathleen. Her mouth was
warm and tender against mine and she tasted of strawber-
ries and champagne. I shut my eyes and reached for her.
The skin of her bare back was warm and the feel of her
small bare breasts pressed against mine through the bar-

rier of my clothes was desperately erotic. I slid my hands up under her hair and kissed her until I had to pull back, gasping.

She was smiling at me and crying, though of course there were no tears on her cheeks. But I could see her clearly and I could hear the sound of tears in her singing breaths.

"Kathleen!" I tried to talk before I thought about it, but instead of choking on water I simply shaped her name and sent it to her.

"It's all right," she said. Her voice seemed to eddy all around me and it sounded even more like singing now than it had in the open air.

"I had one kiss to give," she said—sang. "You can see, breathe, talk. And you should be warmer now, aren't you?"

I hadn't noticed anything but her. Now I registered that I'd stopped shivering.

"Yes," I said. "But how did you know you had one kiss to give? How long will it last? Can I swim like you can?" I thought suddenly to look down at my legs—still legs. Kathleen's laughter burst like bubbles against my ears.

"You're not changed, silly, just gifted." The tears were in her voice again. "For a few minutes."

"And then?"

She shook her head, her hair swirling around her. Underwater it was still red, but darker, with lovely, murky purple shadows in it. "Then I've got to go home."

"To Ireland."

"Yes. Back to my water—do you remember how it made me feel? But—Harry, *look* at me!"

"You're beautiful," I said. Kathleen kissed me again, fumbled at the buttons on my shirt, opened the catch on my bra so we could embrace skin to skin. I shuddered at how good it felt and slid my hands down her back to where the skin became scales. They slipped under my hands like petals of pearl, curved and satiny smooth. Beneath them, she was supple and yielding, undulating against me, taking my sobs into her mouth, then moving her mouth down to my throat, my breasts . . .

I was gasping for breath from the feel of her, then I was just gasping for breath, then suddenly I shut my mouth on the certainty that I couldn't breathe at all.

"Oh damn, damn, it's too soon!" Kathleen cried. She caught me around the waist with one arm and pushed upward. We'd gone very deep. The water was going dark around me and I couldn't even see her, could only feel the press of the water as we rose through it.

Then we broke the surface and my head lolled back on Kathleen's shoulder.

"Breathe!" she snapped. I breathed. I was so tired I couldn't even kick my legs to help her as she swam back into the cove. We'd gone very far, nearly to the open sea.

"Were you planning to take me home with you?" I meant it as a joke, but my voice sounded frightened, not teasing.

"Hush," she said. "Of course not. I just—I lost track of where we were. It was just like my dreams, do you remember, the dreams I used to have of swimming underwater with you? I've never had a dream actually come true before."

She swam us past the creatures still waiting for her near the entrance to the bay. I turned my head and met enormous liquid eyes without any visible whites.

"Are they Selkies?"

Kathleen snorted. "Just seals. I think they're here to guide me home, or some such thing."

"I bet the witches sent them," I said. "You should go see them and tell them what's happened."

"Aren't they supposed to know already?" she asked. "Here. You should be able to touch bottom now."

I could, though I began to shiver again as soon as my feet touched and I wasn't sure how I'd make it all the way back to shore. Robin waded back out to help me but I threw his hand off.

"Listen," she said. "You're going to hate me tomorrow, both of you—all of you—Tom and Tae too. Because I'm leaving you to clean up a mess again, aren't I?"

"I don't care. We don't care."

"Tell Tom I love him. And don't protect me anymore. When you go back, let people—reporters, the police, it doesn't matter—let them all see all the medical records. Tell them I made you bring me here. Stick to the truth, Harry. Tell them"—her smile was delighted—"that I drowned."

"I want to come with you," I said. I'd cried so much that I seemed to have run down. Now it was only hiccupping and the tears on my face.

"You don't want to come with me," she said. "You can't. I will love you forever and ever but you have to stay here and write an opera of *Tam Lin*. And then another one. And another. Write them all and find a girl and love her—"

I gasped. "Stop it. Don't be an idiot," I said.

"Love her and let her love you," she insisted. Her voice was growing stranger and harder to understand, as if the water was rising in it and drowning out the human tones.

"I love you," I whispered.

"Listen to me," she said. "You broke the curse. You saved my life. You set me free."

"It's a happy ending, then?"

She laughed. "It's a happy ending." The water gurgled in her throat and she was already receding from me, letting the tide carry her out.

"Do you promise to live happily ever after?"

"I promise," she said. "Do you?"

What else could I do? She was already half gone.

"I promise," I said.

She'd been laughing at me when we met. She laughed at me now. "You think you're lying," she said. "But you will, Harry. Just wait and see."

She turned fully away—she always had to have the last word, damn her—and dove out toward the sea. I stayed there, in icy water up to my neck, watching the seals turn at some invisible signal that must have been a mermaid swimming under them. They disappeared without a sound. Still I stood, shivering, until she surfaced once more as I'd known she would, right at the entrance to the bay. Any farther out and we wouldn't have been able to see her at all. She blew us a kiss with her shining, webbed hands and showed us the fan of her tail once more as she submerged.

Then she was gone.

*W*hen the knife came back to us, we did not at first recognize it for what it was, for we had ceased to hope for its return like this—in shards, with edges that might scratch or poke the skin but had no power to pierce it. They fell like rain from Above into the chamber where we worked, and we caught them, at first, automatically, knowing only that they must be ours. When we recognized them, holding enough slivers of shark fin in our cupped hands to feel them shift and slide against one another like coins, we rejoiced.

And we grieved, for the death of the girl called Harry, for Kathleen and the pain she had taken on, her lover's blood spilled in exchange for her tail. We even felt a ripple of unease that it should be over now, so suddenly and after so long, and that we had not been ready. Then too, we owed Kathleen for the gifts we had taken from those who had come before her. Our cabinet held a net made from her mother's hair. We sent some guides to lead the mermaid daughter home and told ourselves it was enough.

We took the remains of the knife out to the garden and fed the shards to our oysters, slipping one into each of many rough gray shells. The usual irritant is just a bit of sand or grit, but we have long coaxed our oysters to form pearls around stranger, sharper debris, and we knew even as we sowed the slivers that the pearls they would produce would be exceptional.

We did not expect them to be bloodred, or to grow so quickly. The oysters spat them out only weeks later. We were harvesting the pearls, which were extraordinarily beautiful and gleamed like a basket of berries from Above, when Kathleen came to see us.

We had not expected that either. She swam through the gates without any of the usual hesitation and only stopped at the very entrance to our inner chambers, where she had to knock to be admitted. When we let her in and saw the fine mist of joy still covering her, like sea spray itself, beaded in her hair and over her breasts as though she'd only just been splashed with it, we were frightened for ourselves. That she could feel such joy while her lover lay dead Above by her own hand could only mean that she was mad. We circled her cautiously, herded her away from shelves of fragile, precious things, hid the fresh-picked pearls in a shadowy corner. She looked at us and laughed, a melody of not just joy but also triumph.

"You don't know," she said. And of course, we did not know.

When she told us how the knife had broken, how the curse had been lifted by a false murder, the knife spattered with illusory blood, we could scarcely believe her, though we saw that she spoke the truth. We retrieved the pearls, told her how they had been made. These should not be possible, not without real blood spilled on that blade.

She picked one up and rolled it in her hand. "The

knife should not even have broken the way you say it did, though, should it? You underestimated Harry—and my father. You thought your kind of magic was the only way."

We do not deny our own limitations.

She held out the pearl in her hand. "Can you make a chain for this? And will you give me this one to wear"— there was sorrow now in her face and in her voice—"as a souvenir?"

She asked for a gift, and she had chosen the largest and most beautiful of the whole crop of pearls. To simply agree, to pierce the pearl and thread it on a thin, strong chain and hand it back to her, is not our nature. We deal in bargains and trades, not in gifts. But we owed her much, much more. On a high shelf in another room was a jar filled with the burning embers of Ceara's life.

We gave Kathleen the pearl and she slipped it around her neck.

"Thank you," she said. "There is just one more thing. I came to tell you what had happened because Harry said I should. But I want to ask you to do something for me as well."

We waited. She settled the pearl between her breasts, shook back her hair.

"I want Harry and Robin to know I am happy. Can you send them dreams of me?"

"It would be difficult."

"But you could do it. Maybe just once a year? Enough so they wake up and remember again what they did for me."

We waited. In a chest of a hundred locked drawers we keep the smaller things: the black weight of Fand's regret, the shining bubble of Muirin's fleeting joy, the lock of hair Caolinn was clutching when she drowned. We owed Kathleen the dreams she asked for. Still we waited to see what she would do. We deal in bargains, in magic bought and paid for. But we are also scavengers, and greedy. It is in our nature.

"I'll pay you," Kathleen said.

How will you pay?

"I'll give you a song, of course," she said. "I'll give you the aria that set me free."

Ah.

We had a bottle ready to catch the song. It had come from a shipwreck and it was the kind of bottle used by those Above to hold sparkling wine, but larger than any we'd ever seen.

Kathleen laughed and laughed when she saw it.

"A jeroboam," she said, laughter and tears together in her voice as she pronounced the strange word. "Oh God, Harry would love it."

We remembered the voices that had come before hers—from Fand's to Moira's, each different but all beautiful. We had chosen a vessel that would hold any of these. But when Kathleen began to sing, the bottle nearly shattered; we had to reinforce it magically, which left the bottom thickened and rounded so that it refuses to sit flat but sways like it is caught in a current, like the song inside it is always being sung. She sang a terrible song of grief and pain that shook the dead things in our chambers and reminded them that they were dead, that called for blood until the new red pearls fountained from their basket. It was a song from Above that should not have had power so far Below, but it swept around us like dry wind, impossible and undeniable, until it drained into the bottle and we lunged to put the stopper in.

Kathleen returned to herself, saw the disarray she had created and smiled again. She curled her hand around the pearl at her neck.

"You will send the dreams?"

We will send them. For as long as you live, for as long as they live.

"Good," she said. "Thank you."

Then she turned and swam away. We have not seen her again.

We send the dreams every year. Robin and Harry wake from them with tears of joy and sorrow on their cheeks. They believe that Kathleen sends them the dreams, and indeed, she paid well for them.

But they themselves also paid us well, though they will never know this. The song that swirls in its strangely named bottle is more than Kathleen's voice. It is a lattice-work such as we have never seen and could never hope to weave, words and music as warp and weft. Through their lattice, Kathleen's voice surges and eddies, back and forth, never losing its power, nor its beauty.

It is a song, nothing more, but it is also very much like the sea itself.

The Mermaid at the Opera

A Short Story

The manuscript was gone—pages stacked and bound in twine, then sealed inside an oiled envelope and sent, at considerable expense, on to Denmark. Andersen hurried through the darkening streets of Naples, feeling empty. *The Improvisatore*—it was a good title for a good tale, based on his own vivid experiences of Italy, which had struck his inclination to asceticism and self-abnegation like a blow. But now the book was gone and he faced white paper again, a nearly new bottle of ink, and months left of his planned stay in Naples, without work to give shape and meaning to his days.

Back in his lodgings, he rang for hot water, threw off his cloak, and began to dress for the opera. Even this treat, which he could only just afford, felt flat when Andersen considered that he would return from the Teatro di San Carlo to rooms that were no longer the site of his work. When the maid brought a pitcher, he poured it in the basin and shaved quickly, then dampened his thick hair and patted clove oil onto his jaw, hissing at the sting. He squinted despairingly at the mirror, seeing no great literary figure launched into the world but only a gangling man, narrow in the shoulders and chest but with a great beaky nose and big-knuckled hands, raw from constant scrubbing to get the ink off them. What he needed, Andersen thought as he pulled his cloak back on and settled his hat on his head, was a muse. But while Italy offered muses aplenty—from laughing black-eyed girls to Madonnas whose lips gleamed red under their veils—none of them seemed likely to choose an ugly Dane upon whom to bestow their favors.

THE OPERA HOUSE was sold out, for tonight the great voice herself, Maria Malibran, would sing the lead in Vincenzo Bellini's *Norma*. Andersen's seat was not good, but that hardly mattered when he ducked past the curtains into the box. The opera house fell away before him in glittering waves of velvet and lacquer. Andersen looked so greedily and for so long that he grew dizzy. He no longer worried that this evening would fall flat, nor paid anything but passing attention to the people taking their seats around him. Even before the overture began, the box was full, save for the seat to his right, which had an even more obstructed view of the stage. Then just as the orchestra began to play, a woman slipped into that last chair, her skirts brushing Andersen's arm as she swept them aside to sit down. Andersen turned his head.

He intended to spare her only a glance, but the first glance demanded another, and then, incredulously, he dared not look at her again. She was small and slender, dressed in the unrelieved black of widowhood and heavily veiled. And yet he knew that she was beautiful, the same way that he had known that the sea would be cold when first he saw it. The second glance had gone through him like a sharp pain, for she'd been in the act of adjusting her long glove, exposing a white arm of impossible delicacy. Andersen stared straight ahead at the stage and imagined the sight and feel of her hand in his, palm touching palm, fingers entwined. The overture went on, but he had been abandoned by the music, consumed instead by his awareness of the body beside him. She could not possibly leave the veils on for the performance. They would muffle the sound of the music, make it difficult for her to breathe in the close, perfumed air, obscure the stage in a sooty blur. She would remove the veils and he would see her face. He had to see her face.

A company of druids appeared on the stage in white cambric shirts and linen togas, wreaths in their hair. The leader moved downstage, the top of his head gleaming, his big belly swelling even bigger as he took breath to sing. Andersen closed his eyes. Beside him, he heard the whispering sound of cloth against cloth, and then his nose was abruptly filled with the smell of salt water.

IN THE YEARS since his voice had changed and he had been forced to give up singing, Andersen had discovered a curious paradox within himself. He experienced certain moments with electric intensity, so much so that he made others uncomfortable. Yet he could never claim to be as suffused with feeling as he appeared, because there was always a dispassionate voice in his head observing both the event and his own reaction to it. The cool, sometimes ironic voice was antithetical to Andersen's sense of himself as an *artist*; he came to see it as a growing interior consciousness that he was first and foremost a *writer*, an observer and recorder of human nature and human experience. But during the whole first act of the opera, the woman was there beside him, and as buffer against her he could find no cool, rational voice. She smelled of the sea, and Andersen, who had never liked the sea, found that the fragrance of her made him think not of chilly ocean voyages but of a dimly lit and curtained room, of a tub of steaming bathwater and her damp hair against his body.

He was terribly afraid that she knew his thoughts. He had not been so aroused since his early adolescence and he strove to hide it, to sit rigidly still, to not look at her again. The last glance, after the veils had come off, had been enough. He had never seen hair that color and he smiled bitterly in the darkness, for here was his ironic voice after all, coming not to his aid but to torment him. *Hair like fire inside a piece of coal? Hair like the red-black heart of a late-blooming rose? What pretty compliments can you offer her that she will not have heard before, and from far more attractive admirers?* His self-mocking voice went on: She was a widow. His very response to her violated the reserve and dignity of her state of mourning. And yet her black dress and veils also made an overture possible, did they not? She was a widow and alone. Her sorrowful state demanded the most attentive courtesy, permitted the crossing of certain delicate lines of conduct. The box was stifling, the opera itself wrenching. When the intermission came, might he not offer to fetch her a cup of lemonade?

But the widow vanished as soon as the intermission began, slipping out through the back of the box before Andersen had even risen from his seat. If his perceived attraction to her had driven her away—he cursed himself for succumbing to his basest sensibilities and punished himself by remaining hunched in his chair throughout the interlude. The opera resumed before she took her seat, but not until she was once again beside him and he heard the rustle of her veils could Andersen focus his attention on the stage. He did not steal another glance at the woman until the final scene of the opera, when Norma mounted the sacrificial pyre and Pollione, her unfaithful lover, rushed to be reunited with her in death. The young man was not equal to the role; he sprang up onto the pyre with unseemly athletic enthusiasm and Malibran's voice was so far superior to his that it was like the beating wings of a swan alongside those of a common pigeon. Cast adrift from the story once more by his own critical voice, Andersen turned his head to watch the widow. She was intent on the scene, the fluid line of her profile from throat to jaw like a breaking wave. Above it, her lips were pressed together and the tears streamed unchecked down her cheeks.

Later, Andersen would wonder: If he had not been watching her at that moment, when Pollione sang his final lines, would they have ever encountered one another again? Would he have gotten the courage to speak to her or would she have darted away during the final ovations and left him lurching foolishly after her?

But he *was* watching the woman as Norma chided her lover in majestic tones: *"Qual cor tradisti, qual cor perdesti, quest'ora orrenda ti manifesti!"* The heart you betrayed, the heart you lost, see in this hour what a heart it was! And Pollione answered her, painfully, *"Col mio rimorso è amor rinato, più disperato, furente egli è."* With my remorse, love is reborn, a madder, more desperate love.

Hearing these lines, the woman gasped as if she'd been struck. Her mouth opened, and Andersen, seeing what it revealed, made a choked sound of his own. The woman's head snapped around, her hand coming up to cover her mouth and her eyes meeting his for the first time.

If she had not been so very beautiful, Andersen would have recoiled. But he took in the details of her beauty greedily, even after what he'd just seen. Her eyes were silver one moment and black the next, like the surface of the sea under an uncertain sun, and her face was exquisitely shaped, from the oval sweep of her forehead down to the delicate point of her chin. And as he lowered his gaze to her mouth when she dropped her hand, what he took in first was the fullness and flushed color of her lips and not what he'd glimpsed a moment ago.

The opera was over. Around them rose the applause and cries of acclaim for the diva, "Malibran! Malibran!" Andersen and the woman faced each other and he spoke into a silence that seemed to run like a current between them under the swelling noise.

"Oh, my dear," he said, "who did that to you? And why?"

But of course she couldn't answer. She only shook her head and reached out one slender gloved hand for him to take and bring reverently to his lips. The protocols had been breached, Andersen realized giddily. He could indeed invite her to take supper with him now, offer to escort her home, ask to attend on her again. And she would accept, conveying her acceptance in her fashion, of course. Because he had not recoiled when he had seen, quite by accident, that inside her lovely mouth her tongue had been cut out, cleanly and deliberately, by what could only have been a very sharp knife.

IN POSSESSION OF both her hand and her secret that first night, Andersen forgot to be nervous. He took her to a small café near the opera house, ordered a pot of steamed chocolate and a tray of cakes without a stutter, then watched in bemusement as she produced a notebook and a little gold pencil and wrote out—in English, the only language she could write in, though she understood Italian well and French passably—her very first words to him.

You are a gentleman, sir.

He flushed, smiled, passed the paper back. "It is nothing," he said. "I am honored that you would join me after the performance. It is difficult to go home alone after such a night of music."

The moment the words were out he was aghast, but her head was bent over her pad already and she used three sheets of paper before she finished her response. When he took the pad back from her he saw that she had ignored or not noticed any innuendo in his words; she had written a brief but scathing review of the opera. She had nothing but disdain for the tenor—*Why do they let little boys on the stage? Where are the men?*—this last word underlined so hard that the pencil tip had broken off. And of Malibran she had written something so strange that at first he thought he was not reading the words correctly: *she sings like a bird in a cage.* He read them again and looked up to find her watching him avidly.

"Yes," he said slowly, and heard in that moment a sound like the low notes of the orchestra opening a duet. "That is exactly right. Like a wild bird longing to be set free. I came to hear her sing, of course, didn't we all? And still it was—startling."

He handed back her pad, pages folded back to a fresh sheet, ready for her reply.

She hesitated only a moment, her eyes black in this light,

but sparking with silver in the depths, before she put the pencil to the paper again. *My God*, Andersen thought helplessly, *to kindle those eyes!* He pictured her, fleetingly, lying beneath him, her eyes on fire and her breath coming fast. When he looked at her again, she was holding the notebook out.

I hope I do not presume too much, she had written, *but when I saw your face in the opera box I trusted you. You looked as though you knew what it felt like to have known music and then lost it.*

She cocked her head and Andersen nodded. So she could hear it too, the sound of harmony, the undercurrent of duet between them. They understood each other already. He need only control his own base longings.

The pot of chocolate arrived, steaming deliciously, and the woman waved the serving girl off when the girl would have poured for them both. There was something imperious in her gesture, Andersen noted with amusement as she filled his cup and handed it to him. She might have been a noblewoman in her own salon rather than a widow in a black dress that was revealed, in the bright light of the café, to be shiny with wear at the elbows and the edges of the sleeves. Inspired and touched by her desire to play hostess to him, Andersen told her the tale of how his sweet boyish voice had been captured—overnight, it seemed—by a mysterious bullfrog that sat in the back of his throat and croaked out its presence at unpredictable intervals. Watching her laugh, always with a careful hand to her mouth, Andersen thought, *Ah, if only she could speak! I would have such a muse as any man might envy.* And he realized suddenly that he did not even know her name.

FAND, SHE TOLD him, writing the letters out carefully. It was Irish, apparently, the blunt syllable foreign on his tongue and nothing like what he would have called her. But she gave him no other name to use.

In the months that followed their meeting, they had tea several times a week, dined out after the opera at least one additional night. He always made the suggestion, as was appropriate, and she assented, that tantalizing half-smile of hers dipping out of sight as she bent over her little notepad to scribble her response.

Her penmanship was appalling, no better than an untutored child's. It was a flaw that Andersen found unaccountably endearing even as it maddened him when he had to puzzle over her notes long enough to lose track of his own train of thought. His own penmanship was a source of pride, and how ironic that he did not need to use it with her, this one skill he might have wielded to win her over. If they had been lovers writing letters, his would have been masterful, both the language and the flow of the letters inked onto the page calculated to seduce her, woo her. Hers would have been only poor supplicants in reply. But he had no excuse to write to her. Instead, they fumbled together, she with her little gold pencils worn quickly to nubs and he with his clumsy tongue, always afraid he would say the wrong thing, ask the unforgivable question, or reveal his lust too nakedly.

At first he had restrained himself from even the most delicate of romantic overtures out of concern for her widowhood. As time passed and their intimacy grew, however, he found himself occasionally furious with her, as if she deliberately tempted him. He was a man, after all, and hale—so what if he was ugly! Ugly men enjoyed the pleasures of women all the time. Ugly men married, sired children. Why should he shudder with mingled longing and terror at the sight of her ungloved hands curling around a mug of tea? Why did the sight of her uncovered hair as she sat back in her seat at the opera and loosened her veils, unpinned her hat, leave him panting—panting like a dog, his mouth open and his face averted from her until he could control his response to the scent and sight of that hair, the scent like water and the color like fire, hair that promised to both inflame and quench desire. Her customary chignon was low and heavy at her nape. Unbound, her hair would fall halfway down her back, crimped and wavy from being confined, and intolerably bright against her white skin. Picturing it, Andersen dug his fingernails into his thighs and waited for the spasms of desire to pass. In these moments he hated her.

Then one night as they were leaving the opera, they were caught up in a crush of people avoiding an overturned coach. Swept down a cross street, they made a wrong turn, then another. Fand gripped Andersen's arm and he strode desperately ahead, seeking a way out of the sudden maze of reeking, unlit alleys. At last, he glimpsed a familiar street corner up ahead, but they were only halfway through the narrow corridor that would take them there when a man sprang from the shadows. Fand gave a little choked scream and shied against Andersen, and the strangeness of hearing her voice made Andersen himself jump backward. The man took the advantage to move into the light. He was not armed, did not seem intent on robbery. Instead he fixed his eyes on Fand's face and, with so little fumbling that he must have been waiting for just this opportunity, he exposed his member and waggled it at her, grinning obscenely.

Andersen felt faint. He pulled at Fand, trying to steer her away without manhandling her himself, but she resisted. Appalled—did she not understand what was happening?—Andersen looked at her face. She was staring at the man. Very slowly, she allowed her eyes to drift from his leering face down his body and then her expression changed, from vague interest to total disdain and incredulity. She lifted one delicate winged eyebrow and raised her eyes again to the man's face, and such was the curl of her lip, the arch of her brow, that Andersen felt almost a moment's pity for the fellow. There was no mistaking her implication.

The man's grip slackened, his mouth fell open. Fand picked up her skirts with her free hand and pressed Andersen's arm. As they walked the last few yards back to the main thoroughfare Andersen felt the first stirrings of the panic. This was not the fragile, sheltered woman he had imagined her to be. She was something other, something more. He had been consoled by a belief in his own noble intentions. How much worse it was to have seen that look of imperious disdain, to imagine himself fumbling before her, sweating, no better than a wretch in an alley.

SUMMER BROUGHT HEAT that made the air shimmer in the afternoons and coaxed fetid smells from every alley—horse manure and sweat and rotten food. Andersen longed to leave Naples for someplace cooler, fresher, but he had given his publisher this address. That was what he told himself. When the letter arrived—*The Improvisatore* was marvelous, they would begin printing immediately—Andersen dropped it onto his writing table. It was just as it had been when he'd sent the manuscript off: he knew he should feel proud, excited, but he felt only yawning dread, because there was still no new project. His desk was littered with only the debris of correspondence, to which this latest letter could be added without offering any inspiration. He should sit down immediately and map out a new project. It needn't be a novel. It could be an essay or series of essays. He laughed humorlessly. He'd settle for writing nursery tales now if he could do so with that flaring of excitement that assured him they would be worth writing.

Instead, Andersen pulled out his watch and glared at it. Four hours until he was due to meet Fand. He would need to bathe before he did so, and by the time he'd walked to their favorite teahouse he'd likely be soaked in sweat again. He threw himself onto the bed despairingly. He should leave Naples. He could go to the Alps, up to one of the mountain lakes, up into the Pyrenees—anywhere at a higher elevation would bring relief from this weather. He could even return in the fall if he wished to do so, pay extra to ensure that these same lodgings would be waiting for him.

But then he'd have to leave Fand and face his fear—more palpable than ever since that night in the alley—that while she enjoyed his company, she would not miss him, did not need him, for anything. He lay back and let himself slip into a languorous doze, keeping his hands off his body but dreaming restlessly, feverishly, all the same. When he woke, thirsty and with a headache as if he'd had too much wine, he felt almost unable to get up.

This cannot go on. I cannot go on like this, he thought. *I wanted a muse and instead I've found an enchantress—or a succubus.*

He would go then. And he would tell her today. Andersen pushed himself up and rang for water, knowing even as he planned what he would say to her that what he was truly hoping for was not a severing of ties but a revelation from her—for tears to spill from her silver eyes and a plea from her gold pencil, that he take her with him wherever he went.

FAND WAS OCCASIONALLY late for tea, already pulling her little notebook from her reticule as she slipped into her chair, snatching up the pencil to jot down a fervent excuse: they'd kept her late in the opera's costume room, where she did fine needlework sewing embellishments onto hems and necklines, and she'd sneaked into a rehearsal for *Turandot* and lost track of time. But she'd never failed to arrive, until today. After an hour of waiting, sweating miserably in his coat but unwilling to sit in public in just his shirtsleeves, Andersen stalked from the restaurant and turned toward his rooms, then wheeled abruptly and headed to the boardinghouse where Fand lived. He did not hesitate until he stood in the tiny, sweltering vestibule, the house oppressively silent but for the ticking of the grandfather clock. On previous occasions when Andersen had called here, a maid had appeared after a few minutes, once even the landlady herself. Today he stood long minutes and no one came, but the anger that had carried him all the way to the front hallway of her lodging could carry him no farther. He didn't even know which room was hers.

"Signor?"

It was the maid who usually answered the door, a plump girl with blond hair and startlingly dark eyes under thin, fair brows. Her coloring made her look sly and artificial, like a doll in a shop window. She stood at the back of the vestibule, her shawl still over her head. She must have run some household errand and only just returned.

"You like me to tell the signorina you are here?"

"Is she in her rooms?"

The girl shrugged. "I will knock, signor." She climbed the stairs, straightening her shawl across her shoulders and smoothing her hair. The clock on the landing struck six, nearly an hour and a half past their scheduled tea. Then the maid screamed on a rising note.

"Signor! Signor! Dio mio!" And then even louder, her voice hoarse and urgent, "Signor!"

Andersen took the stairs two at a time, swinging himself around the landings with a hand on the newel posts at each turn. At the third floor he stumbled toward an open door. The maid stood with her back to the wall. She had flung her apron over her face and was sobbing into the folds, her shawl a black heap on the floor. Andersen leapt past her into the room, registering that it was even hotter in there—there was a fire in the hearth, of all things—and saw Fand with her back to him, shoving something into the flames.

"Fand!"

She swung around to face him, and the knife in her hand caught the firelight in a swift dizzying arc. She had cut off all her hair. The fire smoked under the mound of blackening strands, and her face, framed by the ragged remnants, was alien in its beauty, the sockets of her eyes too large, her slender neck too long.

"My dear," Andersen whispered, "oh, my dear, what have you done?" He took a step toward her and his boot heel skidded. He looked down. The floor was smeared with a dark, wet stain all around the fireplace, streaks of it on the hem of Fand's dress. Not water—blood—she'd cut herself badly or she was bleeding from under her dress.

"What have you done?" he said again, his voice raised and roughened this time.

She jerked her head back and put the knife to her throat. Her eyes shone silver in the light of the guttering fire. Her hand on the knife was covered in blood; it trembled as she tried to press the blade closer. Andersen leapt for her, his height an advantage, one hand tight around her upper arm, jerking it down, the other plucking the knife from her fingers. It was shockingly cold to the touch. He flung it behind him and immediately had to support Fand as she wavered, as though the knife had been the only thing keeping her erect. He caught her around the waist when she would have sunk to the floor, put his other arm under her knees, and lifted her—she weighed nothing at all—onto the bed. Here was agony he could not comprehend, and yet it was a thing of grace, like the sound of the music he could no longer sing, because he could save her from this, he could refuse to let her go. She lay with her eyes closed, her face colorless within the coppery frame of her shorn hair. There was a red line across her neck and a trickle of blood sliding sideways, extending it. Andersen walked backward to the door, not taking his eyes off Fand until he had reached the hallway and found the maid still there, hiccupping as her tears ended. The landlady stood beside her, arms folded over her broad bosom, her face impassive.

"Fetch the doctor at once!" Andersen snapped. The maid fled down the stairs.

The landlady waited for him to meet her eyes before she spoke.

"She cannot stay here. You tell her. Not in this house. I keep a good house, a clean house. She must go now. No sickness here."

"She is not sick," he said impatiently. "She is injured and distraught. There can be no concern about contagion."

The woman narrowed her eyes as though he were simpleminded.

"Sick," she said. "That is not what I mean. She cut herself! You see what she did? My girl told me. You see?"

She pushed past him into the room, bringing with her the heavy smells of wood oil and onions, and though Andersen tried to intercept her—went so far as to grip her shoulder to hold her back—she reached the bed before he did and twitched Fand's skirts up above the knee.

He could not restrain his gasp. He had feared, obscurely, some kind of female trouble, but there was no blood seeping down her skirts or petticoats. Instead, her slender feet were bare and sliced to ribbons, both the soles and across the tops, and the deep cuts continued up her legs, encircling her ankles and her calves, joined ladderlike by the blood that had dripped down her legs as she stood by the fire. Andersen fought back a wave of dizziness at the sight. He shuddered to think how sharp that knife was.

"You see," the landlady said. She herself seemed unaffected by the sight of so much blood. "She cannot stay here."

Andersen wrenched his gaze from Fand's legs. He could taste bile in his throat, feel sweat sealing his shirt to his back. He shook the landlady with the hand that still lay upon her shoulder.

"Towels," he said. "Bring towels and hot water."

She jerked her chin toward the washstand in the corner. "There," she said. "Use those." Andersen dropped his hand and hurried around the bed. The landlady hesitated a moment in the doorway.

"I will send the doctor up," she said. Then she turned away, her tread heavy and condemning on the stairs.

Fand shrank into the pillow as Andersen wiped away the trail of blood on her throat, his hand shaking.

"You must lie quietly, Fand," he said. "The doctor will be here soon. You must rest."

He fumbled for the hem of her dress without looking, felt his fingers brush her waist, then her hand, limp at her side. He restored her skirts and drew a breath of relief when the bloody sight was hidden once more. He watched her face as he pressed the cloth to her neck, hoping to see her returned to herself. Her eyes were open now but she looked through him as if into some dream world that lay just over his shoulder.

"I wish you could tell me what you see," he murmured. Her eyes regained their focus and a look of such vivid rage and despair filled her face that his hands faltered.

"Fand—"

She opened her mouth as she had not done since the night they met, opened it obscenely wide to expose her severed tongue. Then she shut her lips again and turned her head away.

Andersen stood frozen a moment, the wet cloth in his hand dripping into his shirt cuff. He felt slapped, brutally reminded of what she had endured. Here he stood dabbing at the least of her wounds, unable even to minister to her for fear of the sight of a little blood, while she had tasted her own blood, choked on it. He shut his eyes against the image and then forced himself to look down the bed. Her feet were still visible, bleeding onto the white sheet. He dipped the towel into the basin beside him, turned her skirt back a few inches to expose her ankles. His hand trembled as he pressed the towel to one of the deeper cuts. He had seen women's legs before, but never like this, limp and exposed on a bed with him bending over her. The watery scent of her was potent even under the stench of burned hair, even under the smell of her blood, like wet iron on his hands.

He leaned in closer, wiping ineffectually at the blood covering her fine-boned feet. The sweep of the clean towel exposed her skin for a moment before blood seeped out again. Andersen stared in horror, wiped again and saw what he thought he had seen—a network of thin, silvery lines on her skin, old scars.

THE DOCTOR WAS a plump man with fine mustaches and an appreciative eye for Fand's profile even as he opened his bag and laid out suturing supplies. He was dismissive of the landlady, assuring Andersen that a few well-chosen words from him would secure Fand her rooms at least until she recovered. Having introduced himself as Fand's brother— impossible to believe, if the doctor's swift look was any indication, but at least they both had red hair—Andersen waited in the sitting room. He felt dangerously faint from the heat, such that he shed his damp coat and tossed it over a chair. He rolled his shoulders a bit under his wet shirt and felt that he could breathe at least. When the doctor called him back, Fand was tucked into fresh sheets, so still she hardly seemed to be breathing. There was a bottle of laudanum on the table by her head. Andersen grimaced; he hated the stuff, the too-sweet odor that clung to lips and teeth, the heavy feel of it in the mouth.

The doctor was washing his hands, looking thoughtful. Andersen realized suddenly that the man expected payment, likely considerable. He opened his mouth to beg forbearance on the bill; he could pay part of it today, but certainly not all. But the doctor forestalled him with a wave of a damp hand. He understood such things. No one could be prepared for a medical emergency such as this, a crisis. There was no need for alarm. He himself had been paid before in kind many times and he was quite happy with such a transaction. He had been given fine jewelry, foodstuffs, several times—and here he raised his eyebrows humorously, as he looked over his shoulder—offered less tangible favors by the grateful wives and daughters of patients he had saved. He knew his worth, the gentleman must be in no doubt of that. He would be returning, certainly, to look in on the young lady, change her bandages, make sure she was comfortable. In the meantime it might resolve the question of payment if the gentleman knew that he, the doctor, was an expert in blades of all kinds: swords, knives, ornamental daggers. He had quite a collection, in fact, in his study at home.

The doctor dried his hands fastidiously while Andersen stared, his mind at first blank as to the fellow's implication. The doctor flicked his eyes to the table where the laudanum sat and Andersen, following his gaze, saw the knife. It had been wiped clean and shone softly in the dim room, the gleam at its core muted by the exquisite carvings along the hilt, a curling pattern like the crests of surging waves. It appeared to be all of a piece, the blade emerging from the hilt without any visible seam in the metal. Andersen could not think how it could have been made. He remembered how cold it had been in his hand.

It was not his to give, but he gave it anyway. He did not want her near that knife, did not want to see it ever again. But only three days passed before it returned.

ANDERSEN CAME TO the boardinghouse every afternoon. Whatever the doctor had said had been persuasive enough that Fand's sheets were changed, her doses of laudanum administered, and her fever cooled by the fresh water sponged on her face by some member of the household, most likely the young maid. One day, Andersen arrived to find the maid gathering up sheets from Fand's room to wash. Warmed and grateful, he pulled a coin from his pocket and offered it to the girl as she passed him. To his surprise, she shook her head, blushing and murmuring something he could not make out.

He caught her arm. "You won't take money? You have been very kind to her, but surely you must allow me to compensate you. I know you have other work."

"She pays me," the girl murmured. "I don't need more."

Andersen frowned. "She pays you? How?" He tightened his grip when she would have pulled away. "Have you been stealing from her?"

"No, signor!" She looked up, terrified. "I am not stealing. She showed me once, asked me how to get money for her jewels. I have done things for her before and she has paid me from the bag. I am happy to do things now, I only take a very, very little thing." She twisted out of his grasp, but only to face him fully, her face open and pleading.

"Please, signor. Do not say it is stealing. I am taking care of her, you said so. I am. She has shown me herself, she has paid me before."

"Where?" Andersen asked. "Show me this bag you are talking about."

The girl looked even more frightened and her eyebrows knitted together in confusion, thinking that perhaps she had committed a greater crime in revealing Fand's secret. She shifted the load of laundry in her arms.

"There," she said, jerking her chin. "In the wall, by the fireplace. The bricks, you see them? Where they are darker? They move." Then she hurried down the stairs.

Andersen glanced at Fand, little more than a huddle of bedclothes. Then he crossed to the fireplace and pulled out the darkened bricks. There was a velvet bag in the space behind them from which Andersen poured a king's ransom in jewels onto the bed. Surely these could not all be real. A necklace of amethysts and black pearls, earrings from which swung emeralds and diamonds, a ring so small his littlest finger could not pass through it, weighed down by a ruby the color of new blood. Gifts from her husband? Andersen looked up at the white face on the pillow. These things did not even suit her. They were heavy and ornate, made for a fleshier woman, or one who delighted in ostentation. They were jewels a man would give a woman when he wanted to show them both off: woman and jewels together, symbols of his wealth. Lifting a necklace of sapphires, alternately dark and light blue, Andersen recalled the night in the alley, the look on Fand's face as she sized up the man. He could picture her, not as she was now, with her poor hair cropped close and her legs crisscrossed with sutures and scars, but as she was still, in his most fevered dreams, wearing this necklace and nothing more, her lovely face uplifted to the caress of the man who gave it to her.

There was something larger in the bag, a box that looked, impossibly, as if it had been crafted from a cross section of a single enormous pearl. But that pearl would have been the size of a schoolroom globe or a streetlamp. And inside, even more impossibly, was the knife he had given the doctor, still shining, and fitted into the case as though it had been made to do so.

He replaced the jewels and the pearl case. He took the knife himself this time. On his way back to his lodgings, he threw it into a pile of refuse behind a public house.

He swept into Fand's chamber the next day with what he almost hoped was visible insolence—for why did she deserve the courtesies he'd bestowed on her, when she'd clearly been deceiving him since they'd met?—then stopped short at the sight of her propped up in bed. Her eyes were nearly black under the heavy fringe of her lashes, and she smiled and held out her hand. He gave her his own, helpless to resist her. She had washed her hair and pulled it back with a ribbon; from the front she might have been wearing her accustomed chignon. There were blue-black shadows under her eyes and a fine tremor in the hand he held, but she was Fand again. He had forgotten.

And then in another moment he was angry. He released her hand and went to the fireplace, pulled out the bricks and brought the bag with him back to the bed. Her smile faded. She watched his face as he poured the jewels into her lap.

"Yours?" he asked. "The girl told me about them. She has been taking them as payment for caring for you here. She insisted to me that you allowed her to do so."

She shrugged, her eyes still fixed on his face.

"And these were gifts to you from whom—from your husband, before he died?"

She lifted her chin and did not break his gaze. After a long moment, she nodded. He wanted to shake her.

"These are the jewels of a princess, Fand," he said, "a princess or a woman whom a man keeps—keeps for show, keeps like a pet or a prize. Was your husband a prince? Were you a princess?"

At that, she suddenly smiled. She very nearly laughed. She looked down at the heap of jewelry in her lap and touched a diamond bracelet with one finger. The tension returned to her face. Andersen realized for the first time since he'd walked into the room that she did not have anything to write with, nor had she sought out her ever-present little notebook. She seemed content not to explain herself to him.

He reached into the bag again then and drew out the pearl case, set it precariously on top of the pile of jewels. She shrank away.

"No, no," he said. "It is gone. I removed it from here while you were insensible and I discarded it. This is only the empty case, you see."

But when he opened it, the knife was there, unblemished. He sat down heavily on the edge of the bed.

"Fand," he said, "I swear to you that I removed it from that very case and discarded it far, far from this room. I did not want you to ever have to see it again."

She nodded.

"It is impossible," he said. Then, carefully, "Can you not . . . will you not tell me—"

She looked around then for her pad, made the familiar gesture with her fingers, of squeezing a pencil. He caught her hand in both of his.

"Will you tell me?" he asked. "Will you tell me all of it? I-I wonder if it might not help you, to tell me, now that I know so much, now that I must believe you. For I've seen it, Fand. I gave this knife to the doctor who tended you and it came back. Then I cast it away myself; I felt it leave my hand, saw it fly through the air and land in a pile of refuse on a city street. And yet here it is again. Will you not tell me?"

She sat with her head bent over their linked hands. He thought that she missed her long hair and her veils, that she wished in this moment to hide her face from him. He waited.

At last she raised her head and nodded, her mouth tremulous, her eyes shimmering black to silver and back again. She tugged her hand free and gestured for her pencil again.

"No," Andersen said. "No. Not that. I will bring you some better paper to write on, and a real ink pen. You shall not scribble this down like something to be discarded on a teahouse table."

Fand nodded again but still gestured for her pad. He found one in the drawer of the bedside table. While she wrote, he scooped up the jewels, shut the knife case, replaced it all in the wall. When he turned back to the bed she was holding the pad out to him. The high flags of color had returned to her cheeks. He took it and read.

It will take a good deal of paper and a long time to tell. I am afraid it will disappoint you.

"Do not worry about that," he said, but she reached for the pad and wrote again, then handed it back.

The story is more like an opera than a fairy tale. It does not have a happy ending.

Andersen looked down at her, his heart pounding the same way it did when he heard the overture beginning, when he would lean forward and forget his cramped seat, the hot, stale air, and lose himself in the soaring voices on the stage below. He did not care if her story had a happy ending. He only wanted to hear it, to lose himself in it, to see the shape of it on the page the way he could close his eyes during a well-sung aria and see the notes stringing themselves together in a shining, ephemeral arc. She could not speak, but she would be his muse yet.

HE WROTE THE words—*To my little mermaid, my muse*—with a flourish inside the front cover and then held the book open with one hand to let the ink dry. He'd bought this particular edition in a shop in London, savoring the peculiarity of paying for his own work, because the size and the softness of the green baize cover reminded him of Fand's little notebooks. He'd sent her a copy of the first edition, in Danish, when it had been published, but this little volume, with the mermaid herself stamped on the cover, appealed to him as the right gift to bring this afternoon.

Sixteen years would have changed her, he reminded himself as he put on his greatcoat. It had changed him, for the better. He had acquired income, acclaim, and confidence in his talent. Even his nose had lost its power to depress him, except on his weariest days. But for a woman of limited means, sixteen years had likely meant a loss of beauty, of grace and freshness. Walking to Fand's latest address, Andersen anticipated encountering a faded version of the vivid woman who had so captivated him. Recalling her struggle to resist injuring herself, he acknowledged that he could even find her wasted by laudanum addiction, or swollen with drink and visibly scarred by that terrible knife.

He was prepared for anything except for the woman who opened the door to his knock: Fand, glowing and vivid. She had not been expecting a caller; she peered around the door at first, then flung it open in exuberant welcome when she recognized Andersen, her lovely face alight. Her hair was loose about her shoulders and she wore no stays but only a flowing gown such as a woman might wear at home, a gown that concealed neither the swell of her bosom—far more abundant than Andersen recalled—nor the larger swell of her belly below.

She tugged him into the house, then shut the door behind him and left her hand on his sleeve, smiling up at him with unfeigned delight. A moment later she had whisked away to snatch up a notebook and pencil, scribbling furiously and glancing up at Andersen as she wrote, as though to reassure herself that he was still there.

Fand was pregnant. Beautiful still, even more beautiful perhaps, made lush where she had been fragile, and *pregnant.* Andersen trembled head to foot as if shaken by a chill. He wanted to flee the house, but he was frozen in place, held captive by all that was familiar in her beauty—the high spots of color in her cheeks, the smell of the sea that wafted from her unbound hair—as well as by all that was new. The shadow between her breasts taunted him, as did her pink and white forearms framed by the lace-edged sleeves of her gown.

She thrust the notebook at him, pushing him into a chair and dropping down onto a footstool beside him, preparing to watch him read with the avidity he suddenly remembered well. Andersen took up the pages and tried to focus on the words. Fand's handwriting was far more familiar than she was herself, for they had corresponded regularly ever since he'd left Naples. And yet he hadn't known she was pregnant, that she had a husband or a lover. She'd written about her delight in the continued success of his stories and about opera. Andersen had come to think of her letters as full of music, both in substance and in cadence, for she often captured a performance with the same spare elegance as when she had first described Malibran to him (*she sings like a bird in a cage*).

The words on the page today were hastily scrawled and hard to make out—but then, his hand was still shaking. *I cannot believe you are here!* she'd written. *After all this time and now you are here just in time for another Bellini, and one that has never been performed in Naples before. We have tickets and Vincenzo will give up his for you to go with me—to think that we will sit in an opera box together again after so many years. You look so fine too, in your cloak and your elegant clothes, but just as young as ever. I worried that you would not come this season though you said*

you would and I worried I would not recognize you or you would not
recognize me. But you have come—the word *have* was underlined three times—*and you are just the same. The tickets are for*
tomorrow night. We can dine first and then go. I would love to go
out afterward to a café as we used to do, but I get too tired now and
Vincenzo likes me home to rest.

Andersen lifted his head from the page.

"Who is Vincenzo?" he asked. "You never wrote to me of
him. Is he your husband?"

Fand seemed amused by the question. She held up her
hands and waggled the fingers so Andersen could see that
they were bare of rings.

"Your lover then."

Andersen tore out the pages she'd written and crumpled
them in his fist. Fand flinched and shrank a little on the
stool.

"And the child," he said, "when is it due?"

She reached for the notebook but he held it out of her
reach.

"What have you done?" he demanded. "Given yourself
to this man, gotten yourself with child by him—what is he,
is he a singer? Is he young and handsome, this Vincenzo?"

Of course he was—all of those things. Fand flushed and
reached again, urgently, for the notebook. Andersen held it
even farther out of her reach.

"You could write a thousand pages and I wouldn't read
them," he said. "You want to talk to me of opera, of music—
did you lie in your lover's arms and write to me? Did you
think you could be both his and mine? You—" He was talking nonsense, but he could not stop. She was pregnant. She
would soon bear some man's child.

"You debase yourself," Andersen said. His throat was so clogged with rage and pain that he could hardly get the words out. "You will bear a child like this, into this shabby world. I made you immortal and you make of yourself just another who—"

She sprang up and hit him in the face before he could finish the word. Andersen fell back in his seat a moment, then jumped to his feet and loomed over her.

"Do you even know what you have done?" he asked. "What if the child suffers your curse, have you thought of that? Does this Vincenzo even know? What will you do if the child wails for water or feels pain in her feet as if she were treading on sharp knives and the blood must flow?"

Those last words were her own, written sixteen years ago while she sat up against her pillows, still recovering from her attempt to mutilate herself and gaining strength from telling him her story. He still had the original pages, folded carefully in a locked drawer in his study in Denmark. He had taken her story and shaped another story around it, thinking as he did so that there was a wonderful metaphor to this particular creative process. He was like an oyster adding luster and polish to a grain of sand and producing—in time—a pearl that was now a beloved story across all of Europe and even America.

He had meant the words to wound her and could see that they had. She backed away from him, then moved to the desk that stood against the back wall of the room and picked up another notebook. From behind, her pregnancy was not even apparent; she was a slender, supple length of skirt and flaming hair.

"What could you possibly say that would explain?" Andersen snarled at her back. The stinging of his cheek where she had struck him felt merely like a physical manifestation of the pain of her betrayal of the chaste bond between them. "Will you tell me how you came to love *Vincenzo*, how he wooed you with his boyish charms and his dark eyes?"

Fand turned, the book and a pencil in her hand, and retraced her steps across the carpet to stand quite close to him, close enough that she had to tip her head back to search his face. She had calmed now, and her expression shifted from perplexity to understanding and then to— Andersen braced himself for it, but then found it unendurable all the same—pity.

She had not known. All these years of agony—first here in Naples, when she had been so close and he had never dared speak of his desire, and since then only from afar, when the mere sight of his name scrawled on a letter from her had been enough to set his heart pounding—she had never known. Andersen might have felt relief that, after all, he had concealed his longing better than he hoped, but for the gentleness with which she touched his sleeve once more.

He jerked away. "You would not hear that word from me," he said. "And I will not say it and risk you striking me again, but that is still what you are now. You cannot love this Vincenzo, who has no idea what you are, what you were. You have sold yourself for physical pleasure, soiled your story—the story I perfected for you—grasping for what, for a *happy ending*? When you do not even know what will become of the child?" He pushed his face down toward hers. "What if it is born with a tail, Fand?" he whispered. "What will you tell your lover then?"

The notebook he had been withholding had fallen to his

side. He held it out to her and she took it, stacked it on top of the one she had taken from the desk. She stood with her head bent. Tears made dark splotches on the top page and the pencil trembled in her hand when she raised it to the paper.

But she did not write. She turned from Andersen again, just a step back and an angling of her body so she could set the notebooks down. Then she straightened and snapped the pencil in her fingers.

"Now you will not speak?" He scoffed. "I confess I am hardly surprised—"

But she was not done. She cut him off with a look as surely as if she *had* spoken aloud. It was the look he had seen only once before, sixteen years ago, and it made him quail now as it had then, when it had not even been directed at him. There were tears on her cheeks and her hands were shaking as violently as his own, but she swept her eyes down Andersen's body and then back up, and when she looked him full in the face, she curled her lip deliberately, arching one eyebrow, and he was instantly reduced to cringing, abject shame.

He fled the house, fumbling with the doorknob and tripping on the step, plunging *away* so desperately that he was halfway down the street before he realized that it was raining. Andersen clutched his coat more tightly about him and quickened his pace. When he felt the lump in his pocket and remembered what it was, he jerked the book out as though it burned him and tossed it in a puddle. He did not look back to see it sink, but pictured the green baize mermaid's smile blurring and smiled savagely. *Let her drown*, he thought. *I've no more need of her. I am done with muses.*

FAND HELD HERSELF still a moment after the door slammed, then clapped a hand to her mouth and stumbled through the front room to the kitchen, where she retched into the sink. When she had finished, she poured a glass of water from the pitcher on the table and rinsed her mouth until she could swallow without gagging. She carried the glass back into the sitting room and sank into the chair at her writing desk. Vincenzo would be home from rehearsal soon. She swiped the tears from her cheeks with the heel of her hand, then set the glass of water down and moved slowly around the room. She picked her notebooks up and closed them, stacked them back on the desk. She tossed the pages he had crumpled and the pencil she had broken into the fire, then stood a moment watching the flames leap to their devouring.

She sat back down. The child surged like a swimmer within her. Fand set her hands over the taut skin of her belly and shut her eyes. After a few moments, she gave voice to a sustained crooning sound. It was wordless, of course, but then the music of her people often was. It was not even a song as Fand had come to understand songs, but it was rhythmic and melodic. It sounded strange in the air, enough so that she wondered if she was remembering it right. It had been sung to her when she was a fretful little girl. Later she had sung it to her grandmother when the old woman was afraid to sleep. *Your voice is a gift*, her grandmother had told her. *When you sing me to sleep my dreams are always beautiful.*

The child, suspended in her own small sea, quieted against her mother's hands. Fand sang on, sang her daughter to sleep, and to dream her own beautiful dreams.

ACKNOWLEDGMENTS

I sent this manuscript out into the world, and not long after received an email: "The first five pages are lovely. May I see more?" So thank you to Cameron McClure for liking how this began and for seeing it through to the end. To Rebecca Lucash, who *loved* that the story was dark; to Elle Keck, who picked me up midstream and didn't let me drown; and to absolutely everyone at William Morrow, who made this book better—thank you.

I love fairy tales and fantasy because of Hans Christian Andersen (even though I think he got this one wrong), Andrew Lang, Angela Carter, Emma Bull, Robin McKinley, and so many others. Without Guy Gavriel Kay's daring to make the impossible happen, for example, this book would never have ended the way it did.

When I realized that Kathleen and Harry were singers and Robin a composer, I set out to understand opera. Thank God I came to love it. And thanks also to Greg Carpenter and to the world he opened up to me, to Dawn Upshaw and Lorraine Hunt Lieberson for their exquisite singing, and to Fred Plotkin for writing *Opera 101*, without which I would not have risked writing a word about opera in performance.

Great writers/teachers along the way have taught me how to write better: cleaner, stronger, truer. From Claire Messud and Reg McKnight to Gail Galloway Adams, Kevin Oderman (I took out all the unnecessary words, I promise!), and Mark Brazaitis (even though he hates italicized sections), I have been unbelievably fortunate and grateful to have worked with all of you. And to Emily Mitchell, who was sort of stuck with me from the beginning (!) and who gave me hope that this book had a shot when I told her how it was going to end and she said not, "Are you crazy?" but "Oh, thank goodness": thank you, thank you.

Finally, there are those who were part of this project because they are my favorite people in the world. Thanks to Paula, who found a way to keep asking how the writing was going even though she was afraid to "poke the bear at the zoo," and to Paul, who doesn't like to be put on the spot but sucked it up and offered brilliant feedback because it's in the sibling contract somewhere. Thanks to Collin, for being at least somewhat proud of me, to Ian, who would like to remind me that Daddy *also* wrote a book, and to Lilah, for keeping me humble. Thanks from the bottom of my heart to Erin, who listened and read and poured more wine and read some more and then asked when she could read some *more*; thank you for reminding me always that my reader is out there and she is you. And thanks to Ryan, who should know all the reasons why but probably doesn't because I'm too busy writing fairy tales. Thank you for refusing to let this book be anything less than the best it could possibly be, for figuring out that tequila is a good incentive for writing the hard parts, and for believing in me, which is its own kind of strange and wonderful magic.

About the author

About the book

Insights,
Interviews
& More...

Brian Persinger

AN INVETERATE READER OF FAIRY TALES, Ann Claycomb believes in the power of faerie, chocolate, and a good workout, in no particular order. She earned her MA in English literature from the University of Maryland, where she baffled her thesis committee with an argument that "Beauty and the Beast" is ruined by the Beast's transformation into just an ordinary prince at the end. She earned her MFA in fiction from West Virginia University, while writing the novel that became *The Mermaid's Daughter*. This took, as her daughter is fond of telling people, "a long time—like, a really long time." Twice nominated for a Pushcart Prize for her realist short fiction, Ann is nonetheless drawn to retelling fairy tales to highlight the thorns around the beautiful castles and the dangers of things that seem too good to be true (they usually are). She lives with her husband, three children, and two cats in Morgantown, West Virginia, where she is at work on her next novel. ◠

Reading Group Guide

1. This novel plays with two versions of "The Little Mermaid"—both the original by Hans Christian Andersen and the Disney film version. How did your own familiarity with either or both of these versions affect your reading of the novel? Were you surprised by the twists in the story?

2. From the very first chapter, Kathleen describes herself as a bit of a "diva" and a "drama queen" and the other characters agree with this self-assessment. What was your initial response to her as a character? How did your feelings about her change as the story unfolded?

3. This story is told by four different characters: Kathleen, Harry, and the sea witches tell the story from their own perspectives, while Robin's story is told in the third person. Did you find this an effective way to tell the story? Was there a voice you liked better than the others, or one that you liked less? Why?

4. The sea witches claim throughout the novel that they've been wrongly portrayed, specifically in Andersen's version, as evil and malicious. They also say they are as trapped by the curse as Fand and her descendants are. What do you think of their arguments? Are they evil or just misunderstood? In what ways are they also trapped?

5. Throughout the book, all of the characters, especially Kathleen and her friend Tom, rely on dark humor as a coping strategy, something that many of us do. Why do you think people turn to this kind of humor in very serious situations? How do you think it helped Kathleen and Tom cope with the circumstances of the novel?

6. Harry and Kathleen's relationship could be seen as full of inequalities: Harry believes that Kathleen is a better singer, more beautiful, and also in need of caretaking, while Kathleen often relies on Harry to be the more practical, grown-up partner. Did their relationship make sense to you? Did you feel that Harry was indeed Kathleen's "true love"?

7. We learn the long history of Kathleen's ancestors well before she and Harry are able to piece it together in Ireland. Did you find the other women's stories compelling? How did their stories affect your outlook on Kathleen's story?

8. Magic enters the "real world" in the novel in Ireland, first with the appearance of the Selkie and then in the sea witches' cave. How did the intrusion of the magical world change your expectations for the rest of the novel? Why do you think it first occurred in Ireland? Do you ▶

believe places can have special properties?

9. Were you surprised by Tae's acceptance of the story that Harry and Kathleen tell when they return from Ireland? What about Tom's? How does the novel set up the element of fantasy to make it plausible enough for other characters to accept? What about for the reader?

10. Robin and Harry become convinced that writing an opera for Kathleen will somehow help her, but they're never quite sure how. What did you think the outcome of the opera would be? Did you ever think, like Kathleen, that they were being selfish and merely pursuing the creative process because they love it?

11. When did you realize what Kathleen's fate would be? Were you surprised? Would you call this a happy ending and do you believe it's the right one?

12. One of the central questions of the book is "Can the transformative power of music overcome a magic that has prevailed for generations?" Do you believe art can have its own kind of magic? Have you experienced that in your own life? How?

13. The bonus short story, "The Mermaid at the Opera," features a relationship between an artist and a muse that is very different from the one between Robin and Harry and their muse, Kathleen. How would you describe the two different relationships? What do you think the relationship *should* be like between artist and muse? ⤳